MILLER'S SECRET

TESS THOMPSON

PRAISE FOR TESS THOMPSON

The School Mistress of Emerson Pass:
"Sometimes we all need to step away from our lives and sink into a safe, happy place where family and love are the main ingredients for surviving. You'll find that and more in The School Mistress of Emerson Pass. I delighted in every turn of the story and when away from it found myself eager to return to Emerson Pass. I can't wait for the next book." - *Kay Bratt, Bestselling author of Wish Me Home and True to Me.*
"I frequently found myself getting lost in the characters and forgetting that I was reading a book." - *Camille Di Maio, Bestselling author of The Memory of Us.*
"Highly recommended." - *Christine Nolfi, Award winning author of The Sweet Lake Series.*
"I loved this book!" - *Karen McQuestion, Bestselling author of Hello Love and Good Man, Dalton.*

Traded: Brody and Kara:
"I loved the sweetness of Tess Thompson's writing - the camaraderie and long-lasting friendships make you want to move to Cliffside and become one of the gang! Rated Hallmark for romance!" - *Stephanie Little BookPage*

"This story was well written. You felt what the characters were going through. It's one of those "I got to know what happens next" books. So intriguing you won't want to put it down." - *Lena Loves Books*

"This story has so much going on, but it intertwines within itself. You get second chance, lost loves, and new love. I could not put this book down! I am excited to start this series and have love for this little Bayside town that I am now fond off!" - *Crystal's Book World*

"This is a small town romance story at its best and I look forward to the next book in the series." - *Gillek2, Vine Voice*

"This is one of those books that make you love to be a reader and fan of the author." -*Pamela Lunder, Vine Voice*

Blue Midnight:
"This is a beautiful book with an unexpected twist that takes the story from romance to mystery and back again. I've already started the 2nd book in the series!" - *Mama O*

"This beautiful book captured my attention and never let it go. I did not want it to end and so very much look forward to reading the next book." - *Pris Shartle*

"I enjoyed this new book cover to cover. I read it on my long flight home from Ireland and it helped the time fly by, I wish it had been longer so my whole flight could have been lost to this lovely novel about second chances and finding the truth. Written with wisdom and humor this novel shares the raw emotions a new divorce can leave behind." - *J. Sorenson*

"Tess Thompson is definitely one of my auto-buy authors! I love her writing style. Her characters are so real to life that you just can't put the book down once you start! Blue Midnight makes you believe in second chances. It makes you believe that everyone deserves an HEA. I loved the twists and turns in this book, the mystery and suspense, the family dynamics and the restoration of trust and security." - *Angela MacIntyre*

"Tess writes books with real characters in them, characters with flaws and baggage and gives them a second chance. (Real people, some remind me of myself and my girlfriends.) Then she cleverly and thoroughly develops those characters and makes you feel deeply for them. Characters are complex and multi-faceted, and the plot seems to unfold naturally, and never feels contrived." - *K. Lescinsky*

Caramel and Magnolias:
"Nobody writes characters like Tess Thompson. It's like she looks into our lives and creates her characters based on our best friends, our lovers, and our neighbors. Caramel and Magnolias, and the authors debut novel Riversong, have some of the best characters I've ever had a chance to fall in love with. I don't like leaving spoilers in reviews so just trust me, Nicholas Sparks has nothing on Tess Thompson, her writing flows so smoothly you can't help but to want to read on!" - *T. M. Frazier*

"I love Tess Thompson's books because I love good writing. Her prose is clean and tight, which are increasingly rare qualities, and manages to evoke a full range of emotions with both subtlety and power. Her fiction goes well beyond art imitating life. Thompson's characters are alive and fully-realized, the action is believable, and the story unfolds with the right balance of tension and exuberance. CARAMEL AND MAGNOLIAS is a pleasure to read." - *Tsuruoka*

"The author has an incredible way of painting an image with her words. Her storytelling is beautiful, and leaves you wanting more! I love that the story is about friendship (2 best friends) and love. The characters are richly drawn and I found myself rooting for them from the very beginning. I think you will, too!" - *Fogvision*

"I got swept off my feet, my heartstrings were pulled, I held my breath, and tightened my muscles in suspense. Tess paints stunning scenery with her words and draws you in to the lives of her characters."- *T. Bean*

Duet For Three Hands:
"Tears trickled down the side of my face when I reached the end of this road. Not because the story left me feeling sad or disappointed, no. Rather, because I already missed them. My friends. Though it isn't goodbye, but see you later. And so I will sit impatiently waiting, with desperate eagerness to hear where life has taken you, what burdens have you downtrodden, and what triumphs warm your heart. And in the meantime, I will go out and live, keeping your lessons and friendship and love close, the light to guide me through any darkness. And to the author I say thank you. My heart, my soul -all of me - needed these words, these friends, this love. I am forever changed by the beauty of your talent." *- Lisa M.Gott*

"I am a great fan of Tess Thompson's books and this new one definitely shows her branching out with an engaging enjoyable historical drama/love story. She is a true pro in the way she weaves her storyline, develops true to life characters that you love! The background and setting is so picturesque and visible just from her words. Each book shows her expanding, growing and excelling in her art. Yet another one not to miss. Buy it you won't be disappointed. The ONLY disappointment is when it ends!!!" *- Sparky's Last*

"There are some definite villains in this book. Ohhhh, how I loved to hate them. But I have to give Thompson credit because they never came off as caricatures or one dimensional. They all felt authentic to me and (sadly) I could easily picture them. I loved to love some and loved to hate others." *- The Baking Bookworm*

"I stayed up the entire night reading Duet For Three Hands and unbeknownst to myself, I fell asleep in the middle of reading the book. I literally woke up the next morning with Tyler the Kindle beside me (thankfully, still safe and intact) with no ounce of battery left. I shouldn't have worried about deadlines because, guess what? Duet For Three Hands was the epitome of unputdownable." - *The Bookish Owl*

Miller's Secret

"From the very first page, I was captivated by this wonderful tale. The cast of characters amazing - very fleshed out and multi-dimensional. The descriptions were perfect - just enough to make you feel like you were transported back to the 20's and 40's.... This book was the perfect escape, filled with so many twists and turns I was on the edge of my seat for the entire read." - *Hilary Grossman*

"The sad story of a freezing-cold orphan looking out the window at his rich benefactors on Christmas Eve started me off with Horatio-Alger expectations for this book. But I quickly got pulled into a completely different world--the complex five-character braid that the plot weaves. The three men and two women characters are so alive I felt I could walk up and start talking to any one of them, and I'd love to have lunch with Henry. Then the plot quickly turned sinister enough to keep me turning the pages.
Class is set against class, poor and rich struggle for happiness and security, yet it is love all but one of them are hungry for. ......Where does love come from? What do you do about it? The story kept me going, and gave me hope. For a little bonus, there are Thompson's delightful observations, like: "You'd never know we could make something this good out of the milk from an animal who eats hats." A really good read!" - *Kay in Seattle*

"She paints vivid word pictures such that I could smell the ocean and hear the doves. Then there are the stories within a story that twist and turn until they all come together in the end. I really had a hard time putting it down. Five stars aren't enough!"

- M.R. Williams

❊ Created with Vellum

MILLER'S SECRET

TESS THOMPSON

For Cliff,
Given the choice of anyone in the world, I would always choose you.

PART I

DECEMBER 1921

1

CAROLINE

C aroline Bennett, nestled into the corner of the sofa in her father's study, organized a stack of letters into alphabetical order. Degrees of handwriting skills aside, each letter was clearly addressed to Santa at the North Pole from one of the forty-two children at Saint Theresa's Home for Orphans. Caroline was cozy in her red flannel nightgown and thick socks, and her legs were almost long enough to reach the floor. A fire crackled behind the metal grid. Fresh fir branches decorated the mantel and filled the room with their spicy scent. Candles flickered on the side tables, casting soft shadows. Outside, December fog sheathed their home so that tonight they lived in a cloud instead of a street in San Francisco where the houses were the size of schools.

Caroline knew there was no Santa. She was twelve now, after all. Her days of childish beliefs were in the past. Her parents were Santa. It was obvious now that she knew. She'd discovered the truth when she accidently saw their house-keeper, Essie, wrapping presents in the same paper that later showed up as gifts from Santa. This new knowledge rested heavily in the middle of her chest. It had been lovely to believe in magic. However, her dismay to learn that her favorite saint

5

was, in fact, fiction was tempered by her delight that this year, for the first time, she would be able to help deliver the gifts to the orphanage. Her stomach did flips just thinking of it. As if that weren't enough, her mother, Sophie, had entrusted Caroline with a sacred task. She was to help find just the right gift for each child.

Her father, Edmund, hidden behind the newspaper in his large chair with nothing but his long legs visible, occasionally grunted or exclaimed over something he read. He'd missed several Christmases when he was fighting overseas. This was his second Christmas home with them, but Caroline had not forgotten how lonely those days were or the worried tears Mother had shed. Edmund Bennett, as Mother often said, could fill up a room like no other. Without him, the house had seemed empty and less like Christmas, his presents stacked up under the tree for his hoped-for return, their deepest fear that they would remain unopened. Now, though, Father was safe at home, and Mother no longer cried by the fire while holding his latest letter in her delicate hands.

Caroline settled back into the sofa, placing the piles of letters next to her. "I've put them in order, Mother. Are you ready for me to read them now?" Working side-by-side with her beautiful mother, Caroline imagined she'd experienced a great transformation from the previous Christmas. She was taller and more sophisticated, and felt almost sorry for her deluded younger self. What a little dolt she'd been, believing that a man could fly around the world in only one night on a sled pulled by reindeer.

Other than telling her parents she knew the truth, she kept mum about this devastating fact. There was no reason her friends should have their belief in magic ruined. Believing in something as wonderful as the idea of Santa made them happy, and it was not her place to take that away from them. The longer one believed, the better.

Essie entered with a plate of sugar cookies, hot chocolate for Caroline, and glasses of sherry for her parents. "Good evening.

Some sweets for the sweet?" Caroline grinned, knowing Essie meant *she* was sweet.

"Essie, you must stop working and retire for the evening," said Mother. "You've been on your feet since dawn."

"Thank you, Mrs. Bennett, and I beg your pardon, but dawn is an exaggeration." Essie, only twenty-five, had come to them four years before as a housemaid but had proven so smart and capable that Mother promoted her to head housekeeper when cranky Mrs. Smith, inherited from Father's mother, had retired. Caroline adored Essie. She was pretty with brown curls that made Caroline want to pull one to see it spring back into place. Essie was never cross, even with Caroline who sometimes forgot that she wasn't supposed to run in the house.

The newspaper lowered. Father's green eyes fixed upon Essie. "Mrs. Bennett exaggerating? Impossible."

Mother laughed. "No one asked for your opinion, Mr. Bennett."

Essie patted Caroline's head, smiling. "Oh, the letters from the children. How wonderful." At the door, she turned back, tears glistening in her eyes. "What you do for those poor orphans—giving them a Christmas. Could've been me but for the grace of God."

"Thank you, Essie. Have a good rest," said Mother. "We have a million cookies to make tomorrow."

The newspaper lowered once again. "We?"

"Well, it's my mother's recipes, anyway." Mother tossed a pillow at Father, which he thwarted by once again hiding behind his newspaper. The sound of Essie's laughter accompanied her clicking heels down the hallway.

Mother held up her pen and paper. "I'm ready, darling. Read away."

The first was from a boy named Miller, who wanted a telescope so he could study the constellations. Caroline put it back into its envelope while left-handed Mother, the paper at a slant

7

so she didn't smear the ink, wrote his wish on the list. Other than Miller's rather forthright letter, the others had deeper wishes.

Please, Santa, bring me a new family for Christmas.

Santa, bring my mother back to me.

Santa, do you know where my brother is?

After the tenth letter, she couldn't continue. Tears slid down her cheeks and onto the paper, blurring the ink. "Mother, please. I can't. They're too sad."

Mother set down her pen. The newspaper came down and Father placed it on the table next to him. "Caroline, I know the letters hurt you," said Mother. "They do us as well. But you must never turn away from truths like these just because it's hard. It's your responsibility as a person with so much to understand that many others have nothing and to let it soften you to do good in the world."

"For whom much is given, much is expected," said Father.

Caroline wiped her eyes with her handkerchief, then ran her fingers over her embroidered initials. "But why do I have so much when others have so little?"

"We're lucky," said Mother. "Because of that we have to serve others as best we can."

"Love instead of hate," said Father. "This is what Jesus taught us. Do you understand?"

"Yes, sir." Caroline picked up the next letter. "Dear Santa."

2

MILLER

I t was Christmas Eve. While sugarplums danced in the heads of the other children, ten-year-old Miller could not sleep, shivering under a thin blanket. An unexpected cold front had come the day before, encasing San Francisco in ice, and the orphanage's fireplaces could not keep up with the frigid temperatures. Before he ventured from his bed, he listened for the sounds of the other boys sleeping. Norm snored, Wesley murmured pleas to his dead mother, and Timmy made a sound with his lips like he was trying to blow a horn. The other four boys were smaller, and in general, uttered nothing, other than falling out of the narrow beds occasionally and crying until one of the big boys shushed them. One grew tough here. Coddling and sympathy were in short supply. There was no room for softness and sadness. It was only tolerated if it was amid dreams, like poor Wesley.

Miller walked in silent steps to the window and drew back the curtain. He stood between it and the glass, looking up at the cloudless sky where stars danced in the black night. He wanted to observe them in the silence, to soak them in without distraction because it made him feel as if anything were possible, like there was more to his paltry existence than the chilled room. He gazed for many minutes until he became a star, too. Silver and shining with heat. Last August, the stars shot across the horizon and he caught them in his hands and hung on, streaking across the sky in splendored glory.

Dust tickled his nose and he rubbed it with the back of his hand to keep from sneezing. He shivered as he placed his hand on the glass of the window. A layer of ice had formed on the inside, and it melted under his warm hand. This proved he did exist and was not invisible like he'd been that afternoon. He didn't care that he wasn't chosen again. No one would ever come for him. He understood that now. Days of hopeful wishes and prayers were with the stars, out of his reach.

That very afternoon a couple had come at lunch, scanning the children lined up in rows at the tables as they waited for a bowl of lukewarm soup and piece of bread. The couple, wearing tweed coats that almost matched and holding rosary beads, presumably for luck, were looking for a child to take home for Christmas. A gift to themselves, thought Miller, as if the children were toys to be handed about to rich people who had everything already. Their earnest expressions and the way they scanned the children's faces, like a miracle was about to happen, made him sick. *Oh, yes, she's the one. Thank you, Lord, for our little miracle.* A bitter taste filled his mouth, like he'd sucked on a handful of coins. He didn't try to catch their eyes like he used to. No one wanted a boy his age. There was no point to try to look endearing any longer. He'd predicted they would choose Patsy, the toddler who'd come to the orphanage just the week before, and he'd been right. The woman's face had lit up like a candle on the Christmas tree the moment she set eyes upon her. "Oh, Frank," she'd said. "Do you see her curls?" It didn't take a genius to see that coming. Sweet little Patsy with her chubby fingers and blond ringlets. He didn't stand a chance.

He'd lived at the orphanage for almost five years, having been dropped there when he was five-years-old in an unceremonious delivery by his deceased mother's only living relative, a cousin with six children of her own and no desire for any further mouths to feed. Before his mother's death, Miller had lived with her in a dirty, one-room shack at the end of a country road. Memories of the time with his mother came to him in a series of fuzzy images, like overexposed photographs. Uneven floorboards, rough on the bottom of his feet. One window, a crack like a spider's web and a layer of dirt so thick that day and night were often indiscernible. A table with one chair next to a woodburning cooking stove. One time when he was small, he burned his wrist on the stove, reaching for a two-day old biscuit. *Greedy boys get burned.* He remembered her voice and the sound of the whiskey bottled as she slammed it on the table. *That'll teach you.* It did. After that he knew not to touch, no matter how hungry he was. He slept in the closet. When his mother did her business with the men, he was to stay there with the door closed and be quiet, putting his fingers in his ears to stifle the sound of creaking bedsprings and frightening moans. Sometimes, she disappeared for days and came back only to sleep for hours and hours, murmuring things he couldn't understand. She did not hug or kiss him like he'd seen mothers do on the few occasions he went into town. Instead, he was smacked or pushed or spanked. He was never sure why.

The memory of smells, more vivid than the images, still lived in his nose. Men's perspiration, wood smoke, whiskey, and the sour smell of his mother. One day, she didn't get out of bed. Men came to the door, smelling of booze and cigarettes, but once they came inside, they quickly retreated. The scent of something rotting from the inside out replaced the sour odor of his mother. One day she didn't wake. He stood over her, unsure what to do. Several flies buzzed around her body, and outside, the shriek of a wild bird pierced the quiet. Her white hand, paper thin, hung from the side of a bed. For five days he remained in the shack alone, surviving on the sack of raw potatoes that had been his companion in the closet. Then, one day, a woman came. She held a paper bag over her nose and offered him her hand. It was the first time he could remember being touched without it being accompanied by a beating.

Now, Miller took his hand from the glass, sticking it between his thighs for warmth. The stars were as close as he'd ever seen them, and a half-moon hung just above the large oak. Not Santa in his sleigh, as some of the younger boys believed. He'd known for years Santa was not real. Just like God, it was a story to make them succumb to authority. Lies told to them by the nuns to keep them placid, well-behaved. *God and Santa are watching.* He knew it was all fiction. He told the others. *There is no Santa.* They were all too young or too stupid to believe him. It wasn't his problem if the little idiots chose to believe the lies. What did he care? Still, he wondered where the presents came from every year. Surely the Sisters couldn't manage to buy all of them.

Miller didn't believe in the birth, death, or rising of Jesus. However, he knew the nuns who cared for them not only believed the stories of the Bible, but wanted the children to believe as well. So, Miller pretended he did, to keep from being smacked with the ruler over the palm of his hand. Who could believe such nonsense? The other children were ridiculous. Who would give up a life in the world for the thankless work of caring for motherless children simply because of a made-up story in a book?

The rumble of a car's engine, and, a few seconds later, the beams of light that appeared between the trees, drew his attention. His stomach flipped over in excitement, despite his disbelief in magical fat men. A visitor of some kind? In the middle of the night? Yes, it *was* a car coming up the lane, headlights like bouncing balls in the dark. The car, black with wide fenders, stopped in front of the orphanage's front doors, and the sound of the engine ceased, bringing back the silent night. A man in a black suit and cap slid from the driver's seat and walked around the car to open the back door. Small feet in patent leather shoes appeared first, reflecting light from the lamppost, attached to thick legs covered in white stockings. Then, the rest of a girl emerged. She wore a fur coat and hat and was short and stout, like the teapot in the song the woman had sung to Patsy earlier. Slightly younger than Miller, if he had his guess, but it was hard for him to judge the age of children who were well fed. They always seemed older than his scrawny companions.

The girl's hands were stuck inside a matching muff, but she shivered despite all her layers. She shifted weight from foot to foot, waiting for whoever was still in the car, her plump face tilted upward, seemingly examining the outside of the building in great detail. Miller pretended to be a statue, hoping she could not see him. A man in a top hat and dark jacket joined her, putting his hand on the top of her head. She looked up at him and smiled. They said something to each other that Miller could not decipher. The man and the chauffer went to the back of the car and pulled out two large boxes. Miller strained his eyes, trying to make out the contents. Packages with bows? Presents for the children. It was not Santa, but this man and his little girl. He was triumphant. He was right. There was no Santa, unless he traveled in a Rolls-Royce and wore a top hat.

The two men, each carrying a box, and the little girl stepped out of sight, under the awning over the front door. Miller crept from his hiding place, tiptoeing to the door of the boys' sleeping quarters. He turned the knob silently, and stepped into the hall-way. Holding his breath, he made his way to the top of the stairs and looked down into the foyer. Their chauffeur and the boxes were out of sight, presumably being delivered into the common room and placed under the tree, but the man and little girl huddled with Sister Catherine, talking in hushed voices. Miller made out every word. "Mr. Bennett, I was afraid you wouldn't make it with all the ice covering the roads. Sister Rosie and I have been beside ourselves with worry."

"Thanks to Mac, we made it just fine. He's driven in worse," said Mr. Bennett, taking off his top hat and holding it in two hands. "We would've walked if we had to. I cannot disappoint Mrs. Bennett. She was also beside herself with worry."

"Bless her," said Sister Catherine. "And who have we here? Is this Miss Caroline?"

The little girl curtsied. "Yes, ma'am. My mother let me come this year. I had to beg her. Because of the roads, she was worried Mac would crash the car and we'd all be lost forever. Well, that and this year I learned the truth about Santa, so Mother allowed me to help shop for the gifts." She had a clear, almost musical voice.

Sister Catherine chuckled. "I'm sorry to hear about Santa, but I'm glad you've come and that you didn't crash."

"Caroline and her mother spent many hours shopping for what they hoped would please the children," said Mr. Bennett. "They were appreciative of the letters to Santa with their specific requests. I think we managed to find everything."

Caroline tugged on her father's sleeve. "No, Father, we didn't. We couldn't find mothers and fathers for them. They had that in their letters." Her voice had the shaky quality that happened when girls were trying not to cry. Girls in the orphanage were crying all the livelong day, so he knew. "I'm so very sorry for them, Sister."

"Ah, well, God has a plan for them all," said Sister Catherine. "So don't you fret." She turned to look at Mr. Bennett. "Edmund, without your contributions, we would surely have shut down by now. We can't thank you enough." She gestured toward the door. "Now, you best be off before it gets any colder."

They exchanged several other pleasantries, but Miller had stopped listening. *I'm so very sorry for them.* The fat little brat. How dare she pity them? He filled with anger, the kind that raged like the color red, burning his face as if he stood before a great fire. How easy it must be to have everything in the world, sipping cream from a silver spoon. He hated her. Gripping the spokes of the railing he imagined kicking her face, stomping on her fingers until she cried.

The chauffer had come back to the foyer. Mr. Bennett said they must go now, and Merry Christmas, and God bless, and all

14

the other absurdities people said on this fake day. Sister Catherine followed the men out, but Caroline, falling slightly behind, looked up to where he crouched by the railing. Her eyes widened. She stared at him. He stared back, not daring to move, for fear she would betray him. Then, in a moment of genius, he put his finger to his lips to indicate she must be quiet. She nodded, put her finger to her lips, and slipped out the door. He ran back to the boys' room on tiptoes, his toes cold and achy, and went to the window. Caroline climbed into the car first, followed by her father. Miller watched their car turn out of the driveway and head down the road until it disappeared from sight.

The next morning, like the other children, he opened his present. It was a telescope, just as he'd asked for. There were also blank notebooks for all of the children. Sister Catherine encouraged them all to keep journals or use it as a place to put their mementos. "If you write down your thoughts and feelings, your life will have clarity and purpose." He wanted to laugh. What mementos, clarity, or purpose did any of them have exactly? He kept the question to himself. Last time he'd been cheeky, Mother Maria had smacked his knuckles with a ruler until she drew blood.

That night, he sat in bed, running his fingers over the velvet fabric that covered the outside of the journal pages and envisioned the little girl and her father. With a pen he'd found on the floor in Mother Maria's office and had stashed under his mattress, he wrote on the first page.

December 25, 1921

This is Miller Dreeser. I am here even though no one sees me. Someday I will be visible. I will be like Edmund Bennett and wear fancy clothes and have more than enough to eat.

When he wrote it down, he knew exactly what it was he wanted. Perhaps Mrs. Bennett understood something he hadn't.

3

CAROLINE

hristmas Eve, her parents surprised Caroline when they said that, yes, she could accompany her father to drop the gifts at the orphanage. The roads, slick with ice from the unexpected freeze, made the journey slower than expected, but Caroline didn't mind. Sitting next to Father in the backseat of their car, she was a princess dressed in her new dress and stockings, plus the delightful fur coat Mother had let her open early so that she might wear it for their festivities tonight. She wanted to wave to her imaginary subjects like she'd seen photos of real princesses do. She closed her eyes for a moment, imagining that she was adored by the masses. Father wore his top hat and formal evening suit. She wriggled closer to him and lay her cheek against the rough material of his jacket. "Thank you for letting me come, Father," she said. "I feel so grownup."

"I'm delighted to have such a worthy traveling companion." He kissed the top of her head. "But don't grow up too fast."

When they arrived, Father said she could come inside with him to meet Sister Catherine. Once she was out of the car, she stood, looking up at the building that loomed large and almost creepy in the dark. She suspected it was cold inside and shivered despite her fur coat. The stars above shone with an intensity she had not seen before, as if the heavens acknowledged the awesomeness of this night before Jesus's birth. She was about to follow Father inside when a movement in one of the upstairs windows caught her eye. Was it a boy, standing in the window? She couldn't be sure, but it appeared to be an outline of a boy. She looked away. It was strange to be watched. Dread washed over her. She shivered. *Don't think of it. Pretend you didn't see him.*

They went inside. Sister Catherine greeted them and they chatted for a few minutes in the foyer, which seemed no warmer than outside. They were about to go when she happened to glance up. A boy crouched low at the top of the stairs, looking down at them. His eyes, the color of coal, stared at her, unblinking. She was about to say something to him when he put his finger to his lips. He didn't want her to speak and let it be known he was there. Perhaps he would get in trouble for being out of bed. She nodded, to let him know she understood, and followed Father out the door.

After their late-night delivery, Mac drove them to the Christmas Eve mass at their local parish. Mother arrived before them and had saved them seats near the front. Like Easter, every seat in the church was taken, forcing men to stand in the back of the church in clumps. Women were dressed in their finest: long, flowing dresses slack at the middle and head pieces with plumes in rich colors. The men were in dark suits, holding fedoras in their hands. The air smelled of incense and ladies' perfume. A silence fell over the parish as the service began, but Caroline didn't pay close attention. Instead, she prayed for the motherless children with so much silent vigor that she worried it might be apparent to others. When she looked around, though, between the kneeling and the chants and the story of Jesus's birth, no one seemed to notice her. She was safe and warm, with more gifts waiting under the tree than most children had in a lifetime. Since the Santa letters, her world had opened. There were children without hope, without a family or a home. She could not stop thinking of them and their letters. Haunted by the phrases in the letters, a heaviness had settled onto her shoulders over the last few weeks. And tonight at the orphanage, the boy standing at the top of the stairs had hollow cheeks that matched his empty eyes, like nothing good had ever filled him, neither food nor love.

As Christmas Eve Mass ended, however, she had sudden clarity. Guilt. She was guilty. For whom much is given, much is expected. Mother and Father conducted themselves in a manner worthy of the directive to their daughter. Yet, somehow it didn't feel like enough. She was a child of privilege. There were others who suffered, while she, Caroline, thrived. She could not understand why. Kneeling in the pew one last time, she vowed to God, "I will do my best to lessen the burden of others, however I can. Please show me the way."

After Mass ended, she accompanied Mother and Father to their club for a late supper. Garlands hung in the windows. A massive tree near the fireplace, decorated with shiny bulbs and red bows, made the lobby smell of pine. In the dining room, a band played Christmas music. Waiters walking around with trays, gave her parents glasses of champagne, and the three of them were enveloped into a swarm of friends. She held on to her mother's hand, afraid to be swallowed by the crowd. Ladies' bare shoulders glistened under the lights, and their perfumes made Caroline's eyes itch. She stifled a yawn. Her bladder was full. "I have to use the ladies' room, Mother."

"All right, darling. Meet us in the dining room," said Mother, waving to a friend standing across the room.

The ladies' lounge was quiet compared the bustle of the lobby. An attendant with skin the color of dark tea stood near the sink. Caroline said hello, politely, as Mother had taught her, before finding an open toilet. She closed the door and sat, delighted to empty her bladder. Voices of two women outside the door reached her. Caroline recognized her friend Elizabeth's mother by her unusual voice. Mrs. Beale had a particularly low timbre for a woman. It could be mistaken for a man's. When she mentioned this to her mother one time, she had pretended to puff an imaginary cigarette and told Caroline she must never smoke, as it made you sound hoarse and gave you wrinkles. This was one of Mother's strange notions. No one else seemed to believe this, as most women smoked. Mrs. Beale was almost never without a cigarette dangling from one of those long holders, the ash always about to drop. "Goodness, did you see the size of Caroline Bennett?" asked Mrs. Beale.

"It's such a shame. Terrible thing to have a beautiful mother and be so homely. And fat! My God, it's like she ate her twin." Caroline did not recognize this brittle voice that sounded like squeaking curds. "Do you think she was adopted?"

"I suppose it's possible. It's hard to believe she came from Edmund and Sophie," said Mrs. Beale.

Caroline stood, pulling her stockings up and her dress back into place, shivering. She should have kept her coat and hat on. It was frigid in the club, like it had been in the orphanage. She walked out to the dressing tables where the two women sat, looking at themselves in the mirror. *I will stand in front of them. Make them see me. Shame them for their cruelty.*

Mrs. Beale's eyes met Caroline's and she made a circle with her mouth. She held a lipstick in her hand, but did not use it, like she'd forgotten it was there. "Caroline, what're you doing here so late? Elizabeth's home in bed."

"My mother and father allow me to stay up as late as them on Christmas Eve. It's important to my mother that I attend Mass." Caroline's voice shook and her cheeks were damp. Had she been crying without knowing? She pulled out her handkerchief from the little pocket of her dress and patted under her eyes.

The other woman's eyes skirted to Mrs. Beale, then back to

Caroline. She looked properly ashamed. They knew she'd heard them. *Good.* "Merry Christmas, Mrs. Beale."

"Merry Christmas, Caroline. Give my best to your mother."

Caroline washed her hands at the basin. Her fingers were like sausages and her cheeks as round as apples. How had she not noticed before? Her thighs pressed against each other. She pushed into her middle, feeling several rolls there, like jelly. She *was* fat. The attendant handed her a towel. After she was finished drying, Caroline handed the attendant a coin. *Good manners were important,* Mother always said, *and these poor women work for tips only.*

Caroline found her parents near the entrance to the dining room. A pain stabbed her stomach, yet she was ravenous, like she hadn't eaten in days. "Mother, will they have pudding?" Pudding and cream. Butter spread over rolls. A thick cut of roast beef. Thinking of the meal ahead made her mouth water, but with that feeling came shame. She was a fat girl, like a pig. No one should have to look at her.

"I believe they will," said Mother. "I'm famished." She held out her hand. "Come along, darling, let's eat."

The next afternoon, she and her mother stood in front of the mirror in her dressing room. They both wore their new Christmas dresses, matching dark blue taffeta. Mother, slim and tall, smiled into the mirror. "I suppose it's a sin to love these dresses as much as I do."

Caroline didn't answer. She stared at herself in the mirror. Mrs. Beale was right. Caroline had been adopted. Perhaps from the orphanage when she was too young to remember? Why else would she look so different from her mother?

"Mother, did you find me at the orphanage when I was a baby?" She met her mother's gaze in the mirror.

Mother turned away from the mirror to look directly at her. "What would make you think such a thing?"

"Because I'm fat and you're not." She pinched the sides of her face. "And I'm homely and you're beautiful."

"You're most certainly not homely or fat." Mother's blue eyes, the same color as the sapphire necklace around her slim neck, filled with tears. "I don't want to ever hear you say that again, do you understand?"

"Other people say it," said Caroline.

"What other people?"

"Elizabeth's mother. I was in the powder room at the club last night and she was in there with another lady and she said, 'It's such a shame about Sophie's daughter. She's such a homely thing.' And the other lady said, 'Yes, and fat as a little piggy. It's hard to believe she came from Edmund and Sophie and maybe she's adopted.' Or, something like that, anyway." Caroline looked at the floor, trying not to cry. "It doesn't bother me, though, Mother, because I want only to be good and smart. I don't care that I'm not pretty."

Mother knelt on the floor, taking Caroline's hands in her own. "Listen to me, my love. You're beautiful inside and out. No one, not even awful Anna Beale, can take that from you. She was feeling particularly mean because her husband has made a bad business deal and they've lost their fortune. It was probably the last time they'll ever be at the club. When people are bitter or disappointed, they're often mean to others."

"But why?"

"Oh, darling, I don't know. It's easy to be kind when your life is filled with security and love, as mine has been. Anna Beale was feeling spiteful because she's jealous of what we have, and it made her unkind. But you, my sweet girl, despite what those women said, look exactly like me."

"I do?" Was Mother lying to spare her feelings?

"Yes, look here now." Mother lifted Caroline's chin to look into the mirror. "Do you see? Same blue eyes."

It was true. The color of sapphires, Father always said.

"And do you see our noses? Same little upturn on the end. See there?"

Yes, it was like a button on the end of their noses. On Mother it looked fashionable, like everyone should have one. Mrs. Beale was probably jealous of her mother's nose. She had a long, pointy one, and skin the texture of tarnished leather despite layers of powder.

"And our hair is the same." Honey blond with curls, although Mother's was piled on top of her head in an elaborate arrangement, whereas Caroline's hung in a bob at her chin. "So is our skin. Your father says we have skin like butterscotch candy." Mother kissed the top of her head. "Someday you'll grow taller, like me, and you'll become slimmer. I was just like you when I was your age."

"Really?"

"Yes, really. And do you think I'm ugly?" asked Mother.

"No. Not one bit."

"So, there you have it." Mother stood. "Now, come along. Your father will think we've run off to the circus if we don't go down for dinner."

She took Caroline's hand as they entered the dining room. "I have a surprise for you."

"You do?"

"Julius and his father are going to spend Christmas with us. They've come up from the beach."

Julius and his father, Doctor Nelson, lived at the beach all year around, not just during the summer like the Bennetts. Occasionally, they came up to the city to stay with her family. Like tonight! Her heart leaped with joy when she saw them, all thoughts of Mrs. Beale slipping from her mind. Julius and Doctor Nelson sat at the table with Father, both dressed in suits. How nice Julius looked. He waved and grinned at her from across the room. *Julius.* Everything was always better when he was there. She glided across the room, newly light. He looked older than when she'd seen him at Thanksgiving with his light blond hair, bleached from the sun, slicked back and smoothed with pomade. Both men and Julius stood as they approached the table. Mother put both hands out to Doctor Nelson. "So lovely to see you."

Doctor Nelson kissed her hand. "Thank you for having us."

"You're looking quite well," said Mother. It was true. Doctor Nelson looked rested and healthy, less thin than the last time they'd seen him.

After they all sat, she squeezed Julius's hand under the table. "I'm happy to see you."

He grinned. "Me too. We're staying the night and everything. I brought you a present."

"I have one for you, too." Mother had found an archery set for him. Ever since they read *Robin Hood*, they'd both become obsessed with archery. She couldn't wait to see his face when he opened it. They had played Robin Hood and Maid Marian many times on the beach, with driftwood as the bow and arrow. "I didn't know you were coming."

"Me either. Father surprised me this morning."

"Has it been lonesome? Christmas without Father was awful."

Julius looked down, as if studying his plate with great intent. "Yeah. For my dad mostly."

Julius's mother had left them last summer. Caroline learned of it listening at the door of Father's study. Mother's voice, sounding strangely shrill, had spoken the unthinkable. "She disappeared into the night. With a man." *Julius's mother had left her child and her husband? How was this possible?*

She and Mother had gone over to see them that afternoon with dinner. Essie had arranged the meal in a basket with a colorful tea towel. Would the beautiful display make someone feel better when their wife or mother had left them? Caroline doubted it.

Doctor Nelson had answered the door, looking just the same as he always did, dressed in a light suit and tie, his hair groomed so that the little ridges from his comb showed. Julius looked different, though. He hadn't combed his hair, and his face looked pale and pinched under his tan. His eyes were bloodshot. He'd been crying. One other time he'd cried, but that was when he broke his arm. Other than that, he was tough. But this? This was too much.

Julius took her into the kitchen while their parents talked. He pointed to the note, still on the table. "There it is." His eyes, flat and dull, would not meet her own.

I'm sorry, but I'm slowly dying here in this place. I was not made to be a small-town doctor's wife.

Why had they left the note on the table? Caroline would have burned it in the fireplace, along with any photographs of the woman's selfish face.

"Remember how I always tried to get her to laugh," he asked. "She never thought I was funny."

"You *are* funny."

"Not funny enough." He picked up the letter and stuffed it in his pocket. "She's not coming back. My father thinks so. He hasn't said it, but I can see by the way he's acting like everything is normal. But I know she's not. I saw her leave last night. She assumed I was asleep, but I was awake, reading *Robin Hood* again, and I heard a car pull into the driveway. I went to the window and I saw a car and this man get out. It was him. She ran to him. She couldn't get away fast enough."

How dare she leave Julius. Caroline's stomach burned. She wanted to smack something or throw an object at the wall. No, she wanted to throw an object at Mrs. Nelson. That was it. She wanted to hurt her like she'd hurt Julius. Mrs. Nelson was cruel and selfish. She tried to imagine her own mother leaving, but it was unfathomable. She would never do it. Mrs. Nelson would be sorry. It was one thing to leave a husband, but how did a mother leave a little boy, especially one like Julius? Caroline understood for the first time the phrase "May she burn in Hell." The last time Caroline had seen Mrs. Nelson was just last week. It was the middle of the afternoon and she was bent over the sink, inspecting something. She had not looked up when the children came into the room, nor had she responded when Julius said they were going into town and could he get anything for her.

He cried, later, sitting on the beach, and she had wrapped her arm around his waist and let his head rest on her shoulder, his tears mixing with the seawater on her shoulder.

"Let's throw the letter into the sea," she said. "We won't ever think of her again."

"All right." They stood together. She took his hand as they walked to the place where the waves crashed onto the shore. Julius retrieved the letter from his pocket and crumpled it into a ball. He threw it hard toward the water. There was no breeze to deter its course as it sailed through the air and fell into a breaking wave. They did not see the paper that broke Julius's heart again, but they both knew because of the time they had spent in the very same surf that it was pulled under the surface now, tossing this way and that until it would be carried out to sea, ultimately disintegrating into fish food. And yet, it was not enough to wipe away her memory. Caroline saw her in the shadows under Julius's eyes.

Since that day, Mother had made sure to include him in everything at the house. Doctor Nelson was often away at night doing house calls or delivering babies, so Julius would stay in their guestroom. "You're family now," Mother said to Julius one night. "Family isn't always blood. Sometimes, when you're lucky, you get to choose who you want for your family."

Now, the waiter, dressed in a black tuxedo, put a small plate in front of her. A sliver of toast with a dollop of caviar and sour cream on top. "Are you going to eat that?" Julius whispered in her ear.

Caroline giggled. "Mother says it's a delicacy."

"How's Essie?" asked Doctor Nelson.

His question yanked Caroline from her conversation with Julius. Why was he asking about Essie? She darted a look to her mother, who held her small appetizer fork in midair. Caroline squeezed Julius's hand under the table and pretended to be absorbed in her food. If the adults realized they were listening, they might stop talking.

"She's fine," said Mother.

"Why do you ask, old man?" Her father's voice held a hint of teasing.

"It's time for me to move on, I suppose," said Doctor Nelson.

"I see no reason not to," said Father. "Everything's been taken care of legally."

"You've been a good friend, Edmund. I thank you for your help."

"Every man needs a good attorney at least once in his lifetime," said Father.

"If only it were only once," said Mother.

"I understand Essie will be at the house on Christmas day," said Doctor Nelson.

"She's a live-in, so yes," said Mother. "But you knew that." Her mother's voice was teasing as well. "I don't suppose you're intending to steal my housekeeper?"

"Something like that," said Doctor Nelson.

Caroline looked over at Julius. His eyes twinkled back at her. "Essie?" she whispered. "And your father?"

"He hasn't said a word to me." He continued to whisper.

"We've been corresponding since Thanksgiving," said Doctor Nelson to Mother. "She's terribly worried you'll mind."

"Doctor Nelson, I'm quite aware of your correspondence. She may be clever, but she's not able to hide everything from me," said Mother.

"Do I have your permission?" asked Doctor Nelson.

Caroline looked up at her mother. She smiled, looking extremely satisfied with herself. "As much as I hate to lose her, she does not belong to me." She stabbed a piece of toast with her fork. "However, she's like family to us, so you're forbidden to hurt her."

"I wouldn't think of it," said Doctor Nelson.

"Let's have a toast," said Father, picking up his champagne glass. "To new beginnings."

Caroline and Julius toasted one another with their glasses of milk. "Merry Christmas, Julius." She smiled at him.

"Merry Christmas, Caroline."

4

MILLER

In the days following Christmas, Miller thought of the Bennetts often, and not just when he used his telescope. Despite the pleasure the gadget gave him, it made him hate them more. It was nothing to them, this gift. Yet, to him it was the difference between wanting to live or not, from having something to look forward to or nothing but flat, dry hunger day after day. For this he hated them. To the Bennetts, it was not a dent in their wealth or their existence. They had anything and everything they wanted. This kindness was just a way for them to feel less guilty about it. People didn't do something for others unless they were getting something for themselves at the same time. He knew this after living in the orphanage for so long. The kids lived by this rule: I'll give you this, if you give me that.

He made it his mission to learn everything he could about Edmund Bennett. He asked Sister Catherine if he might read her discarded newspaper each day, hoping to find mentions of the Bennetts in the paper. She was delighted, for he had shown little interest in anything academic, and Sister Catherine was a kind soul who loved the children, even when they were too old to be endearing. He understood this, especially in the stark contrast to some of the others, who smacked the children's hands with rulers for the smallest offense. Sister Catherine was the first to teach him that kindness was a weakness one could easily exploit.

The first article he saw in the paper was about Edmund Bennett opening a center for veterans of the Great War where they could visit with one another, play games, and have refreshments. Miller cut it out and pasted it in his journal. In the weeks and months to come, he continued to cut and paste several more articles. It seemed the family was always doing some good deed. He cut around the edges of the photograph carefully to make sure he captured the entire article and photograph.

That March, he saw the Bennetts again. The Sisters had taken the children out for the day, a rare treat, to have a picnic at a park, even though the weather was chilly. Miller had found a long stick and declared it a gun. Timmy found another stick, shorter and less satisfying, and they played cowboys and Indians, running and shouting, until they came upon a vendor selling peanuts and popcorn to a well-dressed family of three. Miller stopped, his stick midair, surprised. It was the Bennett family. They stood before the cart, steam rising above their heads. Caroline was dressed in a brown coat and hat, as the sky was dark and moody, threatening a downpour. Miller shivered in his jacket with the holes in the elbows, the cold catching up to him now that he stood motionless. An insect of some kind had caught Timmy's attention, leaving Miller alone to watch them.

The Bennetts—Edmund, Sophie, and little Caroline—out for a stroll in the park. He saw it like a headline in the newspaper, like so many he'd seen in the society section of the newspaper in recent months.

Mrs. Bennett was slender, only reaching Mr. Bennett's shoulder in height. He could not see her face because she wore an enormous hat. Caroline pointed to a bag of peanuts right in the middle of the cart. "I want that one, please, Daddy."

Edmund, a large man, might have been intimidating, but he was not. At least, not at this moment when he was looking down into the eyes of his ten-year-old daughter. "If that's the one you want, you shall have it." He turned to his wife. "And you, my dear? What will you have?"

His wife murmured something that made him laugh. He paid for the purchase and offered each of them his arm, and the three walked away together. They did not notice him. He was invisible.

I want that. I want what he has. I want to be him. That night he wrote in his journal.

March 28, 1920

I saw them in the park. Caroline wanted peanuts, so she got them. I want peanuts and all the rest of it, too. So, I will marry Caroline someday. I will become like Edmund Bennett. No one can stop me.

PART II

SAN FRANCISCO 1929-1930

5

MILLER

Miller stood outside the gate of the Bennett mansion. Enormous and made of bricks, it stood back from the road a hundred feet with a rolling lawn between the gate and front door. The entire property was protected by an iron fence, the top of which had sharp points. No one got in or out unless they didn't mind getting impaled. He rubbed the scar on his left hand, lasting evidence of a grease burn from his fish frying work down at the wharf. Pulling his hat low on his forehead, he gripped the iron rods with both hands and watched the front door. In the three years since the first time he stood outside these gates, he'd never spotted any of the Bennetts coming or going. Servants occasionally, and the chauffer with his stupid hat, but no Bennetts.

It was his birthday. Twenty years he'd been knocking around this unforgiving world. He forced himself to walk here and look at the Bennett mansion at least once a week. No reason to get complacent and start giving up on his goals. No surrender for this kid. He was tough. Eventually he'd get what he wanted. He'd survived this long on his own with no one to ask for help. After he left the orphanage at seventeen, he'd found work as a cook because of his experience working in the kitchen. As he grew older, the nuns started giving him more and more respon-sibilities. Had to earn your keep when you were too old to be adopted but too young to live alone. Turns out, learning how to feed forty hungry kids with very few supplies was a good skill.

His resolve never weakened, despite the passage of time. He would be a Bennett.

After a few minutes—he never stayed long for fear they'd see him and call the authorities—he walked home, stopping once to buy a newspaper and some cigs. He used his key to let himself into the room, exhausted and antsy at the same time. He tossed the cigarettes on his bed and pulled out his handkerchief, bringing it to his nose. What a dump. He hated this place. His room smelled of mildew unless he opened the window. Then, it smelled like fish and let in the damp, bitter cold. The place had come furnished, which meant he had a twin bed and a table and two chairs. No kitchen, which was fine. He usually ate at the restaurant.

He set the paper onto the table and grabbed a cigarette from the pack. Happy goddamn birthday. Twenty years old and no closer to his dream. This was a dead-end life. Nothing but working and sleeping. He opened the window, shoving it up with brute force because it always stuck. He flinched, the shriek of a seagull tearing through his flesh. Fucking birds. Nasty crea-tures with their weird eyes on the sides of their head, staring at you.

Taking a long drag on the cigarette, he sat at his table and opened the newspaper to the society section. The rest of the world was starving to death, but the rich continued to have parties and wear fancy clothes. He hated all the rich bastards, but he had to keep up on what was happening with the Bennetts.

There it was. The something he'd been looking for. A photo-graph of Caroline Bennett on the campus at Mills College orga-nizing a group of women to knit socks for the poor. She was still as plump as a little sausage, but she was pretty, with a lovely halo of blond hair and always dressed in beautiful clothes. If he ever had the chance, he would praise her clothes. He knew it was strange, but Miller loved fashion. He followed all the latest trends in the paper. Sometimes he stood at the newsstand and thumbed through *Vogue* to see what people with money were wearing. What you wore could make you feel like a different person. Wearing nice clothes changed a person on the inside into what was presented on the outside. He knew this only because he owned one suit and when he wore it out to speakeasies and clubs, it made him feel like a gentleman and less invisible. Lately, he'd noticed women staring at him. He'd transformed, finally, from a skinny kid into a man. He was handsome, and he knew it. Honestly, it was the only thing going for him, given everything else was shit.

He cut out the article to paste in his notebook and moved to the classified advertisements. Sometimes there were ads for work, although less and less since the market crashed. That had been a scary day. He'd wondered about the Bennetts in the days following, as the news filled with stories of men who'd lost their fortunes committing suicide. Would the Bennetts lose their fortune like so many of the other idiots? But no, they seemed to be fine. Yet another reason why he wanted to be Edmund Bennett. The man was untouchable. Money swelled at a faster rate for Bennett Industries than it did for anyone else. News of his business expansions were often in the newspaper; everything from munitions to textiles.

A classified ad caught his eye. The pharmacy and soda fountain across the street from Mill's College needed a soda jerk. Near the college that Caroline attended? Would college students frequent a soda shop across the street from campus? It seemed likely. Would Caroline be one of them? It was worth the chance, if he could get the job. Making sodas was better than what he was doing now, frying fish and washing dishes.

The next morning Miller took a trolley over to the soda shop. It was not open this early in the morning, but a sign said Help

Wanted in the storefront window. An older man wearing a dark suit was inside, sweeping the floor. Miller knocked on the window and pointed to the sign as an indication of his intent. The man shuffled to the door and unlocked it. "You here about the job?" he asked.

"Yes, sir. I saw the advertisement in the classifieds. Is it still available?"

"Yes, yes. Come in. I'm the owner, Ernest." The shop smelled like the inside of a cookie jar. To the right of the entrance, eight stools encircled the counter. Above the counter, bottles of soda flavors lined a shelf. A Coca-Cola sign and a list of sandwiches and other menu items hung across the back of the counter.

"I'm Miller Dreeser, sir." They shook hands.

"Sit, please." Ernest indicated one of the small tables scattered across the black-and-white checkerboard floor. Would you care for coffee?"

"No, thank you," said Miller, taking a seat.

"I'm the primary cook." He pointed to the back of the shop as he hobbled over to the table. "Through there is the kitchen. My wife used to run the front here, making sodas and ice cream sundaes and such." Ernest sat across from him, wincing. "Darned arthritis. Anyway, Delores passed away last month, God rest her soul. My daughter's been running things, but she needs to go home to her family."

Miller, hat resting in his lap, launched into his speech. "I'm sorry about your wife, sir. I don't have much family, since I grew up in an orphanage." He liked to use the orphan boy story to evoke sympathy. It worked surprisingly well when looking for work, even on men. "Fortunately, when I was old enough, the nuns taught me to cook in the kitchen for the other children. I've been working at restaurants the last couple years. Bussing tables, washing dishes, doing some cooking. I'm comfortable doing most things in a kitchen. I've never worked at a counter, but I can't imagine I wouldn't be able to pick it up pretty quick."

He had him. Ernest Wentz's expression softened with every

word. "It gets busy some afternoons, so you might have to hustle. College kids love to come in here and study and whatnot. I don't mind, even if they just buy a coffee or a soda."

"No problem. No problem at all."

"You'll need a white jacket and black tie. There's a shop down the street. You can buy on credit if you tell them it's for my shop. Make sure and give them your name so they can stitch it onto the jacket."

"Yes, sir."

"Can you start tomorrow?"

A few days later, Caroline came in with a group of other girls. They sat at one of the tables and ordered coffees and pastries. Miller was invisible to them, in his starched white jacket and bowtie, working behind the counter, which was fine for now. It gave him the opportunity to observe. He must come up with a plan for seduction, narrow in on her weaknesses so that he might exploit them. It would not be easy, given his station behind the counter and her obvious wealth and prestige. She was prettier in person than in the grainy photographs in the newspaper with that fair hair and blue eyes, he had to admit, albeit a little plump for his taste. When she smiled, the room seemed brighter, and she had this graceful way of moving that reminded him of a swan gliding across a still lake. He walked out to their table, carrying his notepad. "What can I get for you, ladies?"

There were four of them, all studying sums; their books open to the same page. He was good at mathematics. He'd flown through the textbooks at the local high school when he was still at the orphanage. Grammar and vocabulary, mathematics—any subject that required memorization or logical thinking—he swallowed whole. Only history and overwrought literature bored him. Who cared to look back? Whiny protagonists left him cold.

The themes in literature, however, did intrigue him. Thomas Hardy and his books of inevitable fate, especially. He seized on to the idea that it was impossible to deny one's fate. He knew his fate. It was sitting in front of him at this very moment.

"I'll have a vanilla soda, please," said Caroline with a polite but distant smile.

The rest also wanted sodas in varying flavors. When he brought them to the table, they all thanked him, not looking up from their books. He went back to his position behind the counter, drying glasses and watching.

Caroline appeared to be the smartest of the group, as the others often asked her for help with their sums. After about an hour, they put their books away and chatted. Caroline didn't speak much. How could she, given the way the others babbled on about nothing? At five, a car arrived outside the windows, and Caroline gathered her books, said her good-byes, and walked out to the sidewalk. The same chauffer Miller remembered from years ago held the car door for her and she climbed in, disappearing down the street.

"She's so smart," said one of the girls. "I would've failed my English paper had she not helped me last week. How do I know what motivated Anna Karenina to take a lover?" She giggled and covered her mouth at the scandalous word.

"I know. It doesn't seem fair that she's smart and nice," said another.

"And pretty," said the first.

"And rich," said the third.

Caroline was kind. Kindness was a weakness to be exploited. He folded his towel into a neat square.

6

CAROLINE

On the second day of January, Caroline shivered, standing under an eave at the train station, rainwater streaming off the roof and splashing the wooden platform. Julius, by her side, inspected his ticket. She didn't need to look to know what it said. *San Francisco to Chicago, leaving at 2:02 in the afternoon.* Having finished his undergraduate work at Stanford in only three years, Julius was departing for medical school.

"This rain. This awful rain," she said. When she woke that morning, dark clouds hovered over the city. Just as they left from home, the tumultuous sky unleashed a downpour that left inches of water on the streets and sidewalks during the time it took to travel from home to the station. "Why would anyone want to live here?"

He would finish medical school in Chicago and marry a socialite or something, given his looks and personality. She'd long ago accepted the inevitable broken heart on the day of future his wedding. The lovely bride coming down the aisle of the church, her gaze locked with Julius's, and she, Caroline, would seethe with jealousy, biting the inside of her mouth to keep from crying. Cake would be her consolation. The largest

41

piece she could get her hands on as she watched Julius twirl his bride around the dance floor. She could not have something as beautiful as Julius, as good as Julius. A beautiful woman was to have him, someone in the future, sent to break Caroline's heart because Julius would never choose her. Not fat, reliable, funny Caroline.

"Don't cry." He took her hands. "I'll be back eventually. Father and I want to work together and I can't think of where else I'd rather be than near the ocean." His blue eyes peered into her and cracked her open so that she was nothing but a beating heart. She wanted to cling to him, to beg him not to go or to take her with him. Anything but to be parted from him. Regardless, she would not do any of those things, because they were not reciprocated. Julius thought of her like a sister. He did not feel about her the way she felt for him, and he never would.

Puffy, she'd whispered that morning when she dressed. *I'm puffy like an overstuffed pillow.* Her mother bought her the finest clothes, but it didn't matter. She looked terrible in everything. Girls like her had to go through life being charming and kind, apologetic. Three years ago, she decided she needed to have a job, despite her parents' wealth. She needed something to occupy her mind, and to feel a sense of purpose, and to distract her from the self-destructive love she had for Julius. She proposed the idea of running her parents' charities and going to college. They had wholeheartedly agreed, and she'd been accepted at Mills College shortly thereafter. What else could she expect from her life but to dedicate herself to the betterment of others? Not a family of her own, she had thought for the thousandth time, staring at herself in the mirror that morning, just as her stomach growled. She craved a piece of soft bread smeared with butter. It would ease the pain, comfort her.

Now, she nodded, and pressed her face to the collar of Julius's jacket. "You'll write to me, won't you?"

"Every week. I promise."

"I know you'll do well. I'm proud of you," she said.

"I'm proud of *you*, Caroline. To think, you'll be a college graduate in a few months."

She smiled through her tears. "I'm grateful to have the chance to go when so many women can't."

"I'll miss you all so much, but I'll be home for a visit before you know it," he said.

The train rolled into the station with an awful clatter and smoke. Trains made her want to weep. Especially this one. *Be brave. Do not sob until the train rolls away, so that Julius doesn't worry.*

"This is it, I guess," he said. "I forgot to mention that Essie and Father asked if you'd come down to visit sometime this spring? They miss you."

"I will. I'm spending the summer there, so I'll be able to see them a lot. I'll take the twins for adventures to get them out of Essie's hair."

He grinned. "Those two. Trouble times two."

"Yes, they are." His twin sisters, beautiful, precocious, and slightly naughty, were turning eight this year. They looked like Julius had at that age, except they had Essie's brown curls.

He let go of her hands and pulled his ticket from his pocket. "I'll see you soon, Caroline."

She nodded and took a step back from him. "Yes, soon."

He turned away, crossing the platform in his characteristic long strides. When he arrived at the entrance to the train, he turned back, waving, before disappearing up the steps. She waited until his face appeared in the window, before she waved and blew a kiss, fighting sobs rising from her chest. "Good-bye, Julius," she whispered before leaving the platform. She would not look back. Instead, she would go to the soda shop to study and have an ice cream. Anything to stifle the pain in her chest. Anything to keep her from thinking that her life was leaving with Julius on that train.

An hour later, Caroline walked into the soda shop. She looked to see if any of her friends were there, but it was nearly empty. It was a Wednesday. Usually they met on Tuesdays and Thursdays to study after their mathematics class. She didn't feel like talking to anyone, anyway, and she needed to study for her first test in art history on the Renaissance period. She was ill-prepared, thus resigned to a day of rote memorization. Nothing rendered more of a state of unfocused boredom than art history. She didn't mind looking at the paintings, although they were all depictions of the Bible and somewhat depressing, but memorizing their titles, artists, and years made her eyes cross. Taking a seat at the counter, she opened the dreadful book and began to read while she waited for the young man behind the counter to finish with another customer.

"May I help you?" The clerk had a low-pitched voice and spoke so softly that she had the urge to lean closer to hear him better. With a trim physique and brown, thick hair slicked back with pomade, he resembled a very young Gregory Peck. He wore a white jacket with his name etched across the front right pocket. *Miller.* Was that his first or last name?

"May I have a vanilla soda? And could you put a scoop of ice cream in it?" She went back to her book.

"You got it." Minutes later, it appeared next to her book, along with a long spoon.

"Thank you." She glanced up. As she picked up the spoon, she gave him a quick smile before going back to her book.

"Pretty dress."

She looked up, adjusting her reading glasses, which had drifted down her nose, and into eyes the color of coal. He held a soda glass, drying it with a towel. The sinewy muscles of his forearms caught her eye, but she looked away before he could catch her staring. "Thank you." Glancing down, unsure of what she wore, cognizant only of the fact that her thighs touched one another under her skirt and that her bare arms were hidden under her sweater.

The young man continued to watch her. "The color looks like a ripe peach." He raised his eyebrows and stared at her, circling the rim of a soda glass with a corner of the towel, a glint in his eye that was either saucy or cruel, she couldn't be sure which. She was exposed, like there were no clothes hiding her naked body. Her nipples hardened, pressing against the material of her undergarment.

She glanced down at her lap once again, warmth starting at her neck and making its way into her cheeks. What *was* she wearing? Oh, yes, the peach dress, made from a beautiful silk her mother had ordered from France. "Yes, it does rather resemble a peach." Her voice shook slightly. *Don't speak. Close your book and go home.*

"Peaches are my favorite fruit." He set the glass on the counter, then reached down, bringing up another and beginning the drying process once more. "I'm Miller Dreeser." Mystery solved. Miller was his first name.

"Caroline Bennett." She couldn't tear her gaze away from his hands. Breathing was suddenly difficult.

"I know who you are," he said.

"How?"

"Newspaper. Plus, your parents were the benefactors at the orphanage where I grew up. Your mother gave me a telescope."

It was like a strong funnel sucked her into the sudden memory. His eyes like black coal. "The boy on top of the stairs. Miller Dreeser: Telescope." She remembered her mother's hand-writing on the white paper. "Oh my goodness. How strange that we've run into each other here."

"I've wanted to introduce myself and ask if you remembered me at all. I figured you wouldn't. Kids like you don't notice invisible kids like me."

"That's not true. That night had a profound effect on me. It changed my perspective on everything. Gave me a purpose."

"A purpose?" he asked. "That sounds kind of serious."

"After college, I plan to help my father run his charities. I'm taking business courses, actually." *What? Did he not believe she could do anything useful?*

"It's obvious you're clever by the way you help the other girls. I've wanted to say thank you and to pass that on to your folks, but you're always with your friends when you come in here. Like a gaggle of geese. You girls can't seem to go anywhere without at least a half-dozen of you clucking and fussing about in tandem."

"Gaggle of geese? That's not a very flattering description." Anger rose from her belly up to the back of her throat. How dare he criticize her friends. They cared about her even though she was fat. Maybe because she was fat. She was the friend they could always go to for advice or cheering. She wasn't competition. She was on the outskirts of it all, therefore the perfect person in which to confide. She kept all their secrets. Who loved whose beau. Who had secret longings for her father's gardener. Everyone had a secret, it seemed, and Caroline was the keeper of them all. "Besides, geese don't cluck. That's a hen," she said, surprising herself with her boldness.

He shrugged, looking unconcerned and arrogant. His looks *were* like Gregory Peck, but there was nothing heroic about him. Wolfish was the better term. If he were cast in a movie, he'd be the villain the heroine loved while the audience knew he was plotting her demise.

"All honking and strutting about," he said. "All of them but you, that is. You're more like a swan. Elegant. Graceful."

How warm it was. She wished she could take off her sweater, but she wouldn't. No reason to show this wickedly handsome man her pudgy arms. She scrutinized his face for a sign of a crack in his self-confidence, but she found none. He knew he was handsome, which she did not care for in a person. Julius was one of the most handsome men she'd ever seen, and it was anyone's guess if he knew it or not. He was humble, gracious, and so polite. There it was. The pang in the middle of her heart. *Don't think of it. Fight the tears. Focus on this horrible young man in front of you.* "Can I have another napkin, please?"

"Sure thing. For months now I was hoping you'd sit at the counter so I could talk to you." He set the napkin in front of her.

"Me?" She picked up the spoon and dug into the ice cream.

"Yes." His eyes mocked her now, daring her...to do what? What did he want? He set aside the glass in his hand and picked up another. "I'd give quite a lot to have half a chance with someone like you."

She stared at him. Surely he was mocking her. This was a cruel man. He hated her because she was rich. She set down her spoon next to the untouched ice cream, and reached to gather her book, fighting tears.

His strong hand reached out, laying it on the top of her book. "Look at me."

She raised her eyes to meet his gaze, feeling angry, and a shot of desire coursed through her. His eyes seemed soft, tender.

"You have no idea you're beautiful, do you?" His voice, husky now, and low, matched his earnest expression.

"I have to go. My mother's expecting me for dinner." She gathered her purse and book and left, walking quickly around the block before stopping to lean against a wall. What had happened? She couldn't understand it. Why would he say she was beautiful when she clearly wasn't? She started to walk home, not bothering to wait for the car her father always sent at five o'clock. The rain pounded the top of her head and ran down her face, but she didn't care. She let it soak through everything. Her jacket, her peach dress. It didn't matter. Nothing mattered.

When she arrived home, instead of going into the sitting room to say hello to her mother, she went up to her room, tossing aside her school bag. She shrugged out of her dress, letting it fall in a wet heap onto the floor, and stood in front of the large, oval mirror. Her stomach bulged and her thighs pressed against one another. Even in the dim afternoon light, dimples on her thighs and stomach were evident. What could she do to reduce? Quit eating altogether? At her last visit, Doctor Nelson had told her she was thirty pounds overweight and that she might consider cutting back her food intake. She had nodded in agreement when he said it, tears of shame slipping from her eyes. *I can't do it. I've always been fat and I always will be.* She went home and ate half a pie standing at the counter, gulping down her shame.

Now, she dressed in dry clothes and went down to find her mother. Mother was in the sitting room, reading. She set aside her book, and smiled. "You're home early. How did you get here?"

"I walked." Caroline sat on the ottoman by Mother's chair. "I need to talk to you."

Mother sat up straighter, peering at her. "Why did you walk in the rain? Have you been crying?"

Mother was still so beautiful and slender, with a long neck and perfect posture. She'd gone to finishing school, as had Caroline, but Caroline suspected it had been innate for her mother. Some women were this way. Not Caroline. No, she was like her father's mother. Plump and homely.

"I don't want to be fat any longer," said Caroline.

"You're not fat, dearest. Big boned. Voluptuous like your grandmother."

"Mother, I love you, but you're wrong. I'm tired of being this way, feeling this way. I want to change."

For once, Mother seemed to have no response. "Well, I don't know. I suppose there are places to send you. Camps and such?"

"A camp for fat girls?"

Mother looked at her hands. "I've looked into it before."

"Mother, you did?" Mother had lied to her all these years? She *had* wanted her to be thinner? She'd even *looked into* a place for fat girls? A painful lump developed in the back of her throat. "Why didn't you ever mention it?"

"I think you're beautiful, sweetheart, and I always will, but I know your weight bothers you. I want you to be happy, and I know you're not. I see you living in the shadows, and it breaks my heart. If you want to try to reduce, I'll do everything possible to assist you. But you have to want it. I can't want it for you."

"I want to, Mother. I really want to."

"Then we'll find you the right help."

"Is that why you've never said anything? Because you wanted me to decide for myself?" asked Caroline.

"I suppose so. I'm not entirely sure, except that I didn't want to hurt you or crush your spirit by making a large fuss over it."

Caroline wiped tears from her cheeks. "My spirit's already crushed, but I'm ready to fight."

"What's made you want this now?"

"A boy." She relayed the interaction with Miller to her mother. "In the end, I don't know if he was being kind or terribly cruel. Either way, I don't want to have to wonder."

Mother, in tears, took her hand. "Oh, dearest."

A week later, Mother had discovered a place to consider. "It's innovative. They believe women should spend time getting exercise every day."

"Exercise?" asked Caroline.

"Tennis and such. Swimming. Horseback riding. That sort of thing." Mother smiled, with a dreamy look in her eyes. "It sounds like fun. I wish I could go with you."

"Will I have to quit school?" asked Caroline.

"Only temporarily. You can take a semester off and return next fall," said Mother.

The camp was in the mountains east of Los Angeles, with horses, a swimming pool, tennis courts, and hiking trails. It was full of young women just like her, varying in ages from sixteen to twenty-two. Pamela Borden, a young woman from Boston, Massachusetts, arrived at camp the same time as Caroline. Pamela, tall and broad-backed, who looked as if she could lift the same weight of any man, was especially thick through her middle section. Her girth did not disguise the stunning beauty of her high cheekbones and wide brown eyes fringed with dark lashes. She wore her thick, glossy hair longer than was in fashion and tied back from her face in a complicated arrangement of pins. As they walked behind the ramrod-straight headmistress, Miss Weible, a single teardrop slid down Pamela's cheek. Caroline moved her satchel to her right hand and slipped the left into Pamela's.

"It'll be all right," said Caroline.

"I'm homesick already, and I've only been here five minutes," whispered Pamela. "And I'm so warm. It was snowing at home."

"Nevermind your homesickness." Miss Weible opened the door to cabin number seven and stepped aside so the girls could pass through. She was a woman one did not question. Every word and movement was efficient and concise, as if extraneous effort bordered on the ridiculous. It was best to simply follow suit. "You're both in Lucky Seven. Only good things always happen here in Seven. You'll be fast friends by the end of the day."

The cabin appeared sturdy, despite being made from rustic boards. Six cots, all with a blanket and pillow, were arranged in two rows on either side of the cabin, with an aisle between. Each cot had a small table and a trunk underneath. "You may store your clothes and such in the trunk under your bed." Miss Weible showed them their cots, which were next to each other on the right side of the cabin. The other four cots were obviously occupied, given the personal items displayed on their pillows, although the girls to whom they belonged were nowhere to be seen. "We ask that you keep your area clean in respect for the others."

"Where do we bathe?" Pamela's soft voice wobbled. "And dress?"

"Showers are across the way. You'll expect to be clean for dinner. Otherwise, you'll be outside a lot, getting exercise. You dress here, in the cabin."

"In front of the other girls?" asked Pamela.

"Yes, Miss Borden. That's correct," said Ms. Weible. "Here at Camp Walden we believe you learn from your peers. The girls in this cabin are all at different stages in their transformations and they will bestow their wisdom upon you. Someday, you will do the same for new girls." She patted her slim hips. "I used to be quite rotund myself. My own experiences and knowledge are the foundation of this camp. I have no doubt that you will both do well here, but our aim is to teach you how to live healthily for the rest of your life. I can promise you won't leave here without that knowledge. It's up to you to make this one life of yours as fulfilling as you want.

"It starts now. You two are to sit here, side-by-side, and tell the other your story, as truthfully as you can. The whole story, as if you've known one another for a long time. We believe in jumping right in. No small talk about the weather or what book you're reading." She rubbed her hands together, as if to rid them of dust. "Now, I must attend to other matters before lunch. The other girls are out on a hike, but should return within the hour. I've asked Susan to give you a full tour and answer any questions. Our midday meal is at noon. Dress in clothes that allow movement. Welcome to the rest of your life."

After Miss Weible left, they sat on their cots, staring at one another. "My God, what have we done?" asked Pamela. She laughed.

Caroline laughed, suddenly feeling lighter. "I don't know. Do you want to go first?"

Pamela had a sweet, soprano voice, which didn't match her stature. "My mother hates that I'm fat. She's ashamed of me. I'm supposed to come out next season, and the idea of me in an evening dress has given her hives. Quite literally. They're covering her entire neck and chest."

"Oh, my."

Pamela continued. "I'm the youngest of two. My sister's pretty and dainty. The picture-perfect debutante. She's getting married next summer to the exact man for her, in the eyes of my mother anyway, but I'm afraid she doesn't love him. She has this awful look in her eyes like a trapped animal. My mother won't listen, though, and my sister and I want to please her, so we swallow anything we want to say. My sister's dying inside, I know it, but she won't defy my mother."

"What about your father?" asked Caroline.

"My father died when I was twelve and that's when the trouble started with my weight. We did everything together, almost like I was a son. He liked to be outside and we used to go on long walks together and play with balls in the front yard. We have a summer home in the country and we swam in the lake and fished together. After he died, I missed him so much. The only thing that made me feel better was to eat cookies and cakes, anything sweet. It only lasted a few minutes, but at the time the food was in my mouth, I felt better. The more I ate, the more my mother tried to stop me. It became this back and forth all the time, until food and shame were all mixed up together."

Her own story spilled from her. Julius. Her mother's delicate beauty and how awful it was to stand next to her at function. She told her of Anna Beale and the shame of that night. She explained her parents' enormous wealth and the pressure Caroline felt to do good in the world. Finally, the interaction with Miller that had ultimately delivered her to this very moment.

By the time the other girls arrived, Miss Weible's prediction had come true. Caroline and Pamela were fast friends.

At that first lunch, they were introduced to the idea of smaller portions and to avoid sweets, including soda. Required to take shifts in the kitchen and dining hall on a rolling schedule, they learned to cook meals that included foods filled with vitamins and minerals. Every afternoon they took long hikes, played tennis, and swam in the heated pool. Day by day, little by little, Caroline's body changed. Muscles replaced fat. Clothes began to hang on her new smaller frame, so her mother sent her new ones. Twice, new clothes were necessary.

In the shared experience, the commiseration, Caroline found hope. Dry mountain air and constant sunshine were like healing balms, as were the other girls. Every afternoon at three, Miss

Weible gathered women into the dining hall for lesson time, where she taught them her innovative ways of thinking about themselves and the world. Caroline didn't have a word for Miss Weible's philosophy other than it was a message of empowerment and self-love, all entwined with the belief that if their inner thoughts of self-hatred could be healed, the outer self would follow. "You must speak to one another with authenticity because in shared experience lies healing."

Miss Weible was to be obeyed. No one questioned this universal truth. During nights on the skinny cots, the women talked to one another, their voices soft in the dark. *Always been this way. I eat the same as everyone else in my family but I'm the only fat one. I want to die from the shame. The only thing that makes me feel better is food.*

I love a boy, but he'll never love me back.

During her first few weeks, she wrote to Julius every Sunday, filling the pages with details of her activities and new friendships. He wrote back of his rigorous curriculum and exhaustion in short notes, scribbled out of duty, Caroline suspected. One day, after they'd been there just shy of two months, Caroline and Pamela hiked the mountain trail. When they reached the peak, they stood side-by-side, looking at the spectacular view of the mountains and blue sky beyond. Caroline took in a large breath of mountain air, filling her taxed lungs to capacity before letting it out slowly, practicing the art of releasing what she could not control, as taught by Miss Weible. "Pam, I'm going to stop writing Julius."

Pamela didn't say anything for a moment. "Miss Weible says we must treat ourselves as well as we treat others."

"Yes."

"We deserve to be loved as we love," said Pamela.

Caroline knelt and picked up an oval stone by her feet. She rubbed her fingertips along the rough surface before putting it in her pocket. The needles of the firs rustled in the breeze. A jay squawked in a tall oak.

"I'm not going home when I'm done here," said Pamela. "I'm staying out West. I can breathe here." Caroline turned to look at her. Pamela's dark hair was in a braid down her back, peeking out from the brim of her straw hat. Slim and tall, with glowing skin, she exuded health and confidence.

"What about your mother? What about your season?" asked Caroline.

"I'm not doing it. I'm done with it. I'm done with her."

"Where will you go? How will you live?"

"I have a trust fund my father set up for me before he died. It's mine. My mother can't touch it or stop me from using it. Maybe I'll buy a piece of property in the country. Have a garden. Take hikes every day if I want to. Maybe I'll move to Oregon and become a mountain lady. I don't know, other than I'm going to travel for a year. I want to see some of the country and decide where to live later. I'll know where it is when I see it."

"A mountain lady?" Caroline laughed.

"I'll grow old and cranky and scare all the children in town with my crazy ways," said Pamela.

"The poor children." Caroline picked up another stone, pointed and jagged, like it had broken away from a larger rock. She threw it as hard as she could off the side of the mountain. "It feels like I've been hoping he'll love me my whole life."

"And I, my mother." Pamela took off her hat and lifted her face to the sun, closing her eyes.

They stood in silence, Caroline gazing at the view, hoping to memorize it for the days and weeks to come and Pamela with her face to the sun. After a moment, Caroline tugged on her arm. "We should go. I want to be at the cabin to welcome the new girl."

Pam placed her hat back on her head. "Lead the way. I'm right behind you."

At the end of three months, Caroline stood in front of the mirror, transformed. A beautiful woman, slender and muscular, stared back at her. Her blond hair, bleached by the sun from all the outdoor activities, contrasted her tanned skin. She did not look away in shame. Instead of food, she wanted to play a game of tennis. Behind her, Pamela stood in the doorway of the cabin, satchel in hand. "The car's here," said Pamela. "It's time to go."

"I'm ready."

7

CAROLINE

O n a warm day in April, Caroline stood outside the soda shop, looking through the window at Miller working the counter. She took in a deep breath, gathering courage. She would march up to the counter and take a seat. She would pretend she didn't remember him. Earlier that morning she had practiced being cold and indifferent in front of the mirror.

She sat on the stool closest the door. It was quiet, only a few customers at tables, chatting quietly. "May I have a water, please? And a tomato sandwich."

He gazed at her with coal black eyes until she was absorbed, penetrated. "You look different."

"Do I?" So much for pretending she didn't remember him.

"Yeah. Where you been?" He set a glass of water on the counter.

"Busy."

"I see. Hang tight. I'll get this order back to the kitchen."

She waited, sipping from the glass of water. Her heart moved to her throat and her pulse thudded there with unusual rapidity. The corner of her eye twitched. She put her index finger over it.

Miller came back, leaning on the counter with his elbow. "It's

7

56

been over three months since you were in here. I imagined your father was having trouble like so many."

"No, we're fine."

A ding of a bell from the kitchen averted Miller's attention. "That'll be your sandwich." He left to fetch it. When he came back, he set it in front of her, along with a paper napkin.

She took half the sandwich and wrapped it in the napkin. There was a man begging on the street. She would give it to him. This was a trick she learned at camp. Eat half of what everyone else eats. Put it aside if you can do so politely.

She looked up to see him watching her. "Not hungry?"

"I'm always hungry." She spoke without emotion, before taking a dainty bite of her sandwich. *Eat slowly. Do not gulp your food. Enjoy the taste.* Would she ever stop hearing the words of the Miss Weible in her head?

He smiled. "I never got enough when I was a kid. It takes a lot not to eat like a hungry kid now that I'm not. We always have a lot of leftovers here, so I'm lucky."

"I went to the mountains," she said, as if he'd asked her again about her whereabouts. "I lost a lot of weight there."

His eyes widened, but he didn't say anything.

"I came in here to say thank you," she said.

"Me? What did I do?"

"You were cruel to me, which made me angry enough to decide to do something about my figure. Every time I thought about putting a treat in my mouth I remembered the way you looked at me."

"Wait now. How did I look at you? How was I cruel to you?"

"Mocking me. Telling me I was beautiful when I was not."

"Caroline Bennett, I meant every word I said. Whether you're curvaceous or slender, you're beautiful."

She didn't know what to say. Her stomach did a flip, like it did when they were teenagers and she saw Julius running toward her on the beach. Was he telling the truth? Had he found her beautiful even when she was plump?

He leaned closer, placing both hands on the counter. "Thinking I hurt you makes me want to die."

"That's outrageous and ridiculous." She laughed, elated, so light she might float to the ceiling. Had she misjudged him?

"Would you like to go dancing with me sometime?" he asked.

"Dancing?"

"Yes. You dance, don't you?"

"I've been to finishing school. I dance."

"This isn't that kind of dancing." He raised his eyebrows and winked. "Don't you worry; I'll take the lead."

"Then, yes. I'll allow you to take me dancing. But you'll have to pick me up at my home. Father will insist on that."

Three months later, while watching a sunset the color of a ripe peach, he told her he loved her, that he could not live without her. "Would you ever consider a penniless dreamer? Because I want you to be my wife."

"Oh, Miller, yes, I want to. But my father. He'll have to agree."

"He'll agree. He won't deny you what you want."

"Why do you say that? How do you know?" she asked.

"I just do." The sunset reflected in his eyes, he shook his fist in the air. "I have big plans, Caroline. I'll be a success someday and nothing will get in my way. I promise you that."

She waited until after dinner that evening to speak to her parents, pouring them all a drink in the study. "I have something important to talk to you about."

Her parents exchanged glances, as if they knew what was coming and had to brace themselves.

"Miller asked me to marry him," she said.

Mother, eyes sharp, leaned forward in her chair. "Why didn't he ask your father?"

"I'm asking for him," she said. "This isn't his world. He doesn't know the rules."

"He's penniless," said Mother.

"Does that matter?" asked Caroline. "We have our own money."

"This is the very same boy who hurt you," said Mother. "You told me he's cruel."

"I misunderstood," said Caroline.

"I question if this young man is worthy of you," said Father. "You have everything to offer and he has nothing."

"How do you know he doesn't just want our money?" asked Mother.

"Mother, I'm surprised at you," said Caroline. "You're so generous to the poor."

Mother sniffed, taking a sip of her brandy. "I want the very best for you. We don't know anything about this young man."

"It's our job to protect you," said Father. "Over my dead body will I let you make a mistake. Who you marry is the most important decision you'll ever make. It taints the rest of your life."

"I love him, Daddy. Isn't that enough to know?"

"What about Julius?" asked Mother.

"Mother, Julius thinks of me like a sister."

"But you love him, don't you?" asked Mother. "You've loved him all your life."

"It doesn't matter," said Caroline. "I deserve someone who loves me back. I can't waste my life pining for Julius."

"Let's have Miller Dreeser to dinner," said Father. "If he wants you, he must do this properly."

Miller came to dinner on Friday evening. The cook made Cornish game hens and rice, served with a bottle of French Chablis. The first course came, a salad with vinaigrette. Miller hesitated. He didn't know which fork to use. His eyes darted to her hand. She tapped the salad fork with her finger. He took the hint.

"What are your plans for the future?" asked Father.

"I'm not entirely sure, sir. I have a decent job now, but times are hard for everyone these days. I would've liked to attend university and become a doctor or something, but it wasn't an option for an orphan boy."

"What is it you think you have to offer my only daughter?" asked Father.

"I have nothing to offer your daughter financially. For now, that is. I'm a hard worker. Whatever path I take, I'll make sure I make the most of every opportunity. I'll do anything to please her, sir, to take care of her."

Caroline might burst from happiness. *Was* it possible to die from delight? How could this be happening to her? Handsome Miller Dreeser loved her. She was desperate for her parents to give their blessing. *Please God*, she prayed silently. *Let them say yes*. After she walked him out that night, she'd headed to her father's study, knowing they would convene there and talk through whether or not Caroline was to have Miller. She stood at the door, listening over the pounding of her heart.

"There's no logical explanation to love," Father was saying. "To deny her the man she loves will only cause us all unnecessary pain."

"But he's penniless. An orphan. We know nothing of his background or what sort of people run through his blood," said Mother. "I assumed she'd marry Julius. It was so obvious how much they loved each other as children."

Caroline brought her hand to her mouth. Julius? Why would they think she'd marry Julius? Wasn't it obvious that he didn't love her? Could never love her?

"Well, darling, no one marries their childhood sweetheart," said Father.

"We did."

"No one besides us," he said, laughing. "Anyway, if Caroline loves him, he must be a good man."

"Well, she's had the best man ever made by which to compare him. The greatest thing a father can do to ensure his daughter marries a good man is to be one himself, and you're certainly that," said Mother. "So there's that comfort."

"Oh, Sophie, you're quite ridiculous." He laughed, obviously pleased. There'd been murmurs after that, and the sound of kissing, which Caroline, in her happiness, did not mind. Let them kiss. Let the whole world kiss. She was to have Miller.

"We'll have to give him a job at the company," said Father. "We can't have her married to a soda jerk."

"Yes. There's no other way."

"Caroline says he's intelligent. I can groom him, teach him, if he's willing to learn."

"How we're going to announce this to the world, I have no idea," said Mother. "What will people think?"

"When have you ever cared what people think?" asked Father.

"Not until now."

"Well, it doesn't matter if Caroline's happy."

"I agree, my darling."

Caroline burst into the room, unable to contain her gratefulness, and rushed into her mother's arms. "Thank you, Mother. I promise you won't be sorry."

Mother's arms tightening around her. "If you're sure this is what you want, we won't stand in your way."

"He's going to need to learn which forks to use before the wedding." Father's voice was gruff. "Have Mac take a message to him that I want to speak with him first chance tomorrow. I have a few things to discuss with him."

Caroline agreed, still floating on air, as she made her way down the hallway to find Mac.

8

MILLER

He arrived at the Bennetts' home at nine the next morning, dressed once again in his only suit, and rapped the front door knocker. Not wanting to arrive disheveled, he'd splurged on the trolley instead of walking, and he straightened his tie as footsteps from inside the house approached. It was a warm autumn day, the leaves not yet turned, and the skies clear. Expecting the housekeeper, he was surprised to see Caroline standing there, her cheeks pink and eyes shining. What a little idiot she was, the way she gazed at him with the eyes of a trusting child. She was ridiculous and trusting. It was obvious how much she loved him. He shouldn't blame her. He was skilled at the practice of deceit, and yet he did. How could she not see that he was an actor on the stage, pretending to love her when all he wanted was to sit at Edmund Bennett's dinner table?

Still, she was lovely. It would not be difficult to take her on their wedding night.

He kissed her quickly on the lips. "Good morning, my beauty."

"My father's waiting," she said. "He wants you to ask permission."

His chest burned. What did they think of him? That he was uncouth? He *would* ask. This is the way it was done. He knew that. Everyone knew that.

Edmund stood when he walked into the study. It was Saturday and the big man was dressed in a casual suit. The windows were open, filling the room with the scent of late-blooming roses. They shook hands. Edmund asked him to take a seat in one of the leather chairs by the unlit fireplace. "I suppose it's too early for a drink," said Edmund, sitting across from him. "But would you care for coffee?"

"No, thank you. I'm fine." He must not allow his voice to shake. "Sir, I would like to ask for your permission to marry your daughter."

"Yes, I understand your intent. I have a few questions for you," said Edmund.

"Yes, sir?"

"I will allow you to marry her, but you need to understand a few rules. You will come to work for me in one of the management positions. It's important to me that you appear a man of prospects, regardless of your humble beginnings. However, you will work for every opportunity and that includes learning from myself and others who have experience. Nothing will be rewarded to you without effort. Do you understand?"

"Absolutely."

"That said, you will never, and I mean never, be given part ownership of any part of my company. We will buy a home for you to live in, but it will be in my name, as will the cars and anything else we allow you to use. There is to be no mistake that it is her money you live on and that it will never be yours. If she decides to divorce you, I will make certain you return to your current penniless state."

Miller nodded, forcing his face into impassivity. "Yes, sir."

"If you do anything to hurt her, I will have you killed and dumped into the bottom of the ocean."

Was he joking? If his deadpan expression was any indication, the answer was no. "I understand."

Edmund scrutinized him. "And you still want to marry her?"

"Very much so. I love her, for richer or poorer."

"It helps that she's mostly the richer than the poorer," he said, dryly. "But it appears we have a deal."

"We have a deal." Miller stood, believing it was time for him to leave.

Edmund stood as well. "A few other points before you go. I've hired a diction coach for you."

"Sir?"

"Yes, a diction coach. He'll clean up your rather casual pronunciations of words. Make you sound a little higher end, shall we say?"

Miller swallowed. He hadn't realized anything was wrong with the way he spoke, but who was he to say? He wanted to be like Edmund Bennett, and if a diction coach helped him do it, he was all for it.

"We have a tailor who will come by to get your measurements. We need to give you a complete wardrobe if you're to publicly court my daughter."

"Nothing would please me more," said Miller.

They walked toward the door to the study. Edmund held out his hand. "Welcome to the family."

"Thank you, sir."

9

HENRY

In the garden of the convalescent hospital in Worcestershire, England, Henry Sayer, Petty Officer Third Class of the United States Navy, turned his face to the sun and closed his eyes, breathing in the scent of grass. Since arriving into the city of Malvern four weeks ago on one of the hospital trains, the weather had been consistently cloudy with temperatures in the upper sixties. Not unusual for early July, the nurses said. That afternoon, however, the clouds broke apart and glorious rays of sun rained down upon them. Good weather must not be wasted, the nurses had said, encouraging him to sit outside and enjoy it while it lasted.

Opening his eyes, he sat on one of the chairs set in the garden for patients, and like a creature trapped too long in darkness, took in his surroundings with eyes unprepared for the bright colors and lights of a sunny afternoon. He squinted, shading his eyes with his left hand. Soldiers with various injuries milled about. Some had nurses by their side, others shuffled along with another soldier. Bees hummed in the wildflowers, gathering pollen, unaware that a war raged through Europe. His right arm, amputated just above the elbow, ached with what Doctor Nelson had described as phantom pain. A bee buzzed close to his ear and he swatted it away with his left hand. *Left-handed*, Doctor Nelson had said at one point. *Very fortunate*. It would soon be time to return home to his cottage in California, the Pacific Ocean, his roses, and the scent of the saltwater and seaweed. Would it remind him of his time at war, of his time on the ship, of the hours in the frigid waters of the Atlantic?

We are expendable on this mission, Lieutenant Commander George Dewey Hoffman had told them. The USS *Corry* was to be the first ship in the ambitious invasion of Normandy on June seventh, leading the other allied vessels to the shores. Their mission was to protect the soldiers on land, firing without mercy at the Nazis. Planes overhead obscured the skies with smoke, hoping to hide the allied ships from the Germans. The plane that was to hide the *Corry* was shot down before it could reach the enemy, leaving the ship vulnerable.

German bombs struck the USS *Corry* with unrelenting fury. She began to sink with great speed, and they were commanded to abandon ship, leaving Henry and the rest of the surviving crewmembers stranded in the frigid waters of the Atlantic. One of his shipmates, clinging to the sinking *Corry*, managed to raise the American flag in the wreckage. Henry fixated on the flag as he struggled in the fifty-four degree water, holding onto one of the rafts carrying his injured brothers. Constant, unrelenting German gunfire cascaded around them, until a shot managed to catch him in the arm. A searing pain had been replaced with numbness, and by the time the rescuers arrived, he was barely conscious. He remembered a member of the USS *Fitch* helping him aboard the rescue ship, along with unclear images of the ship's doctor tending to him, but little else. When he woke in a field hospital set up in Normandy for the inevitable injured soldiers of D-Day, an English nurse stood over him, writing in a chart. Vaguely aware of the moans of other patients, he moved his eyes slightly to the left and saw rows of hospital beds, all filled with injured soldiers.

She spoke to him in her clipped accent, almost like one

would a child, explaining where he was and that she was one of the nurses looking after him.

"I was on the USS *Corry*. How many men did we lose?"

"I wouldn't know exactly," she said. "It was sunk."

"Yes, I know. I saw it go down." Henry turned his face away, not wanting the nurse to see his tears. She poured him water and encouraged him to lift his head, and gave him a small sip. "Is my arm okay?" He experienced no pain. His mind seemed stuffed with cotton balls and he was sleepy, like in one of those dreams where one tried to wake but couldn't.

"I'm sorry, no. Your right arm was nearly destroyed from the bullet. Unfortunately, we had to amputate just above the elbow."

Amputate? But his hand was there. He tried to lift it, but the pain was too much. "Show me," he said.

The nurse lifted the sheet. His arm was bandaged above the elbow. White gauze where his elbow should have been. *They took my arm. The bastards took my arm. So this is it. This is my fate.* He would go home to California, unable to fight any longer, with his arm somewhere in France.

A shout from across the lawn pulled him from his memories. Doctor Julius Nelson, carrying a tray of food, crossed the lawn to Henry and sat in the chair beside him. "Dining al fresco, Doc?" asked Henry.

Setting his tray on his lap, Doctor Nelson smiled and pushed his glasses to the bridge of his nose. "The nurses pushed me out. Said I needed food and fresh air." Blond with a hint of gray at his temples, Doctor Nelson wore circular, wire-rimmed glasses that reflected in the sunlight, making it almost impossible to see his blue eyes behind them. In the first days of his arrival here, the doctor's gentle eyes had reminded him of his mother's. The doctor was like her in other ways, too, quiet and self-deprecating. The hospital demanded more from a man than was fair, but he never complained, just went stoically forward. "How you feeling, Henry? You're looking well."

"My arm that isn't my arm hurts like a son of a bitch."

"It will for a while, I'm afraid." Doctor Nelson took a bite of whatever the brown food was on his tray. "In general, though, your recovery's gone remarkably well, which leads me to my news. You're going home."

"Home?"

"Yes, sir. I hate to see you go, for my sake. I'll miss our conversations."

"As will I." Over the last few weeks, he and the doctor had become friendly after discovering they both were from towns not far from one another on the California coast. Since that time, they'd spent time talking of home and books, without touching on any subject too personal. Henry sensed a deep loneliness from the doctor that matched his own. He missed his fellow seaman and the camaraderie they'd shared on the ship more than he'd thought possible. Henry stared up at the sky. Several fluffy clouds floated in an otherwise silky blue.

"I've not much to go back to," said Henry. His mother and father had died while he was away fighting. His brother-in-law, William, was missing, having fallen or been captured somewhere in France. Only Rose, his twin, was left at home not knowing whether to give up hope that her husband would return. He'd gotten her letter several months before they invaded Normandy. *William's listed as missing. I don't know what it means, Henry. Is he dead? Is he captured by the filthy Germans or Japanese? I'm beside myself with the not knowing.*

"No sweetheart?" asked the doctor.

"No one to speak of, other than my sister. It will be wonderful to see her." Rose had taken over their father's company when he died, since Henry wasn't there to do it. This was the only good that had come out of this awful war. He didn't have to pretend like he was the more capable of the two of them when it came to business simply because he was a man.

"I'm a master furniture builder—I *was* a master furniture builder. Not sure what I'll be now." He smiled to take the heat from the words, but the bitterness was in his throat, tasting of bile.

Doctor Nelson nodded, his eyes sympathetic. "You mumbled something about a table one night in your sleep."

"Probably the table I made for my mother before I enlisted. I was ridiculously proud of it." The beautiful table was at the cottage now, with no one there to use it. His mother, gone. The cancer took her while he was away and he hadn't been able to say good-bye. She hadn't gotten his last letter. He'd gotten one from her, though, arriving after she had passed and was already buried. His aim had been to keep it forever, but it was with the rest of the USS *Corry* at the bottom of the ocean now. "I apprenticed for a man in San Francisco. Taught me everything I know. Not sure he'll want a one-armed furniture maker."

"Over time, your body will get used to only having one hand and you'll be able to do most of what you did before," said the doctor. "Maybe start your own shop? Work at your own pace?"

It was something to consider. Maybe he could open a shop in town and live in one of the cottages? The truth was, his father had left him a wealthy man. There was no need to work, other than he would go insane without something meaningful to do. "I won't go home to San Francisco." Twin cottages had been constructed on the property about a hundred yards from one another, meant to be summer places, let for rent to families on holiday, as both an investment and a gift to Henry's mother, who loved the seaside. When he was a child, Henry's family had stayed in one cottage during the summer months while renting the other to various families. "I'm going to live at the ocean."

"I miss the feeling of salt water on my skin," said Doctor Nelson. "Nothing like it."

"Some good times when I was a kid," said Henry. "The best times." He, Rose, and William had spent leisurely days playing in the sand, riding bicycles along country roads, having picnics. William Thomas was his best friend. Rose's love. He'd lived with his mother and father up the road from the cottages on a small farm. His vision flooded with an image of Rose and William on their wedding day. How full of hope and love they had all been. He shook it off. He must close off his memory. It was like Pandora's box. Open the lid and endless grief came drifting out with no hope for recovery. "My father worked in the city but came down for weekends. I can remember waiting at the end of our dirt road for him to get there."

Doctor Nelson nodded, with a slight smile. "My days at the seaside were the best of my life." An expression of regret or pain crossed the doctor's face. "My father has a practice there. I'm supposed to join him after this is over, but lately I don't know."

"Don't know what?"

"I question how I'll get back to normal life or feel that anything I do has relevance," said Doctor Nelson. "I was on the front lines for most of the war before they sent me out here to set up this operation. It changes a man, operating under a canvas with bombs falling all around you."

A petty officer came by, carrying a mail bag. "Doctor Nelson, sir, I have a letter for you."

"Thank you." They saluted, and he ambled off to track down the next lucky recipient of word from home.

The doctor studied the envelope with what appeared to be great intensity. Then, he traced the tip of his index finger over the return address.

"Letter from home?" asked Henry, curious to know what had made the good doctor's eyes mist.

"Yes, it's from Caroline. She writes the most wonderful letters." The doctor's voice had become husky. "Full of details. I'll save it for later."

"Is Caroline your wife?" Odd he hadn't mentioned her. Most of the men couldn't stop talking about their girls or wives waiting at home.

"No, she's not my wife."

Henry wanted to know more, but he didn't know how to ask, so he remained silent.

"I was in love with her when we were young. While I was away at medical school she married someone else. I never had the courage to tell her my feelings, so I'll never know if there was a chance for us." He paused, swatting at a fly near his head. "But she's my best friend."

"No one's taken her place?" asked Henry.

"I was engaged before the war. She broke it off after I'd been over here for about six months."

"I had someone, too. She met a sailor while I was out to sea. Married him after three days." Henry shook his head. "Women." He said it lightly, hoping to cajole the doctor to smile, but his expression remained dark.

"Ann said she couldn't marry a man in love with someone else."

"I'm sorry, Doc."

"In hindsight, given who Caroline chose instead of me, I needn't have worried about my humble beginnings." His expression darkened. "I have no evidence, but I feel certain he married her for her money."

"What makes you think so?" Henry hadn't been this interested in a conversation since his injury. It felt good, like he was his old self. He was the *story gatherer,* his mother used to say. *People always tell you things.*

"The way he looks at her," said Doctor Nelson.

Henry raised an eyebrow, waiting for more. The doctor had a measured way of speaking. Henry suspected he couldn't be rushed or he might change his mind about sharing his confidence.

"The way my father looks at my stepmother—the way Caroline's father looks at her mother. I know what love looks like when reflected from someone's face. He seems indifferent to her at best. No one sees it but me. They're all fooled by him. Especially Caroline. Lately, in her letters, though, I sense a sadness.

There's something she's not telling me." The doctor glanced at his wristwatch. "My God, man, what am I going on about? Look at the time. I have patients to attend to. I quite lost myself in all that wallowing."

"I appreciated the company. I'm rather sick of my own troubles, if you want to know the truth," said Henry.

"I don't suppose you'd call on Caroline when you return home? I know it would give her comfort to hear how I'm doing."

"It would be my pleasure."

The doctor smiled, looking happier than the moment before. "Would you write to me afterward with a full report?"

"Absolutely. It'll give me a mission when I return."

"Someday, when this is over, we'll have a beer by the sea."

"It's a promise," said Henry.

"Don't let this define your life, my friend. Go home and live. They've taken enough from you. Don't let them take one more moment."

The doctor didn't say it, but Henry understood something else. *Go home and live, because so many others don't get to.*

CAROLINE

A t the end of July Caroline received a phone call. "I'm Henry Sayer," said the pleasant voice. "I was treated by Doctor Nelson in England before I was discharged. We became friends after discovering how close we lived to one another before the war. He asked if I might call on you."

"How wonderful. I would love nothing more. But you must promise to tell me everything. His letters are terrible. He never gives me any details."

"That's the opposite of what he said about yours," said Henry.

She laughed. "I do write a good letter. It's my mother's fault for making me rewrite so many essays when I was young."

They agreed that he would come for lunch the next day. She placed the receiver back on the phone and straightened the framed photograph of her and Miller on their wedding day. How young they looked. She wore a white gown and long veil. Miller wore a tuxedo and a top hat. He'd insisted upon that. They'd had the ceremony at their church with light shining through the stained glass and the reception at the club afterward, all of it a blur. Clearest in her memory was the gown her mother had ordered from France. It weighed five pounds, with an intricate layer of lace over the entire dress and dozens of buttons down the back. Holding onto her father's arm before they entered the church, she started shaking. An intense desire to step backward instead of forward rushed through her. Father nudged her. They walked toward Miller, who stood with the priest and his best friend from the orphanage, Timmy Blick, a small, sharp-eyed man who reminded Caroline of a small dog that either didn't know he was tiny, or was doing everything in his power to hide it. Half way down the aisle, she locked eyes with Julius. He sat with his father and Essie in the second row, behind her mother. He smiled at her reassuringly.

She went to the open window, the sounds of crashing waves and seagulls background to the shouts of her children playing croquet on the lawn. Her parents' beach home, north of Santa Barbara, sat close to the shore, nestled in a cove on a ten-acre piece of property. North of the house, the terrain steepened and, unlike the spot they'd chosen for the house, was suspended above the sea with craggy rocks instead of sand below the grassy knoll. High tide now, the surf crashed close to where their grassy back garden began, with no hint of the sandy beach the children would enjoy later that day. Because of this, her children had resigned themselves to the garden before lunch.

Audrey, seven, wore a yellow sundress, bright against the green of the grass and blues of sea and sky, trying hard to compete with her older brothers. She was naturally thin, thank goodness. She hadn't taken after Caroline and could eat what-ever she wanted without so much as a glimmer of fat anywhere. Pierce, ten, and Sebastian, thirteen, wore blue trousers and white shirts with their sleeves rolled up to their elbows, always complaining they were too hot. None of her children were fat like she had been as a child, all three lanky and long-limbed. Audrey was blond like Caroline, with the same blue eyes, whereas the boys were both dark like their father. Seb, tall and muscular and athletically gifted, took after her father, whereas Pierce favored Miller, lean and quick. The two of them moved like cats, she always teased. Light on their feet and silent, until they pounced upon you.

"Be careful of the mallet, Sebastian. You almost hit your sister." Nanny Brown, large straw hat covering her head of white curls, kept watch over them with an indulgent upturn of her mouth, despite their rambunctiousness. The woman had nerves of steel. She sat in a garden chair in her usual brown suit, plump, white ankles crossed, horrified that during wartime there were no stockings available. Her knitting needles flashed in the sunlight. How she knitted without looking at the needles was beyond Caroline. Knitting had not been one of Caroline's gifts. Why knit when one could read a book, she had thought before the war, but she could no longer evade the click of the needles for the selfish pleasure of reading. The troops needed socks, vests, scarves.

"She shouldn't stand so close," said Seb.

"I wasn't." Audrey stomped her foot and crossed her arms over her chest.

"Do we want to go inside and study our spelling?" asked Nanny Brown.

In unison, they all agreed that, no, studying spelling was not better than playing croquet in the sunshine.

"Then we best control our tempers," said Nanny Brown.

Caroline stepped away from the window and turned on the radio. Since Julius had left, she listened to news of the war in a way that bordered obsession. With his sparse letters, she had some idea of where he was located and listened with rapt attention for news of those battlegrounds. He'd been on the front lines in France, aiding injured soldiers for most of the war. However, six months ago he'd been sent to England to head up the conva-lescent hospital in Worcestershire, England. After this, she'd slept better at night, knowing he was out of the direct line of fire.

Dear Julius. How sweet of him to send Henry Sayer to see her. He knew she would be comforted to hear from someone who had seen him recently.

She sat on the sofa, grabbing her own knitting. It must be done. No idle hands. Everyone must do their part. Edward Murrow's clipped voice came over the radio airwaves, dulled from the crackling of the transmission. The fighting overseas had taken a turn after the invasion of Normandy, he said. The allies were slowly liberating occupied France.

Please God, let it be over by Christmas. Please keep Julius safe.

After he finished medical school, Julius had come back to Santa Barbara and joined his father's practice. He made house calls, earning his money from the wealthy who owned houses along the coastline, giving him the opportunity to tend to the poor for free, or, as he explained to Caroline once, in the "pay what you can" model. After Pearl Harbor, when America entered the war, he'd joined the army as a doctor.

Just before he left for the war, Julius became engaged to Ann, a young woman he'd met through his work. She'd come with Julius to dinner and they'd all liked her. She was pretty and smart and well-spoken. *The perfect doctor's wife,* Caroline thought.

The day before he left, Julius had come to the house to say good-bye. They sat on the back porch, watching the waves come and go.

"I thought Ann would want to marry before you left," she said.

"She wants a big wedding and there simply isn't time to plan it before I go," he said.

She studied his face. There was an evasiveness about him; he wouldn't meet her gaze. "Julius, are you certain about Ann? If you have doubts, it's best to think it all through before making a mistake."

"Are you speaking from experience?" he asked.

"What do you mean?"

"Have you regretted your decision in a husband?" His expression and voice were bland, unreadable.

She shook her head. "No, no. I have a blessed life."

"Are you happy, Caroline?"

"Life isn't a storybook. I'm happy enough." She hesitated, feeling suddenly like she might cry.

"Is 'happy enough' good enough?" he asked.

"It has to be." Tears gathered at the corners of her eyes. She was lonely, that was all. Miller was not a companion. They rarely touched these days. She was often asleep by the time he came home from work. If it weren't for her parents, the children, and Julius, she might have experienced the desolation more keenly, but it was easy to blur it out of her consciousness because of the satisfaction of her other relationships. "It happens over time. We were so young when we married." She traced her finger around a knothole in the porch banister.

"Your parents were young when they married and look at them," he said.

She smiled. "True. Not everyone can be so lucky."

The muscle between his brows scrunched together in the shape of a camel's hump when he took her hands in his. "Take care of yourself while I'm away. Write to me every week with every detail. Can you do that?"

"Yes, yes. I'll write every Saturday."

He closed his eyes for a moment and took in a deep breath. "If I don't come back, I wanted to say something."

She tried to interrupt him, but he put up his hand.

"No, please, just let me say it. These days on this beach with you and your family have been the best of my life. You're quite simply my...favorite person in the whole world."

"Stop it. You're going to make me cry and that can't be the way we say good-bye because you're coming back. We *will* have more good times. Do you hear me?" She wanted to throw her arms around him, cling to him to keep him from leaving. "Just come back to me. To *us*." To *us*. Not *her*. He did not belong to her. When he returned, he would belong to Ann. She must let go of him, not rely on his friendship as much. If he were to marry, he would not have time for her.

They said good-bye. She watched him walk down the beach

to his father's house, feeling like a brick had replaced her heart. During the years between now and then, she had kept her promise, writing to him once a week. She had received letters from him sporadically, depending on where he was and what was happening in the war. One day, about six months after he'd left, he wrote that Ann had broken off the engagement. He did not say why, and she decided it better not to ask.

———

The next day, Henry Sayer arrived at noon. The Bennett's housekeeper, Margaret, brought him into the sitting room where Caroline waited. Her parents had taken everyone into town for a day at the shops and the promise of ice cream, so the house was empty of its usual chaos. Henry was tall and blond with chiseled features and a pair of striking blue eyes that smiled at her when she stood to greet him. "Mrs. Bennett, it's such a pleasure to meet you. Doctor Nelson did not lie about your beauty."

She smiled at him, not bothering to correct him about her married name. Julius sometimes introduced her as Caroline Bennett. An old habit he hadn't been able to let go of when she married Miller. Whether Julius had truly said she was beautiful didn't matter. A compliment at her age was nice, regardless of its origins or truthfulness. "How kind, Mr. Sayer, but you've been away, stuck with men for a while now. Perhaps this clouds your vision." Dressed in a light suit, white shirt and a cornflower blue tie, it took her a moment to realize that the sleeve of his right arm had been sewn to compensate for a lack of limb. His right arm had been amputated. The poor man. This awful war. She fought the ache of injustice that worked its way from her belly to her throat.

He chuckled and shook his head. "I don't think so."

"Please sit." She took one of the chairs, knowing he wouldn't sit until she did. "Would you like something to drink? Fresh lemonade or perhaps something stronger?"

He sat on the couch, long legs crossed at the ankles. His shoes were new, shiny and black. "I'm fine for now, thank you."

"Thank you for taking the time to visit," said Caroline.

"Doctor Nelson was kind to me, not just as a doctor but as a friend. When he asked if I might visit you, I said yes right away." He brushed his golden curls from his forehead. "I've been back several weeks, but the adjustment to being home hasn't been entirely smooth."

"I went away once to a camp for three months, nothing like war, but so entirely different from home life that it was as if I were in a dream for several weeks after my return. People and places I'd known all my life seemed different."

"Yes, that's exactly it," said Henry.

"But it was I who changed, not them."

"I have indeed changed. Not just my arm, but on the inside as well. Doctor Nelson and I spoke of this often during our time together."

"How *is* Julius?" Caroline smoothed the front of her dress. She'd chosen her blue flowered print with the wide collar and sleeves, tucked at the waist with an A-line skirt, made before the war. Even Mother hadn't been able to secure new fabric or dresses during wartime.

"He wanted me to reassure you he's doing well. I don't know the horrors of what he saw at the front, but for now, he's safe." Henry's eyes had dulled.

"As I said, he never gives many details in his letters. I suppose he doesn't want me to know how bad it is."

"Yes, I suspect that's true."

Caroline shivered despite the warm breeze drifting through the windows. "I worry he'll be changed."

"We all are, Mrs. Bennett."

"Please, call me Caroline." She walked to the liquor cabinet. "I suddenly feel like a drink. Would you care for a sherry?"

"Do you have whiskey?"

Caroline smiled as she crossed the room, her heels clicking on the hardwood floors. "This *is* my father's house. We have several different kinds."

"This house is beautiful," he said. "And I'll take whatever's convenient."

"This is my favorite place in the world." She splashed whiskey into a glass and handed it to him. "Tell me, Mr. Sayer, what will you do now?"

He took a sip of his drink before answering. "I was a furniture builder before the war. Commissioned pieces of my own designs. High end—made of the finest materials. My clients were my father's business associates mostly. Their wives have excellent taste. But now? I don't know. I'm unsure if it's possible. Fortunately, I'm left-handed, since that's the one I have left."

"Have you considered getting an assistant?" She sat across from him, tasting her sherry before setting it on the table. "They could do the parts you couldn't. Perhaps you could concentrate on design and finish work?"

"It's odd you should suggest that. Doctor Nelson said the same thing."

"Did he? How funny. I suppose you can tell we practically grew up together. My father's a great one for figuring out a solution to every problem. He taught us that."

"Doctor Nelson also said my body would adjust in time. He claims we have an incredible capacity for adaptation."

"Julius was always the smartest person I ever knew. He still is. The way he thinks, the way his mind works, was always fascinating to me. I've missed him so much." What was she doing? Going on about Julius in front of the sweet young man adjusting to a new life. She must help him somehow. Then, she had an idea. "How would you like to do a piece for me? Just as an experiment." She pointed to her grandmother's old hutch that occupied the corner of the room. "My mother's been talking for years about replacing that with something more modern. This one belonged to my father's mother who, from all accounts, was a quite unpleasant woman. Every time my mother looks at it, she makes some comment about how it reminds her of the old battle-axe. Her words, not mine."

They both laughed. Mr. Sayer's eyes brightened. He sat forward. "What kind of wood does she like?" he asked.

"She loves cherry wood. Do you think you could make something for us?"

"Sure, I could. I could put together a design or two and let you decide which you liked."

"That would be wonderful. I'll surprise my mother with it. I can never think of anything to get her for her birthday."

As if talking out loud, Mr. Sayer continued. "I'm sure I could find someone in town to work with me."

"I'm sure you could."

They chatted for another hour, during which Mr. Sayer asked her to call him Henry, and they shared stories of their childhoods growing up on the beach. Around one, Margaret came in to announce lunch. About that same time, Nanny Brown and the children entered from the porch, bringing their noise and the smell of children playing. Caroline introduced them to Henry before they left to wash up before the meal.

Caroline brought Henry into the dining room. The children and Nanny Brown followed shortly thereafter. She wished she'd had time to warn the children not to ask Henry about his arm. Alas, it was the first question out of Audrey's mouth. "Mr. Sayer, what happened to your arm?"

If it bothered him, Henry didn't show it. "Well, it's quite a story."

"Did it happen in the war?" asked Pierce.

"It did. I was on the USS *Corry*. Have you heard of it?" asked Henry.

Seb nodded. "Sure. She sunk at D-Day, right?"

"She did. And I was there."

The children had stopped eating, staring at him with wide eyes.

"I was a machinist. Do you know what that is?" asked Henry.

"No," said Audrey.

"It's one of the men who makes sure everything on the boat is working well. Anyway, the Germans got us and Commander Hoffman told us we had to abandon ship. So I jumped right into that icy water. And when I was swimming around in there, I got hit with a bullet in my arm."

"Were you scared?" asked Audrey.

"I was, but a seaman has to be brave. We knew we were fighting that day for something important. Fighting for what's right is the best thing you can ever do, so the other boys and me, well, we were proud to go in there, even though we were scared. You know what else? The ship spun around in circles before she sunk. Strangest thing you ever saw."

The boys' eyes were shining. What was it about boys that made them love war?

"Anyway, the USS *Fitch* came by and saved us after we'd been in the water about two hours. I was pretty cold when I got out. And after the surgeons took my arm, they sent me on a train to where Doctor Nelson was the doctor and he helped get me back into good form so I could come home."

"Uncle Julius was your doctor?" asked Pierce, his voice incredulous.

"Yes, and he asked that I call on your mother and you kids to let you all know he's doing very well, and he can't wait to come home and see you all."

"I don't remember him," said Audrey. "It's sad, but there's just not a thing in my mind about him."

Caroline smiled and met Henry's eyes, who also appeared amused. "She was only four when he left," said Caroline.

"But we remember him," said Seb. "He's like a father to us."

Caroline stared at him. What had he said?

"Our real father's very busy with work." Pierce said this matter-of-factly as he buttered a piece of bread. "So he doesn't have time to come to the beach."

Seb pulled a letter from his pocket. "Uncle Julius writes to us, though, and tells us stories of brave things he's seen. He says that there's a lot of bad, but that he sees men do extraordinary things every single day. He told me to remember that if we scared by what's on the news."

Caroline looked at her plate so the children wouldn't see the tears in her eyes. She often snuck a peek at Julius's letters, and what Seb described was true.

"Well, that brings me to one of the other reasons I wanted to come here and meet you all," said Henry. "I'm going to tell you a secret that no one else knows. Doctor Nelson told me you all must keep it a secret."

"We're good at keeping secrets," said Audrey.

"You're the worst secret keeper in the world," said Seb.

Henry continued. "Doctor Nelson was awarded a Medal of Honor for his bravery while working as a surgeon at the field hospital."

Caroline's heart seized. "When did this happen?"

"About a year ago. He told me he never told anyone about it because he's too modest. During our brief friendship, he shared it with me, and he said he wanted you all to know about it." Henry pulled something from his pocket. "As a matter of fact, he sent me home with it so that you might keep it until his return."

Caroline walked Henry out to his car, realizing with a start that she didn't know how he'd driven here, with only one arm to hold the steering wheel and shift gears. As if he read her mind, Henry pointed to the car. "First thing my sister insisted upon was a new car. It's an Oldsmobile with a Hydra-Matic."

"Oh, yes, I remember reading something about it. Didn't the first one come out just before the war?" she asked. "Does it truly work without all the shifting and letting out the clutch nonsense?"

"It does indeed." Henry smiled as he opened the driver's door. "Thank goodness for me."

"You must do the hutch for me," she said. "The children have fallen in love with you. They'll be devastated if you never come back. Besides my father, they don't see very many men around here." She hadn't meant to say the last part. Seb had already given Henry too much information with his statement at lunch about Julius being like their father.

"They're wonderful children. You've done very well with them," said Henry.

"Thank you. They're my pride and joy."

He slid into the car. "I'll call you next week to talk about the hutch and give you an update on how soon I'll be ready."

"I'll look forward to it," she said.

She stood in the driveway, waving, as he made his way around the circular driveway and onto their road. In the middle of the driveway, a ceramic fountain with various foliage surrounding it made a pretty picture, especially this time of year with the flowers in full bloom. She walked over to it, placing her hand in the water stream that cascaded from the top, thinking through the events of the afternoon. Julius had received a medal and he hadn't told her until he was transferred away from the front lines. He'd always been protective of her, like she was fragile. Her legs were unsteady in her high pumps as she crossed the driveway and went into the house.

PHIL

On a morning in late August, Philippa Rains stood on the porch of her parents' Iowa farmhouse, holding the suitcase she'd been given for her seventeenth birthday last spring. She wore her Sunday dress, a white and pink print with a modest tuck at the waist. Acres of tall corn swayed in the breeze, a blanket of green as far as the eye could see, so that one could not see where they ended and the sky began. The scent of freshly cut hay wafted sweetly from across the dirt road where Eddie's family flew their American flag at half-mast. Clouds dangled low on the horizon, but the determined sun hung above them, casting rays like arms of gold across the fields. To the left of the house, a red barn stood proud, and beyond, a pasture where horses grazed on dewy grass. She gripped the porch railing. Soon she would be on her way, an evacuee from her parents' home like a common criminal. She set the suitcase on the steps and went inside to confess to her parents the awful truth.

Her mother and father sat at the kitchen table, a copy of the *newspaper* between them, scents of coffee and baking bread strong in the small kitchen. Phil's mother, Jane, read the funny pages, unsmiling, wearing her light blue housedress. She read them every day, but Phil had yet to see a smile cross her stingy mouth. Her father, Jacob, tapped his thumb against his empty coffee cup, reading news of the battles across the sea. Sunlight streamed through her mother's spotless windows from the east. Birds chirped on the branches of the apple tree in the backyard.

Sunday was a day of rest, other than the two hours they would spend at church listening to Reverend Muller preach of sin and banishment into the fiery depths of hell. Phil hovered at her place by the table, covering the knot in the pine with her index finger. The rectangular table was small so that if the four of them were all together, Jacob, Jane, Phil, and her little sister, Mary, their feet would run into one another if they allowed their legs to stretch. They never did. All four of them kept their feet tucked under their chairs, sitting up straight, like a fire pit divided them. Phil and Mary were not to speak unless spoken to. No one spoke of her brother Ivan. It was as if he had never existed.

"Good morning," said Phil. They were to always greet one another with a polite and pleasant greeting in the mornings. Rules and more rules.

Both her parents looked up, giving her a rote smile. "You're too late for breakfast. We've eaten all the eggs," said Jane. "You should be out the door already."

Phil taught Sunday school to the grade school children at the church. They expected her, but she would let them down. *Do not think of their dear faces or the way they gaze at me as if I know the secrets of the world.* She swallowed the sick that rose to her throat at the mention of eggs. The last several weeks she'd been especially nauseous in the mornings. Eggs were on the list of foods that made her shudder, along with chicken, cheese, and anything made with onions.

"Where's Mary?" asked Phil. She wanted to speak to Mary alone.

"Feeding the chickens." Jane had gone back to the funny pages and didn't look up when she spoke.

Phil sat in her place at the table. She fiddled with the salt and pepper shakers, brushing away specks of salt from where they had fallen near her father's cup. "I'm going to have a baby." The tears came. She fought them, taking in a deep breath and biting her bottom lip.

Her parents' heads jerked up, the color drained from their faces. Jacob's fingers, grasping one corner of his newspaper to turn the page, tightened but remained in midair. Jane's arms fell to her side. Her mouth opened and closed. The large vein that ran down her forehead pulsed. Her father's eyes were wide, like toothpicks held them open against his will. Then their bodies went still, like they were suddenly in a photograph. Phil sat on her trembling hands, waiting for judgment. She tasted blood from where she'd bitten into her lip. Outside, the sound of Mary's voice calling to their dog in her high-pitched voice penetrated the silence. "Boboooo."

Jane's eyes, the color of faded denim, were fixed upon her. She looked old. She'd aged since Ivan's death. A year had passed since the telegraph had come. She now had more gray hair than brown and bags like rolls of raw dough under her eyes. And now Eddie gone, too.

Her thoughts drifted to the night the news had come. Eddie was dead. Killed in action somewhere in the French countryside. Phil cried herself to sleep, but woke when Mary crawled into her bed. Phil moved over to allow her room and Mary snuggled up against her like two little spoons nestled in a drawer. Mary's tears soaked into the sleeve of Phil's dressing gown. "I'm sad, Phil."

"I know, Moo," she whispered and stroked Mary's baby fine hair.

"Did the bullet hurt?"

"I don't think so. The letter said he was killed instantly." A lie. She didn't know how long it had taken him to die. She'd tortured herself with the same questions.

"How do they know?"

"They saw him in battle." *They saw him shot down as he marched toward the enemy. He never had a chance.*

"He was brave, wasn't he?" asked Mary asked.

"Very."

"Remember when he saved me from that mean dog?"

"I do," said Phil. "He was always brave, even when we were little." Her throat closed; tears leaked from her eyes into Mary's hair.

"You won't die, will you, Phil?"

"No, Moo. Not for a long time."

"Can I sleep here with you?"

"Yes, my lamb. Now go to sleep. You have school in the morning."

"School seems dumb now."

"I know. But we have to go anyway."

Now, her mother jerked again, this time with her upper torso, like someone had smacked her between the shoulder blades. "How far along?"

"Three months."

"Before he left?" asked her mother.

Phil nodded, her cheeks on fire with shame. *I wasn't sure he'd ever come back. I had to give him what he'd begged for so many times before he left.* Something to assure him she would be here when he returned from battle, ready to marry him and start the life they'd talked about for so long.

Three years after the news of Pearl Harbor and America's entry into the war, when they were both just sixteen, he enlisted, lying about his age.

"I can't sit here and do nothing." They were in the hayloft above his father's barn, his cheeks flushed from kissing and his attempts to get her to let him inside her. Strands of straw were tangled in his dark hair and there was that hardness to his eyes since the telegram had come about Ivan. The two families had neighboring farms and the boys had been best friends, as close as brothers, even though Ivan was several years older. No one, except her parents, took his death harder than Eddie.

She hadn't bothered to beg him to stay. He was not the type of boy to listen to a girl, even the one he loved. He enlisted the next day. A week later, knowing he might never return, she gave herself to him, body and soul. Six weeks later she discovered she was pregnant. Sixteen weeks after that, he was killed fighting the Germans.

"Did he know?" Her father set down the paper and smoothed his hand over the front page. Ink stained the palm of his hand.

"No. I wrote to him, but he was gone by the time it would've reached him."

"How could you do this?" asked Jacob. "After all we've done for you?"

Phil let the tears spill down her cheeks, knowing what would come next.

"You have to go," he said. "Pack your suitcase. Leave and don't come back."

"My suitcase is already packed." Anger fueled her now, both at herself and them. She was stupid. There was a part of her that hoped they might surprise her. What an idiot she was to think so. And yet, it was Eddie's child after all. They loved Eddie. Everyone knew from the time they were kids that they would get married someday. *Damn you, Eddie.* Why did he have to lie about his age and enlist? *Why did you leave me alone with a baby?* It didn't matter now. She must go and make a new life. California awaited. Anything was possible there. Opportunity, jobs, the Pacific Ocean.

"You'll be sorry not to know this baby. I won't ever come back, don't you worry. But I won't be the one who wishes it was different."

She grabbed a biscuit from the stove on her way out the back door. The money she'd made taking care of Mrs. Betz's children down the road was tucked into the inside pocket of her dress. Her friend, Susan, was meeting her at the end of the dirt road to take her to the train station. She took her suitcase from where she had left it on the front porch and crossed the yard to the barn, anger replaced by tears. She must say good-bye to her darling Mary. She found her in the hayloft of the barn, sitting cross-legged, petting their barn cat, Stripes. Phil left her suitcase outside the door and climbed up the ladder to the loft. Mary was dusty and Phil knew she'd been crying because there were streaks of tears in her dirty face.

"Why're you crying, Moo?" asked Phil.

"I heard you talking with Mother and Father," she said. "You're going away."

"I have to, but not forever."

"Take me with you."

"When I get settled, I'll send for you," said Phil. She knew this was nearly impossible to do, but both needed the dream.

"Promise."

"Cross my heart," said Phil.

"Where are you going?"

"California."

Mary's eyes went wide. "But that's so far away."

"There's work out there. Seamstress work in factories. And it's sunny all the time. I could live by the ocean. Would you like to live by the ocean?" Absolutely none of this she had planned to say or even thought about for herself, but as she said it, she knew it to be true. San Francisco. The ocean. A job as a seamstress.

"How will I know when I can come?" asked Mary.

"I've arranged with Susan to take letters to you, and she'll take ones from you and mail them to me."

"Will her father find out?"

Susan lived with her widowed father, a kind, quiet man, weak from various ailments, so she took care of him, not the other way around. "Susan mails the letters and picks them up."

"Okay."

"I have to go now, Moo. I'll write soon."

Mary sobbed with her head in her knees. "Please, don't go."

Phil pulled her onto her lap. "You must be brave. Just for a little while. Someday, you, me, and the baby can all live together."

"It'll be like Eddie's with us, won't it, Phil? When his baby's here?"

"Yes, lamb, it will." She stood with Mary clinging to her, skinny legs around her waist. She was the size of a four-year-old, not a girl of six. They'd both been fat babies. Their mother, concerned, rationed out their food like they were kin to the animals in the barn rather than her own children. When she had her baby, she would let it eat until it was full.

"Listen, Moo, you have to let me go. Don't follow me down the road, or Mother will see you and punish you for it."

Mary nodded but clung tighter.

"Can you be brave for me?" asked Phil. "Be brave like Eddie, okay?"

Mary lessened her grip and let Phil set her on the floor of the loft.

"Pet kitty. It'll distract you," said Phil.

The light had gone out of Mary's eyes. She nodded, dully. "Bye, Phil."

"Bye, Moo."

She cried as she walked to the end of the road. Susan's truck was there, waiting. She got in and stared straight ahead, not allowing herself a glance back.

———————

Five days later, she exited the train in San Francisco. Other than her transfer in Chicago, it had been a continuous trip. Grimy, she washed as best she could in the station restroom and changed clothes. She had not been able to afford the cost of the sleeper car, so she had slept sitting up and now felt at least a hundred years old as she crossed the floor. It was late afternoon and the station smelled of urine and engine oil and bustled with people, all walking fast, bumping into her with satchels, purses, and shoulders. Heart pounding, she headed to the doors, praying that her next step would be apparent.

Once outside, she looked up and down the street. The weather was cool and cloudy. Wasn't California supposed to be sunny all the time? She had no idea where she was and knew the only solution was to ask someone for help. An older woman, well-dressed, stood near a lamppost, seemingly waiting for someone. Phil approached, putting on her best smile, glad she'd taken a moment to put red lipstick on so that she might look a few years older than she was. "Excuse me, ma'am."

"Yes, dear?"

"I'm Philippa Rains." She held out her hand.

The woman took it, and they shook. "Mrs. Crowson."

"I'm new to town, and I wonder if you might point me in the direction of the factories?"

Mrs. Crowson's mouth twitched, like she was trying not to smile. "Factories? Which kind?"

"I'm a seamstress. Needing work."

An expression of understanding crossed her face. "I see. Well, some of the Bennetts' factories are hiring, I know. They're always hiring it seems, making uniforms for the troops, and all this dreadful ready-to-wear clothing."

"Would you be so kind as to tell me how to get there? Could I walk?"

"Oh, no. It would be much too far." A black car, fancier than Phil had ever seen, pulled alongside the woman. "Come with me. We'll take you."

Phil hesitated. Her mother always said never to get into the car with a stranger. Yet, this was an extreme circumstance and the woman looked harmless enough. "All right, yes. Thank you," said Phil.

The driver was out of the car by now, opening the back door.

He wore a black suit and a hat. A chauffer. A real live chauffer, like in books. Phil, despite her anxiety, she shivered with excitement. If only she had someone to tell. They settled into the back seat of the car. Mrs. Crowson wore stockings. Where had she gotten them? Perhaps the black market wasn't just a rumor.

"Mrs. Crowson, we headed home?" asked the driver, taking off his hat. He was young with freckles and red hair.

"Not yet, Frederick. Do you know where the Bennett clothing factories are?"

"Yes, Mrs. Crowson, up in the Northeast Waterfront," he said. "Warehouse District. Greenwich Street."

"Excellent. We're going to drop this young woman over that direction before we head home."

"Yes, ma'am."

Mrs. Crowson settled back in her seat. "Tell me, Miss Rains, what brings you to San Francisco?"

"My husband died in the war and I have no family, so I decided to come west. To the land of opportunity." She had planned her story on the train, but was surprised how easily it rolled from her tongue. "Now that I'm here, I feel frightened. There are so many people."

Mrs. Crowson made a sympathetic clicking sound with her tongue. "I'm sorry for your loss. Too many young widows these days."

"Thank you. We were only married a short time, but I knew him all my life." Although half the sentence was a lie, she choked up, thinking of Eddie. "He died in combat."

"How awful. You poor dear," said Mrs. Crowson. "How old are you, Mrs. Rains?"

"Twenty," she lied.

"You don't look older than sixteen. I suppose the city will age you fast enough."

Phil turned her gaze to the sights. They passed buildings with ornate trim and houses built in a row with very little room between them. The streets were up and down and narrow. How did people drive here? The main street of her hometown was wide enough for cars to park at an angle on both sides of the street. The sky seemed closer here, obscured by all the buildings. *Jail Bonds* was etched into a building. What on earth were those? They crested a hill and the Golden Gate Bridge and the bay appeared.

"Breathtaking," said Phil.

"They don't have that in Iowa, I expect."

"No, ma'am, we do not."

They passed a trolley, creeping up a steep street. How did it not fall backward? People hung from the sides, perched precariously. How did they not fall out?

"Your eyes, Mrs. Rains, are as big as saucers." Mrs. Crowson chuckled. "It's refreshing to see it from your eyes. A person gets used to something and hardly sees it any longer."

"When I left home, I tried to memorize certain things that I'd taken for granted," said Phil.

"I hope you won't be too homesick."

"It's so different here. Different than I expected," said Phil.

"What did you expect?" asked Mrs. Crowson.

"Palm trees."

"That's farther south, dear.

Mrs. Crowson told her they were at Fisherman's Wharf now. It bustled with activity. Boats of all shapes and sizes populated the piers. Phil spotted tugboats, fishing boats, and even a few luxury liners. Men and women hocked goods in front of the wharf in an open market: fish, crab, flowers, even taffy. On the shores, fishermen were pulling a large net. Women and men dressed in beautiful clothing dined outside on the patio of a café, with waiters dressed in red uniforms. "It's glorious," said Phil.

"You won't think so after a time. Smells like fish and dirty people."

After a few minutes the scenery changed to large brick buildings. "This is where a lot of manufacturing goes on," said Mrs. Crowson. "Frederick, which do the Bennetts own?"

"Practically this whole area," he said. "They manufacture munitions, ship parts, clothing. You name it and they make it."

"The Bennetts are an old-time San Francisco family. Money goes back to the 1800s. Gold Rush money, I believe," said Mrs. Crowson. "Mrs. Bennett—Sophie—and I came out together. We both married well, but she married a little more well than I." Mrs. Crowson chuckled, waving her hand in front of her face like she was trying to get rid of a fly buzzing around her head. "Anyway, despite their wealth, they're lovely people. They put the rest of us to shame with their philanthropy. You could do worse than to work for them."

Frederick had pulled the car over to the curb in front of the brick building. "Mrs. Rains, if you please, I will escort you to the front doors."

"No, no, that won't be necessary," said Phil. "You've been so kind to bring me here. Do you think there are rooms to rent anywhere around here?"

Frederick met her eyes in his rearview mirror. "If you get hired, mention you're looking for a place to stay. The other girls will know where to send you."

She thanked them again and got out of the car, carrying her small suitcase toward the front of the building. Sure enough, on the door was a sign listing all the different positions they were hiring, including seamstresses. She walked in and ventured down a dark hallway until she saw an office. A young woman sat at a desk, typing, but looked up when Phil tapped on the door. "I'm here about work. Sewing."

"Have a seat. Mr. Dreeser will be with you in a moment." The secretary was blond, with a long face and rather large nose, both of which made her look like one of Eddie's horses.

"Mr. Dreeser?"

"Yes, Miller Dreeser. The boss." She went back to her typing, the clicking of the keys in a steady rhythm, interrupted by the sound of the bell and the lever when she came to the end of a line.

After a few minutes, two men came out of the office, both in dark suits. One, of a slight build with black eyes and hair, patted the other man's a shoulder. "Good to see you, Timmy. Can't thank you enough for taking care of this for me. It was getting too close for my comfort."

Timmy, short and stout with a rather long nose and unfortunate double chin, stuck a piece of paper into the inside pocket of his jacket. "You got it, Miller. Easy enough to take care of, so don't lose any sleep over it. We orphans gotta stick together."

"Always."

Miller. The boss. Phil sat taller, holding her breath as he turned to look at her.

"Are you here about a position, miss?"

He talked like he was on the radio. His suit draped like he was an actor in a movie. Although old, like her father, he didn't look defeated and stooped. He looked proud and sharp. Like a fox. A sleek, quick, intelligent little fox. "Yes, sir." She stood. "I'm Phil Rains." Was she to hold out her hand like men did?

"I'm Mr. Dreeser. Come into my office, please."

She followed him. Her breath sounded like she'd just run across the yard, for heaven's sake. Although she'd washed and changed at the station, she prayed she didn't smell as bad as she suspected she did.

"What brings you here?" he asked.

"I need a job."

"Yes, I assumed that, Miss Rains. Why here?"

"I've just come from Iowa," she said. "A little town not far from Des Moines called Albertville."

"And?" He raised his eyebrows, looking impatient.

"I have a lot of experience sewing. We sewed all our own clothes."

He nodded, as if nothing she said surprised him. "A farm girl."

She smiled, trying to appear sophisticated, but her hands were shaking, as was her voice. "Yes, sir."

"We'll try you out for a morning. If you're fast enough, you can come back after lunch."

"I'll be fast enough," she said.

His mouth moved into a smirk. "Can you begin now?"

"Yes. Absolutely, yes."

He picked up the phone. "Mrs. Kramer will take you to the factory and explain everything. She's the supervisor."

The factory was arranged in rows, at least a dozen deep and six wide, many women of all shapes and ages sitting in chairs and hunched over sewing machines.

Mrs. Kramer led her to a machine at the end of the first row. Each station had its own table and sewing machine, along with thread and replacement needles. The bodice, skirt, and sleeve pieces of a dress were arranged in stacks.

"Today it's dresses. Tomorrow might be uniforms for the army. You'll be responsible for doing good work, no matter what we're making. Cutters cut them from patterns. You sew them." She twisted, pointing to a door on the other end of the factory. "When you've finished your stack, you take them through there to packaging."

"May I ask you something?" asked Phil.

"Yep," said Mrs. Kramer.

"Do you know of any places to live? Like rooms for rent? Cheap?"

She called over to one of the other girls. "Martha, does your building have any rooms for rent?"

Martha, a tall brunette with stooped shoulders and bad teeth, looked up and shrugged. "They got rooms, but they ain't nice. About all we can afford, though. You can follow me home later."

"All right. Thanks," said Phil.

"Don't mention it," said Martha, before she hunched over her sewing machine.

After Phil's shift ended, she walked with Martha over several blocks to a building that leaned slightly to the right. "Suffered some damage in one of our minor earthquakes ten years ago or so. It looks like it might tumble at any minute, but it's lasted this long, so I figure we're fine. Come on. I'll take you to the landlord. Goes by Mrs. Beale. She's mean as the day is long, so don't cross her." With that, she disappeared down the hallway.

Mrs. Beale, bony and angular with uneven features that seemed as lopsided as the building she ran, opened the door almost immediately when Phil knocked. "What you want?" She lurched close to Phil's face, her breath acidic. It took Phil a moment to realize it was booze. Once, Eddie and Ivan had come across a bottle of moonshine in the woods, presumably from one of the illegal distilleries, and had sampled a drink or two, much to Phil's horror. If her father had caught them, they would have been beaten within an inch of their lives. Fortunately, their indiscretion was not discovered, but their breath had smelled like Mrs. Beale's.

"I'm looking for a room to rent," said Phil.

"You got money?"

"Yes. And I have a job at Bennett textiles."

A sour look crossed the Mrs. Beale's face. For a split second, Phil thought she might spit. Instead she backed away, reaching for a set of keys hanging on the wall. "I got one. Just vacated today, so you're in luck."

Phil followed her up a flight of stairs and down a narrow hallway. Everything was narrow here compared to home. Mrs. Beale threw open the door. "It's furnished. More luck for you."

The room was no bigger than a closet with a twin bed, small table, and one chair. It smelled like the attic of their barn: rat droppings and mold. Phil wanted to cry. "Where do we bathe?"

"Shared bath for the floor. From what I hear, it's best to take a shower at night. Fewer people."

"How much?"

"Two dollars a week."

"I'll take it."

"No men allowed, you understand?"

"Yes, Mrs. Beale."

Initially, although fast enough for Mrs. Kramer, she wasn't as fast as the other girls, but as the weeks turned to months, she matched them and subsequently exceeded their output. Her stomach grew larger and larger. During her off hours she made a dress big enough to cover the growing bump, hoping to keep her pregnancy from the other seamstresses. The work made her back ache, acerbated by her growing midsection. She had no way to cook, so for food she bought a loaf of bread, bologna, and whatever fruit she could find when she received her weekly wages. She stretched this throughout the week, but often went to bed hungry. She worried whether she ate enough to provide for the baby. Each week she set a portion aside to live on after the baby came, hiding it under her the lumpy mattress in her "furnished" apartment.

From time to time, Mr. Dreeser walked through the factory, examining their work. Often he lingered at her station for longer than he did the other girls. She assumed he was checking on her because she was new, making sure the quality was as good as the other girls. In about her eighth month of pregnancy, he asked her to follow him to his office.

His desk was bare except for several stacks of papers, a telephone, and an adding machine. The chair behind his desk creaked when he sat. She stood in front of the desk, unsure what she should do. "Sit, please."

She reached behind her for the arm of the chair, lowering herself slowly.

"You're going to have a baby," he said, his gaze directed at her midsection. "You've done well to hide it, but I'm more aware of these things than other men."

Her cheeks flushed. She began a fervent prayer that this interaction would be over soon. The work at her station was much preferable.

"I have three children of my own." He laced his fingers together and rested them on his desk. "What do you plan to do once the baby comes?"

"I don't know."

"May I ask about the father?"

"My husband died in the war." The way he'd asked the question, she wondered if he guessed the truth. There was no husband and never had been.

"How old are you?"

"Seventeen."

"You can't bring the baby here."

"I know, sir."

He gazed at her with half-lidded eyes. "You're beautiful. Arrestingly so. Has anyone ever told you that?"

"I guess." Eddie had told her that a few times, although he wasn't one to compliment a woman on a regular basis. "Although, not the arresting part."

The corners of his mouth twitched.

"There's no man in your life?"

"No, sir."

"All right. Back to work you go."

Dismissed? What had he wanted? She couldn't imagine why he'd asked her into his office. Perhaps it was to give her the message that she would not be able to come back to work after the baby came?

That night she went home to find her door wide open. Her mattress had been overturned, the stash of money gone. She sat on the floor and cried. What would she do once the baby came? How would she work with a baby? How would they survive?

The next day her water broke, soaking her dress and dripping onto the floor under her chair. The girl next to her, Betty, stopped sewing. "Your waters break?"

Waters? Plural. How many were there? "How did you know?"

"I have four kids."

"What do I do now?"

Betty scrawled an address on a scrap of paper. "This here's my mother. She's birthed a lot of babies. You'll have to take a taxi to get there. You got money?"

"Enough for fare, I guess." She had no idea, having never taken a taxi before now.

By this time, Mrs. Kramer had rushed over to ascertain exactly what was unfolding. "Her waters broke," said Betty.

Mrs. Kramer nodded. "Wondered when that baby was coming. By the looks of you I knew it couldn't be long." She pointed toward the door. "Come along, now. I'll help get you on your way. We don't want a baby born in here. Mr. Dreeser would not care for that, no."

Phil arrived at the midwife's house within fifteen minutes. The midwife, Mrs. Able, took her to the back of the house where there was a double bed and various tubs and pots, apparently what one needed to help a baby come into the world. A horrible pain caused her to double over, panting. The contractions came hard and fast after that and at regular intervals. All good, according to Mrs. Able. She screamed with each contraction, but went through labor quickly, and the baby came out without much trouble. He was small, just under six pounds Mrs. Able said, and facing the right direction. "Slipped right out. Round head, this one. Your milk will come in soon. You're skinny as can be, though. You need a little meat on your bones or your milk will dry up."

She held her little baby boy in her arms. He was beautiful, perfect, even with his face squished from childbirth. A rush of love, of protectiveness, washed over her. She must take care of him, keep him safe from harm.

"What will you name him?" asked Mrs. Able.

"Edward, after his father. But I'll call him Teddy." She imagined a freight train hurled toward them. They were stuck to the tracks. She would cover his body with her own to save him from a train or anything else that might come their way. There would be a way to take care of him. She would figure out something. What other choice was there?

The midwife told her to put his mouth on her breast. "He'll know what to do," she said, crossing her arms over her own ample bosom.

The midwife was right. He opened his rosebud mouth and sucked. Nothing had seemed more right than this moment. And yet, this glorious feeling of love was tempered with terror.

She had just switched the baby to the other breast when the midwife returned. "There's a gentleman here to see you."

"A gentleman?"

"A Mr. Dreeser. He won't go away before speaking to you. He says it must be now."

Mr. Dreeser? Whatever could he want? Her mind frantically searched for an answer, but nothing came. "I'm not decent."

Mrs. Able held out her arms. "Give the baby to me. Pull up your blouse. That's right."

A few minutes later, Mr. Dreeser walked into the room. Phil stared at him, too frightened and surprised to speak.

He sat in the hardback chair next to the bed. In his hand, he held his hat and a paper bag decorated with grease spots that smelled of salami and fresh bread. Despite her fear, her stomach growled. "I've come with a sandwich and a proposal," he said.

"A proposal?"

"One which I hope you'll accept."

She stayed quiet, feeling as if she were out of her body, watching the scene from the ceiling.

"Your beauty's gotten under my skin. When I see something beautiful that I want, I take it. And I want you."

"Me?" She couldn't follow what he meant. Wanted her? How?

"I'll put you up in an apartment. You and the baby can live there. You'll want for nothing, including food and clothes. I'll come and go as I please. Our visits will be pleasurable."

Pleasurable? Did he mean? She started to perspire.

"There will be no other men." He sat on the edge of the bed and pushed her damp and stringy hair off her forehead. "You're lovely, even after just giving birth. With some care and proper nutrition, I'll transform you, make you stunning. You should shine."

Her gaze moved from his face to his hand where his wedding ring shone under the light.

"But you must be a secret. Do you understand?"

Teddy cried from the other room. Her stomach growled once again. "Yes, I understand."

"And you can agree to my terms?"

She remembered the empty place under her mattress. "Yes."

"Excellent. I'll pay to have you moved to a hotel tomorrow. You can finish your recovery there. I'll come by and see you once you're settled."

"What about my job?"

His brow furrowed. "Job? This will be your job now. You'll never have to see a sewing machine for the rest of your life."

What if I want to? "May I have that sandwich?" She was desperate for something to eat.

He smiled. "You certainly may."

MILLER

He had found the apartment for Phil through Timmy, who had arranged the lease for him so there was no way to trace the diversion of funds. It was important that he'd taken every precaution for discretion.

Three years ago she'd come to the factory to apply for work as a seamstress. Thin and pale, with the slightest hint of a pink rose petal blush to her cheeks and a fragility mixed with intelligence that made him feel drunk in her presence. He had to have her. He watched her from the window of his office, looking down on the factory floor, hiding behind the curtain so no one would see him. It took several months before he figured out she was pregnant. Pregnant, unwed, and only seventeen years old. Had he used that to his advantage? Yes, he had. That's what men with power did. He wasn't about to apologize for it. At first she'd been only a physical obsession, but now, three years later, he loved her. All he wanted was to be with her. To possess her. To have her on his arm while he ruled over Bennett Industries.

PART III

JUNE 1946

13

CAROLINE

The Sunday before they left for the beach house, Caroline and the children attended church with her parents. As they walked down the steps of the cathedral after the service, her father took her arm. "Darling, will you make sure Miller comes for dinner tonight?"

"You know I don't have much control over him." She spoke lightly, disguising how it hurt. A habit now. Seventeen years of marriage did that.

Audrey, skipping, led the way to the street where the car was parked. Joseph, hat in hand, stood waiting. The boys, arms linked with their grandmother, walked ahead of them.

"I ask little from him, but I want him there tonight. It's important."

She glanced up at him, wondering why tonight was different than any other Sunday evening. His profile gave away nothing. "I'll do my best, Father." They were upon the car now. The children had already slipped inside, while Mother exchanged pleasantries with Joseph about the fortunate weather.

"Thank you, sweetheart. In you go." He kissed the top of her head as he guided her into the back of the car.

After church, she found Miller in their bedroom. He stood at the mirror, tying his tie.

"You need to come for dinner tonight. Father asked specifically that we all be there."

"I can't." He grabbed his jacket from the back of a chair. "I have to go into the factory."

She caught a whiff of his cologne. He'd started wearing a different brand in the last few months that smelled like musk mixed with cinnamon. "You work for my father. If he wants you at dinner, it takes precedence over whatever's happening at the factory."

He turned to look at her, the skin between his eyebrows furrowed into the shape of a camel's hump. "Why do we have a family dinner every Sunday night?"

"It's what we do," she said. "The rest of us, anyway. You haven't joined us for years." In truth, she hadn't minded, enjoying the evenings much more without Miller. There was an underlying tension between her parents and her husband that made her feel apologetic and anxious. Lately, Seb and Miller seemed to have developed the same unspoken hostility. Fifteen was a particularly hard age for a boy, and Miller wasn't the type of father her father was. Distant, at best, might describe him. Neglectful might describe him better. Work over family. Always.

"I don't understand," said Miller. "It's not like you all don't spend an inordinate amount of time together already."

His tone, clipped and detached, made her hands itch. That speech coach years ago made him sound like an actor in a movie. It was unnatural. She flexed her fingers hanging by her sides. "My father asks for very little of us, considering what he's done for you."

The muscle in his jaw twitched. "Fair enough. I'll step out now, but I'll be back by dinner."

"Thank you."

He left the room without another word. She sat at her vanity and looked in the mirror as she took the pins from her hat.

Staring at her reflection, she wondered if the recent years had changed her. Would Julius think she'd aged since his time overseas? She opened a drawer and took out his last letter, opening it to the familiar words.

March 23, 1946

Dearest Caroline,

I leave at the end of the May for the long trip home. I've bought a first-class ticket on an ocean liner, an indulgent gift to myself after this long war. I'll be home by the time you all arrive at the beach house for the summer. I know it probably seemed insensible to you that I stayed after the war was over, but the people of Europe were left with a broken world, Caroline. Cities in ruins with no facilities in which to treat women and children, neglected for too long. It was my duty to God to stay and help. I know you understand giving to those less fortunate, so I needn't explain it to you, I suppose. I knew you would have done the same. In truth, I haven't much to return to anyway. No family of my own, other than Father and Essie and the twins, but not a wife or children of my own. The people here needed me more than anyone at home.

I can't say the war hasn't changed me, Caroline, but I'll return unharmed, on the outside, at least. Counting the moments until I see you all.

Love,

Julius.

She folded it, careful not to tear the thin paper, and set it back on top of the pile. There were at least a hundred letters, although she hadn't counted them. Saving his letters was probably foolish, but it had given her comfort to see his neat handwriting on the envelopes every time she opened the drawer, despite the nondescript nature of their content. Like Henry Sayer had said when he had come to visit her years ago, it was unlikely Julius would share any horrid details. He had never wanted anything harmful to ever touch her.

When she received the letter about his return home, she'd written back a letter she would never send. If he kept painful and frightening details of his war experience from her, she should return the favor. Writing it, however, had helped.

Dear Julius,

I'm afraid you'll find me changed as well. I look in the mirror some days and I see an old woman staring back at me. It feels as if all the joy has been sucked from my life. I love my work and the children, but I'm lonely. My marriage is solitary. I live with a person I hardly know. He leaves in the morning before I wake and comes home after I'm asleep. Some nights he doesn't come home at all. He claims he sleeps at the office, but I know it's a lie. We barely touch. I think he has someone else on the side. I wonder if he ever loved me at all or if he married me for my money? His relationship with the children is almost nonexistent. If it weren't for my father, I don't know where we'd be. They look up to Father, like we always did. Children and dogs always know good people. Sadly, despite everything, I can still remember what it was like to be in love with Miller. The remnants are there in my heart, like shrapnel. I know there's nothing I can do. Divorce isn't an option. Plus, who would want me now that I'm old?

I know, too, that I never stopped loving you. All these years, our friendship continued to grow deeper, perhaps because we both knew it was safe, given that I was a married woman. It's always been you. I know you've never felt the same, so it's best I married Miller. We have the beautiful children because of it.

She had stopped at that point, her self-pitying tears leaking onto the paper and blurring the ink. Now, she folded it carefully and put it at the back of the drawer. Miller wouldn't look in here anyway. He didn't care enough.

That evening, the temperatures were unchanged from that afternoon, warm and without a breeze. Mother and Caroline, discussing it over the phone, had decided it would be particularly festive to dine outside in the garden. The staff had set up a long table, adorning it with lanterns, candles, and fresh roses.

Now, sitting around the table in the flickering light, the children's eyes shone like the stars twinkling above them. Scents of roses and red wine permeated the air. They'd finished the first course, a lovely cucumber and tomato salad, when her father picked up his wineglass. He'd opened a particularly good vintage, although Caroline couldn't remember what it was, only that he'd mentioned it, making her wonder again what made tonight so special.

"I have an announcement," said Father.

Caroline glanced at her mother. She gazed at her husband with an expression of adoration mixed with excitement. What could it be? Were they taking a trip? Or had they purchased a new home somewhere? Despite their immense wealth, other than the two homes, the Bennetts were not extravagant people. Over the years, as their wealth continued to rise, they gave more and more money to their philanthropic causes. They traveled some, but did not collect objects like cars and fur coats and thousands of hats like some of her parents' friends.

They were both approaching sixty. She was thirty-seven. Thirty-seven! How had the years flown by so quickly? It was that way when one had children. They kept her so occupied and busy that the days and months slipped through her hands, even as she tried desperately to make time stand still. This was one of the lessons of motherhood. One must make them into wonderful adults only to let them go. How was this fair? To make us love them, only to have them leave? When the children left, she would have no one.

Father set down his glass and looked at each of them around the table. Caroline sat between her two sons, with Audrey and Miller on the opposite side of the table. She tried to catch Miller's eye, but his gaze was fixed on her father.

"As I look at each of you," said Father, "I know that no matter my accomplishments in the outside world, my greatest joys are sitting right here in front of me. As you know, I inherited great responsibility from my own father. Not only to carry on his wealth and the companies he worked hard to build, but also to the good people who worked for him. I know he would be proud to see what we've done, sustaining through the Depression and adjusting to the new world during this war." He chuckled. "I can't imagine what he would've thought of his munitions factories full of women workers."

"Your mother would've loved it," said Mother. "She was a suffragette."

Audrey's eyes shone. "I saw her name in a book at the library the other day."

"Did you?" asked Father, smiling.

Audrey smiled as her eyes skirted to Caroline. "I'm ashamed to say I bragged to the other girls about it."

"Audrey. You know how I feel about boasting," said Caroline.

"I'm sorry, Mama."

"Never mind that," said Father. "I'm sure God and your mother can forgive you just this once." He cleared his throat. "Anyway, back to the subject at hand. Enough stalling." He picked up his wineglass and swirled and sniffed. "I'm retiring."

"Retiring?" asked Caroline. "You mean from work?"

"Yes, from work. I've decided it's time to give the reins to the younger generation. I'm a bit of a dinosaur these days. And I want to spend more time with all of you. Perhaps we can take some trips together, see more of the country."

Miller. What did this mean to him? Would he be given the president position? She stole a look at him. Was he wondering the same? His face was impassive, as it often was. She couldn't imagine his thoughts.

Father put his glass up. "Let's toast to new beginnings."

They all lifted their glasses—milk and wine—and cheered. After they set their glasses down, Margaret, on cue, sent the young man in to serve their dinners. He was new, and with all the excitement, Caroline couldn't remember his name. As he set her plate in front of her, she noticed a scar on his right hand, red and angry looking. Mostly likely from the war. Did it spread farther up his arm? Regardless, it hadn't marred his abilities, as he appeared strong and without tremors. "Thank you," she said. Was it Martin? Marvin? She made a mental note to ask Mother after dinner.

After they all had their dishes, Miller tapped his glass. "May I offer a toast, Mr. Bennett?"

"Yes, Miller, please," said Father.

Miller raised his glass. "Congratulations on a lengthy and successful career. You have surely carried on your father's legacy with grace and intelligence. Thank you for the opportunities you've given me. I hope you know how grateful I am. And here's to the younger generation. May we do you justice."

They all toasted again. Miller had come so far after starting with so little. It was true that Father had given him the opportunity by providing a position in his company, but Miller had worked hard all these years. Currently, Miller ran the textile arm of the company, but he was capable of running the entire conglomerate. She hoped with all her heart that Father planned to give him the presidency. Stewart had been with her father since he was a young man, but even so, Miller was the obvious choice. Miller was family. Stewart was simply an employee, albeit a competent and loyal one. Maybe Father would give Miller part ownership finally? She took a hearty sip of wine. Would it be better or worse if Miller became the president? It probably didn't matter. Either way, she and the children wouldn't see him. She took another sip of wine, ambivalent and tired.

She declined dessert, even though it was strawberry shortcake that made her mouth water. She placed her hand on her flat stomach and decided to have an after-dinner brandy with her parents when the children had finished. It didn't take long for them to inhale their cake and ask to be excused, giving the adults time to retire to the sitting room to enjoy after-dinner drinks as they did on Sunday nights. Father surprised her, however, by asking if he might speak with her in the study. Alone.

Standing, she looked over at Miller. He appeared nonplussed by this deviation from routine, offering his arm to Mother. "Mrs. Bennett, may I get you a brandy?"

"That would be lovely, thank you."

Miller and Mother walked out of the dining room together, chatting about flowers. Caroline followed Father to his study. The room had changed little over the years, other than new drapes and wallpaper and replacement of furniture that looked remarkably the same as the furniture from her childhood. She sat in one of the chairs by the fireplace, which stood dark tonight. Instead, the room was dimly lit by the two lamps on the small tables next to the chairs, giving everything a comforting orange glow. Father poured her a brandy. "What is it? Is something wrong?"

He sat in the chair next to her, patting her hand that rested on the arm of the chair. "Nothing wrong, per se. Rather, it's a somewhat uncomfortable matter I need to discuss with you. I will preface by saying I've given this a lot of thought and my decision has not been made in haste." Father, tall and broad chested, was a man who had aged well. More salt than pepper to his thick hair these days made him appear distinguished and authoritative. He'd remained active, playing tennis and golf, keeping him tanned and fit. "Who I name as my predecessor is enormously important to all of us. We're in an uncertain time now, after this war. Many hard decisions must be made about what choices we make going forward. The world's changed, as you know, and I'm not the man to take us forth. It's taken a lot of soul-searching to realize that."

"I know you're not impulsive, Daddy. Whatever you've

decided, I'm sure is the best thing." She always called him Daddy in this room.

He patted her hand again and took a drink from his brandy. "I don't know what you or Miller have assumed about who will take my place. He and I have never talked about it."

"We've discussed it." She cleared her throat, hoping to think of the most tactful way to describe their hopes for the future. "That, and he wishes you'd allow him to be a full partner in the business."

"Give him part ownership, you mean?"

"Yes," she said.

"We don't think ownership should go out of the family, sweetheart. You know that."

"Daddy, I've been married to Miller for almost seventeen years. How much longer before you consider him family?"

Father was quiet for a moment, looking into the fireplace as if it were lit. "It was something of a leap of faith for your mother and I to agree to the marriage, and as the years have unfolded, our fears have increased, not lessened."

"But why, Daddy?" Shock expanded the space between her shoulders. "I've always been grateful that you gave your blessing, knowing what you hoped instead." *Who* he had hoped for her. *Julius Nelson.* "Is it because of where he came from?" Her voice cracked. She folded her hands in her lap to keep them from shaking

"Absolutely not. His upbringing, although unfortunate, is not the reason for our feelings."

"What is it? No one could've worked harder over the years to prove his worth to you."

He sighed. "Sweetheart, although he's worked hard and he's charming and obviously clever, your mother and I do not think of him as family. We can't explain why exactly."

"Try."

He undid the top button of his shirt and pulled at his tie, loosening it so that it hung slack at his neck. "We think he's like an actor on the stage. A bad actor, that is. He says all the right lines but there's a lack of credibility somehow. We don't trust him."

She stared at him, unable to think of a single thing to say. Had her parents always felt this way? How could she not have seen it?

"Anyway, regardless of our personal feelings, we don't think Miller's the best choice for taking my place," he said.

"Why?"

Impatience crept into his voice. "Simply because he's our son-in-law doesn't mean we should choose him over someone with more experience or wisdom, especially when it comes to running the company. As much as I want to keep the peace between us, Caroline, I can't make a decision based solely on you. I have hundreds of employees who rely on us for their livelihood. We need the right man at the helm."

"And Miller's not that man?"

"I'm afraid not."

"Is it Stewart Young?" she asked.

"Yes, I'm giving the presidency to Stewart. He's fifty years old, which means he's been with me for twenty-seven years. He's been my right hand all this time. No one knows the company better than he. His character is above reproach. He's a family man, you know, and that means a lot to me. Over the years I've seen men do all kinds of things when they think no one's watching. Stewart's not one of them."

"How do you know? I mean, if no one's watching him."

"I'm watching. He just doesn't know it." Father chuckled. The skin around his eyes crinkled in the way Caroline loved. As angry as she was in the moment, the love between them remained. That would never change.

She took another sip of her brandy, hoping it would warm the sudden chill that had come upon her. "When will you tell him?"

"Tonight. After this."

"Nothing has been more important to him than to be esteemed by you," she said. Nothing. Not her, not the children. "He's not going to understand."

"I hope to let him down gently."

"It would lessen the hurt, if you gave him part ownership in at least the textiles."

He patted her hand again. "Everything will go to you after our deaths. I've made sure it's clear that all of it will be yours, not Miller's. I need to feel sure that you're protected. Do you understand this has all been for you? You're the rightful heir to this family's fortune. Not an orphan kid with a lot to prove."

"Daddy!"

"I'm sorry. That was a cruel thing to say. It's not what I mean." He looked remorseful for a moment. "Caroline, what do we know about him? Truly. After all these years, neither your mother nor I feel like we know him."

"He's just what he seems to be. A loyal employee, husband, son-in-law."

"I find it interesting that you didn't say father."

"I meant to. He's a wonderful father," she said.

"He's an absent father. You've raised these children alone."

"Because he's been trying to please you all these years." Her voice had raised an octave. Tears came again. Angry, hot tears. "All he's done is work to prove to you that he has what it takes to become you."

"He's not me." Father's usual soft, low voice had deepened, grown combative, not so much a shout as a growl. "That's just it. I finished my workday and rushed home to your mother and you. I knew that all of it, the houses and wealth could vanish, but if I had you two I would still be a rich man. I learned that lesson during the First World War. When I was crawling through the trenches, all I could think about was you and your mother. Just getting back to you. The bargains I made with God..." He finished off his brandy and went to the cabinet to pour another. With his back to her, he sighed. When he turned back around, his voice sounded softer. "Miller doesn't understand the value of what he has at home. He knows only ambition and position and money. I've never said this to you, Caroline, because I wanted to keep the peace between us, but he's not the man I wanted for you. There's never anything so important that it keeps you from your family."

"Daddy, you realize you're the only man I've ever met who thinks that." Other men didn't think this way. She was certain of it. Most men were concerned with who they were and what they did.

He leaned against the cabinet, dwarfing it with his wide shoulders and tall stature. "I may be, but that doesn't mean I'm not right." He crossed the room and sat again in the chair, leaning forward with his long legs bent at a ninety-degree angle. Dangling the drink between his legs, he bowed his head. "I'm sorry to upset you, sweetheart. I've never understood how anyone could resist either you or your mother. To me, you are perfect."

"You're mistaken." She wiped under her eyes, managing a smile. "But we think the same about you."

"And you're mistaken." A pause, as he sat straighter and looked over at her. "Miller needs to spend more time at home. That's what I want. I want to see him here with us this summer, spending time with the children, treating you like a queen."

Ice flooded her veins. Was there more to this than her father's belief that men should spend time with their wife and children? Did he suspect there was a woman? Or women? "Daddy, is there something you're not telling me?"

Father set his drink aside and patted her knee. "No, love."

She knew not to press further. Father had his ways. Peculiar and dear as they might be, he was a man of integrity who mulled all matters with care and diligence. Once he'd decided, there would be no changing of his mind, no matter how she pleaded Miller's plight.

"Could you ask him to come in now?" asked Father.

She agreed, rising from her chair, suddenly fatigued. She hadn't felt herself for a week or so, unusually tired. If she didn't know better, she'd think she was pregnant. With as little as she and Miller had relations, it was unlikely. What had it been? Once in the last six months? He wasn't interested in her, claiming tiredness by the time he came to her at night. She put that out of her mind. The most important thing was to get Miller through this disappointment as best she could.

14

MILLER

The old man poured Miller a brandy and asked him to sit in one of the chairs near the fireplace, which was still warm from Caroline's body. Edmund always sat in the chair to the right. Edmund's chair. The big man's chair. It always struck Miller what a masculine room Edmund's study was, with its mahogany trim and dark drapes and furniture, misplaced in a house of soft hues and textures. He waited, excited, knowing what was coming. Finally, after all his hard work, his years of pretending, he would become the leader of Bennett Industries. He had no misconception that Caroline's father would ever step completely aside and let him run things as he wanted. There would be advice and interference, and Edmund would still be chairman of the board. Yet still, it would be Miller's turn to be in charge, to be the ultimate authority. When he imagined the job, he envisioned the top hat Edmund wore. *Big man. Big hat.* This new position was like that hat. And, it was his. Finally.

Edmund settled in the chair next to him. "I'll come right out with this, Miller. I'm giving the presidency to Stewart."

It took him a moment for the content of the sentence to reach his brain. It was as if he heard the words, *congratulations, it's about time you took over, can't imagine anyone better,* only they came out in the wrong order or language or something. Stewart. He was giving the job to fucking Stewart? He was giving it to someone outside of the family?

Miller sat in stunned silence for a moment. He'd heard that phrase before and wondered what it meant exactly. Now he knew. He was paralyzed, like one of those stupid birds that fly into a glass window and knock themselves out and fall to the ground.

"I'm sorry, Miller. I understand you're disappointed, but Stewart has more experience and maturity for the position. You're still a young man."

His mouth was dry. He took a sip of brandy. He should have seen this coming. The old man had never treated him like family. He was still just Caroline's husband instead of a son-in-law or a son. *I love him like a son,* he had expected him to say after just a few months. *The son I never had.* Instead, Sophie and Edmund had kept their distance. He'd expected that their kindness was exploitable, but he'd miscalculated. They loved the children and Caroline with something bordering madness. But him? Nothing but politeness, like a distant relative they tolerated and slightly distrusted. No matter how he poured on the charm or melded himself into their world. Nothing worked. Not even being the children's father. Surely he would get some credit for them? But no, it was like Caroline had conceived them by herself. Despite Edmund's outward warmth, Miller knew that he would never be allowed into the inner circle. He was still an outsider.

All this went through his mind as he prepared the latest falsity. *Be gracious. Pretend it doesn't matter. Act humble.* He must hide the seething anger that now coursed through his body. "I assumed it would be Stewart. So kind of you to consider me at all. I had no expectations. My God, no, none at all." He forced a laugh, like he was delighted the old man had considered *poor old orphan Miller* as a candidate. "I'm happy to be where I am, considering where I've come from. I still have much to learn, Mr.

Bennett, and I hope your retirement doesn't mean I can't still come to you for advice." *Mr. Bennett*, never *Edmund*. The epitome of politeness. Well-bred. Well-mannered. This was part of his act. The voice coach had taught him how to speak without dropping "-ings" at the end of words. *Mending, not mendin'.* Clipped, with aspirated T sounds, like the Bennetts.

"Yes, please." His words were polite, but Edmund's eyes were locked upon him, like Miller was a predator threatening his family. Even after his big act, he didn't believe him. Edmund was like Sister Catherine from the orphanage. That battle-axe never bought into his act, either.

"As a matter of fact, Mr. Bennett, I have an idea about how to increase productivity in the factory. I'd like your thoughts. See if there's a flaw in my reasoning."

"You can come to me anytime." Edmund put up his hand in a gesture of weary dismissal. "However, not tonight. I'm tired. This decision has taken its toll. And now that I think of it, perhaps it would better if you talked it over with Stewart. Other than keeping a close eye on my own financials, I plan to step aside, and let Stewart steer the ship. I want to spend more time with my family while I still feel well and fit. In addition, I have my charity work to attend to. More and more, I find it's the legacy I'd like to leave. Ah, well, never mind. I'm becoming one of those old bores obsessed with his own mortality."

Miller smiled at Edmund's self-deprecating humor. Since the beginning, Miller had observed him closely, imitating his charisma. There was no denying that his father-in-law was not only sharp-minded and charismatic, but also warm and compassionate, just like his daughter.

"I agree, Mr. Bennett. Tonight should be about celebration." He raised his glass. "To your next adventures."

They clinked glasses.

Later, in his own study, Miller sat at his desk with his notebook open, staring at the wall. He had his feet on the desk, sipping a glass of whiskey, not up, like Edmund preferred, but on the rocks. In his own house, he would drink his drink how he wanted it. He grabbed a pen to write in his notebook. When he first married Caroline, he noticed that Edmund, too, used a notebook. "My wife's idea years ago," he told Miller. Apparently, he'd forgotten that Mrs. Bennett had also provided the children at the orphanage with the same journals.

He wrote business ideas or thoughts in it, Edmund explained, so that he didn't lose the thread of anything. The idea of a thread caught Miller's imagination. He pictured this thread as a long string connecting all aspects of a life. One does this, this leads to that, and so forth. Connecting threads. Getting what he wanted. When he wrote something in his notebook, it became reality.

Of late, he found himself pondering whether it had all been worth it in the end. Was the obsession, the planning that led him to Caroline, whom he did not love, in exchange for her money, lifestyle, and the opportunity to work with one of the most powerful families in the country worth it all? Three years ago he would have said, yes, without a doubt. However, Philippa Rains had changed everything. He had not understood the seduction of romantic love, how it colored one's life, brightened and changed the hue of everything. He had not known that he could want a woman as he wanted Phil.

Lately, he'd started doodling in his notebook, writing Phil's name like a schoolboy. He couldn't stop himself. One day, the phrase had come to him. The thread. *Someone had to die.* This was the only way to be happy. Either he must die, and be put out of his misery, or Caroline must die. After what happened tonight— this rejection of him for what should be his rightful position—it was the frayed end of the thread.

He tossed back the rest of the whiskey and rose to his feet, pacing back and forth between his desk and the window. He could not divorce Caroline and remain sheltered under the umbrella of his father-in-law's wealth. They would decimate him. Edmund would take everything away, all of it that he'd worked hard for over the past seventeen years. He would be dismissed from his position and unable to secure another executive position because Edmund would ruin any opportunity for him. Edmund knew everyone and had his greedy hands in businesses all over the state. Even the government was in his pocket. Not once over the years had he ever loosened the reins and given Miller autonomy or trust. None of this was Miller's. He was still an interloper, a borrower of time and money.

It was simple math. There were three people involved. One must go.

The fantasies of Caroline's death had started a year ago. At first, they were only fantasies, daydreams from the backseat of his car while Joseph drove him to work. What if something happened to his wife, through no fault of his own, so that he might be free? What if she were hit by a car, or fell off the cliff on one of those interminable walks she took. Maybe a horse riding accident? Or, one night she had too much wine and slipped on the stairs, hitting her head on the marble floor? These were all common occurrences. Why couldn't one happen to her?

It became habitual, these musings and imaginings over her death. With each passing day, the fantasies became more detailed. The way in which the accidents could unfold played in front of his eyes like a moving picture. Yesterday morning, on his way down the stairs, he saw her lifeless body crumpled on the floor. He had blinked, unsure for a moment if somehow his wish had come true.

He settled on the notion of the cliff. It would take only a swift, deft move and she would tumble over the side of the cliff to the jagged rocks below. No one would be the wiser. He could be free. He would be happy the way he deserved to be. Why shouldn't he have what he wanted just once in his life? After everything he'd been through? The awful nuns at the orphanage.

The rapping of his knuckles until they bled. The nights and nights of an empty stomach. The good life should be his now. No matter the cost.

The way he would mourn and put on a show! Wailing. Trying to jump into the grave with her. *How he loved her*, they would all say. *He's devastated. The poor man. I hope he finds someone eventually. And those poor children.* Then, after an appropriate time, and with everyone's blessings, he would introduce the idea of Phil. She might come to dinner. The children would not be able to resist her beauty. No one could. A few months later, after they were all in love with her, he would announce their plans to wed. She could come live with them—help take care of the children. None of this he could be faulted for. After all, the children needed a mother. He needed a wife. And Phil was young and beautiful. The perfect solution to their problems.

Before now, it was only fantasy. When he'd rented the house in Stowaway, he believed it was the perfect solution. She could remain a secret, stowed away at the edge of the world. His perfect secret. At least he would have a few nights a week with her, and she could be comfortable there, but the more time with her he had, the more he wanted. Why should he have to leave her? Phil was his home. He couldn't survive without her. Just as he learned as a child, it was his only choice. Survival. He couldn't think of anyone but himself.

And tonight? The way he'd been tossed aside, after his years of loyalty? He sat back at the desk and turned to a fresh page in his notebook. *No more*, he wrote. *I will have what I want. He'll be sorry.*

Caroline and the children would leave for Edmund's beach house next week. He couldn't do it himself. There were men to hire, he knew, from Timmy Blick. Good old Timmy from the orphanage. Years ago, over drinks, Timmy told him that the bar he owned was only a front for the real money.

"Cash exchanged for services," Timmy said. "I'm like a conduit for people with things they need taken care of."

"What kind of things?" They were drunk, making Miller bold.

"Well, let's say you had a person you wanted to vanish. I arrange it."

"Do you take care of them, or *it*, yourself?" asked Miller.

"Nah, I got people." He raised his hands in the air. "These babies don't like to get dirty with the details."

Timmy got rid of people for a living. Timmy was dangerous. But he was loyal, too. They went back. They knew the same demons. They were family. Timmy would know what to do. A professional would know how to make it look like an accident.

He wrote in his notebook. *Call Timmy.*

15

HENRY

The scent of parched earth after a rainfall blended with the briny breeze of the sea and drifted into Henry's bedroom from an open window, waking him from a dream in which bombs still fell, the blasts in rhythm to his beating heart. In the moment before full consciousness, he opened his eyes, unsure of what sights and sounds would greet him. Gauzy curtains that moved in the breeze softened bright sunlight and brought the sounds of waves crashing against the shore. Seagulls screamed to one another, or was it to him? *The sea. You're home. Alive. Almost intact.*

He'd been home for several years now and still he woke from nightmares almost every morning. How long until the dreams ceased? How many more mornings before he knew with certainty that he no longer woke to the horrors of war but of a world in peace? When would he stop wondering, *Why me? Why did I return when so many others didn't?*

His pajamas were soaked with perspiration. Shivering, he rolled to his side, suspecting he'd slept late. The clock on the bedside table confirmed his suspicions, reading a little after nine a.m. His mother, gone, her ashes mingled with the sea, but her clock remained as a reminder that time marched forward regardless of loss, uncaring of whether the bereaved cursed the passage of time, wishing for one more moment with the one they once took for granted. The ache shot through him with sudden ferocity. He missed her. He missed his father. The happy days of his youth were no more. They could not return. Time moved forward despite the waves of grief.

He pulled the blanket closer, watching the light play on the hardwood floors. It was a simple room, sparsely furnished with work from his own hands before the war, each piece carved and sanded with meticulous care, as if it were art he made from walnut slabs instead of a dresser and four-poster bed. His phantom arm was quiet now, without pain, succumbing, for now, to the knowledge that it was no longer part of the physical world. Last night when he wanted nothing more than to sleep, his stub had itched and the phantom pain nearly drove him mad. So, this morning, he'd indulged and slept late, something he never would have done before the war. *After the war*; the phrase was like the title of the book.

He relaxed into the softness of the pillow behind his head. Perhaps he would remain a while longer, read another chapter of the novel that had been his redemptive companion during his sleepless night. What was so urgent it couldn't wait? The patchwork quilt, in the pattern of tulips, was twisted around his legs from restless sleep. With the fingers of his remaining hand, he touched the hand-sewn stitches, evoking the memory of his mother's never idle hands. Her work ethic was enough to dismiss his reluctance to begin his day. His sister, in one of her devoted weekly letters when he was overseas, had written that even at the end when their mother was dreadfully ill from the cancer that eventually took her life, she had not stopped making useful, beautiful objects with her hands. "Self-pity gets you nowhere," she had often said to them while they were growing up. "Best to figure out a way to get where you want to be instead of acting like a victim."

Tossing the blanket and quilt aside, he yawned and slid from bed. In bare feet, he went to the window and lifted the filmy curtain with delighted expectation, for there was not a morning when he was not thrilled to see his garden and the sea beyond. He pushed one pane of the window open wider and breathed in the morning. His garden and the sea and the sky, ever changing, yet the same. When he was scared or homesick while overseas, he had conjured this very image, like a photograph, and it had sustained him. *I will see it once more*, he had told himself again and again. *I am fighting for it, so that all might be free to look out the windows of their homes whenever they choose.* He had come back to this place he had once been happy, hoping that it might ease his haunted mind. The hope for happiness had been replaced by its paler sister: peace. Existence was hard enough without putting unrealistic expectations on himself.

Rain had come during the night. The garden sparkled with drops of water. Overhead, clear skies. Morning fog, common on the coast of California, had either rolled out while he slept or not come at all. Roses bloomed in reds and pinks. The lawn, deep green from daily watering, ended at the edge of the cliff that overlooked the Pacific, and native grasses grew along the precipice in varying shades of yellow and green, creating a shield from the wind like a man-made structure, but without obscuring the view of the ocean. Over the last several days, working slowly, still trying to figure out the best way to manage with only one arm, he'd constructed a fence from native pine to encompass the garden, and it stood pale and knotty, waiting for whitewashing from Henry's paintbrush. A tenant was coming with a little boy to stay in the cottage next door and he did not want the small one to fall to the rocks below.

Late yesterday, a car had come, a Rolls-Royce, delivering his new tenants, a young woman and her little son. The attorney had told him her name: Philippa Rains, and the boy was called Teddy. He'd been out when they'd arrived, buying groceries from town, but on his way home, he'd come upon the departing car, a chauffeur at the wheel. After Henry parked his truck under the shade of the large maple, he'd hesitated, wondering if he should go next door and welcome them, but had decided it was late, nearing dinner, and that he would not disturb them. He had not spoken with Mrs. Rains; the details of the lease were negotiated through an attorney. The client must be rich, Henry decided, for the attorney had given him a check for a year's rent in entirety. He was curious why a young woman and her son were to live here alone but did not ask. It was most likely a tale like so many women of his generation. Her husband had died in the war, leaving her care to either his family or hers. Yet, the question lingered. Why would she have picked such a remote location? There were no other neighbors for miles, and Stowaway, five miles away, was nothing more than a village with little to interest a young woman. His sister, Rose, had no interest in living in Stowaway, saying it was a place for old people and tourists. *Old people, tourists, and Henry.* She hadn't said, but he knew she was thinking it.

So now, he was taken aback, having almost forgotten the presence of his new tenants, to see a woman on the lawn. It must be no other than Philippa Rains who sat in one of the lawn chairs he'd put out for her, a pencil between her teeth, gazing at an open pad. She wore a yellow blouse that moved like a ribbon in the breeze and black pants fitted and tapered at the ankles. From this distance and angle, he could not ascertain her stature, other than she was slim with long legs and a rather short torso.

Pants. Women wore pants now, after the war. No wonder, considering the jobs they'd all taken on while the men were away fighting. There were aspects of life before the war that would never return, and although it was a somewhat frivolous example, that women wore pants now seemed to encompass how the country had changed. He sensed a difference in women now, a streak of independence in their eyes he had not seen before, as if this façade they'd all lived under, that women were the weaker sex, that there were tasks and work only men could do, were no longer lies the collective masses believed. His sister, for one, was happy about pants and having a career. Despite the war being over for a year now, she continued running the company left to them by their father. This had been their arrangement. Rose was to run the company. He was to return to the sea and make his furniture with the one hand he had left. *I can't do it, Rosie*, he'd said to her. *I can't sit behind a desk.* There had been no disagreement between them. They knew one another, knew their parts. Two parts of a whole, he'd always suspected. He'd gotten the heart and Rose the brain.

After the visit with Caroline, Henry opened his own studio in Stowaway, buying a brick building long empty, big enough for both a workspace and a modest storefront. He concentrated on design and finish work, and hired a young man back from the war to do what he couldn't. The townspeople, made up of fishermen, loggers, and farmers, rarely frequented his shop other than to stop in to admire his workmanship and encourage him, treating him like a hero but unable to spend hard fought income for pieces that were not useful. Regardless, his reputation continued to build, after the piece he made for Caroline, with the wealthy of San Francisco keen on custom pieces. With this patronage, he kept busy and earned enough to pay for costs, with enough left over for a comfortable life without dipping into the inheritance left by his father. He didn't need much, being on his own, and he figured the family money should be saved, not squandered on frivolity. Someday Rose would have children, and the money should be protected for them.

He drew away from the window with some reluctance. A beautiful woman on his lawn was not an everyday occurrence. Perhaps later he would introduce himself, offer his services, and explain about the lack of paint on the fence. First, however, he must get cleaned up and fill his empty belly with sustenance before leaving for his studio. He was working on a commissioned piece for a wealthy widow in San Francisco, taking his time to ensure fine craftsmanship. She'd asked for a walnut wood cabinet to display her collection of dozens of teapots, gathered from her travels around the globe. Well on the way, he was in the final stages of the finishing work, sanding the wood until it was like silk beneath his fingers.

After bathing, carefully avoiding the sight of his torso in the mirror, he dressed in jeans and a button-down shirt. The right arm of all his shirts had been shortened by Mrs. Thomas, stitched straight across like a hem on pants. In the kitchen, he put eggs on the stove to boil and made a pot of coffee in the percolator. When he'd moved in months ago, most of his mother's kitchen items were still there, hiding in cabinets. He'd pulled them out one by one, cleaning or polishing as needed, before lovingly setting them back in their places. The twin houses were built during the summer of 1931, and his mother had been thrifty, not only because they were in the middle of the Great Depression, but because it was in her nature. Growing up in modest circumstances in a mill town up north, she had never quite adjusted to both the wealth and generosity of her husband. Thus, the original appliances had stayed, despite the changes of the modern age, including the percolator, which he now filled with water, then scooped coffee into the top.

Rose asked every time she came to visit if he would like to change out a few things, join the modern era, as she put it, worried about his potential starvation. He politely dismissed the idea, preferring his mother's old pans and dishes. They seemed familiar, made him feel safe, and evoked memories of happy times. He abhorred the idea that the horrific years of the war were the only recollections that he would carry forth.

The kitchen itself was small, in equal proportion to the rest of the house, without adornment or opulence, but spacious enough for Henry's purposes. A vase of roses gathered yesterday had opened and their sweet scent filled the room, mixing with the aroma of the percolating coffee. The original appliances, installed by his father in 1932, included an electric stove and refrigerator, and a deep sink set before the window so that the person washing the dishes might glance up to view the sea. A square table, made of a dark cherry, had been Henry's gift to his mother after he'd learned his trade, every inch of wood carved, grooved, and sanded with love. Now, he lifted a corner of the yellow and white gingham tablecloth and rubbed his thumb on the smooth wood.

What would be the best way to greet the young woman? Would she like a cup of coffee? Should he bring one to her, or ask her if she would like one? Some people didn't drink coffee. Maybe she was a tea drinker? Did he have tea? He opened the pantry and scanned the shelves: flour, sugar, baking soda, baking powder, yeast, a loaf of sourdough bread—fresh yesterday from Stowaway's only bakery. Perhaps he should offer her a slice of buttered bread and a bit of Mrs. Thomas's strawberry jam? He could explain to her where the Thomas's farm was located, even offer to take her for a visit so that she might meet them. Given that she was in the company of men most days, Mrs. Thomas would be thrilled to meet another woman, especially now that Henry's mother was gone. Perhaps it would help distract her from her grief over William. The little boy might cheer her. Or would it have the opposite effect? Remind her of her only son lost to war?

He opened the refrigerator and grabbed a full jar of jam, along with the loaf of bread, and set them on the table. How best to present his offering? A basket with a pretty cloth? He needed a woman to advise him. Men were no good at these things. Again, he opened the pantry and reached to the top shelf where a basket his mother used for picnics huddled under a cloth to keep it from collecting dust. He set the bread, jam, and fresh butter inside, covering them with a yellow tea towel.

The sun blinded him as he stepped outside. He hesitated, letting his eyes adjust to the light. Mrs. Rains was still sketching, but perhaps sensing his presence, she set her pencil aside and turned in his direction. She stood. *Too thin. And fragile, like the sea breeze might knock her to her knees at any moment.*

"Mrs. Rains?" he asked.

"Yes. Mr. Sayer?" She put out her small and very pale hand. Her fingernails were cut short and painted red. This close, he smelled her perfume: a mixture of gardenias and vanilla. Her gaze skirted to his missing arm and away a split second later. Then, her cheeks turned pink.

He held the basket, therefore unable to take her outstretched hand. Feeling awkward, he set the basket at his feet, but it was too late. She'd withdrawn her hand. "Nice to meet you, Mrs. Rains. I brought you bread. And homemade jam and butter."

"Did your wife make it?" Her shoes, black, were flat, like ballerina slippers. Tied back with a white string, her dark hair glistened under the sun except for the strands that had come loose and danced about her face.

"Oh no. I have no wife. Mrs. Thomas made it. She and her husband live just up the road a mile or two. They're old friends of mine." He pointed in the direction of the Thomas's farm. "You can't see it from here, but you passed it on your way to our cottages—the white farmhouse."

"The one with the enormous porch?" she asked.

"Yes, that's the one."

"It made me think of my home in Iowa. Aren't porches lovely?"

"I think so," he said. *She* was lovely. Pale skin against dark hair, nose dusted with nutmeg-colored freckles, a perfect row of white teeth. Small features except for enormous brown eyes that were almond shaped and long-lashed. Her blouse, a filmy material, shuddered in the breeze, occasionally pressing against her small breasts. *No older than twenty-five, but possibly younger.* Her was face unlined, taut and well-scrubbed, with a splash of red lipstick and rouge on her cheeks.

"I'm sorry I wasn't here to welcome you yesterday," he said. "I work in town and usually don't come home until it's time for supper."

"What do you do? For work?"

"I'm a woodworker. Furniture mostly."

"Are the pieces in my cottage yours?"

"Most. Yes. I made them before I left for the war. My mother fretted for years about the state of the place, that the furniture should be nicer for our renters. I'm a bit out of practice as a landlord."

"So far, everything's been wonderful," she said. "The key was just where you said it would be."

"You won't need it. No one locks their door around here."

She smiled and brushed a strand of hair from her eyes. "Like my hometown." He stole a glance at her left hand: no wedding ring.

"Where's your little boy?" he asked.

"Inside. Having a nap. He had a tantrum this morning, indicating to me he needed more rest. Yesterday was a long day and I couldn't get him to settle when it was time for him to go to sleep."

"That's understandable, being a new home and all."

"I suppose," she said.

"Where're you coming from?"

"San Francisco. I worked there. At a dress factory."

"You were a seamstress?" he asked.

"At a factory. Many of us hunched over sewing machines for hours and hours a day."

He knew of them, and their reputation for working the girls hard. This did not concur with his original assumptions. A woman who worked in one of these factories was not from wealth. He resisted the urge to ask further questions.

"I'm going to paint the fence," he said. "I'm sorry it looks rough. I built it just last week, after I learned you had a little boy. This way he can roam the yard without fear of the edge." He pointed toward the sea. "It's a steep drop."

"Thank you. Would you like help?"

He wasn't sure what to say. Help from a woman? One who appeared so delicate? He didn't think that was an appropriate task, especially since he was supposed to be providing a place for her to live. "No, thank you." What he said next surprised him. He hadn't planned to say it, but suddenly it was out of his mouth. "Would you and Teddy care to join me for supper this evening? Every Friday, Mrs. Thomas fries up a chicken for my weekend meals." As way of explanation, he added, "She looks after me. Housekeeping and cooking, a couple days a week."

"I don't know, Mr. Sayer. Teddy's a rambunctious boy."

"That won't bother me, Mrs. Rains. I used to be a rambunctious boy myself." He smiled. "Less rambunctious without my arm."

She shuffled weight from one foot to the other, like a dancer doing the two-step.

"It's all right," he said. "Best I talk about it so folks aren't uncomfortable."

"Was it the war?"

"Yes. Normandy. USS *Corry*."

"My husband died in combat. Somewhere in France."

"I'm sorry, Mrs. Rains."

"Thank you." She crossed her arms over her chest, looking out to sea. "I think about it all the time. What he must have been thinking right before he was killed."

"Who's to say? When we invaded Normandy, it was our job to protect the men on the beach. I'm not sure any of us had time, in that moment, to think of anything but our assigned tasks."

"Were you and your shipmates scared? It must have been a long journey. Too much time to think about what might happen?"

The way she asked, he knew it was important that he answer with only half the truth. No reason to break her heart. He would not describe the way his shipmates' eyes had looked like deer chased by a pack of wolves, sure of their inevitable demise. "The day before the invasions we were told to turn around, that the mission was called off, then suddenly, it was back on. We wanted to fight and were disappointed when we had to turn back, and jubilated when we were told to continue as previously planned. We were proud, Mrs. Rains. That we could possibly make a difference in the ultimate victory for the allies was something that gave us courage."

"Well, one can be afraid and courageous at the same time."

"Very true. I didn't know that before the war," he said.

"Me either," she said.

"We all sacrificed. Some more than others. I lost a lot of friends that day."

"Please, call me by my first name. My friends and family have always called me Phil, short for Philippa."

"Then you must call me Henry." He smiled, leaning down to retrieve the basket. "This is for your lunch. I'm off to work now. Say six for dinner? Is that too late for Teddy?"

"How thoughtful of you to ask," she said. "Most men don't think of the habits of little ones. Six will be just fine."

"Also, it's not safe to swim on our beach. The current would pull Teddy out to sea, but he can splash around in the tide pools."

"Is there a place to swim that's safe?" she asked.

"Just north of here, at the edge of town, there are several long stretches of sandy beaches, perfect for swimming and picnicking."

"I grew up swimming in lakes and rivers. I've never swum in salt water before. Is it true that it makes you float?"

"Yes, it does make you more buoyant. It feels nice on your skin, too. I don't swim any longer, but I grew up in the ocean with my sister and William. Ever since I spent two hours in the Atlantic, I haven't been able to go back in. Plus, not sure how I'd do without my arm." Snapping his fingers, he pointed to a shed on the other side of his cottage. "I have buckets and a small shovel in my shed, if I remember right. It's unlocked. If you decide to go down to our beach, grab whatever interests Teddy. Just over the fence, there's a path that leads to steps. I recently checked and they're solid, but hold on to the railing, just in case.

Sometimes it's slippery. And now I must be getting along." He tipped his hat. "Until tonight."

"Until then." She smiled, brushing back strands of hair and peering up at him with those soft, sweet eyes that reminded him of Mr. Thomas's most recent calf.

16

PHIL

After Henry walked away, Phil returned to her chair. The ocean breeze cooled her skin, despite the bright sun on her back. Without enthusiasm, she picked up her sketchpad and examined the new dress design she'd scrawled on the page, her morning spoiled with this new complication. Henry Sayer. The landlord. He was not what she'd expected. She hadn't had a concrete image of him, nor had she given him much thought, but had assumed, quite wrongly, that Mr. Sayer was an elderly seaman, spending his twilight years by the beach. Why a young man would live here in the middle of nowhere she couldn't be sure. She was surprised, too, that he had no wife or family. He was quite handsome, with that thicket of dark blond curls that fell over his forehead, and he was charming, well-spoken—refined even. His eyes were a pretty shade of light blue, and he was tall and muscular, despite his missing arm. She'd noticed his arm, embarrassingly enough, after she had stuck out her hand. He'd recovered gracefully, pretending that it hadn't happened, which told her he was a kind man. Thoughtful, as well, to think of Teddy's bedtime in relation to the dinner hour, not to mention the new fence.

Miller wouldn't like this. A young and handsome landlord?

Less had caused Miller's jealousy. She shivered. *Stay away from him. Make it so Miller never knows of his existence. Otherwise it will not be safe here.*

She picked up her abandoned pencil. It calmed her to draw, especially outdoors. The movement of her hand, the focus on a task, eased her mind, kept the terrible bouts of anxiety at bay. Perhaps she should take up a physical activity as well? Collecting seashells? Walking the beach? Simply staring at the view didn't seem like a useful task. It was breathtaking today— the endless blue and the sound of waves crashing against the shore. To the right, craggy boulders jutted out of the water, the waves doing their best to mold it, change it, but it resisted, for now, or at least the changes were not visible. Like a person, the battering changed one little by little.

It used to be God, family, Iowa soil, in that order. She could hardly remember the girl she'd once been. The choices she had to make to protect her child had hardened her. Even this. Her eyes scanned the sea. Miller had suggested a house by the ocean and she'd agreed. Far away from the city and Miller Dreeser's wife and family. Tucked away. Hidden. The cost to her own young life? She did not have the luxury to calculate it. She was not the first woman in the world to trade her body for nourishment, for a roof over one's head. Sacrifices had to be made. For Teddy.

Henry's car rumbled in the driveway. She turned and gave him a small wave. He unrolled the window and waved at her with his hat. Henry Sayer. He'd unsettled her, made her feel anxious. Why had she agreed to dinner? There were rules. There were to be no friends, no attachments, no other men.

From inside the house, Teddy called to her. "Mama, I be nice now." He was talking a lot these last couple weeks. Her baby becoming a boy right before her eyes. How long until he understood things he shouldn't have to?

Setting her pencil aside, she abandoned her unfinished piece for the only thing she'd ever made that was exactly perfect:

Teddy. She was almost to the kitchen door when she remembered Henry Sayer's basket and went back to retrieve it. *Lunch, at least, was taken care of. The rest I'll sort out later.*

Teddy stood in the middle of his bedroom, wearing only short pants, his chubby arms crossed over his middle. His face, flushed from the warmth of his bed and the room, had an imprint of the pillowcase on his cheek. He grinned and held out his arms. She went to him, kneeling to gather him against her. "Hi, Mama."

"Hi, Ducky. Let's get you dressed. I have a special treat for your lunch."

"Wookies?" His name for cookies.

She smiled. "No, but delicious bread and butter. And strawberry jam."

MILLER

Miller lay supine in bed, watching the ceiling fan go around and around, making dust dance in the beam of sunlight that stole in from under the drawn shade. From the bathroom came the awful noise of Caroline's vomiting. He rolled to his side, toward the windows that faced the street. Damn if his wife wasn't going to have another baby. Caroline had yet to tell him, but he knew, having witnessed three of her previous pregnancies. Her breasts were swollen, especially noticeable because they were small, no bigger than a child's fist, so that any increase was obvious, and they were tender to the touch. Just last night, he'd noticed her wince when Audrey had given Caroline one of her enthusiastic hugs. There was no denying it. She was pregnant. Thirty-seven and pregnant with their fourth child. A lapse in judgment, to say the least.

The only night he and Caroline had been intimate for months, he'd come home late from work slightly tipsy. To his surprise, Caroline had stayed up for him, and when he slipped into bed, she pressed her body against him. It had been a week since he'd been able to spend time with Phil. He imagined it was her, not his wife. The dark made this possible.

The sound of running water came from the bathroom. Caroline was taking a bath, providing an opportunity for him to paste his latest article in his journal. He padded to the window in his bare feet and opened the curtains to San Francisco in all her glorious shades of gray. Fog covered the city, hiding buildings and the bay, giving everything a feeling of quiet in direct juxtaposition to his home. Downstairs, the children were yelling to one another and running through the house like a bunch of animals. Did anyone ever walk in this house? He pulled at the collar of his pajamas and tried to breathe, but it was no good. He was suffocating. His family was an albatross around his neck, yoking him to the chaos they inevitably brought with them. No matter that the house was enormous, there was not one empty room. Not ever. Servants coming and going, the nanny, and their three children, always movement, noise, distraction. Caroline never ceased talking. Every detail of every child, of the book she was reading, of something funny her father said. He wanted to shout at them all: *be quiet*. Regardless of his desires, he held it inside, like he always did, like he'd trained himself to do.

He reached under the bed and pulled out a small box. He doubted anyone, including Caroline, even knew it was under the bed, except for the maid. Regardless, he kept a lock on it, the key hidden in plain sight on his keychain which he stored each night on the bedside table, no matter which house he happened to sleep in that night. Lately, though, he knew the box belonged at the beach with Phil. It seemed wrong here, under Caroline's bed, when it held his world. His real world. He opened it now, pulling the eighth journal in a series started all those years ago at the orphanage. From his wallet, also on the bedside table, he pulled the latest article on the Bennett family and pasted it on the second to last blank page.

Edmund Bennett names Stewart Young his predecessor.

When he was finished, he placed it in the box with the rest. Then, he reached for the house phone, calling the kitchen. Mae, their housekeeper, answered. "Yes, Mr. Dreeser?"

"Send up breakfast, please. Mrs. Dreeser doesn't feel well. Make it dry toast and weak tea. A few pieces of bacon and some fruit for me. And send Joseph up. I have something I need delivered this morning."

In minutes, Joseph was at the bedroom door. Miller pointed to the box, speaking just above a whisper. "Take this out to Phil's this morning. Ask her to store it under her bed."

"Yes, sir."

Miller handed him a few dollars in cash: insurance that Joseph kept his secrets. As he closed the door, Caroline came out of the bathroom. The master suite was opulent, decorated in light blues with everything made of something either shiny or soft, with cushions and chairs and a four-poster bed practically the size of the room he'd shared with six other boys in the orphanage. Dressed in her cotton nightgown, Caroline's skin had the green hue of pregnancy, and dark circles under her eyes marred her usual attractiveness. He had to admit, she'd aged well. Despite three pregnancies, other than stretch marks on her stomach, she remained rather unchanged over the years. She ate almost nothing, afraid to return to the fat girl of her childhood, and was small-boned yet muscular from tennis and horseback riding. White blond hair set in waves contrasted her California suntan.

She came to bed, pulling back the heavy covers, and climbed in next to him. "Good morning." She smelled of her bath soap.

"Nice bath?" he asked.

"Yes. I wasn't feeling well and hoped a warm bath would help." She yawned. "It didn't do much for me, unfortunately."

"I've ordered breakfast up," he said.

"I should cancel my tennis game with Meredith."

"Meredith will give you hell for that," he said.

She turned on her side to look at him, her fair hair splayed against the pillow. She gave him a weak smile. "I'm pregnant."

He must pretend to be excited. "I thought as much."

Her eyes filled with tears. "Are you angry?"

He swallowed, preparing his answer, knowing he had to be convincing. "Why would I be angry?"

"You're not particularly interested in the ones we already have." She smiled in a way that softened the words. She'd always had such a gentle smile, almost indulgent, especially with him and the children. It did nothing but fill him with disdain. This ridiculous woman wouldn't know the truth if it hit her in the head.

"Don't be ridiculous. I adore our children." He tickled the side of her face with a strand of her pale hair. "Another baby will keep us young."

"Daddy said he wanted you to spend more time with us. That if you did, he might consider giving you partial ownership in the textiles."

"More time with you. What does that mean? Come to the beach house this summer?" Edmund, the big man. The top hat, demanding what he wanted in exchange for money and power.

"At least for some of it. He wants to see you be more of a family man," Caroline said. "It's important to him."

His stomach clenched. The damn beach house. They were all mad about that house. It was all anyone could ever talk about. They would all depart in the next day or so, not to return until the last weekend of August. He'd hoped this would give him ample time with Phil, but once again, the Bennetts had ruined his plans. "I will make it a priority," he said.

"Thank you, darling."

"I know the children love the time at the beach. I would've loved it as a kid, I can assure you of that." Bringing up his childhood always evoked sympathy from her.

"Oh, my poor Miller." She kissed his shoulder. "Anyway, my father and Seb can spend time together. There's something troubling Seb. I'm not sure what."

"Seb? He's fifteen. What isn't troubling him? It's probably a girl. They can do wicked things to your brain, you know." He said it with just the right connotations, so that she would think it was her to whom he referred. "I think it's a splendid idea for you, not just the children. Sea air is just what you need to grow a healthy baby. And I'll get down as often as I can."

"Thank you, sweetheart. I feel better just thinking of it."

18

PHIL

Teddy sat at the table on a stack of books, short legs dangling, face smeared pink with jam, and gulped the last of a glass of milk. When the glass was empty, he picked up another piece of buttered bread covered with jam and split it apart before taking a large bite from the middle, making murmuring noises of appreciation. Her Teddy loved his meals. The sacrifice was worth it, she reminded herself. *Remember what it would be like without Miller. Don't ever forget.*

Phil leaned against the sink and folded her arms over her stomach, clutching at the skin around her waist—a habit when she was nervous. Dinner. What could she say to get out of it? She could lie. Teddy woke up sick. No, that wouldn't work. He would see Teddy bouncing around the yard and know she'd fibbed to get out of dinner. She could feign a headache. This sometimes worked with Miller when he was amorous and she couldn't stomach one more minute of his hands on her. Other times he took what he wanted, regardless. It depended on the number of drinks.

The sound of a car coming up the driveway distracted her. She crossed through the kitchen and went to look out the living room window. "Oh, no," she whispered. Miller's Rolls-Royce slowly made its way up the long driveway. What was he doing here in the middle of a Friday afternoon? Now that he'd found a place to stash her, he planned to visit several nights a week. This way he could tell his wife he had business meetings and would be late. But a Friday during the day? This was unprecedented.

She went out to the front steps. They were newly built, she noticed for the first time. Fresh paint. Not a creak as she stepped down onto the lawn. Henry had made sure they were safe, that neither she nor Teddy would slip and fall. The sun, directly above, shone with intensity. She shielded her eyes with her hand as the front door of the car opened. Miller's chauffer, Joseph, was so tall that when he came out of the car it always looked uncomfortable, like he was unfolding from a space much too small. In his early fifties, his once dark hair was almost completely white, but thick and always in exact placement. He had a slight paunch, mostly hidden by his dark jacket, a jowly face that reminded Phil of a bulldog, and a deep voice he did not often use. When he did, he spoke softly as if to mask the resonance, which gave the impression of humility combined with dignity.

Crossing the yard with long strides, she reached him just as he was closing the car door. "Good afternoon, Joseph."

He yanked his hat from his head, holding it at his waistline in a way that always made him seem apologetic. "Miss, I'm sorry to disturb you. I have a message and a delivery from Mr. Dreeser."

"Is everything all right?"

"Yes, fine. He wanted to tell you that he'll be visiting tomorrow. Returning to the city Sunday."

Joseph: chauffer and secret keeper.

"Mrs. Dreeser and the children are leaving for their beach house in Santa Barbara." He opened the back of the car and pulled out a wooden box with a lock on it.

"I see." She flushed, ducking her head, examining her fingernails. Mrs. Dreeser. The wife. The mother of his children. With her absence, Miller could safely come to her. He would stay the night.

"Mr. Dreeser asked if you would keep this box for him. He asked that you put it under the bed," said Joseph.

"Thank you, Joseph. I'll take it." He placed it in her arms. "Would you care for something to drink? A glass of cold water?"

"No, thank you, miss. I've been instructed, however, to take you and Teddy into town for supplies."

It hadn't fully occurred to her until that moment that she was without a car, stuck miles away from town. Yes, she would have to rely on others to take her shopping. Another way in which she was trapped like an animal. "That would be lovely, Joseph. Can you wait a moment? I'll put this away and fetch Teddy."

Moments later, they were settled in the back of the car, Teddy snuggled close against her legs. He loved riding in the car. It had the lucky effect of quieting him, as he was too busy gazing out the window to squirm or ask a hundred questions.

After five miles, they arrived in the town of Stowaway. The main street, flush with businesses, bustled with activity. Joseph slowed as they passed the city sign, inching along now behind another car that had its windows down, with the arms and legs of young women and men hanging out the sides, skin exposed to the bright sun. No one seemed to be wearing many clothes. She almost smiled, imagining her mother's horrified expression as they passed two women in two-piece bathing suits walking barefooted toward the beach. Her mother's shrill voice invaded her mind. *Practically naked, just strutting through the middle of town.*

At the end of the main street, the town met the sea in a long strand of sandy beach spotted with copious people reclining or picnicking, all in brightly colored swimsuits. Children ran from waves. Women chatted in clumps, smoking cigarettes or drinking sodas from bottles. In the surf, men rode long boards. An old man held the hand of a small girl in a pink bathing suit as they ran from a wave. Even from the car, Phil heard the child's delighted shrieks. *Mary*. She remembered the plump legs of her baby sister and her laughter like chiming bells as Phil chased her across the lawn. Fury, jealousy, and self-pity came roaring in like one of the waves. Why was she the only one here now? Why couldn't Eddie be here holding Teddy's hand with Mary running ahead to chase a wave? It all played before her as if it had happened once, like a memory or a photograph or home movie, and when it was over, the homesickness came and she was like a washrag hung out to dry, dirty and useless. She lived in a state of memory or imagination. This is what it was like to be banished from your world and sent to a strange land for punishment. No matter how pretty the new world, one still longed for home, for those who had made it home by their presence.

"Miss, will this do?" Joseph had found a place to park near the beach.

"Oh, yes, Joseph. This is fine."

They got out of the car, the scent of marine life and seaweed and salt air greeting her like a soft kiss.

"Shall I take the young master for a walk along the beach, miss, while you shop?"

"Yes, please." She turned to Teddy. "Be a good boy and don't run away from Mr. Joseph."

"Yes, yes." He nodded, jumping up and down in excitement.

"Try not to get too sandy," she said, planting a kiss on his fat cheek.

Joseph reached into his pocket. "Mr. Dreeser said to give you this." He handed her an envelope. It would be full of cash, she knew. He gave her a generous allowance every week, and often, like now, extra spending money. "He said to buy yourself something pretty besides just supplies."

Something pretty? A new dress to wear for him? A new hat? She needed nothing. Her closet was full, as was her stomach. Regardless, Miller liked to see her in new dresses, made her put them on and walk in front of him, proud that she had such good taste and a slender figure.

She parted ways with Teddy and Joseph and made her way down the main street, quickly spotting the butcher shop and the produce stand. A barber, a doctor, and drug store rounded out the necessities. In an alley, a sign for a tailor shop hung above a door, but no dress shop.

She needn't have worried to change into a decent dress. Ladies were dressed in bathing suits and shorts, walking around town, brown from the sun. California was a strange land. She came upon an attractive brick building. Sayer Fine Furniture. Henry's studio. She paused at the window, looking inside. He stood, sanding a large piece of dark wood. Should she go inside and say hello? Before she could decide, Henry looked up, his face changing as he recognized her. Grinning, he set aside his sanding tool and strode to the door, swinging it open to meet her on the sidewalk. "Mrs. Rains, you've found me."

"I'm just here doing some shopping. I'd forgotten to look for your shop, I was busy getting acclimated, and there you were." Why did her voice sound odd? She sounded nervous. Indeed, she was nervous. Henry Sayer made her nervous.

"It's nice to see you." He smiled at her again. *Such a nice smile. So genuine and disarming.*

"Thank you for all the work you put into the cottage and yard to make it safe for Teddy. The more I'm there, the more I notice what you've done."

"Oh, you're most welcome. You must let me know if you need anything. Anything at all." He raised an eyebrow, almost flirtatiously, but in a way that seemed out of practice. She imagined him before the war, handsome, whole, the world before him, no lady impervious to his charms.

"The awful place I had to live before..." She could have kicked herself. Why had she revealed so much? Thankfully, he did not ask any follow up questions. Too well-mannered. His mother had taught him properly.

They chatted for a few more minutes, during which time Henry gave her advice on where to shop, offering to bring home anything she couldn't carry. "That won't be necessary. A friend brought me to town." To change the subject, she continued without pause. "Stowaway isn't what I expected."

He nodded, glancing down the street at the water, the bright light illumining the golden highlights in his dark blond curls as he squinted into the sun. "It's changed since I was a kid. The surfers have discovered us."

"I've seen them in the city, but it seemed such a silly thing to do I couldn't imagine it being anything more than a fleeting interest. Apparently, I was wrong."

"Fortunately, I never picked it up. Can you imagine trying to surf with one arm?" He continued to watch the shore, smiling.

She followed his gaze toward the beach. Young women lined the coastline, watching the surfers catching breakers, some riding them almost to shore, others falling, only to get back up again. She spotted Joseph holding Teddy's hand, both running from a wave. What was it about the seashore that made everyone feel young?

"On a day like today it feels like the war never happened," she said. "They all seem lighthearted, like they haven't a care in the world except how to catch the next wave."

"May they be so lucky," he said.

"It doesn't make you bitter?" she asked.

"Others having fun?"

"Yes."

"I fought so that they might do exactly that."

She turned her gaze back to him. He spoke without pride or boastfulness. It was a fact to him, she supposed, an inevitability that his generation must bear. He fought so that the world, their world here in America, could remain free from terrorist reign. Eddie and her brother Ivan had not come back. They would not ever frolic under a warm sky again. She wasn't like Henry. She could not let it go, this bitterness that lived at the back of her throat, poisoning everything. But she didn't say it out loud. It was best to keep her darkness away from men like Henry, who had given so much and yet could still look for the light.

For the moment, she was no longer in the place between memory and imagination, but right here. Was she absorbing Henry Sayer's light? "You should make boards."

"Excuse me?" he asked.

She gestured toward his shop. "Surfboards. Surely they couldn't be any harder than the exquisite furniture you make."

He stared at her. "I hadn't ever thought of it before."

"There could be a fortune to be made from others' fun," she said.

"I suppose. Something to think about anyway."

"Well, I should be on my way. I have more than a few items on my list."

"It was a pleasure to see you, Mrs. Rains. I'll look forward to tonight."

"Yes. Shall I buy a bottle of wine for dinner?"

"There's no need. My father left an extensive wine collection when he passed. It'll be nice to have someone to share it with."

After they said good-bye, it occurred to her that she had had every intention of canceling their dinner, and yet it hadn't crossed her mind for a moment when she was in the presence of Henry. The feeling she'd had earlier, this nervousness around Henry, what was it? She halted, right there in the middle of the sidewalk. That was the feeling earlier. Not nervousness, but excitement. Desire. Smitten. She'd forgotten the pleasurable flutter of desire.

A creature buzzed past her ear. A planter hung in front of the store's window. Inside it, a hibiscus dripped with pink and purple flowers, and a hummingbird with his slender, graceful beak drank from the flower's sweet nectar, drawn to it despite the scent of the salty sea that might distract a less sensitive creature.

Henry Sayer's a problem. I'm a hummingbird to a hibiscus.

After Joseph carried her parcels into the cottage, he accepted a glass of water and a sandwich before he left for the long drive back to the city. When he finished his late lunch, he insisted that it was time he was on his way home. She walked him to the car, the sun hot on her dark hair. "I'm sorry, Joseph."

"Whatever for, miss?"

"Well, this. Me."

With downcast eyes, he removed his hat and took a handkerchief from his pocket and patted his forehead. "Miss, we all do what we must to survive, to take care of little ones entrusted to our care. This world's cruel to young ladies without a man; everyone knows that. Been that way since the dawn of time. My mother came here from England with me and no husband. My mother was the finest woman that ever lived, despite falling in love with the wrong man."

Phil's eyes burned. *Please don't cry,* she told herself. Why, when people were kind, did it always make her want to cry?

He stuck his hat back on his head and put his handkerchief back into his pocket. "Don't despair, Miss Rains. Everything will work out as it's supposed to. It always does."

She remained standing in the yard, the grasses rustling about in a lovely symphony of sound, watching until the car disappeared. Throughout the last three years, the infinite kindness of some, equaled only by the treachery and cruelty of others, amazed her. They seemed to be parceled out in equal measures. One could not decide if more people were good than bad.

Later, up to her elbows in sudsy water, Phil looked longingly at the ocean, wondering what it would feel like to be submerged in its depth. Behind her, Teddy played with his truck, running it up and down the soft leg of the armchair. She dried her hands on her apron, leaving the wet dishes in the rack to dry. Her mother had never allowed such things, insisting that everything be dried and put away before leaving the kitchen. But her mother wasn't here. She would never be here or in Phil's life ever again. *Do not cry. Fold the towel and walk away from the kitchen without thinking of her, without wondering what she's doing at this very moment.*

Teddy had fallen asleep on the couch, sitting straight up with his face tucked into his own neck, never one to give up the fight and admit he needed another nap. She carried him to his bed before wandering into her own room. She lay on the bed, planning on resting her eyes for only a few moments, but she fell fast asleep.

Teddy woke her up an hour later, staring at her with a worried expression in his brown eyes as her stroked her bare arm with his little hand. "Mama, wake up." "Yes, yes. I'm awake."

"Beach now?"

"Yes, beach now. Mr. Sayer said there were buckets and maybe even a shovel. We could build a sandcastle."

His round eyes, brown like her own, went wide. "A bucket?"

"Yes. You can dig a hole or whatever you like." She rose from bed, straightening her blouse. "We will only put our toes in or the waves might take us out to sea."

He bounced off the bed, nodding with great solemnity. "Okay, Mama."

She held out her hand. "Come on, let's get our swim clothes on."

It took them only moments to take off their clothes and dress in their swimming wear. Phil's bathing suit, a gift from Miller, came in two pieces, the top no larger than a brassiere. The bottoms came up to her waist and stopped at the beginning of her thighs. A bare midriff and exposed legs were more revealing than she was comfortable with, but Miller had insisted upon it. "You're too young for an old lady suit," he said when she'd opened the box.

"A swim costume?" she asked. "Whatever for?"

"I've found you a cottage by the ocean. Out of the way." A solution to both their problems, he said.

Now, she stood at the full mirror in her bedroom, staring at her own reflection. Thinner than she was before she'd gotten pregnant with Teddy, her ribs stood out and her arms and legs looked like trunks of a birch sapling, pale and breakable. She covered her mouth with red lipstick, vivid against her pale skin. Slender all her life, with long legs, small breasts, and a short torso, she had never given much thought to her appearance but was under no illusions that when God had given out curves He'd forgotten to include her. She had not minded. Growing up on a farm, she'd always been thankful for strength and ease of movement, and there was no place for vanity in their strict religious upbringing. Mirrors were discouraged, as were clothes that revealed one's figure. Hair styled in any way other than long and worn in a braid or bun was not allowed. But of late, she'd dwelled more on her appearance, given that it had saved Teddy's life. Miller found her beautiful, arrestingly so, he'd told her that first night when he'd made his offer. Because of her outward appearance, she'd secured a home for Teddy. Was she beautiful? Before Teddy and the hardships of the last three years, she might have said, yes. But now, her cheeks were hollow and her clavicle bones, missing flesh and muscle, were more visible than they should have been. Shadows under her eyes made her seem either tired or troubled. Perhaps both? Her eyes stared back at her with a wariness, like a dog expecting to be hit.

She covered in a loose cotton dress. Teddy was at the door, calling out to her that he was ready and could she please hurry?

Minutes later, they searched the shed. It was neatly organized, everything arranged on shelves, and they found sand toys and a bucket with no trouble. Teddy bounced with happiness.

They held hands going down the stairs to the beach. It was a sharp incline but the steps were well made, with nary a loose board. Soon, they were settled on a blanket under the shade of a tree. A large piece of driftwood at her back made a nice chair. Teddy played in the wet sand, far from the incoming tide. He was afraid of the waves. Well, good. She wanted him to be cautious. From her bag, she pulled out a book, put on her sunhat, and settled back to read. It was no use. She couldn't relax and keep an eye on Teddy at the same time.

Instead, she surveyed their little cove. Above, on the cliff, grasses swayed, but here in a cleft of the hillside, it was warm, sheltered from the breeze. The small stretch of sand was no more than a hundred feet wide, surrounded by rocks on both sides. The tide, low now, would enable one to walk beyond the cove, but Phil had decided against any kind of walk, afraid to get stuck. On both sides, tide pools housed sea anemone, small fish, and even a starfish. Incoming waves crashed against rocks, breaking their strength so that only soft waves came to their shore.

She'd brought with them the bread, butter, and jam, along with several boiled eggs and a jar of water, in case Teddy grew hungry. She salted an egg, devouring it in two bites. The fresh air made her hungry. She buttered a piece of bread, smeared it with jam, and bit into it. Heaven. The jam was extraordinary. Sweet but not overly, like the taste of a strawberry warm from the sun. Her mother had made good jam, but nothing like this. Perhaps it was impossible to make something sweet if you were mean and stingy? She was about to take another bite when footsteps coming down the stairs distracted her. Setting the bread back into the basket, she turned to look. It was a woman in her late forties, wearing an enormous pink straw hat. It flapped in the breeze, almost as wide as the woman was tall. Petite, no taller than five feet, she wore a loose sundress that engulfed her small frame. Her legs and arms were muscular and browned from the sun, although no bigger than a prepubescent boy's. She carried a muslin bag, from which a long loaf of bread bounced from side to side. A shotgun rested over her shoulder. Phil tensed.

The woman had reached the bottom of the steps. With some

effort—sitting on the ground had made her stiff—Phil unfolded her long legs and stood to greet her. "Hello there."

"You must be Mrs. Rains," she said. "I'm Mrs. Thomas. Dear Henry stopped at the farm earlier to tell me of your arrival. Mortified, I was, to think you'd moved in yesterday and I hadn't been by to welcome you and bring you some food. Such a bother to get settled, I said to myself. You best get over there and offer your neighborly services." Mrs. Thomas ripped off her hat and tossed it onto the blanket, setting her gun next to it. She wore her curly red hair, with just a hint of gray, short and cropped attractively around her face. Her eyes, the color of a pine needle, sparkled like she knew a delightful secret and couldn't wait to share it with you.

"Oh my, you're having my bread and jam. I'm enormously pleased. Don't you know, I've had that sourdough starter from the time I was first married? No older than you, come to think of it." With both hands, she raked her fingers through her hair, causing it to bounce like coiled springs as she turned to look at Teddy. He'd stopped playing—a rather unusual event—and gaped at her with his mouth open far enough a bug could quite easily fly inside, as if the last thing he expected was to see another person, especially this one who obviously carried a bag of good things to eat. "And this is the wee one? Dearie, he's a darling. Look at those cheeks." She perched on the edge of the driftwood piece. "My son was always such a skinny thing when he young. Used to worry myself sick whenever he was ill, afraid he'd perish before the morning." She sighed, and wiped the corners of her eyes. "At the end there was nothing a mother could do, with this awful war taking all our boys. Anyway, never mind that. It's a lovely day God's made for us, and we should revel in it. I do love this cove. Many happy memories, right here, with Henry's mother, God rest her soul. We were the very best of friends. She knew everything about me, even more than my poor Mr. Thomas. Women have their secrets they can tell only one another. Men, bless them for trying, just never understand nuances like other women do. I miss her terribly. Cancer took her. She went fast, which I was glad of at the end, as she was in terrible pain. Just three summers ago we spent almost every day here, enjoying our picnics and one another's company, both of us beside ourselves with worry over our boys fighting overseas, and just like that, she started feeling awful and three months later she was gone. Wouldn't you know, this is the exact spot we used to make our picnics. Speaking of which, I've brought some yummies. Like I said, Henry stopped by, asking if I'd make a little extra for your supper tonight, and I said to myself, it would be best if I put a few things together for you and me, maybe trap you into a chat. I get lonely, I'm not ashamed to say. I love every inch of my property and this view here, but it *is* a bit isolated. May I sit with you on the blanket?"

"Please." Even though Mrs. Thomas had not stopped talking, except to take in a breath here or there, Phil immediately liked her. No wonder she was lonely, given all she'd lost. A boy and a best friend in such a short amount of time. Despite the warmth, Phil shivered.

"We have a grocer in town, but sometimes his stock is limited, and we make almost all our own food. I don't frequent his shop much except to buy toiletries or certain items for the house. I've probably supported his entire family with the number of canning jars I've bought over the years. Anyway, between my vegetable garden and the livestock, chickens, goats, and all, we don't have much need for store bought. Yes, we have goats." She paused, pursing lips. "Goats, the most awful crea-tures. One ate my hat the other day. I had to buy this new one when the other one would've lasted me many, many more years to come. I regret the day I brought them home, but they were the cutest baby animals, bleating to beat all. The most pitiful sound. And Henry told you about the strawberries?" While she talked, Mrs. Thomas emptied the cloth bag. First she pulled out the baguette, several knives, plates, napkins, a jar of pickles, a flat of raspberries, a metal tin, and a chunk of white cheese. Last, she pulled out two brown bottles, holding what, Phil couldn't guess.

"No, he didn't." Phil had resumed her place and stretched her legs out, enjoying the kisses of the late afternoon sun.

She put her head in her hands in a dramatic gesture of despair, before looking back at Phil. "A half acre we planted last spring. Poor Mr. Thomas didn't say a word about it, just planted and planted, and wouldn't you know they're all thriving, producing fruit like plants possessed. And now we have all this jam."

Teddy had approached, looking shy, but his love of food had outweighed his wariness of strangers. "Teddy, can you say hello?" asked Phil. "This is Mrs. Thomas, and she's brought you some delicious food."

"Hallo, Mrs. Thomas."

"Hello, Teddy."

Teddy pointed at the flat of raspberries. "What those?"

"Raspberries, dearie. Would you like one?"

"Yes, please."

"What nice manners you have." Mrs. Thomas put a half-dozen raspberries on one of the plates and handed it to Teddy. "Will we spoil his dinner? It's after four."

"He's always hungry, Mrs. Thomas. Dinner is not usually spoiled."

Mrs. Thomas smiled. "We'll call this tea time. My mother came from England and we always had tea around this hour. I've gotten out of the habit of it, serving poor Mr. Thomas his supper around six. He works himself to death, and he's not getting any younger. He's half-starved by six and ready for bed by eight." She pulled a metal object from her pocket, using it to pop the top off both bottles. "Ginger beer. Best thing you ever tasted. Poor Mr. Thomas fetches it for me from the city. Only thing I can't make myself, I always tell him. He likes his whiskey after supper, so he can't say much, now can he? Plus, ginger's good for your complexion. Did you know?"

Phil, taking the drink from Mrs. Thomas's outstretched hand, confessed that, no, she did not know ginger was good for one's complexion. She took a tentative sip. It was cold and spiced with ginger. Unlike a soda, it was only slightly sweet. "Delicious. Thank you. Will it make me drunk?"

"Oh, heavens no. There's no alcohol in it, but I always feel like I'm doing something terribly wicked when I drink it." Mrs. Thomas had set her drink aside and was breaking pieces off the baguette. Then, slicing into the cheese, which Phil was surprised to see was soft, spread it onto the bread. "You eat this, Mrs. Rains. We need to fatten you up. This is cheese made from our goats, the appalling creatures. It's not like cheese made from cows, so you might not like it at first, but give it another try, because it grows on a person. Like coffee, I always say. You'd never know we could make something this good out of the milk from an animal who eats hats."

Phil laughed, accepting the plate Mrs. Thomas had made for her, and took a bite. The bread was slightly warm but the layer of cheese cool and creamy with a zesty taste. "I love it," she said.

"Oh, but that does make me happy." Mrs. Thomas smiled and settled back to lean against the driftwood log. Phil assumed she would begin to ask questions. Where did she come from? Why here? Where's Teddy's father? Instead, her unexpected companion drank her ginger beer and nibbled on a piece of bread with the cheese made from a hat-eater's milk and watched, with apparent delight, Teddy gobble almost the entire bowl of berries. Phil relaxed. The food satiated her hunger. Between her full stomach and the soft light of late afternoon with the sound of the waves crashing, she became drowsy and lazy, unworried.

After the berries were gone and Teddy had polished off a piece of bread with cheese and jam, he was ready to play. Toddling off with his bucket in his hand, he returned to the wet sand, plopped to the ground, and began to dig.

"Have you always lived here?" asked Phil.

"I grew up a couple hundred miles north in a small fishing town. Mr. Thomas's family has owned our land for a century. Early pioneers. I married Mr. Thomas when I was only seventeen years old. I suppose you could say I've grown up here."

A flock of birds flew overhead. Mrs. Thomas jumped to her feet, snatched her shotgun, aimed into the sky, and fired a shot. A bird, whatever kind it was Phil couldn't say, fell from the sky, landing about ten feet from them. Mrs. Thomas put the safety back on—at least Phil assumed it was a safety—and set it back by the log.

Both Phil and Teddy were speechless. She worried he might cry, having never seen or heard a gun fired, but instead he gazed at Mrs. Thomas with his lips pursed, like he was trying to figure out what in heaven's name had just happened.

"Don't mind me," said Mrs. Thomas. "I can't ever pass up the chance for a pheasant for poor Mr. Thomas's dinner, now could I?" She marched over to the dead bird, picked it up by its feet and carried it over to the basket where she pulled out a newspaper and proceeded to wrap up poor Mr. Thomas's dinner. When she was done, she walked to the water and washed her hands in the surf, drying them on her dress. She came back to sit by Phil, grabbing her ginger beer and taking a large swig.

"Where did you learn to hunt birds?" asked Phil.

"My grandfather taught me. He was from England and bird hunting's big over there. He said no granddaughter of his was going through this life not knowing how to kill a pheasant. I've particularly good aim. My son, William, inherited my keen shot. He was specially trained in the army to shoot long range."

"I'm sorry for your loss, Mrs. Thomas."

"Thank you, dear. I'd just turned nineteen when he was born. I grew up overnight. The minute you hold that baby in your arms you know life requires more of you. Well, you know, Mrs. Rains. You must be better, stronger, smarter. I was blessed to have Mr. Thomas by my side. A more devoted father you'd never meet. He's a quiet one but still waters run deep, as they say."

It was true what she said about motherhood. The moment she'd known that Teddy grew in her belly, she knew the only purpose of her life was to take care of him. "William's such a nice name."

"We said we'd call him Will or Bill, but he was a William. Tall and lanky like his father, and handsome. Quiet like Mr. Thomas, and dignified. I always imagined he'd become an attorney and ultimately a judge. Fair-minded. He had a sweetheart from the time he was just a boy. Rose. Henry's twin sister. We all figured they'd be married with babies running around this beach by now. He lost his life protecting another soldier. Received a Medal of Honor for it. He made me proud all his life, up until the very end. It gives me comfort, knowing he saved another mother's boy. They didn't have a body for me, though. I didn't get to bury him." Mrs. Thomas, although her voice had not wavered from its cheery cadence, swiped at the corners of her eyes.

"What's happened to Rose?" asked Phil.

"Rose? She lives in the city. Took over her father's business. Quite different than dear Henry. She's one of those people so quick-witted and smart that you can practically see her mind solving problems."

"It must be strange to be a twin."

"I can't imagine. He was the social one, such an athlete, always making something or throwing something or figuring out how to make a game out of nothing. Whereas Rose was more in her brain...what's the word I'm thinking of?"

"Cerebral?"

"Yes, right-o. Cerebral. Nose in a book. Doing figures. Never had any interest in sports or making things with her hands like her mother, but had a head for business like their father. 'Girl things bore me,' she used to say when we asked her to help us in the kitchen. She would've rather been out with the men talking politics or business. They built the twin cottages for them, figuring they could live next door to one another. Always close, those two, finishing each other's sentences. Funny, being twins and all, that Henry took after his mother and Rose after her father. Inga was good with her hands, like Henry. Wasn't a thing she couldn't cook or sew or knit. 'I like to do,' she used to say to me. 'Makes me feel useful.' Sure as anything, when we were down here at the beach together, Inga's fingers were always flying, knitting needles making that clicking sound, half blinding me when they caught the light. I used to say she made me tired just looking at her." She chuckled, shaking her head.

"Seems I spend all my time missing them. I've lost Rose, too. She doesn't like to come back here—says it's too painful without William. She couldn't think of what to do with her grief but to work like a mad woman. Henry says she won't hardly leave the office. She looks different now, too. Skin and bones with this hard set to her mouth. Not that I can blame her. Besides Henry, she lost everyone she loved the most in five years' time. Life's cruel sometimes. We thank the good Lord for Henry. He's all we have left of the old days." She wiped the corners of her eyes again. They were red and chapped.

"We lost my brother. Ivan. In 1943." Even as she said it, Phil knew it opened the possibility of questions, and she instantly regretted the slippage of her tongue. This genuine, intimate exchange, as if it were possible for them to be real friends, was the exact thing she could not do. She must remain isolated. Miller was clear on that point. Yet, here she was on the first day here, letting this endearing woman inside her secret world.

"And Teddy's father? Mr. Rains?" asked Mrs. Thomas.

"Yes, just a year later."

"You poor dear."

"I understand how Rose must feel. Just this morning I was looking at myself in the mirror, thinking how skinny and pale I am. Hardly recognize myself anymore." Phil kept one eye on her son, but he was not near enough to the surf to be in danger.

Having dug one hole, he was now working on another and did not look up from his task.

"Did he ever meet his father?" asked Mrs. Thomas.

"No."

"Sometimes I wonder how we all bear it." Mrs. Thomas, as if only just remembering, snatched her hat from where it lay at her feet and plunked it on her head. "My mother was always telling me to wear my hat. She'd be horrified to see me now; brown as can be."

"My mother had the same affinity for hats," said Phil.

"When did she pass?"

"Oh, she's very much alive. She's too mean to die young."

"I see." Mrs. Thomas threw her head back, laughing.

"When I came out here, I cut ties with my family. They're all in Iowa where I grew up. We grew corn, mostly. Eddie, Teddy's father, lived on the neighboring farm. They were horse people and his father was a preacher, too. I knew Eddie all my life. I never loved anyone but him."

Mrs. Thomas, with the front brim of her hat folded back, watched her. "What brings you here?"

"I wanted to live by the ocean." A lie. "Start somewhere new. Fresh."

"Without all the ghosts?"

"I suppose that's one way to say it. I have an uncle in San Francisco." Miller had told her to tell anyone who asked that he was her uncle. "He was kind enough to send for Teddy and me and rented this cottage for us. I'm trained as a seamstress and hoping to find work. Is there a dressmaker in town?"

"We have a tailor, Mr. Mullen, but more and more people buy their clothes mail order. It's not how it used to be. Anyway, he makes clothes for men. Women have to go into San Francisco for a decent dress."

Phil nodded, excitement growing in the pit of her stomach. She had designs, masses of them, for dresses that mimicked the latest fashions from London and New York. With careful planning, she could make them for a quarter of the price of a designer piece. Surely there would be ladies interested here in town? Independence. Freedom. If she saved every nickel, it would only be a matter of time before she could escape from Miller and start a new life with Teddy.

The sun, low in the sky now, indicated it was time for them all to go home and get cleaned up for supper. Phil didn't want the day to end. It had been a long time since she'd sat with another woman talking the afternoon away. For the second time that day, she remembered the person she once was.

19

CAROLINE

Caroline sat on the covered patio of her parents' beach house, watching Audrey and Pierce play in the surf. Mother sat in the chair next to her, reading a novel. The sun hung between sea and sky, swathing the June afternoon in warmth. In the rafters a pair of mourning doves cooed to one another like a sigh mixed with a moan, and the sound always evoked a feeling of loss and regret in Caroline. On the beach, Audrey shrieked as she ran from a wave.

"Mother, I'm feeling terribly guilty for my idleness," said Caroline.

Mother put her book facedown on her lap and reached across the arms of their lounge chairs to take her daughter's hand. "Darling, you must give in and let yourself rest. If not for you, for the baby. Sit here in the shade this afternoon. Watch the sun move toward the sea. Let the staff do for you. They're beside themselves with joy to have you all here. As am I. When all the children are here, it feels like when you and Julius were young. It's good to hear the children's voices and their laughter. And to think we'll have another."

"Oh, Mother, I can't believe I'm about to start it all again. It's been too long since we had a baby. What if I've forgotten what to do?"

"That's what Nanny Brown's for," said Mother.

"I hate to ask the staff to do more than their usual load," said Caroline.

"That's ridiculous. A new baby will give Nanny something to do. The older children don't need her anymore. I've worried she would sink into despair if she had to leave you all for another job."

"Poor Nanny."

"Darling, truly, you need to let people take care of you, including me."

"I hate to have anyone make a fuss," said Caroline.

"That's ridiculous." Mother scrutinized her. "I blame Anna Beale."

Caroline laughed. "Yes, Anna Beale should have part of the blame. Do you remember how I thought I was adopted?"

Her mother smiled, cocking her head to the side. "Yes, I do."

All these many years later, and Caroline still experienced the sting of that night.

Mother tapped her arm. "I'm very proud of you. Do you know that?" she asked. "You're a good mother and a good person. I couldn't ask for anyone better than you for a daughter."

"Mother, stop. You'll make me cry."

The ocean was bright blue under the afternoon sun. Seagulls cried out to one another, swooping near the waves and back up again. Audrey and Pierce had stopped playing in the surf and were sitting side-by-side on a blanket, eating the sandwiches the cook had made for them. Everything tasted better on the beach, Julius always said.

"I think you should stay here at the beach until the baby comes. Maybe afterward, too. For the first year, at least. We could enroll the children into the academy in Santa Barbara."

"Mother, I can't just leave Miller in San Francisco alone. It's at least five hours from us."

Her mother's mouth made a flat line, like it did when Miller was mentioned. "If he chooses to make the drive, he can come weekends." She waved her hand in the air, chasing away a small fly. "Plus, the staff is there to take care of him."

Her parents had kept their house in the city, but they were hardly there, spending most of their time here, even during the winter months. They could easily stay, and like her mother said, enroll the children at the academy. They wouldn't know anyone, but perhaps they wouldn't care. Should she? For the first year? Would Miller care if they didn't come home? No, he wouldn't.

"I'll think about it," said Caroline. "Let's see how the rest of the summer goes."

"That seems fair," said Mother.

"They look like Julius and me at that age, don't they?" Caroline pointed at Audrey and Pierce, who were working on their second sandwich. They were not talking, just sitting in compatible silence. Audrey knew her brother's need for contemplative silence and adjusted appropriately, even though she was always bursting with something to say. Audrey and Pierce, although opposites and three years apart, were especially close. Audrey was outgoing and talkative, with a self-assurance and grace that mimicked her grandmother Sophie, whereas Pierce was quiet, reserved, and small for his age, making him and Audrey appear almost the same age. He loved science and mathematics and wanted to be a doctor, like Julius. "Mother, tell me about Julius, before he gets here. Is he much changed?"

Mother looked out to sea, her eyes seeming to focus just above where the children sat on the shore. "I'm afraid all the men who've come back from the war are changed."

"Can you describe him to me?" asked Caroline.

"He looks older. I'm afraid you'll be shocked when you see him. He's quieter, too. There's a sadness in his eyes, like he still sees the atrocities."

"The dreadful war," said Caroline.

"And the one before it," said Mother. "Your father still wakes from nightmares. Says he can still feel the mud from the trenches."

"Well, I'll be glad to see him, however he's come back to us."

As if she'd conjured him with her words, she saw Julius walking up the beach. She stood, waving, her heart in her throat. "Mother, here he is."

He waved back and set off running for their house.

She ran down the steps and onto the sand, forgetting she was barefoot. She let out a yelp. "Hot, hot, hot."

Mother laughed. "Have you forgotten what the sand feels like in the summer?"

She laughed, too, running back up the stairs and clinging to her mother's arm, jumping up and down like a child. "It's him. It's Julius."

"I'm going inside to discuss lunch with Margaret, my darling," said Mother. "And leave you two to visit."

"Thank you, Mother."

Seconds later, Julius reached the porch. He was dressed in a gray linen suit, crisp white shirt, and carried his medical bag. Tossing the bag onto the steps, he reached for her and Caroline leaped into his arms, not caring if it was appropriate or not. Her Julius had returned safely. She drew away from him, examining him for damage. Her mother was right. He did look older. Or perhaps the word was *weary*. Regardless, he was more handsome than ever. He'd always had a baby face and looked too young to be a real doctor, but the lines around his eyes and the half-moon crevices on the sides of his mouth gave him an air of sophistication. She shuddered to think what he had seen and done. "Julius Nelson, it's about time you came home."

"I'm sorry it took such a long time." Julius stared into her face, examining her as she had examined him. "Caroline, you look beautiful." He had a soft, low-toned voice that always made her feel relaxed.

"I do not." She smacked his arm. "I've been sick all morning. Miller told me I look green."

"No, not green. As pretty as you've always been. Prettier." Julius was of medium stature in both height and weight and wore wire-rimmed glasses. His hair was the color of late-September hay and fell against his forehead in waves. His dark blue eyes were often serious, making him seem both scholarly and sad.

"I have to make a house call after this, thus I can't stay long, but I had to see you as soon as possible." He escorted her over to the chairs. "Let's sit. Your mother tells me you're not feeling well."

"Just nauseous. Nothing to worry over. Can you believe it? Another baby after all this time." She gestured toward the water. The children were now building a sand castle together. "Audrey's nine. And now a new baby."

He turned to the beach. "That's Audrey? And Pierce?"

"Yes, they've grown up."

"I've missed so much." He took off his glasses and wiped his eyes.

"But you're here now. We can make up for lost time this summer."

He replaced his glasses and looked over at her. "There's no way to make up for lost time. We can't get it back, no matter how much we want to." His face twitched like someone had flicked his left cheek with their fingertip.

"Where are you staying?" she asked.

"At Father's and Essie's for the time being. They have plenty of room since the twins are married now," he said. "I hated missing their weddings."

"You didn't miss much. They were small affairs, arranged between the grooms' leaves," she said.

"I'm grateful they both returned safely," he said.

"Me too. Everything was gloomy during the war. It was hard

to be happy at a wedding when you knew days later the groom would be off to fight."

"Caroline, your letters—they often came in bunches, and I would organize them by the postmark date to make sure I read them in the right order. I read them over and over and have saved them all. The way you write made me feel like I was here. Someday we can put them in a book and send it off to a publisher. *Letters from Home* or some such title." He smiled. "You'll be famous."

She'd almost forgotten how slowly he talked, as if he had the rest of his life in which to converse. "I don't think anyone but you would be interested in the details of my rather mundane life." She waved her hand in a dismissive gesture, feeling more pleased than she should.

"The work you did for the servicemen's families was not mundane."

"It was nothing. Not compared to your contribution," she said.

He let out a long sigh. "It was never enough. We lost so many good men, and I couldn't do a thing to stop it." He held up his hands. "No matter how much I washed, they still smelled of blood."

"Oh, Julius." The back of her throat ached. She wanted to take him in her arms and make his unseen wounds disappear.

"I thought of you and your parents and the children and this stretch of beach when things were bad and it gave me hope that I'd see something beautiful again."

He was less guarded than before the war. Perhaps being close to death every day changed a person. One would feel the fragility of life more keenly. It would seep into you, waken you to the possibility that life could be snatched from you at any moment. Say what you want to say now, not later. She wondered what would change in her own life if she followed that simple rule.

He took her forearm in his hand, feeling her pulse. "Shall I take a look at you while I'm here?"

"No, no. I'm fine. It's the usual first trimester nausea. My doctor in the city says there's no reason to worry."

"I seem to remember the same ailments when you had Audrey." His warm hand remained wrapped around her forearm.

"Yes, I'm afraid so. Maybe it means we'll have another girl."

"How's Miller? Will he be down this weekend?" His voice changed when he spoke of her husband, like he was faking his interest.

"No. He can't get away. Work, you know." The rims of her eyes stung. *No tears, you ninny. Not after what he's gone through.*

"The world nearly perished and yet some things never seem to change." She guessed he meant it to come out as a tease, but it sounded angry instead. He dropped her arm to reach into his pants pocket for a handkerchief and handed it to her.

"I'm sorry. I'm weepy. Don't think anything of it." She dabbed under eyes.

"No reason to be sorry. We've always told one another everything. There's no reason to stop now." His statement wasn't completely true. She hadn't told him of her true feelings back when they were young, too afraid of his pity.

For a moment, he simply looked into her eyes and she let herself sink into the comfort she found there.

"You were away too long," she said.

He brushed a curl from her wet cheek with his fingertip. "You'd let me know if you ever needed anything?"

"Yes, thank you."

He seemed to be thinking of something else he wanted to say, but decided against it. "I should get along. Mrs. Peterson gave birth to a baby boy yesterday and I want to make sure they're both doing well." He looked out to where the children were running from a wave, squealing in delight. "It was nice to bring a life in rather than escort it out." He cleared his throat as he reached down for his bag. "I'm still acclimating. I have these moments that feel unreal, like I'm in a dream." He paused. "Seeing you, though, it's as if I were never away."

"When can I see you next? Can you come to dinner?"

"Yes, I'd love to." He leaned down and kissed her on the cheek. "Take it easy today, especially with the heat. Maybe rest later with a fan on you.

"Yes, Doctor."

"I'll say hello to Essie and your mother before I go." He smiled and turned away, crossing in front of her with his familiar long strides, like he was always in a hurry. She fluttered her fingertips as he opened the screen door and disappeared inside the house.

When she could no longer hear his footsteps, she brought his handkerchief to her nose and breathed in his scent and let the tears slide from the corners of her eyes. Overhead, the mourning doves cooed.

20

HENRY

Billows of dust in his wake, Henry pushed the gas pedal
of his car harder, wanting to get home. He knew why.
Obviously. Phil Rains. Her unexpected appearance at
his shop had left him distracted for the rest of the afternoon.
He'd even found himself counting the hours until it was time to
close up shop, which wasn't something he could remember
feeling since his return home. Usually, his work was a grateful
distraction from his troubles, but today he had felt alive, happy
to be home.

He bounced in a pothole and lifted several inches off the seat.
Out of nowhere, he had a sudden memory, like a photograph
before his eyes. It was of William, Rose, and him at the cove,
sitting on a blanket with their backs against the large piece of
driftwood that Rose called their bench. With Rose in the middle,
they sipped from cold beers and watched the sun set over the
Pacific. It was before Pearl Harbor, when they could still believe
America wouldn't enter the war, when they supposed they were
safe from harm. What he wouldn't give for just one more second
of that moment. How could he have known how few they had
left?

He shook off the dark reflection. Perhaps he would call Rose when he returned home? She would still be at the office, but maybe he could convince her to drive over in the morning and spend the weekend. Rose loved children. Maybe she would play with Teddy in the sand? He knew the answer would be no. It was easier for Rose to stay in the city where the shadows of the past did not lurk in every pothole.

Promptly at seven, Phil and Teddy knocked on his cottage door. It took great willpower not to gasp at his new tenant's beauty. Her hair was down, attractively arranged in large, loose curls just above her shoulders. A light blue dress, gathered at the waist with a flared skirt, made from a soft, silky material, displayed her slender body to its full advantage. She held a white cardigan sweater, which he asked if he could hang in the closet for her, trying to remember his manners when all he wanted to do was stare at her.

Teddy, hair neatly combed, wore dungarees and a blue shirt. He carried a bucket Henry recognized from his own childhood. "I see you found my old bucket," said Henry.

"He refused to let it go," she said. "I washed the sand off."

"A little sand never hurt anything," said Henry. "Come in, come in."

Her black pumps that made her long legs look even longer clicked on the hardwood floor. What a lovely sound. The bodice of her dress, sleeveless with a sweetheart neckline, flattered her narrow shoulders. She'd been in the sun that afternoon. A strip where her bathing suit straps had lain across her shoulders remained alabaster, but the rest of her glowed with the first hints of a California tan. "You've been kissed by the sun."

A hand flew to the bare skin above her décolletage. "Yes, we were out this afternoon. Down below, in your cove. It was lovely. Mrs. Thomas came for a visit and we started chatting. Before I knew it, the afternoon had passed." She placed a hand on Teddy's head. "This one may be a bear. He played hard."

Teddy put his bucket by his feet and held up his hands to show Henry. "Blister."

Henry knelt and took the boy's outstretched hands. "Yes, I see." A pink blister had developed on his left hand between his index finger and thumb. "Is he left-handed?"

"Yes. They'll make him change in school," said Phil.

"Nonsense. Don't let them," said Henry. "I'm a lefty, and a good thing, too, or I'd be in more trouble than I already am." He raised his left arm. "Do you see, Teddy, I only have one arm to dig holes with and I'm sure glad it's the left one I still have."

Teddy nodded his head, eyes wide.

"Please, sit. We could have a drink before dinner, if it suited you. I've set the table in the dining room. It's not often I have guests, so I pulled out the good dishes." He smiled at Phil, wishing he would stop talking too fast. He was giving himself away acting like a foolish schoolboy. "My mother always fed us in the kitchen except when my father was here for the weekends. I find I do the same, since it's just me. But tonight, we'll be fancy."

"Me no fancy," said Teddy. He wrinkled his brow in apparent perplexity as Henry led them into the living room. Always tidy, thanks to Mrs. Thomas, and decorated in light greens and creams with maple wood furniture, including a coffee table and cabinet. It was presentable for a lady. This was good. He hadn't changed it much since his mother passed, except to add several photos of his parents and a few of the pieces of pottery from the big house in San Francisco. A bouquet of roses from his garden was displayed in the middle of the coffee table. The rich aroma of rose petals, warm from the sun, infused the room.

"Teddy, I dug around in the shed this evening and I found some of my old toys. Trucks mostly. Would you like to play with them?" he asked.

Teddy nodded, eyes wide. Henry held out his hand. "Come

along. I have them in the spare bedroom. We'll think of it as your bedroom while you're here." He turned to Phil. "I'll get him settled and be right back."

After Teddy was occupied with the box of toys, Henry returned to the living room. Phil sat on the couch near the window, gazing into the yard, the orange light of the setting sun softening her features. Worried he might startle her, he tapped his knuckles against the doorframe. She rotated to look at him, a slight smile turning up the corners of her mouth. Her lips, not plump, but full enough to beg for a kiss, were painted red. She had mascara and blush on tonight as well, both of which made her appear glamorous in addition to pretty. He wondered what her lipstick would taste like if he were to kiss her. *Stop that*, he told himself. *Behave like a gentleman. This is not a date, simply a welcome dinner to my new tenants.* A woman like Phil would not be interested in a man like him, especially now. He walked all the way into the room. "Before dinner, my parents always had a cocktail. Would you care for one?"

"I've only ever had a Manhattan. Do you know how to make one of those?" she asked.

"I do. What American man doesn't know how to make a Manhattan?" He moved over to the cabinet where he kept alcohol and cocktail tumblers. His father had enjoyed his before dinner drink and had a tumbler and a glass pitcher for just such a purpose. "My father loved Manhattans."

"What did your mother drink?" she asked.

"She always had what he had."

"I suppose most women do," she said.

He took ice from the bowl he'd filled before they arrived and dropped a generous amount into the glass pitcher, and then poured whiskey, sweet vermouth, and a dash of bitters before stirring. "I don't think all women, necessarily. My sister, Rose, for example, makes it a point never to do what any of the men around her are doing. If William was having a Manhattan, she would most surely choose a martini."

"She must be very independent."

"Rose? Yes, independent. Stubborn. Bull-headed. And brilliant. Like my father." He poured the amber concoction into two glasses. "However, in the spirit of the times, I shall have what you're having."

"I wish I was more like Rose," said Phil. For the first time, he sensed weakness, a quaver to her voice that belied her general composure. She reminded him of a remote ballerina, straight backed, always contained, like she knew what every muscle of her body should be doing and did it.

Walking over to her, he placed a drink in her outstretched hand. He spoke gently, not wanting to spook her. "How do you mean?"

"Independent. My parents believed that women should always be subservient to men. That doesn't serve one in a situation like mine." She took a sip, cautiously, like it was a hot cup of broth. "Nice. Thank you."

"It must be frightening for you, alone with Teddy. You mustn't hesitate to call on me if you need anything. Even with my lack of a few limbs, I'm quite handy." He grinned as he sat in the armchair opposite her and took a sip of his own drink. "Not bad, if I do say so myself."

Phil smoothed the skirt of her dress and crossed her ankles before taking another sip, less cautiously this time. "I never dreamt I would ever be alone with a child. Eddie, Teddy's father, was my childhood sweetheart. I was naïve enough to think we would grow old together, raising children, then enjoying grandchildren, all of it right there on the same land our fathers cultivated." She told him how they lived on neighboring farms. "There was never anyone else but Eddie. Everything thought out and agreed upon between the two of us when we were fifteen years old. You know the rest."

"The war."

"Yes. Every dream vanished. The hardest part is Teddy.

Knowing he'll never meet his father. And, being alone without any family."

"They're still in Iowa, I take it?" he asked.

"Yes. My little sister's only ten. You can't imagine how I miss her. I haven't seen her since the day I left over three years ago. It broke my heart to leave her."

"And your parents?"

She smiled. "They were easier to leave."

"What made you come out here, alone, with Teddy?"

She shrugged, staring at her lap, her voice soft. "It's a long story, but I suppose you could say that my parents and I had a disagreement. It was best for me to leave. I have an uncle out here, wealthy, and he offered to find a place for me at the beach. So here I am."

Her past made her sad and isolated, he knew, despite her casual tone. He paused before speaking. What could he say to make her feel better, less alone? For some reason he wanted nothing more in the world than to comfort her. "My mother always said God never gives us more than we can handle."

She flashed him a sad smile. "I hate that expression."

He laughed. "Most people do, especially if they have a problem that prompts someone to say such a thing."

"Right." She chuckled before taking another sip of her drink. "Henry, why is it you're not married? Or do you have a sweetheart?"

"Ah, well, this is a sad story indeed." He let his eyes twinkle at her. "Do you truly want to hear it?"

"It can't only be my sad story."

"It's a simple story and not terribly original. My sweetheart married someone else while I was away."

Phil's eyes flew open and she made an adorable expression with her mouth like she had just tasted a lemon. "She didn't wait for you? Did she think you were dead?" She popped her hand over her mouth. "I'm sorry. How rude of me. It's this cocktail."

He couldn't help but smile at her distress. She was pretty

when flustered. "Don't be sorry. No, she didn't think I was dead. Apparently, absence does not always make the heart grow fonder. She wrote to me that she'd met someone else. She'd moved to Los Angeles for work and met a sailor there. It was a three-day romance. They married before the day he shipped out."

"Did he make it home?"

"Yes. Thankfully. They're very happy, from what I hear. Her parents live here in town and stop into the shop from time to time to give me news of her." He finished his drink and set it on the coffee table. "It's all for the best. I changed a lot while overseas. Life no longer seemed simple. Things were no longer black and white, good or evil. There were all these areas in between where I saw men at their worst and at their best but mostly a mixture of both. She was a nice girl looking for a party." He rose from the couch and fetched the pitcher from the bar. "More?"

She shook her head. He poured another glass for himself before sitting. "That's my sad story. Do you feel terrible for me?"

"Yes, quite." She smiled and glanced out the window. "I was raised in a strict Christian home and taught to believe every choice was black and white. Now I live in the gray and I realize what a lie they told me." She spread her hands in the air. "Nothing they taught me is of any use. Not when it comes to the hard decisions, the ones that come down to survival. I no longer have the luxury of believing it's as simple as good versus evil. Perhaps that comes with motherhood. There isn't anything I wouldn't do for Teddy. Evil be damned." She set her half-empty drink on the coffee table. "Goodness, this drink's gone to my head. I never talk this much."

"I bargained a few times with God when I was overseas, promising to be a better person if He'd get me home, or heal my mother, or let them find William. One time I even told Him to take me and send William back to Rose." He rattled the ice in his glass. "What we're prepared to do to save the people we love was proven over and over again with this war. We fought to ensure that those we left behind would be safe. But if war isn't gray, I don't know what is."

She had picked up her drink again and held the glass to her lips, looking at him with eyes like cups of coffee. "Do you think we're forgiven for doing something bad if it's for someone we love?"

He hesitated. The way in which she gazed at him made him feel as if how he answered was vital, like the difference between life and death. "I believe so, yes."

"I *am* sorry about William and your mother. And to lose your parents within a couple years' time must've been terribly hard."

Her eyes were glassy and so sympathetic it made a lump develop at the back of his throat. Terrified he might start to tear up, he took a quick sip of his drink. "They hated to be apart, so I suppose it was fate." He set his drink next to hers on the coffee table. "Well, this is hardly dinner conversation. Shouldn't we talk about my roses or the weather?"

She giggled. "Yes, we must immediately."

"Would you care for some bread and cheese?"

For some reason, they both found this enormously funny and burst into uncontrollable laughter. They might have laughed themselves silly if Teddy hadn't appeared right at that moment.

"Me hungee, Mama."

"He can't say his r's yet," said Phil, whispering. "It's going to break my heart when he learns."

Henry cocked his head to the right, observing Teddy, his heart full, grateful for the sunshine these beauties had brought into his house, if only for the moment. "That makes two of us."

They dined on Mrs. Thomas's delicious fried chicken and baby red potatoes, dug that evening and smothered in butter, and green beans Henry had brought from town. Teddy, perched atop a stack of books on one of the dining chairs, ate with gusto, devouring everything on his plate and washing it down with cold milk, developing a white mustache until his mother reminded him of the napkin in his lap. Henry opened a bottle of French Chablis from his father's cellar and poured them both conservative portions. After the drinks before dinner, which he rarely had, it was necessary to keep his wits about him. They spoke of more casual subjects during dinner—books and the history of the community. Phil confessed to her love of film, mostly because she loved to see the costumes. "Can you imagine how wonderful it would be to work on a film, designing clothes for the actresses?" she asked.

He put down his knife and fork and wiped his mouth before setting the napkin back in his lap. "I can't imagine anything more daunting. I can barely dress myself, and I don't mean because I have only one arm."

"Is it hard? Dressing, I mean?" She gazed at him with a complete lack of guile. He was surprised by the question. Most people didn't ask about his arm.

"I've developed certain techniques," he said. "At first, everything was difficult. Things you take for granted that you never realize require two hands. But after a while I adjusted. Not much choice. My work is slower, obviously. I have a boy who comes in to help cut the wood and such if I need him. I have devices that hold the wood steady. It's amazing how humans can adapt to their circumstance. We always find a way to keep going."

"Yes, we have a keen sense of survival." A bitter expression crossed her face. It reminded him for a moment of Rose. That hard set of the mouth and glint of anger in her eyes. He didn't like it. He must distract her from whatever it was she was feeling.

"Did you design and sew your dress?" he asked. "It's lovely."

She smiled, and the hardness evaporated. "Yes, thank you. I have a lot of designs. I study the fashion that comes out of New York and Paris. Milan even, now that the war's over. I try to emulate the trends with my own ideas, using less expensive fabrics." Stabbing a small piece of potato with her fork, she held it, suspended, between the plate and her mouth, obviously captivated by her subject. "My dream is to have my own dress shop."

Her own shop? "In San Francisco?"

"I thought so, once, but since talking with Mrs. Thomas, I've been unable to let go of an idea of a shop right here in Stowaway."

"Bathing suits," he said.

"Pardon me?"

"Surfboards and bathing suits. That's what people here want. Both those visiting and those who live here. And dresses made for outdoor living. For warm environments."

She was staring at him now, still holding the fork with the unlucky potato hanging in limbo. "Bathing suits." It was not a question. "Bathing suits. And beachwear."

"Yes, like for actresses starring in a film set at the beach," he said. "Honestly, I think you're on to something about the surfboards. I feel kind of dumb I didn't think of it myself."

"I'm feeling something similar," she said. "Town was swarming with people today."

"Yes, and they're almost all from somewhere else, come to enjoy a day at the beach. Your shop could be one of their stops." He smiled, imagining the storefront. "Window dressings of beach scenes. I could do them for you. I'm quite good at that kind of thing."

"You are?"

"Yes, I'm artistic that way."

She set her fork down on her plate. "You're making me imagine it."

"I can see it quite perfectly in my mind. An attractive shop, run by the prettiest woman in California."

"You're very kind." But she'd changed. Her face had become impassive, closed, like a blind abruptly closed on a sunny day.

She gestured toward Teddy. "It's getting late. We should probably be going home now. Teddy's up way past his bedtime."

Teddy started to shake his head, no. "Stay at Henry's."

"No, little man, listen to your mother. You can come back any time and play with the trucks," said Henry.

Teddy's eyes filled with tears. "Play now."

Henry stood and offered Teddy his hand. "How about this? You go on home without making a fuss and I'll let you pick out one truck to take with you."

Teddy's face, although still sad, went slack in agreement. "All 'ight." He slipped his small, pudgy hand into Henry's. "Will you be my friend, Henry?"

"I already am, pal. Now come along."

Later, he sat in his living room, an open book on his lap and the radio playing a Mozart piano concerto. He wasn't sure which one. His mother knew them all, but he found listening without knowing was as pleasurable. Next to his reading chair, a lamp shed soft light, but the rest of the room was in darkness. He'd poured another glass of wine instead of making coffee or having a whiskey, the condensation from the glass soaking into a napkin. It didn't taste nearly as good without Phil to share it with. Since her polite but distant departure, he'd been silently chastising himself. Why had he said what he said? They'd been having fun, developing a friendship, which is all she wanted, if her reaction was any indication. He'd been comfortable with her, like his old flirtatious, confident self. Back in the day, there was no woman he couldn't charm, and, if he were honest, he'd been a bit unscrupulous with his flirtations and certainly not discreet. Any of the girls from the old high school crowd would have described him as a shameless flirt without any regard to the way his lack of seriousness broke more than one heart. Until Sheila, he'd never had a serious girlfriend.

His wine glass was empty. He entertained the idea of another. Good grief, he should get control of himself. No one liked a melancholy man feeling sorry for himself. Another glass of wine wouldn't help. It was better that Phil had made her feelings known to him. Less likely to make a fool of himself this way. It would do neither of them any good if he was the inappropriate landlord, making her feel uncomfortable. He would apologize in the morning, reassure her that he was there for her like a brother would be.

At the hum of a motor car coming up the driveway, he crossed the room to look out the front window. Two headlights bounced, headed toward the cottages. Who could it be? No one ever came to visit this late at night. He glanced at the clock on the mantel. Almost ten. The car was at the end of the driveway, but instead of turning right, it turned left, parking in front of Phil's cottage. She had a visitor? At this time of night?

Before the lights went out, Henry caught a glimpse of the car —a Jaguar MK V. A man dressed in a dark suit and hat got out of the car and stretched his arms over his head, like one does after a long drive. In the dim light from the porch light of Phil's cottage, Henry could not see the man's face, only that he was tall and slender. Henry, feeling both jealousy and protectiveness, was out his front door and trudging toward the man before he could think twice and talk himself out of it. "May I help you?"

The man turned at the foot of the steps. "Hello there. You must be Henry Sayer."

His voice, on the deep side, possessed perfect diction. He thrust out his hand. "Miller Dreeser. Phil's uncle."

Henry, taken aback by the man's friendly manner, held out his own hand. They shook. Firm handshake but soft hands. A man who worked indoors. "Nice to meet you. Phil told me of your generosity earlier. I hadn't realized it was her uncle who made the arrangements."

"Oh, yes, how impolite of me. My attorney deals with such

matters. Perhaps he didn't mention it was her uncle providing for her?"

"No, I didn't ask, actually." He smiled. "None of my business, I suppose. Anyway, they're settling in nicely. Rest assured I'm here if she needs anything."

Miller shoved his hands into his pants' pockets. "That's good to hear. A woman on her own can't have enough help. I appreciate it." In the light from the porch it was difficult to see his face exactly, but from what he gathered, Miller was a handsome man, with a full mouth, deep-set eyes, high cheekbones, and a full set of white teeth. There was an aura of authority about him. This was a man used to running things with people at his immediate disposal in which to do his bidding.

"Well, excuse my interruption," said Henry. "I don't have many visitors this time of night. Wanted to make sure it wasn't trouble arriving."

"Landlord and watchdog. What could be better for my Phil? I feel quite assured of her safety." There was a glint in his eyes, hinting at cruelty under his handsome exterior. Or was it a threat? No, it couldn't be. This was a kind man taking care of his niece. *You're letting your imagination go wild. Jealous because of your ridiculous crush on Phil.*

"Good night," said Henry.

"Good night."

A cloud cover had rolled in after dusk, and now the night was starless with a muddy darkness. He could not see his feet as he crossed the yard. His steps in the gravel driveway made crunching sounds too loud for the black night, like he was a thief attempting a quiet advance into his own yard, with the possibility of capture at any moment. He quickened his pace, his stomach muscles clenched. As he neared his house, Miller's gaze bored into his back. He stopped at the bottom of his front porch steps to turn and look up to the sky. *See that, Dreeser. I have not a care in the world. Just a man looking up at the sky, unworried.*

Once inside his cottage, he shut the front door and locked it, something he rarely did. *Ridiculous, it's Phil's uncle. Obviously, he's not a threat.* Yet, his hand hovered over the knob, the hairs on his arms standing upright, like they did when he was frightened. He checked the lock from the inside, and finding it secure, went back to the living room, sitting in his armchair once more, looking out the window toward Phil's house. The light in her living room came on, yellow behind the thin curtains. Then, like the window was a movie screen, two shadows appeared. Phil and Miller, standing close, facing one another. He leaned over her. Their face merged into one shape.

A long, lingering kiss. The show was for him.

Miller Dreeser was not Phil's uncle. His instincts had been correct. He had the sudden urge to throw something as the truth of Phil's situation fell into place.

21

PHIL

Phil was in bed, wide awake. Above the bed, a crack in the ceiling zigzagged from one side of the room to the other. In the morning light she'd spotted it, but now in the darkness it was no longer evident. Regardless, she knew it existed, caused by the natural settling of a house over time, and it bothered her, made her worried with an irrational fear that the entire house might come down while she and Teddy slept. This was ridiculous, she knew. Houses did not fall from one crack. She rolled to her side, carefully as her hair was set in rags, pulled the cool sheet up to her neck, and closed her eyes. A vision of Henry appeared, his cheeks flushed after the cocktail. His curls had unfurled from the neat way he combed them, falling over his forehead. She wanted to brush them away with her fingertips. Throughout the evening, she'd smelled his aftershave, and now she wished it had followed her home. What would it feel like to put her lips in the spot between his chin and neck and breathe him in for as long as she liked?

She found it more than unsettling to contemplate her intense reaction to him. During her time with him, the whiskey soothed her nerves, made the back of her throat and cheeks warm, but it wasn't the drink. It was him. Almost always, when she was with

Miller, he made them Manhattans. Often she had two. It eased everything that came later in the evening, lulling her into a state of compliance. The drink with Henry was different. It tasted better and made her warm instead of numb. She had enjoyed herself, without any of her usual worries. It was like there was nothing but the three of them and that everything else was simply a bad dream, and for a split second, she had allowed herself to contemplate what it would be like if she were free to build a life with a man like him.

She was not free and she might not ever be again.

She considered getting out of bed, making a cup of tea and reading through the night, but was distracted from that musing when the low growl of a car coming up the driveway made the house quiver. She went hot, then cold. Miller with an unexpected visit? This was Friday and he was supposed to come Sunday. She dismissed the idea almost as soon as it entered her mind, knowing he was not a spontaneous man, both because of his nature and his circumstance. It was most likely someone for Henry. This made her curious, which dismayed her, but she tumbled from bed, running hands through her hair, and grabbed her robe, throwing it over the cotton pajamas she wore. On her way down the hall, she peeked in on Teddy. He was asleep, his thumb in his mouth and half-covered by the blanket. Ducks on his pajamas. Still a baby. *My baby.*

She went to the front window and lifted the edge of the curtain. A car, headlights bobbing from the rough road, turned right, toward her cottage. It stopped, the engine idling for several seconds. When the sound of the engine ceased, the car's headlights remained on as Miller unfolded from the driver's seat. He was not supposed to be here yet. Why was he here now? She squinted and watched as he crossed through the beams of light not toward the cottage but in the other direction. It was Henry, wearing the same clothes he'd had on when she left him earlier. The men shook hands. Mouths moved, but she could not make out the conversation because of the pounding of her heart

between her ears. Miller's shoulders were squared, his strong
jaw set. He looked like a rooster. Henry stood with his legs
shoulder length apart, his torso stiff like he was braced against a
strong wind.

Cursing under her breath, she moved away from the window
and stood at the fireplace, wringing her hands. Why had she
gone to dinner at Henry's home? She'd told him too much, let
him inside her world, and had found herself charmed and entertained, even understood. Less alone. A feeling she had not had
since home, since Eddie. Yet, she and Henry were adults,
survivors of great difficulties, more complicated than the innocent child she'd been when Eddie was her world. She seldom
allowed herself to think about the days preceding her departure
for California. Over the years, she taught herself to put it aside,
like a package in the back of a closet. Nonetheless, her evening
with Henry had stirred up memories and emotions.

———

She let Miller in, silently. He shoved the door closed with his foot
and grabbed her into his arms, pushing her against the wall. "I
couldn't go another day without seeing you." He spoke into her
neck, his lips pressed against her skin. Hungry. Always hungry
for her.

"How did you get away?"

"They left for the beach early," said Miller. "It's dark in here.
Turn on the light. I want to see you."

She went to the lamp and flipped the switch; the room
flooded with light, blinding her. Her hands flew to her hair,
remembering that it was set in rags. "My hair. It's not fixed."

"Never mind that. Women curl their hair at night. You look
fine." Miller crossed the room and took her hand, pulling her,
until they stood in front of the window that faced Henry's
cottage. The houses were mirror images of one another. She'd
noticed it earlier that her living room faced his. At the window,

Miller stopped, drawing her into another embrace, kissing her on the mouth, sliding his hands under her dressing gown to pull her hips to his. She fought the instinct to push him away, thinking of Henry. He might see them at the window. A sensation of betrayal came over her, but why? Henry was her landlord. A pleasant evening had passed between them. That was all. And yet, she could not shake the feeling. She did not want him to know about Miller. It was inevitable. She opened her eyes, sliding her gaze without moving her face, and reaching out to touch the thin material of the curtains. They were closed all the way. No gaps. Henry could not see, even if he happened to be looking this direction. "Would you like a drink?" she asked against Miller's mouth.

"No. I want you," he said.

———

After Miller was done, he'd fallen almost immediately to sleep, with his leg flung over her hips, pinning her to the mattress. With some effort, she'd removed his leg and slid from the bed, rising to open the bedroom window before heading into the bathroom. Sitting on the toilet, she washed his climax from her thighs with a warm, damp cloth. She inspected her hair rags in the mirror. Amazingly, none were out of place. In the bedroom, she found her nightgown crumpled on the armchair and put it on, smoothing it over her bruised and tender skin. She covered Miller with the sheet and climbed in next to him. It was nearing midnight, but instead of sleeping, she lay in the dark, listening to Miller's soft snore. He slept on his back, with one arm thrown over his face, as if shielding his eyes from light, even though the room was dark and quiet, except for the flutter of the curtain hanging over the open window.

The night air, smelling of the sea, pushed the scent of their lovemaking from the room. Still, Miller's cologne and perspiration were on her hands and skin. In the morning, she would scrub her body in the bath and afterward douse her skin in powder and the scent Miller had given her at Christmas. No amount of scrubbing and scent would matter. It remained, imagined or not, like the guilt-induced blood on Lady Macbeth's hands, not replaced by her perfume that smelled of lilacs and vanilla, but of him. She drew the sheet to her chin and closed her eyes, concentrating on the sounds of the waves. Two nights here and the crash of the roaring sea already soothed her threadbare nerves, like she'd always been here, like this was her home.

Her eyes were scratchy, tired, yet she could not sleep. What would she convey to Teddy in the morning about why Miller was here? Prior to this, when Miller arrived for one of their late-night sessions, Teddy had been asleep. Miller murmured something in his sleep, his eyes moved under his closed lids, as he rolled to his side. She relaxed, her body overcoming her mind, and drifted into sleep. She dreamt she was on a train headed west, hot sun withering rows of corn outside the window.

***

When she woke, it was morning. She sat up with a start. The other side of the bed was empty, an imprint of Miller's head in the pillow and the twisted sheets evidence that last night had not been a dream. It was after nine. Teddy would have been awake for at least an hour. She threw on a robe over her nightgown and went down the hall to the kitchen that smelled of fresh coffee. Miller was at the table, wearing his glasses, reading a magazine of some kind, which he must have brought with him. Teddy sat in a chair at the table, chewing on a piece of dry bread, his short, chubby legs hanging loose above the floor. She stood in the doorway, unsure what to do. Miller looked up and gave her a smile. "Good morning."

She mumbled a reply, her heart pounding, watching the back of Teddy's head.

"Teddy and I are getting better acquainted," said Miller. "I told him Uncle Miller would buy him a train set for Christmas if he's a good boy."

Teddy turned to look at her, grinning. "Trains."

"You love trains, don't you, sweetheart?" *Uncle Miller?* She went to the refrigerator and grabbed the butter and strawberry jam, and fixed a piece for Teddy. "Eat this up, ducky." She set it in front of him.

"I told him I'll be visiting a lot this summer. To keep an eye on you," said Miller.

Teddy popped a piece of bread into his mouth.

Keep an eye on us?

"The landlord came by. Brought your sweater over. Apparently, you left it at his cottage last night." Miller's gaze was on his magazine. He turned the pages one by one. For the first time, she noticed her sweater, hanging on the back of Teddy's chair.

"Yes. Did I not mention he invited us for dinner? It was very gracious, especially for a landlord." She poured a cup of coffee, then held it with two hands to control the sudden shaking, and looked out the kitchen window. Henry was outside, painting the fence white.

"Yes, poor fella," said Miller. "Disfigured. I'm gathering he's mostly a recluse, living out here all on his own."

She turned away from the window to look at him. He continued to turn pages of the magazine. "You mean like me?"

"Pardon me?" He set aside the magazine and looked over at her.

"Living out here alone, like a recluse. A secret."

Miller pushed the magazine to the middle of the table and crossed one leg over the other. "You're certainly not a recluse. You have Teddy. And you have me." He picked up his coffee cup and held it out to her. "Would you pour me another, please? This has turned cold."

She took the cup from him without comment, her insides clenching. His veiled message was clear. She had Teddy and therefore had no choice but to live here, alone. Miller's plaything in a cage. She poured the last of the coffee into his cup. Loose grounds floated to the top. She would leave them, let them get stuck in his perfect teeth. After setting the cup on the table in front of him, she turned away, finding her spot by the sink and leaned against it with her hands on the rim, looking out the window. Henry had finished two more rungs of the fence and was on his knees painting the bottom of the next one. A seagull landed on one of the painted sections. He stood, shooing it away with his brush, before leaning to paint over the spot where the bird's feet had made an imprint.

Behind her, the chair creaked. Miller's heavy footsteps as he crossed the small kitchen caused the floorboards to groan. He stood behind her, pressing her into the sink with his body. Near her ear, he whispered, as he gripped her wrists with his hands. "I don't want you spending time with him. Not for dinner. Not for anything."

"What harm can come of it?" She said it with no expression, as if they were talking about what to have for dinner.

He tightened his grip. "You're a beautiful woman. It's natural that he'll want to enjoy your company. But you're not available."

"You can't control who I'm friends with. I get lonely." Why was she pushing him? She knew it was dangerous; she knew it would get her nowhere except to agitate him.

"Men have no interest in friendship."

"He's a nice man, a gentleman. He was simply being polite."

"I will not have it." He elongated every word with pauses between. "You belong to me, and that means I decide everything you do."

Not what I think. You can't control what I think.

"So help me God, Phil, I will kill before I let another man touch you. Am I clear?"

Tears started. She fought them, her lip trembling.

"Am I clear? Dammit, Phil, answer me." His grip hurt now and she winced from the pain.

"Yes."

197

"Teddy." Miller's authoritative voice gave the little boy no choice but to listen. "Go play in your room."

"I'll be in to help you get dressed in a minute. Until then, play with your new trucks," said Phil.

"Okay, Mama." The innocence in Teddy's voice made her cry harder.

"Where did he get the trucks?" Miller turned her around to face him. He lifted her chin. She stared into his eyes. "You have one chance to tell me the truth."

"Henry gave them to him."

"You let him give Teddy toys?"

"It was nothing. Just some old things he had in the shed."

"I'm not paying for you to flirt with other men. You're mine." He moved his hands down her bare arms, pressing hard into her flesh, stopping at her wrists.

"I know. It was nothing."

"Tell me you're sorry." He tightened his grip on her wrists and pushed them toward the counter. She winced.

"I'm sorry."

"Promise me you won't see him." His voice was husky now.

"I won't see him. Please, Miller, you're hurting me."

He loosened his grip, but not enough to let her go, and kissed her neck, speaking into her ear. "You've made me lose my mind, but God help me, I want you. Now. Go to the bedroom. Get ready for me."

———

Teddy played on his floor, making noises at the back of his throat like a truck, and didn't look up as she passed by. She figured they had about ten minutes before he came looking for her. In her bedroom, she stripped off her robe and nightgown and perched on the edge of the bed, waiting. A few seconds later, Miller was there. "Lock the door," she said. "In case Teddy decides to wander in."

After he locked the door, he strode across the room, peeling off his shirt. At the chair, he sat, taking off his pants and underclothes. The most intimate of acts; stripping naked in front of someone. She was not his wife. This was not how it should be. She should be in Iowa with Eddie right now. They should be having lunch at his parents, then driving into town for an ice cream.

Miller, unclothed now, knelt at the side of the bed, pulling her legs apart and wrapping them around his waist. "I love you, Phil. Don't ever forget that." He pushed her onto her back.

She stared at the crack in the ceiling as he thrust in and out of her, a tear leaking from the corner of her right eye.

Afterward, Miller bathed and dressed, whistling while he shaved, then announced he would drive into town for groceries. A steak and potato sounded good for dinner, he said, as if this were the most ordinary of circumstances. He sat on the edge of the bed where she remained, curled up like a child, and stroked her cheek, speaking gently. "While I'm gone, fix your hair. Put on something pretty. I should get you some real curlers." He picked up one of her curls. "These rags make you look like a maid."

After the front door slammed, she got up to check on Teddy. He was still happily playing in his room, but she wanted him in her room so she could watch him while she bathed. Compliant, if he could bring his trucks, he followed her into her bedroom. "Play here in front of the door."

"Yes, Mama."

"Good boy." She went to the window. Henry had finished the fence and was no longer in the yard.

When the tub was filled with the hottest water she could tolerate, she climbed in and scrubbed until her skin was raw, but not lingering, worried that Teddy would need her. After drying with one of the soft towels Henry had left for them, she chose a yellow, bell-sleeved sundress. At the mirror, she took the rags from her hair and fixed it into waves with a roll at the top, and applied red lipstick, rouge, and mascara. Just as she finished,

Teddy came into the bathroom. Staring up at her, he patted her fanny. "Mama pretty."

Smiling, she knelt next to him and hugged him. "Thank you, my little man."

A loud knock on the door caused her to jump. Heart thumping, thinking it might be Henry, she strode to the front door. She would tell him they were busy today, to not bother them.

It was not Henry but the postman, holding a letter. "Sorry to disturb you, but I didn't see a box, ma'am." He handed her a letter. It was an Iowa address. From Susan. She thanked him and went inside, closing the door behind her. She sat in one of the armchairs as Teddy settled at her feet, leaning his head against her leg.

June 17, 1946

Dearest Phil,

Thank you for writing with your new address. I'm afraid I have sad news. Your parents were killed today in a car accident while coming home from church. A hay truck unexpectedly lost its brakes. The driver panicked and swerved into their lane. Both were killed instantly. Mary, thank God, wasn't with them. I'd asked if I might take her home and they agreed. I wanted to give Mary your latest letter.

Mary has been staying with my father and me. Your parents had no instructions about what to do if something like this happened. The bank is taking the farm; too much debt, apparently. It's awful to leave you and Mary with nothing, but I suppose the banks own all the farms out here in one way or another. You know I love Mary and would be happy to keep her with me, even though I have my hands full with my father, plus teaching, but I feel it would be best for both of you if I sent her out to California. As luck would have it, there is a young woman from church who is willing to accompany her on the train if you wire money for her ticket, as well as for Mary. Her name is Holly Moore and she has plans to move to Los Angeles at the end of July. After she drops Mary with you, she'll continue south. If you agree, please send a telegram that you will be there to meet them. I will keep Mary safe until then.

I'm sorry you didn't have a chance to say good-bye to your parents. They tried their best to do the right things, unfortunately they never quite did.

With all my love,
Susan

The letter fell to her lap. She waited for tears to come. Instead, she went numb. Her parents were dead? Mary would have to come. Mary. She would have Mary. A second knock on the front door pulled her from her contemplation. Mrs. Thomas, dressed in a cotton dress, her sunhat hanging down her back from a string, stood on the steps.

"I thought Teddy might like to come with me to the farm. Our mama cat gave birth to six kittens in the middle of the night," said Mrs. Thomas.

Teddy stood behind Phil, peering out from behind her skirt. Phil moved back from the door to invite Mrs. Thomas inside the house. "Come in, please. Would you care for coffee?"

"No, thank you. Had my cup of tea already this morning," said Mrs. Thomas. "Would you like to see tiny kittens, Teddy?"

He nodded, reaching for Phil's hand. "Mama come?"

"She's welcome to, but I think she might like to have a little time to herself."

Teddy wrinkled his brow, looking up at Phil as if in disbelief that anyone would want to be away from him, especially his mama.

"Can you be a brave boy and go without me?" asked Phil.

He nodded, with great solemnity. "I can."

"Go get your shoes, please."

He scampered away, singing, "Kitty, kitty, kitty."

"It's kind of you to think of him. It would be nice to have a moment to myself. I've had a bit of a shock, actually."

Mrs. Thomas's expression immediately changed to one of concern. "What's happened?"

"A letter from home. My parents have died," said Phil. "And my little sister is only ten. She'll have to come here."

"You poor thing." Mrs. Thomas patted her arm.

"I haven't seen her in over three years."

"Oh, dear."

"She'll have to share a room with Teddy, I suppose."

"You'll have a full house, Phil. But I'm just a moment away. I'll help you however I can."

"There's school to think of," said Phil.

"We have a good one in town, although small with twelve grades in one building. Probably fifty kids all told. But we have all summer before we need to worry about that."

They chatted for a few more minutes, then she was off, taking an excited Teddy with her. As she scooted Teddy into her truck, Mrs. Thomas said, "Now, you won't be able to touch the kitties because they're too little."

Still holding the letter, Phil wandered into the backyard and sat in the chair that faced the sea, unsure what to do. There was no wind, yet it was cooler than yesterday. She sat there for a few minutes, and then Henry appeared, whistling under his breath, carrying his bucket and brush. He stopped when he saw her. The sun was high in the sky, bright; she shielded her eyes with her hand. He set his paintbrush in the bucket by his feet. "Good morning, Mrs. Rains."

Mrs. Rains? Hadn't they agreed on first names?

She stood. "Teddy's gone with Mrs. Thomas. Something about kittens."

"I saw."

She smoothed her hair and bit the lipstick off her bottom lip. It would be gone soon, succumbing to her anxious biting. She'd have to reapply it before Miller returned.

"Is your uncle staying all weekend?" asked Henry.

"Until Sunday morning."

"I see." He took off his hat, letting it dangle in his hand. Soft curls, the color of butter and damp with perspiration, fell over his forehead.

He understood. There would be no keeping the truth from him. She clutched the letter tighter between her fingers. Overhead a seagull let out a long, terrible screech.

Settling his hat back on his head, he gestured toward the fence. "I should put on another coat. A lot to do this afternoon."

"I'm sorry I lied to you."

"It's none of my business. I'm simply your landlord." He smiled at her, kindly, but with none of the intimacy of their budding friendship from last night.

"I'm to be invisible except to him. He's possessive. Jealous."

He took off his hat once more, gazing down into her eyes. "Phil, I understand how these things work."

"Men always do." A slight breeze rose from the sea, carrying the smell of saltwater. A ship, miles from shore made its way across the ocean at a speed imperceptible to the human eye. It appeared to be unmoving, anchored to the bottom of the sea. She crossed her arms over her stomach, still clutching the letter in one hand, imagining what it would be like to be free enough to be on that ship. Where would she go if she could? She looked back at Henry. He was staring at her arm, his eyes narrowed.

"Phil, what happened here?" He brushed her forearm with the brim of his hat, a look of concern in his eyes. "You're bruised."

A series of bruises. Deep purple. Fingerprints in her white skin. She uncurled her arms, covering the bruises with her hand. "Nothing."

"You didn't have them last night."

"Please, Henry, don't make trouble."

"Is he dangerous, Phil?"

"I have nowhere else to go. He takes care of us. And something's happened that's made it even more important that I have that." Her voice wavered. She swallowed the painful lump at the back of her throat.

His voice, gentler than the moment before, "What is it?"

She waved the letter at him. "My parents were killed in a car accident. I haven't spoken to them since I left Iowa. When they found out I was pregnant, they made me leave, which is how I ended up out here. I'm sending for Mary. She's only ten. I'll have another child to take care of."

"I don't understand. Why did your parents force you to leave home?"

"I wasn't married to Eddie, Henry."

"Oh, I see." His face deflated as the truth of her sins washed over him. It was best he knew. She couldn't pretend to be a normal girl, available for dinner dates and car rides.

"I have to go. He'll be home soon. I'm sorry, Henry." She turned and ran across the lawn to her cottage.

When Miller arrived, carrying packages from the market and the butcher, she was in the kitchen, staring into her coffee cup, the open letter on the table. He set the packages on the counter, then tipped her face up, running a finger along her jaw line.

"You look pretty."

"Thank you."

"Where's Teddy?"

"Mrs. Thomas took him over to her farm to see baby kittens."

"Baby kittens is redundant. Kitten means baby cat." He smiled at her like one might do to a child. "Who's Mrs. Thomas?" A brittle edge now in his voice. *That's how suddenly he could change. You must remember this. Do not make him angry.*

"She lives up the road. I met her yesterday. She's lovely. Sadly, she lost her boy in the war." She reached for the letter, holding it in her lap. "I've had a letter from home."

"Home?"

"Iowa. From my friend, Susan. My parents died in an accident last week."

"I'm sorry, darling." He sat next to her at the table and took her hand. "What does it matter, after how they treated you? You and me, both orphans."

"My little sister, Mary. She's nowhere to go. She's only ten."

His eyes glittered, almost black. "Excellent. She'll come here. We'll send her to boarding school."

"Boarding school? Why can't she stay with me?"

"Darling, she should have every opportunity. Here in Stowaway is not the place for a proper young lady to receive her schooling."

"But I'll have only just gotten her back. I'll want her here, at least for a while."

"You'll have the rest of the summer with her. Then we'll decide what to do next," said Miller. "You'll want her to have the best schools."

The summer would not be long enough, but she knew enough not to argue. It was only important that she get her here. She needed Miller's help to make sure that happened.

"Will you wire the money to Susan for the fare? And send the telegram?" she asked.

"I'll have my secretary do it the moment I'm back in the city."

She smiled. "Thank you."

"I'll do anything for you, Phil. You know that."

A knock on the kitchen door interrupted any further discussion. It was Mrs. Thomas back with Teddy. Phil rose to open the door. Teddy, pulling on his ear in the way he did when he was tired, threw himself into her arms. "Mama, me not touch the kitties. I got eggs." He rested his head on her shoulder and sighed, then stuck his thumb in his mouth.

"Tired, little man?" she asked.

He nodded against her neck, his soft eyelashes fluttering against her skin. His hair smelled of sunshine and strawberry jam. Mrs. Thomas stood in the doorway, the screen door in one hand, smiling at the back of Teddy's head. "We had a perfect time. Thank you for letting me take him." Then, she seemed to notice Miller for the first time. "Ah, who do we have here?" She held out her hand. "I'm Mrs. Thomas."

"Miller Dreeser. Phil's uncle," he said.

"Pleasure to make your acquaintance. Well, I should be pushing off. Poor Mr. Thomas needs his supper."

Phil escorted her out, thanking her for taking Teddy. "Do you need anything before you go?" asked Phil.

"You're a dear, but no. I have to pop in and ask Henry a quick question and then I'm off. You enjoy your family time, dear."

Teddy was heavy, his limp legs dangled down her sides as she walked back into the house. "Time for a little nap, ducky."

He didn't answer, asleep already. "I'll put him down," she said to Miller as she passed through the kitchen.

"I'll open some wine for us," he said.

As she walked through the kitchen and down the hallway to the bedroom, she fought a growing sense of despair. Being here made her feel more isolated and hopeless than she had at the apartment Miller had rented for her in the city. Perhaps Mrs. Thomas and Henry pursuing a friendship with her had reminded her that she was not free.

Mary would be here in a month. That was all that counted. She must focus on Mary and keeping Miller happy.

22

HENRY

Monday morning, at his studio in town, the scent of the stain made his eyes itch. He yawned, then his stomach rumbled. He'd come in early, unable to sleep after a dream of his mother had woken him from a restless sleep. After he was done with this coat, he would walk over to the bakery and buy a loaf of bread and some cheese for his lunch. Maybe he'd take it down to the beach and watch the surfers. The bell over the door tinkled. He looked up to see Mrs. Thomas. He set aside his brush. "Mrs. Thomas, what're you doing here?"

She set a bag on his desk. "I had to come to town for a few items. I brought some vegetables from the garden for Phil and Teddy. Would you mind taking them over to her this evening?" Dressed in a light brown suit, Mrs. Thomas looked unusually dignified. Since he'd been home, he couldn't remember the last time he'd seen her in town. Usually she sent Mr. Thomas. It was the stares of sympathy, she had told him once, that she couldn't tolerate.

"For Phil? What about me?" asked Henry, teasing. "Have I been replaced in your affections?"

"Perhaps." She grinned as she unpinned her hat and set it next to the bag of vegetables.

"You look very nice. New suit?" he asked.

"Phil designed and made it for me. She said I'm too petite to wear the ready-made clothes from Sears and insisted on making something for me."

He smiled. "The suit suits you."

She rolled her eyes, chuckling. "Never mind that. I came by to discuss something with you."

He put his hand up, shaking his head. "I already know what you're going to say, and we should keep out of it."

She cocked her head to the side and widened her eyes, as if she were the epitome of innocence. "I don't know what you're talking about."

"You're here about Phil and Teddy and their situation. And, again, it's none of our business," he said.

"I don't know how you can say it's none of our business. The poor thing's no more than twenty and that *married* man is forty if he's a day. It's not right. Keeping her stashed away out here. Like a dirty secret."

"No offense, but she is rather a dirty secret."

"Henry! She's a fine young lady with a terrible circumstance. She has no one. Her husband taken by the war," said Mrs. Thomas.

"He wasn't her husband," said Henry. "Her parents made her leave home when she told them she was having a child out of wedlock."

"I'm surprised at your old-fashioned ways, Henry Miles Sayer. They're certainly not the only ones to have ever jumped the gun before marriage."

"I'll have you know, using my middle name no longer intimidates me." He shook his head, smirking, amused and irritated at the same time. "And, you're the one shocking me. What's gotten in to you? If it had been Rose and William, you would have not been happy."

"First of all, it's not for us to judge, Henry. That's Jesus's job. Your mother taught you this. I don't want to hear one word to the contrary. And, second of all, I'd give anything to have a grandchild, no matter whether he or she had come a little earlier than expected." Mrs. Thomas's eyes snapped. Two pink blotches had appeared on each cheek. He fully expected smoke to start coming out of her ears. She looked good, even in her agitated state. Better rested? He looked at her more closely. That was it. The chapped area around her eyes had disappeared. She wasn't crying as much. "Are you listening, young man?"

"What? Yes. Yes, I'm listening. I noticed the skin around your eyes looks better."

"*I'm* better," she said. "These last two weeks have been good for me."

"Because of Phil and Teddy?"

"Yes, genius. Because of them. Teddy brings life back to our house. You should see poor Mr. Thomas. He's a changed man. We need to figure out a way to help her."

"Mrs. Thomas, you know my affection for you and Mr. Thomas has no limits, right?"

"Yes, dear."

"I would do anything for you, but I don't think it's a good idea for either of us to get involved with Phil. My instincts tell me Miller Dreeser's a mean man, and I don't want you getting hurt."

"This is my point exactly. How can you sit by and allow a sweet girl like Phil and that adorable little boy to be caught in that man's web?"

He sighed, then ran his fingers through his hair. "What did you have in mind?"

She crossed her arms over her chest, with a satisfied smile. "I call it Operation Henry."

"I don't like the sound of this."

"You and Phil obviously have a connection."

"We do?"

"Don't play dumb with me. The day after she moved in, there was a distinct skip in your step. I haven't forgotten the look on your face when I brought over the chicken that night. You liked her."

"Maybe. But all that changed when I realized she belongs to someone else."

"She does not belong to that horrible man. She belongs to herself—and to Teddy. She's in survival mode, Henry. Surely you know what that feels like?"

He perched on the side of his desk. The aroma of fresh basil wafted from the bag. "Yes, I do. But I still don't see what this has to do with me."

"It's everything to do with you. Poor Mr. Thomas didn't seem able to grasp this, either. Men are sadly simple sometimes. You and Phil are meant to be together."

He stared at her. "Mrs. Thomas, you've lost your mind." Now he was alarmed. He'd never heard her talk foolishly. She was practical and tough. She shot birds out of midair without so much as a second thought.

"I have not lost my mind, contrary to popular belief. I'm a religious woman, Henry. I have no doubt that someday we'll all be reunited in Heaven with William and your parents. For now, however, we're here on earth, and God has spoken. You are to pursue Phil with all you have until you win her heart."

"God spoke to you?"

"Well, actually it was your mother in my dream last week, but she was sending His message."

Henry couldn't decide whether to laugh or cry. "Mother was in your dream?"

"Yes. She looked beautiful. Apparently, we all get to look twenty-five in Heaven, which is wonderful news for me, because I'm quite sick of wearing a sunhat."

He had no idea how that correlated, but he decided it was best not to ask.

She continued. "What you're going to do is insist that you spend time with them, regardless of *that* man's wishes. You're going to take them on picnics and have them for dinner. You'll take her on romantic drives up the coast and to nice dinners."

He opened his mouth to say something, but she stopped him with a stern look. "You can afford it, so don't start in on that. I'll take care of Teddy."

"She told me to stay away. That he's dangerous. Did you see her bruises?" he asked. "I don't want her to get hurt."

Mrs. Thomas snapped her fingers and glared at him with a dogmatic expression. "There it is. There's the look in your eyes that gave you away in the first place. You know, you can fall in love with someone at first sight. Mr. Thomas did. It took me a while longer. He grew on me. Which is what you need to do to Phil."

She had lost her mind. It was the grief. Her mind had finally snapped. Dreaming of messages from God via a dream with his mother? Advocating getting involved with a situation clearly complicated and fraught with danger? Grief was the only explanation.

"Henry Sayer, did you survive in the cold waters of the Atlantic for two hours with a gunshot wound through your arm?"

"Yes, ma'am."

"Then you can do this. You'll go home tonight and ask her for dinner. There's a lovely fish place up the highway." She grabbed her hat, fixing it on her head, then sticking the needles through, rather viciously. "Have I ever asked you for anything?"

"All the time."

She smiled. "Good then. You're used to it."

That evening, bag of vegetables in hand, he crossed the yard to Phil's cottage and knocked on the back door. Miller's car was nowhere to be seen.

She answered the door barefoot, wearing pants and an untucked blouse. She'd piled her hair on top of her head. Tendrils of hair framed her face, and several straight pins dangled between her teeth. Behind her, dozens of dress and swimsuit designs were scattered across the kitchen table. A dummy wore a soft yellow dress, the hem pinned.

"Hi, Henry." She seemed surprised to see him. She would be. They exchanged no more than friendly waves after their last exchange. A pang of guilt stabbed him in the gut. *She's not your responsibility*. Despite Mrs. Thomas and her crazy ideas.

He held up the bag. "Vegetables from Mrs. Thomas."

"How thoughtful. Come in." Speaking with the pins still in her mouth, she moved aside. He stepped into the kitchen.

"You've been designing swimsuits?" He couldn't keep the delight from his voice.

She took the pins from her mouth and set them on the table. "Yes. Just a few." She blushed. "It was such a good idea, I decided to try a few."

"They look swell." My God, she was pretty. How was it possible not to think so? No man in his right mind would be immune. No wonder Dreeser wanted to keep her to himself. If she were his girl, would he be the same? An image of her in bed with Dreeser popped in his mind. No, he would not allow himself to go there. If he thought of her with him, he would not be able to be her friend. Mrs. Thomas might be able to overlook it, but it was impossible for him to see anything about her but the fact that she slept with a man for money, unless he separated that part of her from the woman in front of him now.

"I have some new dress designs, too."

"Quite a few," he said, moving to the table. He picked up a sheet of paper with one of her pieces. Outlined in black ink, she'd colored in the bodice and skirt of the dress with a bright pink color. "Pretty color. Reminds me of a peony."

"The style's going toward lively colors, now the war's over. Vogue says everyone wants to feel cheerier." She picked up one of the dress designs. "Ladies want to have hourglass figures, like the actresses. Take me, for example, I'm like a boy." She tapped the sides of her hips. "But with shoulder pads and an A-line angle to the skirt, it can change a woman's silhouette. See here." She pointed to another design. "This has a high waist, tucked tight. High waists are flattering on almost all body types. This would be a great dress for going to the office or out to lunch somewhere nice."

"Oh, yes. I see it." Half sleeves, and wide, tall shoulders, with a skirt shaped like an A. He wouldn't have noticed before, but it was plain as day now. He'd always assumed a dress was just a dress.

"I'm making one for myself from this design." She pointed to a design labeled: Summer Dress, then walked over to the dummy. "This is made of a light cotton. Softer colors are good for warm weather. And see here, I've pleated the skirt, another popular choice."

He picked up another design, labeled: Evening Dress. The drawing was colored in with a dark blue pencil.

"That's for fancy. Maybe a cocktail party or night at the theatre," she said. "Made with velvet. And you see the sleeves, how they're gathered and reach to the elbow? Very elegant." She picked up another design. "I designed this one for Mrs. Thomas. It's a pencil skirt, which works great because she's petite. And do you see the how the sleeves are short but kind of flowy? Perfect for dinner and dancing. She told me she has no use for such a thing, but you should've seen her eyes light up when she saw it. I need fabric, though, and nothing in town will do," she said.

"What kind of fabric?"

"A light cotton. I want a flower print of some kind. Something that will complement her skin and hair. Not orange or red. Pink would be disastrous. But romantic, nonetheless."

"I saw her today. She was wearing her new suit. She looked like a new woman."

Phil's face lit up in a wide smile. "Doesn't she look magnificent? It's like dressing up a doll."

"She hasn't had anyone making a fuss over her since my mother died. They used to do girl things together, but now, you know, it's only Mr. Thomas and me. We're poor substitutes for other women." He'd never seen Phil this animated, even during their pleasant evening together. Her enthusiasm and obvious love for her craft was contagious. It made him want to be better. Better how, he wasn't sure. More alive, perhaps. He didn't know. My God, the woman befuddled him. She was special. Smart and talented.

Stop now, you fool. Focus on what she is saying.

Phil sat at the table. "She's been kind to me. The last few weeks she's come by every day to check on us. She's always bringing food of some kind, usually from her garden. I don't understand how she gets so many things accomplished in a day."

"She gets up at five a.m. Always has."

"I admire her very much."

"It would be impossible not to." This pleased him, like she'd given him a compliment, instead of Mrs. Thomas. *Keep control of yourself. You cannot let yourself get too attached to an outcome.* He would be her friend, and that was all. After a time, Mrs. Thomas would see this was a futile enterprise.

"What did you come by for? Do you need something?" asked Phil.

He cleared his throat. "I thought you and Teddy might like to take a drive tomorrow evening. Up the coast? I know a great fish and chips place. A roadside type of joint. Great food. We could watch the sunset."

"I don't know, Henry."

"Not a date." The tips of his ears started burning. "Just friends. I understand your situation, but there's no reason we can't be friends."

"We have to be discreet."

He wanted to say something snide, pointing out the irony of that statement, but he nodded sympathetically instead. "Sure."

"That sounds fun. Teddy would love it."

"Excellent. I'll pick you both up at five tomorrow."

The next day was Saturday. He didn't go into the studio. Instead, he wandered around the cottage, looking for something to do that would occupy his hands but found nothing. Finally, it was five, and he headed next door. As he crossed the yard, he spotted Teddy in the window, bouncing up and down. He knocked on the door, then waited for Teddy to jump from the couch and come open the door, which took longer than expected. Finally, the door burst open and there stood a three-foot-tall ray of sunshine.

"Hi, Henree!" No "r" sound.

"Hello, Teddy. Are you excited to go for a ride?"

He nodded. "Yep."

Phil came from the back, bringing the heavenly scent of her perfume. She wore the yellow summer dress he'd seen on the dummy last night. The dummy had not done it justice. With short sleeves and a belt around her tiny waist, she looked cool and fresh. Regardless if curves were her wish, he liked her slim, straight figure. She wasn't as thin as when she'd first arrived, either. Her hair was fixed in one of those twists in the front that always reminded him of a fancy dinner roll, and she wore makeup. On her feet were sandals with a bow on the top. Her little toes were painted red. He tore his gaze from her feet to take in her lovely face. She had the prettiest mouth. Small, but plump, with an even row of white teeth that sparkled against her tanned skin.

"You look...stunning," he said. So much for keeping his emotions controlled. How many freckles did she have on her nose? More than the last time. He wanted to count them, then gather them and put them in his pocket. *Holy cow, man, get it together.*

"Thank you, Henry. I'm pleased with the dress."

"Rightly so. Shall we go?" asked Henry.

"Yes, please, Henree," said Teddy.

Phil

Phil stood on the front steps watching Mrs. Thomas's truck bounce through potholes and make dust billows toward the cottage. Teddy stood on the front seat, waving and grinning. In the four weeks since they'd arrived, Teddy had turned brown in the sun, with even plumper cheeks and shining hair. *The picture of health*, Mrs. Thomas had said yesterday.

Phil crossed the yard, meeting the truck when it stopped. She opened the door for Teddy, and he jumped into her arms. "Mama, goat ate my sock."

"One of the nasty creatures got hold of his sock on the wash line." Mrs. Thomas rolled her eyes as she exited the truck from the other side. "The biggest nuisance you ever saw."

Teddy wore a pair of new pajamas and his hair looked damp. "Did you bathe Teddy?" asked Phil. "You shouldn't have gone to so much trouble."

"He spent some time with Mr. Thomas in the fields and was simply too dirty to bring home to his pretty mother."

He nuzzled against Phil's neck, smelling of fresh soap and talcum powder. "And new pajamas?" They were dark blue cotton, scattered with sailboats, and soft against her skin.

"I saw them in town the other day and couldn't resist." Mrs.

Thomas grinned sheepishly. "You won't deny an old woman a little spoiling of her special friend, now would you?"

"No, I wouldn't think of it." Phil chuckled. "Did you have fun, ducky?"

He nodded. "Pie."

"Oh, I see." They began to walk toward the house. "It's such a treat to have an evening to myself, Mrs. Thomas. Thank you." They were at the steps now. "Do you want to come in for a moment? I have cold beer in the fridge."

"I did have something I wanted to ask you," said Mrs. Thomas.

"I'll get Teddy to bed," said Phil

He didn't make a fuss when she brushed his teeth and tucked him into his bed. "Did you wear yourself out chasing after Mr. Thomas today?"

Teddy hugged his special bear to his chest and nodded, his eyelids drooping. She kissed him on the forehead.

"Good night, ducky."

"Night, Mama."

She lingered at the doorway for only a moment, gazing at her boy as he fell almost instantly asleep. Her rambunctious terror looked like an angel when he was sleeping.

Mrs. Thomas was outside sitting in one of the chairs that faced the sea when she came out with two bottles of beer. After seven, the sun hung low in the sky.

She sat in the other chair and handed Mrs. Thomas a beer. "I can't thank you enough for all the experiences he's having on your farm. He's already fast asleep. It's good for a boy to be outside all day."

"We feel awful lucky to have him. He's brought life back to our little farm. He gives such joy to my poor Mr. Thomas. It's good to have a child around, especially one as special as this little tyke. When Mary comes, I hope she'll want to join us, too. I know she's going to need some mothering and, well, I seem to have some left in me." She paused for a moment, swatting away a fly. "Listen now, I know that Mr. Dreeser's not your uncle."

"What?" The transition was so abrupt, Phil wondered if she'd heard her correctly.

"I hate to bring up something delicate, but I feel I must."

"Did Henry tell you?" asked Phil. How dare he. It wasn't his right to share her secrets.

"No, dear. He would rather die than talk about something like this with me. I've been around long enough to see with my own eyes what's going on here. No one's uncle would be around as often as he is, given the distance between here and the city. His wedding ring tells me he's married?"

"Yes."

"He's stashed you away here? You have no one else and a little boy to take care of."

"That's the extent of it, yes." Phil drank from her beer. Here it comes. The judgment. The chastising. Perhaps Mrs. Thomas would suggest she give her the children so they might have a proper home.

"Of course you don't love him," said Mrs. Thomas.

"Why, 'of course'?" she asked.

"I mean to say, I know you don't love him. You haven't the look of a woman in love. So, my conclusion is this is an arrangement of convenience for you. Or rather, of necessity."

"Correct." She wanted to rise, chuck her beer as far as she could into the Pacific, and let out a primal scream.

"I understand how hard it is for you. Knowing how these things happen and you being all alone. If you're inclined, Mr. Thomas and I are willing to help."

Here it comes. She clenched her teeth, bracing herself.

"If you and the children want to come live with us until you got on your feet, we would be happy to have you."

"Me and the children?"

"You can't be separated from Teddy, or Mary, for that matter. But we could offer assistance. Henry and I were discussing it."

"You and Henry?" They'd been discussing her? Deciding her life?

"Now don't get agitated. He believes you're very talented and he's willing to offer you a loan if you wanted to start a dress shop in town. Dresses and bathing suits, that is."

"Why didn't Henry ask me himself?"

"He doesn't want you to think there are any strings attached, like the ones you have here." Mrs. Thomas took a drink from her beer, looking toward the sea.

Shame caused her to flush. How could she have thought the worst of either Henry or Mrs. Thomas? They were her friends. They cared about Teddy. Dare she dream? Was there hope? Her own dress shop? A chance to get back on her feet. Living with Mr. and Mrs. Thomas on their farm, protected from Miller? Was it possible? No, it was not possible. No matter what she did, he would never let her go. "It's generous of both of you. But I can't ever get away from him."

Mrs. Thomas's expression didn't change. She had a determined purse to her mouth. "That's why you'd live with us. Henry agrees you're not safe here alone."

"It's not only me in danger. It's Henry, too. He's threatened to kill Henry simply because I went there for dinner. If you and Mr. Thomas were to take us in, you would not be safe, either. He will stop at nothing to have me. His jealousy is irrational now; think if I moved in with you. He has no idea that we've continued to spend time with Henry. If he knew, I'm afraid he might make us move away or worse, he would hurt Henry. Or me. Maybe both." She might start to hyperventilate, her breath coming in gasps. "I'm trapped forever. I made my bed with the devil, and now I lie in it. I did this to myself and I will not have you or Henry put in danger because of my mistakes.

After everything I've lost—I could not bear it if anything happened to either one of you."

Mrs. Thomas was silent. A cricket began to sing somewhere in the yard. The sun sank farther in the horizon. Then, she smacked her beer against the arm of the lawn chair. "No. This is not the end of the story." She turned to Phil, gesturing at her with the beer bottle. "This man will not win. I don't know how exactly, but he will not win. The world's lost too many good people. The Holocaust. The brave soldiers. Those who remain are obligated to carry forth without fear, to rebuild the world. You deserve a second chance. Teddy deserves men in his life that he can respect and admire. Not one who hurts his mother. Henry told me about your bruises. I will not allow this to continue."

Phil, shocked by the outburst, stared at Mrs. Thomas. She began to laugh.

Mrs. Thomas cocked her head to the side. "What exactly is funny?"

"You're funny. What are you? A hundred pounds soaking wet?" Her laughter turned to tears. "Don't you see? My situation is hopeless. My only choice is to be grateful that Teddy's fed and clothed with a roof over his head. I knew the day he was born that only his life mattered and that mine was over."

"I do believe you know the story of David and Goliath?"

"Yes, Mrs. Thomas, I do."

"Well, then, you need to have a little faith."

A week after their excursion to the fish and chips roadside hut, Henry picked them up for a day at the beach in Stowaway. Instead of heading to the beach parking, Henry stopped the car in front of his shop. "I have a surprise." He ran around the front of his truck to help Phil and Teddy out. "Careful now. It's a big step down."

Teddy wore his sailor suit, blue short pants, a white shirt with a blue tie, and the appropriate strut go with it. They followed Henry to the studio. The room smelled of wood shavings and stain. Shades were drawn, making the room dark and cool. Henry switched on the electric light, explaining that he kept it dark when he wasn't there so the sunlight didn't fade any of his wood. "Heat warps wood, as well. I keep it dark and cool during the summer months."

Various pieces were displayed near the front of the shop, including a large dining room table and chairs, a tall dresser, and delicate secretary's desk. "Follow me," he said. "It's in the back."

Teddy ran ahead of them. "Mama, look." He pointed to a bunk bed made of light wood.

"This is for you," said Henry. "For Mary to share with Teddy."

Phil's hands flew to her mouth. "Henry, it's beautiful. How did you do this so quickly?"

"I was already working on it when I learned that Mary was coming to you."

"For a client?" she asked.

"No, to display here in the shop. I sell quite a few of them. I like to have one made already if I can."

"It's too generous, Henry. Thank you."

"I ordered mattresses, too."

His kindness brought tears to her eyes. What would Miller think, though? How would she explain it? Simply, that she ordered them from town. He needn't know they were from Henry's shop. Miller didn't know Henry was a woodworker. He wouldn't guess, given Henry's arm.

"How did you know I was worried about where she would sleep?" she asked.

"I assumed. I have my helper bringing it out later today while we're at the beach, if that's all right."

Teddy was climbing the ladder of the bunk bed. Phil snatched him from the third rung. "You will sleep on the bottom, little man."

"No. Me top."

"Aunt Mary will sleep on the top," she said. "Now come along. Let's get down to the beach."

The mention of the beach distracted Teddy from his pursuit

of the top bunk. He marched toward the door with a determined look upon his face before turning back and waving to them. "Hu'ey." Hurry? Still no "r" sound.

In Henry's car once more, they headed to the public beach where Stowaway emptied into the ocean as if a river. The dirt parking area was nearly full. They had to drive to the very end before finding a spot. Henry once again barreled around the front of the car to open the door for her and Teddy.

She squinted under the bright sun and reached into the bed of the truck to grab their sun hats. "You wear this, young man, and don't take it off unless I say it's all right."

Teddy nodded in agreement as she slipped it on his head. He would do anything she asked to get his hands on the bucket and shovel and all that sand.

Henry had grabbed their picnic basket, an umbrella, a blanket, and several towels from the back of the truck. "You two ready?"

"Yes, yes, yes," said Teddy.

They set out across the parking lot. Teddy held on to her hand, eyes wide, staring at a cluster of surfers with salt-encrusted hair and bare chests chatting near the strangest looking car Phil had ever seen. It looked like a car made in the thirties, but the surfers had cut off the top so that their tall surfboards would fit upright. "They all ride in there at once," said Henry. "Standing, with their surfboards next to them. It's quite a sight."

Nearing noon, the air was warm with a slight breeze and the tide was low. The flat, sandy beach stretched about a half mile before being interrupted by rocks and hillside. This afternoon it was speckled with families, young women in two-piece bathing suits lounging on blankets, and clumps of young men throwing balls or playing badminton with one eye on the ladies. They found a spot several feet from the wet sand. Phil spread out their blanket while Henry put up the umbrella. Teddy, holding his bucket and shovel, plopped down in the wet sand and began to dig.

Phil wore her bathing suit under a simple housedress. Before she took it off, she hesitated, feeling shy. Looking around, though, it seemed as if all the young ladies were wearing one. Times had changed, she supposed. She slipped off her dress and folded it neatly, placing it behind her, and settled under the shade of the umbrella with her legs straight out in front of her. Henry set the picnic basket between them.

"Here, use this to lean against." He folded the extra blanket to make it taller and placed it behind her. He did the same for himself with the pile of towels. "You hungry? Would you like a sandwich?"

"Starving," she said.

Henry pulled out two cold sodas, popped their tops, and handed her one. "Teddy, do you want a sandwich?"

Teddy, shovel in midair, nodded with distinct enthusiasm. "Butter?"

"Yes, butter sandwiches," said Henry. "Your mom made them special."

Henry ran to them, then sat cross-legged on the edge of the blanket and held out his hand. "Yes, please."

After lunch Teddy went back to playing, and the two of them watched him, sipping their sodas. "Did you come here as a kid?" she asked.

He smiled, raking a hand through his hair. "Yeah, all the time. Especially during high school years. Rose and William and I were here every chance we had. William had to help his dad in the mornings at the farm. We'd wait for him, then swing by and spend the rest of the day here." Henry's blue eyes were set on the sea as he spoke softly. "A lot of good memories. You don't know when you're young how little time you have with people you love."

"Mrs. Thomas talked to me last night about your offer," said Phil.

"Yes, she told me." His voice sounded careful, like he didn't want to spook a frightened puppy.

"It's very generous of you, but I can't accept. He wants complete control over everything I do, for one. Not to mention that he'll see it as disloyalty. His jealously is not rational, Henry. I don't want either of you involved in my mess."

"Your concern for us is admirable, but we don't need it," said Henry.

He was wrong, but she didn't say anything further, distracted by the waves. They seemed larger than when they'd first arrived, peaked high and crashed hard, eating sand. "Do the waves seem larger than before?" she asked. Surfers dotted the water, some catching waves, others falling.

He stood, putting his hand over his eyes. Teddy played on wet sand, scooping it into his bucket. "Yes, and the tide's coming in."

"I think Teddy's too close to the water," she said at the same time.

"I'll get him," said Henry.

Just then, another wave crested and broke close to shore, reaching Teddy and his bucket. Teddy cried out, and turned to them, attempting to run, but his feet were seized by the sand and swirling seawater. He dropped his shovel. The sea snatched it and his bucket, carrying them out to sea with a fierce quickness. The water had disappeared from the shore. Teddy's feet were free. Holding both hands out in front of him, he turned away from them and trudged toward the retreating wave. *He's going after his shovel and bucket.* Her heart seemed to stop beating.

"Henry!" she screamed. "He's going after his shovel."

They ran toward the water in tandem. Teddy continued after his shovel. Another wave was coming, cresting high. It broke with a terrible speed and sucked Teddy under. He disappeared under the water. Phil screamed and ran faster. Henry sprinted, his long legs leaving her behind. The wave was on its way back to sea. It was only Teddy's hand that reached out of the water.

Phil continued to scream. At the water's edge, she fell to her knees. Surfers, who must have heard her scream, were headed into the ocean, too, but Henry was already in the water, headed toward the spot where they had seen Teddy's hand a split second before. He dove into the water headfirst. She held her breath, waiting. Another wave crested.

Then, Henry stood, clutching Teddy. The wave crashed against his back, seeming to propel him forward. On the shore, he ran toward their umbrella, cradling Henry with his good arm. Phil ran after them, arriving seconds after he set Teddy on the blanket. Henry moved Teddy's head to the side and swept his mouth with his index finger. He put his face close to the child's mouth and blew into it, then pumped his chest with the palms of his hands. Teddy coughed and Henry turned him over. He spewed sea water before he took in a large breath of air and started to cry. Phil was by their side by now and took Teddy into her arms, rocking him. "It's all right now, ducky. You're safe." She repeated this three times, at least, grateful tears running down her cheeks. "Henry, thank you."

"It's my fault. He shouldn't have been that close to shore." He knelt on his knees next to them, and touched a shaking hand on top of Teddy's head.

Teddy had stopped crying. "Me scared, Mama."

"I know, but you're very brave. Henry's brave, too. He saved you."

"Henry saved me," he repeated. His wet, salty head was cool against the Phil's bare skin. He yawned and nestled closer to her, then stuck his thumb in his mouth and closed his eyes.

"I think he's going to sleep," she said. "Is it all right, do you think?"

"Let's pack up and take him to the Doc. Just to make sure."

She held Teddy tighter against her, as his breathing evened. He was asleep. Her precious baby. What if she'd lost him? She wouldn't have wanted to live. "How did you know what to do?" she asked.

"They taught us in the Navy. A lot of water, you know." Henry sat back against the towels. His wet shirt clung to him. For the first time, she saw the outline of his stump. He pulled on the front of his shirt to detach the wet cloth from his skin, visibly shaking.

With Teddy still in her lap, she handed him a towel. "It's all right now. Put that around your shoulders."

He wiped his nose with the corner the towel, then did as she asked. "When I dove in there I actually forgot I didn't have my arm. Jesus. We both could've been lost."

"But you were strong enough without it," she said.

He lifted his eyes to the sky. "Yeah, I guess I was."

"And you went in the water. You didn't even hesitate."

"I did, didn't I? Didn't even think about it." He shivered. "I think I'm good for another few years now."

She smiled. "You and Teddy both."

"Come on, let's go. I won't feel right until the doc takes a look at him." He brought his long legs up to his chest and rested his chin on his knees. This is what he must have looked like as a boy. "Phil, I try my hardest not to feel sorry for myself, but some days it's harder than others. Sometimes I wonder if it's worth all this effort to keep my chin up. Everywhere I look is evidence of everything I've lost. I haven't been here since before the war."

"Oh, Henry."

"I haven't been able to face it without my sister and William. It's easier not to remember if I stay away from places where we were happy."

"I understand, Henry. I do." She sat cross-legged, forgetting for a moment she was a grownup lady that wasn't supposed to sit this way. "I can't believe this is my life. I didn't ask for much. I was willing to live the life everyone expected of me, even though I had dreams, even back then, of designing my own clothes." Her voice quavered as the tears came. "And I'm mad at Eddie. Mad at him for lying about his age and talking me into being intimate, and most of all for dying and leaving me here all alone with Teddy. I'm mad he's not here to see this beautiful boy." She sobbed. Her makeup would be a wreck and she was probably pitiful in front of this brave man, but she no longer cared.

"Phil, don't cry. It's going to be all right." He moved so that his back was to the water, and reached out with his left arm, wrapping it around her shoulders and holding her close. "We're all going to be fine."

For a moment, she allowed herself to believe he was right.

23

CAROLINE

Caroline woke Saturday morning feeling better. She bathed and slipped into a light cotton dress and went downstairs to find her family. The children and her parents were all at the dining room table, eating breakfast.

"Good morning," said Caroline.

They all turned to look at her. Audrey jumped up from her chair, clapping her hands. "Mother, you're feeling better?"

"Yes, much better." She looked over at the buffet, set with scones, bacon, and fresh orange juice. "Actually, I'm feeling quite ravenous."

Seb was already up, filling a plate for her.

"Sit here, Mother. By me," said Audrey.

Pierce rose to his feet, pulling the chair out for her. "You look pretty, Mother," he said.

"Not quite so green?" she asked.

"Let's say your true color is back," said Mother.

"Between a good night's rest and seeing Julius last night, I feel like I'm ready to join the living. I'm even going to take my walk this morning. The sea air agrees with me."

"It agrees with me, too," said Audrey.

Father smacked the table. "Great news, darling."

"Maybe you're through the worst of it?" asked Mother with a hopeful lift to her voice.

Father and Seb went back to their sections of the newspaper, immediately absorbed, while the younger children and Mother chatted about the sea lions they'd spotted yesterday on their walk.

"The baby sea lion was my favorite," said Audrey. "Her big brown eyes were cute." She stabbed her fork into a piece of melon.

"How do you know it was a girl?" Pierce, eyebrows scrunched, peered at his sister in genuine curiosity.

"I just know." Audrey held her fork midair, the melon precariously perched on two out of four prongs. "Some things you know."

"I don't," said Pierce. "I never seem to know anything."

"You know lots of things," said Audrey. "Gobs."

"I agree." Mother buttered a portion of her scone, then gazed back and forth between the children with an expression of enchantment, as if they were the two cleverest children ever born. "You're both brilliant."

Pierce blushed, looking down at his plate. "I'm good at school work. Not everything."

"School work is a wonderful thing to be good at," said Mother.

Seb showed something to Father from the newspaper and they both chuckled. Caroline blinked. Seb looked more like a man than a boy this morning. What had happened to her little boy? He wanted to study law and become a judge, his whole life mapped out before him, which frightened her, knowing how way leads to way, as Robert Frost said. She wished he were more open to the possibility of diversions, rather than being sure of what he wanted. There were many ways he could be disappointed, wanting things the way he did. She hated to think of anything disappointing her children or breaking their hearts. Her mother claimed that this was the fundamental lie of motherhood: by our simple will or actions, we could keep our children from harm.

In the past week, Julius had come to dinner three times. To see him at their dinner table interacting with the children, hungry for details of their lives since he'd last saw them, had filled her with joy. Only once did she think of Miller. *You're missing it all. And for what?*

She dismissed further dwelling. Here she was at the beach house with her parents and her beautiful children, and Julius. *This is enough.* Look at all she had, and one couldn't have everything.

"What's everyone doing today?" she asked, as she took a bite of eggs.

The three children all started talking at once, but fortunately, Caroline had ears enough for all three.

Later that morning, after her walk and a bath, she sat on the porch with a book. Behind her, the screen door opened and closed. It was Seb with a glass of lemonade in his hand. He set the drink on the small table between them, then sat next to her. "Margaret wondered if you were thirsty. She sent this out for you."

She patted his arm. He was warm, his skin flushed. "How kind."

"She wants to know what you would like for lunch. 'Anything her heart desires' was the exact instruction." He smiled at her. Seb, rosy-cheeked, wore tennis clothes, his long legs already brown from the sun. Given his sleek face and sweaty hair, she gathered he'd just returned from the courts.

"Chicken salad sandwiches sound delicious," she said.

"They always remind me of picnics here with Nana," he said.

"Me too. You look warm. Perhaps you should drink the lemonade?"

"Margaret said specifically it was for you." He grinned and shuddered.

Caroline laughed. "Yes, she's not to be disobeyed."

"Mother, I've been invited to Robert's for a few days. His parents are having their annual garden party and the whole gang will be there. Would it be all right if I went?"

"How lovely. We'll send some wine for his parents as a thank you," she said. "When will you go?"

"Next week, if it's all right with you."

"I'll miss you, but you must go. I want you to enjoy every moment of your youth. It goes too quickly." She shivered, imagining if she'd had to send him off to war.

"Mama, are you cold?" asked Seb.

"No. I was thinking of the war. I'm thankful it's over."

"Were you worried I'd have to go?"

"Night and day. Between that and fretting over Julius, I'm surprised I slept a wink the last four years."

"Julius was brave, wasn't he?"

"Yes. Very brave."

"He doesn't want to talk about anything that happened over there, does he?" asked Seb.

"I think he wants to forget."

Seb looked out to sea, then ran his hand through his hair before turning back to her. "Mother, may I ask you a question?" He shifted in his seat, shuffling his feet before intertwining them.

"Anything."

"What does Father think of the new baby coming?"

"Well, let's see." Caroline stalled, wanting to answer carefully, knowing that Seb would see through it if she was too ebullient in description. "He was surprised. He guessed the truth, actually, because I've been ill."

"Why isn't he here with us?" asked Seb.

"You know the answer to that question. Work."

"I'll be here for you, to help and do anything you need."

"You're a good boy, but I have Mother and Nanny Brown. She's been with us so long and through three babies, I think we'll be fine." She smiled at him, feeling worried. Something *was* bothering him.

He stared down at his hands. "Why didn't Father fight in the war?"

She blinked. What was this about? "He tried to enlist, but they wouldn't take him."

"Because of his heart condition?"

"That's right."

"But some men lied about stuff like that and went anyway. Isn't that true?" asked Seb.

"I don't know, sweetheart."

"Well, I do," he said.

"Is that what's bothering you?" she asked.

He let out a long sigh. "Several things are bothering me. Do you know for certain he has a heart condition?"

She cocked her head to the right, observing him. His voice had wobbled when he asked the question. "He wasn't properly cared for as an infant and it did something to his heart—you know, before he was brought to the orphanage."

"Has Uncle Julius ever examined him?" asked Seb.

"No, he has his own doctor. Anyway, your father's private about these things."

"It doesn't seem to bother him when he plays tennis or golf. Yet he couldn't fight in the war?"

"Seb, what's gotten into you?"

"I don't believe him, that's what. And I can't decide which is worse. Lying about an illness you don't have or not lying to the army so he could fight with the rest of the men of this country."

"Seb. I don't want to ever hear anything like this out of your mouth again. Do you understand?"

"Yes, Mother." He rose to his feet, his eyes glistening with tears. "I'll go tell Margaret about lunch."

"Thank you."

Seb wiped his nose before walking back in the house, letting the screen door slam behind him. The mourning doves cooed.

24

PHIL

Henry drove them south on Highway 101, with the front windows of his Oldsmobile rolled down, letting in the glorious sea air. Phil wore a scarf around her head and sunglasses Henry had bought her last week during their trip to San Francisco to buy fabric for her designs. "I noticed you squinting when we went to the beach, and we can't have that," he said. "You're a Californian now."

She smiled, adjusting her glasses, feeling like a movie star. Strands of her hair occasionally escaped and stuck in her lipstick until she brushed them away with her hand. Clear sky reflected in the endless sea. Sun, shining through the front glass, relaxed her. She was free in Henry's car. Nothing and no one could get her.

Over the last four weeks, Henry had appeared on her doorstep a half-dozen times to ask them to accompany him somewhere. He always made it seem as if it were something he would do with or without them. Each time she wanted to tell him no. It was too risky, given Miller's decree, but as was the way when it came to Henry, she agreed each time. It helped that Miller's visits had changed to only weekdays. He had to be at the beach house with his family on the weekends, he explained.

His father-in-law had insisted. Phil suspected there was more to the story, but she didn't ask, too happy to have weekends with Henry.

Today, they were driving to Carmel. An artist community, he explained, when he asked her to join him. "I'm looking for a painting for my cottage. Would you like to come?" Teddy had left an hour ago with Mrs. Thomas for an overnight sleepover. "To give you a good night's sleep," Mrs. Thomas had said. She agreed when Henry asked, feeling excited. A day away, looking at art, how could she say no?

Carmel-by-Sea, the sign said as they turned off the highway into the little town. Henry parked, and they strolled down the main street of town. The community exploded with people around 1910. "Artists, writers, sculptors started coming here."

They spent the afternoon strolling through small galleries and a bookstore. Henry bought Teddy a book about trucks and a copy of *Little Women* for Mary, even though they had no idea if she'd read it already. The last gallery they walked into had more traditional paintings than the abstract work in the others. They agreed that although they appreciated the abstracts for their artistic qualities, a more traditional work might be better for Henry's simple décor. They meandered separately through the gallery. Phil was especially drawn to the watercolors, of mostly still lifes and landscapes. She liked the way the colors blended together and were less precise than oil or charcoal. Like life. A little messy.

She rounded a corner to find Henry in front of a large oil painting. It was of two little boys and a girl sitting on the beach, dressed in overalls. She guessed the subjects to be around eight, given their sizes. They faced the ocean, arms linked around one another's waists. One of the boys had dark hair, as did the girl, but the boy on the right had unruly blond hair. It looked like Henry's hair today after their car ride.

Henry sat on a bench in front of the painting. She walked over to him, about to tease him about the little boy's hair, but stopped a few feet from him, alarmed. Tears ran down his face, which he wiped occasionally with his handkerchief. Phil sat to his left. It only took her a second to realize what made him cry. The painting reminded him of his sister and William, of their days at the beach. She moved closer and rested the side of her head against his shoulder. "I'm sorry, Henry."

He laughed through his tears. "I feel about Teddy's age right now. This is not a way for a man to act."

"It's okay. I won't tell anyone."

He covered her hand with his. They sat like that for a few minutes. "You hungry?" he asked.

"Starving."

"Good. All this blubbering has me quite famished."

They found a bistro at the end of town and were seated by a severe-looking host outside on the patio under an umbrella, with a view of the ocean. Overhead, the screams of seagulls merged with the chatter of other guests and an occasional clatter from inside the restaurant. The waiter came by with glasses of water, then explained to them about the menu. "It's a four-course meal. Chef's discretion."

"Meaning what, exactly?" asked Henry.

"Meaning we bring you four courses of the most delicious food you'll ever have."

"Okay, then," said Henry. "May we also have wine? A bottle of chilled Chablis."

"Coming right up," he said.

They sat in silence, enjoying the view. What Henry pondered now could be anyone's guess. It was as if his show of emotion had not happened. After the waiter poured their wine, Henry lifted his glass. "To you, Phil."

"Why me?"

"Because you're helping me make new memories, driving out the ghosts. The last time I came here was with William and Rose. And now, we're here, and I'll have this day to remember."

"Thank you for bringing me, Henry. I feel at home here."

He smiled, his usual good humor apparently restored after his bout of grief at the gallery. "You belong here with the other artists."

"You think I'm an artist?"

"What else would you be? Your designs? Your vision?"

. "I don't know. I never thought of myself that way. I always figured I was simply good with the sewing machine."

"You know it's more than that," he said.

She sipped her wine before answering. "I guess I do."

He slapped the table, hard enough that two bohemian-looking women dressed in peasant blouses at the table next to them turned to look. "It's about time you admitted how talented you are."

"Oh, Henry, you're impossible."

The sun set as they dined. The waiter had not lied. It was the most delicious food either of them had ever had. Something called Caesar salad, which the waiter informed her was invented in 1924 at a restaurant in San Diego by Caesar Cardini when he ran out of the usual ingredients for salad dressing and made up a new one with what he had on hand. However it came to be, Phil was glad it had as she dug into the crunchy lettuce with the tangy dressing. The next course, fresh linguini and clams, was possibly the best food she'd ever tasted. When the grilled trout came out, she changed her mind. "The trout's my favorite. Definitely the trout," she told Henry. Dessert was a lemon sorbet that melted on her tongue. At some point, Henry ordered another bottle of wine. By the end of the meal, Phil was full and a little tipsy. The sun had set while they dined, and the waiters lit candles along the railings and the tables. They moved empty tables aside to make a dance floor, as a three-string band began to play. Several couples got up to dance.

"Phil, I haven't danced since I lost my arm, but would you care to see if it's improved my unfortunate two left feet?"

She laughed. "I have sandals on. You won't hurt my toes, will you?"

He stood, holding out his hand. "I can make no promises."

They walked out to the middle of the floor and she wrapped her arms around his neck, all inhibitions gone with the second bottle of wine. He held her close with his good arm. "There'll be no swinging."

"Thank goodness," she murmured. "I'm too drunk for that."

The band continued to play as they swayed to the music. The candles created a feeling of estrangement from the rest of the world, and it was only her and Henry and the music. They danced for an hour, until Phil could no longer feel her toes in the high sandals. "My feet hurt," she whispered.

"Take them off. We'll go down to the beach," said Henry. "You can put your toes in the sand."

Henry asked the waiter if they could take the rest of their wine and glasses out to the beach. "Yes, sir." He appeared two minutes later with a blanket, the rest of the wine and their glasses arranged in a bucket, and a lantern, as if it were the most ordinary request. "Watch your step on the way down to the beach," he said.

They could still hear the music from the sand, background music to the waves. In the dark, only the white caps of the surf were visible. Henry spread the blanket out and Phil plopped down, feeling loose like a rag doll. And happy. Being with Henry made her happy. That's all. Just happy. And smart. And brilliant. Yes, all those things. He made her feel like a better person, not the compromised woman she had become, but a merging of her innocent self with this new, artistic self. If only she were free. If only.

Henry handed her a glass of wine. She took a tiny sip, knowing she'd had enough, and leaned back on her elbows. "I had no idea this kind of life existed. Not in Iowa. No, definitely there's no Caesar salad in Iowa."

"Phil?"

"Yes?"

"What're we doing?" His voice sounded serious in the dark. She set her glass in the sand. Her heart started to pound.

"Having fun?" she asked.

"Yes. Fun. Every minute with you is more fun than I've ever had in my life."

"We just have to keep it like this, Henry. We can't have any of the rest of it." She'd turned to look at him, making out his handsome face in the lamplight. His eyes glittered as he leaned closer.

"I'm going to kiss you," he said.

"No, please don't." She sounded breathless, like she'd run up hill. "If you do, I don't know if I can go back to pretending."

"Pretending?"

"Pretending I don't want you to."

He leaned closer. "I'm going to kiss you."

She held her breath as he lifted her chin, then caught her lips with his, pressing gently. Frozen for an instant, she let him kiss her, until her mouth betrayed her and she began to kiss him back. She sighed when his tongue flicked hers. As the kiss deepened, she lost all sense of place or the passage of time. It was Henry and only Henry. Finally, he pulled away and gazed at her under the starlit sky, his eyes sparkling in the lamplight. "Phil, there's something between us that I've never experienced before."

"I feel it, too. But, Henry, it's too late for me. I'll never be free of him." She started to cry.

He pulled her close. "Listen to me. You have to have a little faith."

She buried her face in his neck. "That's what Mrs. Thomas said."

"Just be here with me, right now. We'll worry about the rest later, okay?" asked Henry.

"Okay."

He brushed her hair from where it had stuck to her wet cheek and kissed her for the second time that night.

"The bigger problem is how we're going to get home," said Henry.

"What do you mean?" asked Phil.

"I've had way too much wine."

"The road's treacherous in the dark."

"We'll have to find a place to stay here in town. Separate rooms. In the morning, we can have croissants at that bakery we saw," said Henry.

She giggled. "You and Teddy. Always with the food."

He laughed, then kissed her. "Let's pretend, for tonight, that we don't ever have to leave here."

"But we do, Henry."

"Shhh…be here with me now."

She answered him with a kiss.

Two days later, Miller drove them to San Francisco to pick up Mary at the train station. Joseph had gone down to pick up one of the sons to take him to a weekend gathering, he explained to Phil. She didn't care. All she wanted was to get to the station on time and see her sister, hold her in her arms. The highway to San Francisco was curvy and Phil had to look out the window to the road to keep from being nauseous. From the backseat, Teddy played with his trucks, making sounds like an engine until Miller told him it was silent time if he wanted to have a cookie later. Teddy was quiet after that. Anything for a cookie.

They arrived at the station fifteen minutes before the train was supposed to arrive. It was crowded with people, all pushing and shoving to get to where they needed to be. Miller kept hold of her arm and she carried Teddy, afraid he would be swallowed by the swarm of humanity. When they reached the doors to the platform, they settled by the window to wait. After a few minutes, Miller, obviously restless, offered to fetch sodas. Phil let out a sigh of relief as she watched him depart.

A few minutes later, the train came roaring into the station, loud and clanging. Teddy buried his face in her neck. "Too loud."

She hoisted him to her hip, then patted his back and kissed his sweaty head. "It's merely a train, ducky. Nothing to be scared of. And it will have Aunt Mary on it."

Finally, the doors opened and passengers started to unload. She might not recognize her sister. She was ten now. What if she no longer looked like the little girl she'd left that day? People continued out of the train and onto the platform. Still no Mary. She started to panic. What if she'd gotten into trouble somehow? What if the companion had abandoned her? Maybe they hadn't made the train for some reason. Then, she spotted a girl and a young lady. There she was! Her Mary. She was taller and her face thinner, but it was Mary with the same dark brown curls and big brown eyes. She and Teddy could be siblings. Beside herself with joy, she jiggled Teddy. "It's her. There, see? That's Aunt Mary." They both waved. The young woman must have spotted them because she waved back and said something to Mary. Mary's eyes locked upon them, wide, unsure. The young lady was hustling them inside, and they disappeared for a moment in a sea of people. Phil made her way through the crowd, using her free shoulder to nudge her way through.

They reached her at last. Mary stood in front of her, holding a small bag. Phil began to cry, which made Teddy increase his grip on her. She drew her sister to her with her free arm, squeezing her against her shoulder. "You grew tall, Mary."

Mary didn't speak, peering at her with unblinking eyes. Did she not remember her? "Do you know me, Mary?"

Mary nodded, yes, but her expression remained impassive.

"And this is Teddy. He's my baby. Your nephew."

Her gaze flickered to him. She brought her hand up in a gesture that was almost a wave.

Using his thumb, he pointed at this chest. "Me Teddy. You like sandwiches?"

Mary nodded.

"Mama make you," said Teddy.

The young lady—what was her name? Suddenly Phil couldn't remember. But she needn't have worried, for she introduced herself. "Miss Rains, I'm Holly Moore." Holly was a blonde beauty with porcelain skin, wearing a fitted dress that accentuated her copious curves.

"Thank you for bringing Mary to us," said Phil.

"It was my pleasure. She's not much of a talker. Susan tells me she hasn't spoken much since the accident."

Phil looked back at Mary. She'd clasped her hands together and stared at the floor. What was she thinking? This was not the girl she'd left in Iowa.

Behind them, Miller appeared, carrying several bottles of Coca-Cola. "What have we here? Is this Mary?" He smiled at her, showing his teeth. Heavens, he was charming when he chose to be. Mary elevated her gaze to look at him, and a slight smile lifted the corners of her mouth. Suddenly, there she was. The Mary she remembered. "I'm Miller. A friend of your sister and of Teddy, and now hopefully of you." He handed her the bottle of Coke. "I bet you're thirsty."

She nodded, taking it from his outstretched hand. She took a tentative sip, then smiled.

"Yes, they're very good," said Phil. "But you can't have them all the time. Right, Teddy?"

"Yes, Mama."

"And you, young lady?" he asked Holly. "Would you care for the other soda?"

"I would give almost anything for it," she said, laughing.

"I'm Miller Dreeser." He handed Holly the bottle. "Welcome to California."

"Thank you." Holly performed a hint of a curtsy and gave him a dazzling smile worthy of a magazine advertisement.

Miller focused once again on Mary. "Don't feel like talking?" he asked her.

She shook her head, then took another sip of her Coke.

"Well, there's no reason to talk if you don't feel like it," he said. "Did your sister tell you she lives in a cottage by the sea?"

Again, Mary shook her head.

"We're going there now. You can play in the sand with Teddy here." He turned back to Holly. "May we take you somewhere?"

"No, thank you. I'm catching the next train to Los Angeles."

Miller reached into his jacket pocket and pulled out an envelope. "This is for your trouble, Miss Moore. It should get you started in your new city." He tapped the edge of the envelope into the palm of his hand. Phil imagined a puppeteer, controlling his subjects with the flick of his wrist.

Holly blushed. "Thank you, but it's not necessary. Susan already gave me the money you wired for our fares." She was charmed by Miller. It was this way he had of making his subject feel like they were the only person in the world. Why was she not charmed in this way? Her life would be much easier if she loved him, if she craved his attention. Why was she immune when others were not?

"This is a little extra to say thank you for your troubles. I imagine traveling across the country with a child wasn't a party. Anyway, everyone could use a little extra cash."

"Well, thank you then. It will help. I don't know a soul there. My parents say Hollywood's full of nothing but the devil in fancy clothes. They think I've lost my mind." Holly held the envelope loosely; she had the good manners not to look inside, but Phil knew she must be itching to see how much he'd given her.

"We should be off now," said Phil.

"Mary, I'll miss you." Holly stooped, holding out her arms to the child. Mary hugged her, laying her cheek against Holly's shoulder for a moment before letting go. Then, Mary held out her hand to Phil, looking up at her with solemn eyes.

Phil, settling Teddy on her hip, took her sister's hand. They made their way through the crowd.

Miller insisted they stop at his favorite diner on the way out of town to have a meal and some ice cream. They sat in a booth by the front window. Miller and Phil on one side, the children on the other. They ordered hamburgers and milkshakes. While they waited, Phil told Mary about the cottage and the beach. "We'll have the rest of the summer to play and swim. Would you like that?"

Mary turned a knife from one side to the other and nodded.

Teddy had not stopped staring at his small aunt since they left the station, clearly enamored with her. In the bright light from the window, Phil took a good look at her sister. She was too thin, and there were half-moon shadows under her eyes.

"Was the sleeper car good to sleep in?" asked Phil. She hadn't had a sleeper car when she traveled. The five-day trip had been exhausting and grimy, with every smell known to humanity passing through the car at one point or other during the trip.

Mary shrugged.

"I didn't have a sleeper car ticket when I came out," said Phil. "I learned to sleep sitting up."

Miller put his arm around her shoulders and kissed the top of her head. "You'll never have to travel that way again."

Mary's eyes darted from Phil to Miller and back again. Given their background, Mary had not seen men and women sitting together like this unless they were married. How was she to explain all this to her?

Their food came then. Phil cut her burger in half and put it on a napkin for Teddy, along with some of the crispy French fries. He tucked in right away, as did Miller. "Feels like we haven't eaten in days," he said.

"This has been a long day," said Phil.

Mary chewed on the end of a fry, watching Teddy. After a moment she smiled and turned back to her plate. She picked up her burger and took a small bite. Her eyes widened in what looked like appreciation as she chewed. Then, she took a sip of her vanilla milkshake. Another smile.

"Did you eat on the train?" asked Phil.

Her sister gave her the same noncommittal shrug as she had when Phil asked about the sleeping car.

"Was Holly good to you? Did she feed you?" asked Phil.

Mary nodded.

"Well, when you're ready to talk, I'd like to hear your voice," said Phil. She teared up and looked out the window. On the sidewalk, a young man stood near a streetlight, looking at them. When he saw her peering back, he averted his eyes and walked away. *Terrible manners to stare at a person.* People were different in California. Perhaps the sunshine made everyone bolder, freer. She turned back to look at Mary. Half of her burger was gone. She was eating. That's all that mattered right now. Whatever trauma she'd experienced, at least she hadn't lost her appetite.

Teddy held one of his french fries out to Mary. "Me share."

Mary smiled at him and picked up one of her own fries. She took the fry from his outstretched hand and shook the other at him. Teddy's eyes darted to his mother.

"Yes, it's all right," said Phil. "She wants to share with you, too."

He grinned, then snatched the fry, popping the entire thing into his mouth.

Miller cleared his throat and straightened his tie before slipping from the booth. "Excuse me, I have to make a phone call before we go home. I won't be long."

When he was out of earshot, Phil wiped Teddy's mouth. "Moo, do you remember when I left home."

"Yes. I remember."

Mary's voice. She spoke. Thank God. "It was a long time ago now." Phil kept her tone even, afraid to spook her with too much excitement.

"Twelve-hundred and twenty-one days," said Mary.

She stared at her sister. Mary had picked up another fry and, head down, seemed to be studying it.

"You counted the days?" asked Phil.

"Yes, and I wished every day you would send for me. Then one day they died and it finally came true." Her voice trembled and giant tears fell down her cheeks. "It's all my fault."

"That they died? Because you wanted to be with me? Is that what you think?"

"Yes."

"Oh, Moo, no, no. Just because you wanted to escape from them doesn't mean you caused their death. It was more likely Father's terrible driving. He drove way too fast. Around corners especially."

"What does it mean when they say a car was wrapped around a tree?" asked Mary.

"It means the accident was very bad."

"Mother made an apple pie before we left for church. It smelled good and she caught me sniffing it real close and called me a pig and said I couldn't have any now that I chose to put my dirty nose so close to it. Said I was bound to grow up fat."

"Oh, little Moo, you're not a pig," said Phil. *You're my precious baby sister. I will not let anyone call you a name ever again.* That hateful, awful woman. *Damn you to hell, Mother.*

"Why did you call me Moo? I can't remember that part," asked Mary.

"That's what you called yourself when you were small. You couldn't say Mary, I guess. It came out 'Moo.' It was adorable. You were adorable."

When Miller came back, they paid the bill and got up to leave.

"Is everything all right?" asked Phil as they walked out the door of the restaurant and onto the crowded street. She adjusted the brim of her hat against the bright afternoon sun.

He tapped the brim of her hat with his index fingers. "Yes,

my beautiful. I have something unpleasant to take care of in the next few weeks."

"Something unpleasant?"

"But necessary."

She assumed it was something to with his job and didn't ask any further questions. Miller didn't like it when she asked questions. Taking Mary's hand, she pointed down the street. "Come along, Moo. We'll take you home so you can see the ocean."

When they walked in, the cottage smelled of wood shavings. A hammer pounded furiously for a moment, then stopped. "What's that horrific noise?" asked Miller.

It was Henry. Putting together the bed. Phil chose her words carefully. "It's a bunk bed for the kids to share."

Teddy tugged on her arm and jumped up and down with excitement. "Bed."

"From where?" asked Miller.

"Henry's shop," said Phil.

"I see." Darkness, like a mask, covered his features. He looked like a monster. "What did I tell you?"

"I know." She lowered her voice, hoping he would do the same. "He offered, knowing Mary was coming. A landlord's responsibility, or something like that. Is what he said, I mean." Stuttering. She was stuttering. Hatred rose to her throat from the pits of her stomach. She loathed this man. How dare make her bow down and grovel. Her hands itched, wanting to claw at his face, make him suffer.

"He's quite a landlord," said Miller.

She set her purse on the table near the front door, her insides twisting, praying that he let it go. "Moo, do you want to see your room? You'll have to share with Teddy because it's not a very big house."

Teddy toddled over to Mary and held out his hand. "Me show Mary."

Mary took Teddy's hand, speaking in a motherly tone. "When I was your age, I shared a room with your mother. I loved it."

"You, me, share?" asked Teddy.

"That's right. And you won't have to be scared any longer," said Mary.

"Me never scared," said Teddy.

"Well, me neither," said Mary. "I'm ten years old, you know."

"Me is three," said Teddy. "Wave scared me, right, Mommy?"

"Yes, darling. It scared us all," said Phil. "But we'll tell Mary about that some other time."

They disappeared down the hallway, Teddy babbling about his bucket and the wave.

"You need to do something about how that boy talks," said Miller.

"He's fine," said Phil. She followed them to the bedroom. Henry must have just finished. The banging had stopped and the bed was put together. "Ah, good timing." Henry placed his hammer into his toolbox. "Everyone arrive then?"

"Yes, this is Mary. And Mary, this is Henry. He's our landlord and lives in the cottage next door." She sensed Miller's presence in the doorway, like a heat lamp on a hot day, permeating the room.

Mary fluttered her fingers, then moved closer to Teddy.

"It's a pleasure to meet you, Mary," said Henry.

Miller crossed over to stand next to Phil. "Thank you for this lovely piece, Mr. Sayer. I think we can take it from here."

"Sure," said Henry. "I'm on my way over to the Thomas's. Mrs. Thomas has a jam delivery she needs help with." He held out his hand to Miller. They shook. "Pleasure to see you again." He nodded at the rest of them. "Enjoy the rest of your day." His footsteps were heavy down the hallway. All she wanted was for him to be here with them. For a moment, she couldn't move. It was impossible to continue without Henry. Pain pierced her chest.

Teddy started to show Mary all his toys, naming each one in his breathy voice. Teddy and Mary. She must stay strong for them. This was all for them. Her own feelings and desires must be secondary.

"I need a drink," said Miller. He strode out of the room, and on feet made of lead, she followed him. He went to the liquor cabinet and poured whiskey into a glass. "You want one?" he asked.

"No, thank you."

"I have to leave, get back to the city, and then I'm headed south for a few days. Family obligations."

"Think nothing of it."

He took a drink from his glass, then set it on a table near the sofa, pulling on his tie. "Can I trust you, Phil?"

"What do you mean?"

"Are you fucking the one-armed landlord?"

"Miller, my God." She glanced toward the bedrooms, hoping the children hadn't overheard him.

He sat on the sofa, pulling his tie completely from his neck and picking up his drink. "I'll send Joseph out here for the rest of the bloody summer if I have to."

"It's not necessary." She went to the liquor cabinet, keeping her voice steady and light. Suddenly, a drink sounded good. "I have the children here, for heaven's sake. What do you think could happen?"

He grunted, emptied his glass, then thumped it onto the coffee table.

She poured a drink with her back to him, counting the seconds of silence, then took a sip. The drink was warm and smooth down her throat. Mary was here. Mary was hers to care for. Mary was hers to heal from the abuses of their mother. Phil fought a growing sense of terror. Keeping Miller happy was paramount. Turning to him as she sipped her drink, she looked at him over the rim of her glass. "Miller, you have to trust me. I think you know I can't live without you."

"You can't live without my money."

She knelt at his feet, setting her drink aside, and put her hand on his thigh. "That's not the only reason. I was positively green with envy this afternoon. Holly Moore's a beauty. You could have her or anyone you wanted. I know how special it is that you chose me."

He placed his fingers around her wrist. "Tell me you love me."

"You know I do."

"Say it. I want to hear the words."

"I love you."

"You don't."

"I do. Yes, it was an arrangement that kept me off the streets, but that was then. You saw something between us that I didn't. I've grown to love you, Miller."

He gazed into her eyes and let go of her wrist. A flicker of triumph crossed his face. "Phil, I'm willing to blow up my entire life to be with you. I want to marry you. Make this official. You won't have to hide anymore. I want to give you everything."

"This is enough." Her pulse throbbed at her neck. What did he mean? *I'm willing to blow up my entire life.* "I understand you have responsibilities to your wife and family. I'm satisfied with the arrangements as they are."

"But for how long? How long until Henry Sayer starts to look good to you? Until he manages to steal you from me."

Lie. Think of something. Convince him. "Darling, Henry Sayer has absolutely no appeal to me. He's about as interesting as watching towels dry on the line. He builds furniture for a living. Do you think a man like him is appealing after being with you? Truly. You have nothing to worry about."

He stared at her, as if trying to decipher a code to open the inside of her brain. "Are you saying I'm being a jealous idiot?"

She bit the inside of her mouth, hoping to draw blood, so

tears would flood to her eyes. He always believed her when she cried. "Yes, you're being silly. Don't you know by now how loyal I am to you?"

"Yes, yes, I do. I can't think rationally when I'm with you." He put both hands in her hair, brushing his thumbs against her neck, making her shiver.

She must let him think she shivered from desire, not repulsion. "Think of how I feel about your wife. It's awful. I can't sleep or eat, thinking of you with her."

Something akin to anger passed over his features. He glanced at the ceiling, like a fly had suddenly caught his interest. "You've made me very happy. Do you know that? I can't stand the thought of leaving you, but I have to go. This thing I have to take care of is important."

"I understand you have to keep up appearances and I'm happy for whatever time we have together." If only she could cry on demand, act as if his leaving was devastating as opposed to the opposite. When he left, she would be able to breathe again. Now, the room was airless. "We'll be like a family when you're here."

He closed his eyes. An expression of peacefulness crossed his features, like a man suddenly relieved of pain. "That's all I want. All of us to be together."

PART IV

AUGUST 1946

25

CAROLINE

Morning fog floated over the sea like translucent fabric. Beyond, a strip of blue promised another bright August afternoon. Caroline wore a loose, sleeveless dress and her walking shoes, a layer of perspiration on her skin. She walked fast, swinging her arms, until she was near her parents' house, the grass on the cliff still wet with dew, making a dark patch on the top of her shoes. At the edge of the cliff she stopped to sit and cool down on the bench Father had placed there to watch the sunset or read a book or sit and dream. A stick lay at her feet, about four feet tall and at least two inches in diameter and bent slightly at the end. She had picked it up earlier for Audrey, who had been looking for the perfect walking stick for weeks.

It was Audrey's latest romantic notion after reading an English novel about a young man who used a walking stick when escorting his betrothed on their daily walk. Audrey had described to her the need for such a stick, with a dreamy look in her eyes. Caroline had been romantic at that age, too. They were ten the year she made Julius marry her on the beach. She'd made a dress and veil out of seaweed, and stuck a large piece of drift-wood into the sand for the preacher. Julius made rings from the long grasses, twisting several strands together and tying them in a circle.

Footsteps behind her made her turn. Julius waved a greeting as he approached. She smiled, her spirits immediately lifted at the sight of him, dressed as usual in a tan linen suit and light blue tie, his sun-bleached hair falling into his eyes. No medical bag. He must not be on his way somewhere. Maybe he would stay for lunch? "Speaking of the devil," she called out to him. "I was just thinking of you."

"Well, then, we're even, because I was thinking of you and decided to come by and see how you were feeling."

They greeted one another with a swift embrace, and then he sat next to her on the bench. "You're looking particularly pretty this morning," he said. "Exercise always makes your cheeks such a lovely pink."

She flushed. "Thank you, Julius. You know how I love compliments."

He chuckled. "Yes, I do."

"Are you on your way somewhere without your bag?" she asked.

"I'm taking the day off, unless someone calls. How are you feeling?"

"Better. Still nauseous when I first wake up, but it's a little better, I think."

"Good to hear."

She waved the stick at him. "Audrey's been looking for a walking stick. I think I found one."

He smiled and took the stick from her. "She told me the other day when I was at the house. She's one of a kind. Like her mother." From his pocket, he pulled out a small knife. "I'll carve a sharp end for her. It'll make it easier to stick in the ground."

She cocked her head, observing him. "Am I one of a kind? I always think I'm quite ordinary."

"No, not ordinary." With a flick of the knife, he cut into the wood. The shavings fell at their feet.

She wondered what he meant exactly, but was too shy to ask. "I was thinking of the time I made you marry me on the beach. Do you remember?"

He turned to look at her, smiling. "Sure. I remember it well. I made rings out of grass."

"Yes, that's right. You were good to me, playing my silly games." She closed her eyes and drew a deep breath through her nose, feeling drowsy and content with Julius beside her, the noise of his whittling in rhythm to the waves. "I love the smell of the sea. It always makes me think of you—you and the sea intermingled in my mind. I was in love with you back then. Since I can remember, it was always you."

The sound of his carving stopped. She opened her eyes. He was staring at her, his complexion ashen, like he'd seen a ghost. "What's the matter? Are you feeling ill?" she asked.

"I didn't know."

"Didn't know what?" she asked.

"That you loved me."

"Of course you knew."

"I had no idea," he said.

She patted his hand with her own. "Sometimes I wonder how we can be a patriarchal society. Men are so stupid."

"How come you never told me? I mean, back then," he asked.

"I expected you knew. It seemed obvious to me."

He shook his head. "No, not to me. Not at all."

"Anyway, I would've rather died rather than have you know. I knew you could never love a fat girl."

"Why do you always say that? You were *not* fat."

She laughed. "Julius, I was fat."

"I never saw you that way. To me you were strong, athletic. You could do anything I could do. Run up a hill, swim, dig giant holes in the sand."

"Athletic maybe. Like my father. But I had a few too many pieces of cake back then." She laughed. "Remember how we used to make homemade ice cream? We should make some for the children."

He had looked away from her, staring out to sea with a stony expression, his eyelids at half-mast. "You were perfect the way you were. I wouldn't have asked you to be anything but what you are. I loved you, too, Caroline. All my life."

Her pulse quickened. What had he said? *All my life.* She would make a joke of it, disguise the fact that her heart was in her throat. "What? No, you didn't." She kept her voice light, teasing, but spots of pain widened her chest, expanded her until she was nothing but a beating heart. It couldn't be true that he had loved her. If that were true, then she had made a terrible mistake. She had married Miller. No, that hadn't been a mistake. She couldn't think that way. Choices were made. Julius left. She had the children.

"I planned on coming back," he said. "I planned on coming back for you when I was worthy of you."

She stared at him. "Why didn't you tell me?"

"I don't know. Because I'm an idiot. I presumed I'd have more time. I wanted to prove to myself that I was good enough for you. My mother leaving...well, it made me doubt certain things. When I came home, you were engaged to Miller. And you were different. Cowed. And thin. It seemed like Miller had you under some kind of spell." With the tip of his shoe, he dug a hole in the sand. "I should've fought for you then. It's the biggest regret of my life." He pointed to the sea with his knife. "I've envisioned that day we played wedding many times."

She closed her eyes, replaying the moments in her mind. The smell of the seaweed veil, the feel of the twisted sea grass around her finger. They exchanged vows, like she'd read about it a book. *For better or worse. Richer or poorer.* Then, he kissed her, lingering for a moment, tasting of saltwater and smelling of sunshine.

He continued to stare at the sea, his face impassive, the tremor in his voice the only indication of his emotions. "I've never been able to move on from you. No woman has ever seemed close to as perfect for me as you."

"Julius," she whispered. "I had no idea."

He turned to look at her, his hat low on his forehead, casting a shadow over his face. "Would it have made any difference? If I'd told you long ago, would you have loved me, too?"

She didn't know how to answer and searched her hands as if there were instructions written on the knuckles. The words, the truth, came out of her, like he was dragging it with a rope from her insides. "I would've loved you, too. I *did* love you, but I didn't think there was ever a chance you felt the same way. And now I'm married, Julius. I married someone else, for real, before God and my parents."

"Yes, I know. I do know. The years unfold, one by one." He went back to carving the end of the stick. A few more slices and it would be sharp, like the end of a pencil. "Do you have any idea why Ann broke off our engagement?"

"I've wondered," she said.

He was quiet, his hands warm over her cold ones. "She said I didn't love her as I should. She said I loved someone else. You, in fact."

She closed her eyes. He must stop talking immediately. They were on the precipice of something. They could not recover if either of them allowed themselves to fall.

"When I was over there and it got bad—oh, Caroline, the noise of the bombs at night—you can't imagine. I'd sit there, sometimes monitoring an injured soldier, or in surgery under nothing but a tarp, wondering if I would make it to see the morning light. And do you know what I remembered? It was that day when we were kids. I replayed every moment. The way the salt water made your hair stiff, the freckles over your nose that reminded me of the Milky Way, your blue eyes that mimicked the sea, the way it felt when I kissed you, like the world made sense for the first time. Every time I was frightened, sure I would die, I thought of you, Caroline. I vowed to myself, to God, that if I ever got back here, if I ever had the chance to see you again, I would tell you that I love you. I've never loved anyone else. It's always been you. I know nothing can come of it because you love Miller like I love you, but I promised myself I would tell you the truth because if I didn't, if I kept it inside any longer, I might as well be dead."

She was crying. He handed her the handkerchief from his pocket, and she dabbed at her cheeks. "I'm sorry, Julius."

"For what?"

"That we kept our secrets."

"I think about what our life together would've been like. I'm ashamed to say I do."

"I never allow myself that luxury," she said. "I'm afraid of where that path might lead."

"Would you have married Miller if you'd known I loved you?"

She sighed. "We wouldn't have the children if I hadn't."

"Yes, but that wasn't my question."

"If I'd known you loved me, I would never have noticed another man existed. It's as simple as that."

"I don't know how he does it," said Julius.

"What's that?"

"Stays away from you for a minute longer than he has to."

"That's just it. He has to."

"Right. The orphanage and all," said Julius, his tone bitter. "A better man could've gotten past it, Caroline. My mother left me, too. I know what it feels like to be abandoned, but I haven't let it keep me from the people I love."

It was all clear to her now. She understood what had happened to his heart that kept him from her. "You did, though, Julius. You didn't feel good enough for me because of what she did, how she abandoned you. You're the same as Miller."

"As much as it hurts me to admit it, I guess you're right. But here's the difference between the two of us. If you were mine, I would spend every moment of my life making sure you never experienced the hurt I felt as a kid. I would love you so well that you'd feel nothing but safe and adored. I would not spend all my time away from you," Julius stood, shoving the stick into the ground and smiling down at her in a way that didn't reach his sad eyes. "I'm meeting someone in town for lunch." He brushed a lock of her hair from where it had stuck to her damp cheek. "I'll see you later for dinner."

Tears blurred her vision as she watched him stroll down the path from which she had come.

She walked to toward the house, wiping her eyes. She would try and sneak inside without seeing her mother. Mother always knew when she'd been crying and she was not ready to speak about what had happened now with Julius. His confession had stunned her. The possibility that she might have had a life with Julius made it feel like the world had tipped and she might fall off at any moment and float about the atmosphere for all eternity, muttering *what if, what if, what if?* She must put it aside, however. She'd devoted herself to her marriage, to her husband. Loyalty to Miller was the most important thing. He was the father of her children.

Seb sat on the porch, slumped in a chair, staring into his hands. Alarmed, she hurried up the steps. He was back a whole day earlier than expected. Had something happened with Oscar? Did they fight? Had they gotten into trouble?

"Darling, what's the matter?"

He raised his face. Traces of tears streaked down his dusty face. "Hi, Mother."

She sat next to him, brushing his hair back from his hot forehead. "What is it? Why are you home early?"

"I called the house and asked Papa to send Frederick for me."

"Yes, but why?" she asked.

"I have something I have to tell you." His voice was wobbly, like when he was little and a bad dream had scared him in the middle of the night.

What had he done? Her heart started thumping harder for the second time that day, afraid of what someone she loved was about to say.

"I was with Oscar yesterday. We were at the Wharf with some other of the boys." His voice broke.

"Yes." *Steel yourself. He's made a terrible mistake.*

"It was Father."

"Father?"

"I saw him through a window. He was with another family."

"Sweetheart, I don't understand," said Caroline.

"I saw him, Mother. I saw him." He began to sob.

"What did you see?"

"He was with a woman and two children. He had his arm around her and there was a little boy and a girl the same age as Audrey. They were having milkshakes. Father kissed her head."

Ice water merged with the blood that coursed through Caroline's veins. With great restraint, she kept her voice steady. "An employee, perhaps?"

"No, Mother. It wasn't like that. He wouldn't have his arm around an employee. He wouldn't kiss them." Tears ran down his face, in that way boys could cry without any of the muscles of their faces moving. "And she's..." He trailed off, flushing a deeper red and brushing tears from his cheeks. She imagined they were hot against his smooth cheek. Regardless of her shock, she yearned to take away his pain. "She's..."

"She's pretty?"

"Yes. And young, Mother. Very young."

"There were children with them?" The questions came automatically. She had detached now and sought only facts.

"Yes. Two. Like they were a family."

"I think I'm going to be sick." Caroline lurched forward and vomited into the hydrangeas. When she was done, she placed her forehead on the edge of the porch railing. Grains of sand, scattered across the surface, dug into her skin. *This can't be. He's mistaken. What he saw wasn't what he thought. Miller. No, no. This cannot be true.*

Her son was behind her, taking her arm and leading her inside the house. "Seb, let's keep this between us for now."

"You should tell Papa and Nana, Mother. They can help figure out what to do."

"I know. Just not yet. Can you do that for me?"

"If that's what you want." He squeezed her hand as they walked through the door.

Mother lounged on one of the couches, reading a book. She looked up, a smile ready for them, but upon seeing Caroline, tossed aside her book and jumped to her feet. "Are you ill?"

"Yes, I need to rest, that's all. Just nauseous."

"Seb, go fetch Margaret. Ask her to bring a cold compress for her head," said Mother.

Caroline leaned against her mother, trying not to sob as they made their way to her room at the far north end of the house. The main sitting room, large and facing the sea, normally airy and light, seemed suffocating and the aroma of frying onions from the kitchen caused the nausea to come back in full force. Black dots danced before her eyes. Her legs were boiled spaghetti. Mother called for Seb. "Sebastian, come help me. I think she's going to faint."

Then, it went black.

2 6

MILLER

iller drove the coastal highway toward San Francisco, his hands sweaty. He could barely hang on to the steering wheel. What the hell was the matter with him? It was this meeting with Timmy that had him flustered. He didn't want to do it, but it had to happen. It was time. His old friend said to meet him at his place of business, a bar near the wharf. They could talk over what he needed. The last time he'd seen him, Timmy had delivered paperwork from some doctor he had in his pocket to keep Miller out of the Army. Official diagnosis of a heart condition. No draft for Miller. Timmy could make things happen.

He took a turn too fast and slammed on the brakes to keep from veering off the road. The moment he'd left Phil, his elation at her words had turned to agitation. Caroline and her blasted family dinners. How many dinners could one family have? He'd tried to get out of it when he'd called last night, pretending to be at the office, but his mother-in-law was insistent. Caroline didn't feel well and needed him. It would mean the world to them all to have him there for the weekend. For all the weekends. Miller snatched a cigarette from the pack he'd set on the other seat but tossed it aside, realizing he couldn't light it while driving, especially with these curves. A drink was what he needed. Anything to calm his nerves. Could he do what he needed to do? The life he wanted was elusive if he continued the way he was. *Someone had to die.*

It was time.

The highway was uncrowded and Miller took advantage of that fact, combined with his anger, to drive faster than he probably should, especially since Caroline wasn't there sucking in her breath every time he turned a corner. Miller cursed under his breath. He was hot. Why hadn't he rolled up his shirtsleeves before he left, and now he'd have to roll down the car window. He hated the blasted air blowing his hair this way and that.

His mind jumped to the landlord. Goddamn it if Henry Sayer hadn't turned into problem. A man knew these things about another man. The way he'd examined Miller when they came back from picking up Mary, his tone of voice when he'd said Phil's name. He'd noticed it months ago, the way Sayer had glanced, more than a few times, at the door of Phil's cottage when he was painting the fence. Protective and curious, jealous even, like he was considering knocking on the door to see if she was safe. The toys for Teddy and the bed for Mary. A worried and thoughtful man was a man halfway in love. And then, there was Phil. It was easy to see how she cared about him from the way her eyes softened when she talked about him. Yet today, she'd said he bored her. Was that true? Could he trust her? It didn't matter. What mattered is that he could make her his wife, give her a legitimate life. He must make it so that the Henry Sayers of the world held no power. A white dress and a wedding. A fancy house and servants. Nannies and private schools. These were the things that would keep Phil happy. There was no choice.

He cursed again, thinking of Sayer. He should have vetted the landlord before agreeing to put Phil there. He'd assumed Sayer was an old man, no threat at all. He was, though, despite his missing arm. He was young and handsome and a blasted war hero. A secluded cottage was supposed to keep her away from other men, especially ones like Sayer. The streets of San Francisco were full of eligible men back from the war in droves, all considered heroes with their medals and their stories of courage. Who knew what went on over there anyway? A man wasn't going to confess to a woman what it was truly like, or what he did in the dark when fear and doubt were like metal in his mouth.

Before he left Phil's cottage, Miller had called his attorney, a recommendation from Timmy years ago. Robert Sizemore had access to information he shouldn't. Miller didn't ask how. What Robert discovered did not please him. Henry Sayer was a rich man, sharing his father's substantial fortune with a twin sister. Land, passed down generations from early settlers, all along the coastline, not to mention buildings on entire city blocks in both San Francisco and Los Angeles. The one commodity that continued to grow, especially now the war was over and the need for military equipment had lessoned. Land in California? This was to be coveted. Therefore, it was unlikely Sayer could be bought off, coerced to leave by the enticement of a large check. Plus, he wasn't the sort of fellow to be persuaded by money. A man who made furniture with his one fucking arm when he could easily live off his father's fortune was not the type of man persuaded to do anything because of money.

Sayer took care of the woman he loved. This they had in common. Sayer also had the means to do so. And, Henry Sayer had no wife or family to get in the way of what he wanted. He was free. Miller was not.

He needed the means to take care of Phil once he was free. A life insurance policy on Caroline was the only answer. Edmund Bennett might throw him out on the street once Caroline was gone. He had to ensure his future was secure. For Phil. He had to do it for Phil.

Yes. Full circle. He always came back to the place he'd started. Caroline had to die. Henry Sayer had to die.

He met Timmy at his bar, leaving his car on the street. The neighborhood was dark, even in the middle of a summer afternoon, like an invisible veil hovered over the narrow streets. Timmy owned the building, using the bottom for a bar, the top for his living space, and conducted business in the back, away from other customers.

He was at his usual table in the back when Miller entered. Cigarette smoke hovered near the ceiling and mingled with the smell of stale beer. A half-dozen men sat at the bar, slouched over their drinks. Miller kept his gaze from them, not wanting any trouble. They were mean drunks, Timmy told him last time he was here. Regulars, always looking for a fight.

Timmy stood when he saw Miller, holding out his arms. They embraced, and he caught the scent of bourbon and hair oil. Barrel-chested, with thick black hair and pock marks on his cheeks, the man before him bore no resemblance to the boy from the orphanage, other than his ice blue eyes.

"Good to see you. What're you drinking?" asked Timmy.

"Whiskey. Up. And a beer." He needed a stiff drink to steady his nerves.

Timmy called out to the bartender, then gestured toward a chair. "Sit. Tell me what you need."

Miller glanced behind him and to the side. They appeared to be out of hearing distance from any of the drunks at the bar. "I have some trouble."

"Yeah?"

"It's my wife." He hesitated, looking over his shoulder and lowering his voice. How to say it? "I love someone else. I want to start a new life. But you know, I married her for her money."

"Yeah, I remember. The wedding her folks threw her...holy crap. I'd never seen a house like that one before. I remember thinking, my man Miller got it good from now on." He touched a hand to his heart. "I was touched you got me an invite."

"Well, heck yeah, we were practically like brothers."

The bartender came with their drinks. Miller downed the entire two fingers of whiskey, feeling it burn the back of his throat before warmth spread through his chest. His hands were shaking. He needed to get control of himself. Timmy wouldn't take kindly to cowardice. When they were kids, Miller was the boss of their little orphanage gang because he was smarter than the rest of them. They relied on him for answers. But now? Timmy lived a kind of life Miller couldn't fathom, with ties to the seedy underbelly of San Francisco.

Timmy took a cigarette from the package next to his whiskey, then offered one to Miller. He took it and leaned forward for Timmy to light the end for him, then inhaled deep into his chest.

"You need her taken care of?" Timmy lit his own cigarette.

"I need it to look like an accident."

Timmy looked at him with those ice blue eyes, blowing smoke rings. "Obviously."

"I don't want her to suffer."

"We'll make sure she doesn't." He sipped his drink. "You sure this is what you want to do?"

The condensation from his beer had made a ring on the table. There were others, too. Hundreds of them all over the table. How many people had sat here over the years? Had they all been here to see Timmy? To have a problem erased? He swiped his finger down the glass, then placed it on his forehead. "You ever feel like we never had a chance? You know, like no one ever gave a shit about us. We figured we'd take the best we could get."

"No one did give a shit about us." Timmy laughed and picked up his cigarette, waving it like a conductor with his baton. "I got this bar by the skin of my teeth. Just like you, man. We're scrappy. No silver spoons in our fucking mouths, you know. We gotta make things happen for ourselves because no one else will."

"See, that's what I've been thinking, too. Why shouldn't I get what I want? It's not like the Bennetts with everything handed to them, right?" Like he did when he spent time with Timmy, he slipped back into the way he used to talk. The drink gave him a new sense of boldness. "I ever tell you how I came up with the plan to marry fat Caroline?"

"No, I don't believe so." Timmy waved to the bartender for another round. "I always figured it was a happy coincidence you ran into her down there at the soda shop. You're handsome, you bastard. It didn't surprise me you got her to fall in love with you."

The bartender delivered another couple whiskeys to the table. Miller, enjoying himself now, drank from it with a greedy thirst. "I had a plan for a long time. You remember how we always used to get those Christmas presents from Santa."

"Sure, yeah. We used to write letters every year, right?"

"That's right. Well, it turns out it was the Bennetts. They were Santa. The year I was twelve, which would've made you ten, I was awake when they delivered the presents on Christmas Eve. Caroline and her father, all dressed up in furs, delivering those gifts to us poor orphans. She was a fat thing. Looked like a white seal in her fur coat and hat. I stood up there on that railing and watched them, and it's hard to explain, but I hated the bastards. Then, later that year we were at the park, and I saw them again, and I thought to myself, I'm gonna make that girl mine, get that life for myself."

"You telling me you had a plan since you were twelve?"

"Yep, that's what I'm telling you. And I did it. Followed them in the newspaper, got a job where I knew I'd see her, then turned on the old Miller charm. She was still fat when I caught up to her. Then she went off to some camp or something and came back skinny. I thought I might lose her then to one of her rich cronies on the account I was figuring on her being fat, you know, so she'd feel like she couldn't get anyone else. But damn if she didn't fall in love with me. Seriously, it was easy. Even her folks, which I figured would be only too happy to get rid of me, were fine. It was like they all thought she was still fat."

"You always did have a way with the ladies. Even the nuns, when they weren't beating the crap out of you with one of those rulers." Timmy laughed, stubbing out his cigarette.

"Sister Theresa always had it out for me. One time she looked me straight in the eye and said she saw the devil." He chuckled, taking the last drag of his cigarette. "She was the meanest woman alive."

"Yeah, one time she left me in that hallway closet all night long. I was only six." Timmy shivered. "Can't stand small spaces to this day."

"I was in there more than once. It was usually my big mouth got me in trouble. One time I dared question the existence of God. I thought Sister Theresa's head was going to spin around and fly off her body. What did you do to get in there?"

"Stole an extra breakfast roll one morning." Timmy patted his stomach. "I was a hungry kid, what can I say? They didn't feed us enough to keep even the little girls from feeling half-starved." He paused to take a sip of his drink. "I never did anything ever again to get that punishment. Still have nightmares over it."

Miller didn't say anything for a moment, before looking up at his old friend. "Yeah, so the way I figure it, life owes us whatever we want now. The world rejected us. We don't have to play by the rules." He swirled the whiskey around his glass. "You know you're the only person I ever tell the truth to? The rest of the time I'm an actor. I could be in the movies. I'm that good."

"We gotta do what we gotta do," said Timmy. "Can't blame you for that. You were always the smartest kid around, always figuring out how to get away with shit before the rest of us could get the fuzz out of our navels."

"Nah, that's you." Miller waved his hand to indicate the bar. "Look what you've done here. You made a life for yourself."

"I live well. I do."

Miller, feeling a little tight, watched a fly scoot along the window. "You sure you can make it look like an accident?"

"It's not a problem. My man does this kind of thing all the time. You'd be surprised how many people have someone in their life they want dead."

"That right?"

"Yeah. Tell me, is there anything she does every day? Anything we could count on that's a habit or something."

"Almost every day she takes a walk along the coastline by her parents' beach house at nine in the morning. It's above the water, you know, like a cliff. She walks to this one point that kind of juts out and always stops there to look at the view before she heads back. There are tall grasses that someone could crouch in and be hidden. One shove and she'd be over the edge. It's rocky. No one could survive it."

"Good." Timmy tapped the ashtray. The fiery tip fell and turned to ash. "We'll make it look like she slipped and fell. You want us to do it soon?"

"Yeah. Next day or two would be best. I'll pay whatever."

"He'll want cash," said Timmy. "A thousand bucks."

"Yeah, fine. I got another problem, too. His name's Henry Sayer." He explained the situation to Timmy. "He's only got one arm. Easy target. You think your guy could make it look like an accident? I don't know Sayer's habits or whatnot, but he has a shop in town there."

"My man can figure out the best way," said Timmy. "When do you want it done?"

"A day or two after Caroline."

"You got it."

27

CAROLINE

She spent half the night crying, silent sobs so as not to wake the children or her parents, until she fell into a dreamless sleep as dawn broke. It was after eight when she wakened to the familiar nausea, fled to the toilet, and vomited. Afterward, she ran a bath, as hot as she could stand it, and crawled into the water, wrapping her arms around bent knees, and sobbed. The same questions came, again and again. How could Miller have done this to her, to the children? And this girl? Who was she? What right had she to take a woman's husband? The children? Were they his? How long had this been going on? After thirty minutes, shivering, she got out of the bath. The pain was worse than any physical pain. One moment she wanted to scream and break something, the next she was crying again and thinking, *no it cannot be true*. Just as soon as that idea came, she moved to the next. Seb hadn't imagined this. He was a smart boy. Her husband had a mistress and a pregnant wife. She hated him.

At her vanity, she stared at her reflection, thinking she looked a hundred years old. Puffy eyes. Blotched skin. Tangled hair. She fixed her hair and tried to even out her face with foundation and lipstick, adding blush, but it all made her look ghoulish. She must stop crying and find Father and Mother. Seb was right. They could help her sort it all out. She needed a plan. Her parents would know what to do. They always did.

Father was in the dining room lingering over coffee and the newspaper. As soon as she entered, he set it aside, an expression of concern on his face. "Sweetheart, you look exhausted."

She sat opposite him, and touched the raw areas under her eyes with the tips of her fingers, fighting tears. "I didn't sleep much."

"Poor girl," he said.

"Where are the children?" she asked.

"Frederick took them into town for some shopping and lunch. Your mother said you needed some peace this morning."

Mother came into the dining room, a stack of mail in her hands. "Oh, darling, you're up. Are you feeling any better?" She sat at the table next to Caroline, setting aside the letters. "Did you sleep?"

"Not much." She put her face in her hands and took in a deep breath before looking at them both in turn. "I've something to discuss with you." She choked and started to cry.

"What the hell has happened? Is it one of the children? Are they ill?" asked Father.

"You're scaring us." Mother sat at the table.

Father looked younger since his retirement. Tall and athletic, his skin tanned from the California sun, he was as handsome as he'd ever been. What she was about to say would break his heart. She knew it, and yet, it had to be done.

"It's Miller," said Caroline.

Father's eyes, sharp, fixed upon her. "What about him?"

Mother, at the same time in a high-pitched, frightened voice said, "Miller?"

Speaking succinctly, she managed to keep from crying as she told her parents what Seb had seen, finishing as Margaret entered with a bowl of breakfast rolls. She took one look at Caroline and immediately started making her a cup of tea. "Here you are, Miss Caroline. This'll settle your stomach."

Caroline saw Margaret and Mother exchange glances and knew that Margaret had heard the majority of her story. The sympathy on her face was almost too much to bear. "Try a roll, too."

"Thank you, Margaret," said Caroline.

Margaret excused herself and left the room. No one spoke for a moment. Caroline took a sip of tea.

"I need to know if it's true," said Caroline.

"Yes, we need to know if it's true." Father rolled the newspaper into a cylinder, then smacked it against the side of the table. "But it can't be. Not Miller. He's been very loyal to this family. To you."

"How do you know he's been loyal to Caroline?" asked Mother. "Men cheat on their wives all the time. Why should he be any different?"

"I don't know," said Father.

"I think it's true." The tears started, stinging the raw area under eyes. "He's been more distant than usual. One time I suspected I smelled perfume on his jacket. I dismissed it all, pretended like I was imagining things. But a woman knows, I think. I know he's with her right now. It's not work that has him away from us."

"That bastard," said Mother. "That goddamn bastard."

Both Caroline and her father looked at Mother in shock. Caroline couldn't remember ever hearing her mother curse.

"I'll hire someone. A private detective. Have him followed," said Father. "Whatever it takes."

"I don't think that's necessary. If anyone knows the truth, it's Joseph. He drives him everywhere. He'll know." She sipped from her coffee, then set it aside when her stomach turned. "I spent all night thinking about this. If there's another woman— it's not a fling. It's an obsession, like everything is with him. If there *is* someone, he loves her, which means he has her somewhere. An apartment or something. We need Joseph to tell us where he's stashed her."

"It's not like Joseph to betray a confidence. He's loyal to Miller," said Father.

"Everyone has a price. You taught me that, Daddy."

Father grimaced. "Right."

"Seb said a little boy and a girl about Audrey's age were with them." She broke down once again, sobbing into her hands, until she felt her father's arm around her shoulders.

"My darling girl," said Father

Wiping under eyes, she took in a deep breath. "They might be his children."

"How old was the little boy?" Mother, having risen, paced back and forth in front of the bay window. Pink roses pressed against the glass, like peering faces.

"Seb guessed two or three," said Caroline.

Father's reading glasses had slipped down to the end of his nose. He took them off, dangling them in one hand and rubbing his eyes with the other. "Another entire family? It cannot be."

"It's entirely possible. He's gone so much," said Caroline.

Mother faced the window, her shoulders hunched. "He's charming and handsome and intelligent. He always says the right thing at the right time." She turned to them. "He's been gracious about the successor decision, but every once in a while, when he thinks no one's observing him, I catch a glimmer of something else. Something almost sinister."

"Mother? What do you mean?" asked Caroline.

"It bothers me, as you two know, that he chooses to spend most of his time away from his family. The children understand he has no interest in them, but that's not unusual. There are many fathers like him. Perhaps more like him than like Edmund. Beyond that, though, there's this sense I have sometimes that he's playing a part."

"Mother, what're you saying? That you think he married me for the money? That he never loved me?" The pain was unbearable. She got up from the table, wringing her hands, wanting to throw the china against the wall. All of it, every piece.

Mother was beside her, taking her into her arms. Caroline crumpled into them, sobbing into her shoulder. "My whole life's been a lie."

"You have the children. And us, my love. We will be here no matter what happens next." Mother led her over the settee by the window. "Sit for a moment."

Caroline obeyed. Mother sat next to her, and Father came to sit on the other side. They each took one of her hands. "It's going to be all right," said Father. "We'll find a new path."

"What should I do, Daddy?"

"Divorce him," he said. "You're protected financially. I made sure of that when you married him. Everything is mine. The house you live in. The cars. If he's not married to you, these will no longer be available to him. But first, I'll call your house in the city and see if I can get Joseph on the phone."

After her father left them alone, Mother turned to her. "What can I do?" she asked.

"There's nothing to be done for me. We have to think of the children first and foremost. There's Seb. He's beside himself. And the other two will be confused and hurt. He's their father no matter what he's done to me," said Caroline.

"What he's done to you is what he's done to them," said Mother. "Don't you ever doubt that for a minute. He chose this woman over his family."

"He may have another family, Mother. I have to prepare myself for that."

"He won't ever see this one again, I can assure you," said Mother. "It'll be over my dead body if he ever sets foot in our home again."

Caroline rose from the settee and turned to look at the view. "Mother, I could kill him."

"I understand, dearest, but there's no reason to go to prison over this piece of trash."

An hour later, Father joined her in the sitting room. He came to stand next to her chair, his expression grave.

"Just say it."

"You were right. He has her stashed somewhere. A beach cottage about seventy-five miles down the coast from the city. Stowaway. I was there once, years ago. Small town."

"What does Joseph know about her?"

"She's twenty years old. Used to work at one of the factories as a seamstress. She has a little boy, but he's not Miller's."

"How does he know?"

"She came with him. Born out of wedlock, he's assuming, although Miller hasn't said anything to him about their relationship or her. Joseph drives her places. Brings her supplies." He withdrew a slip of paper from his shirt pocket. "He gave me the address."

"What about the girl Audrey's age?" asked Caroline.

"It's her younger sister. Just arrived from the Midwest. Their parents were killed in an accident."

"How much did it cost you to get the truth out of him?" she asked.

"Not a thing. And he quit. Said he's leaving and won't be back," he said. "He told me to convey how sorry he is for his part in Miller's secret."

She'd held out hope that Seb had misconstrued something, that their family was what she believed it was. She couldn't deny it any longer. The truth was clear. He loved someone else. He had her stashed at the seaside. "Twenty years old? She's practically Seb's age."

"I'm sorry, sweetheart." He sat in the chair across from her, his arms dangling between his legs. Never had she seen him at a loss. It occurred to her that this was not only a betrayal to her but to all of them, most especially her father, who had given Miller opportunity. "I'll call Ernie. Get the divorce proceedings started.

In the meantime, I'll hire someone to go out there, take some pictures of the two of them together. We can prove adultery. I'll ruin the son of a bitch."

"What do I say to the children?" she asked.

"The truth. It'll come out eventually."

"They'll never want to see him again," said Caroline.

"Good, because I have every intention of making sure they never do."

"Is that the right thing?" she asked. "For them, not us?"

"I believe it is, but you're their mother. You should decide, not me," said Father. "Either way, we don't have to make any rash decisions, I suppose. I need to keep myself in check, which feels impossible."

"I know, Daddy. I know."

―――――

The next morning, Caroline woke minutes before sunrise with one idea. *I must see this girl for myself and force her to look me in the eye.* She dressed in the silence of the house, and fussed with her hair, arranging every curl, then squirted hairspray around her head to ensure no slippage. Mascara and rouge and lipstick, all applied with care. She left a note on the dining room table for her father, telling him that she would be gone for the day but would be home in time for dinner. Knowing it would worry her parents, she added that she was simply taking a drive to clear her head, that she needed a little time alone. She took a carton of crackers from the kitchen. Then, she went out to the garage, got into her car, spread the state of California map on the passenger seat, and took in several deep breaths before starting the engine.

Minutes later, she was on the highway. The Pacific, encased in fog, was invisible as the sun came up in dancing beams through the firs. It was an hour before the fog cleared and suddenly the ocean appeared in endless blue as she wove along the curves of the coast. She stopped once, to vomit into a bush on the side of the road, then got back in the car, eating crackers to sooth the nausea, the crumbs cascading down her dress and onto the floor. Miller didn't allow food in the car. The children were not allowed to speak in the car. She must wear a scarf over her hair, even though he refused to open the windows unless he deemed it too hot to bear. For years she'd abided by his rules, all his idiosyncrasies and controlling ways, but no more. *I will eat crackers in the car whenever I want.* And later, when it grew warm, she would roll down the windows and let the wind blow through her hair and remember what it felt like before he was in her life; when it was the three of them driving to the beach, and she was in the backseat behind her father, and she put her face close to the door and let the wind fill her with the possibilities of her life. Who was she, then? That girl before Miller? Was she in there somewhere, still, screaming to get out? Shouting to her. *Roll the window down! Roll it all the way down!*

She had not let herself think much about Julius's confession. Put it aside for now, she had told herself. Julius was something separate. He was her oldest friend. He remembered the girl she was. He'd been there for all of it, the before and after. Did she love him? Yes. She did. She always had. But in the same ways he did? She wasn't sure. Her feelings were in such turmoil that it was impossible to decipher the truth. All these years she'd loved her husband for better or worse and that was all she'd had room for in her heart. Her hands gripped the steering wheel, as she slowed to take a curve. Julius was her childhood. She'd been a happy child, perhaps over-indulged, spoiled, by both her parents and Julius. They'd loved her so well. It had never occurred to her that the man she married would not treat her as they had.

Again, she dismissed reflecting upon Julius, concentrating instead on where she was headed. With the map, she found Stowaway without trouble, stopping in town to ask directions out to the cottage. The attendant took off his hat, wiping his brow. "Sure, that's Henry's place. You renting the other cottage?"

"Are there two?" she asked.

"Sure. He lives in one, rents out the other to summer vacationers and such."

"I'm fairly certain he already has a tenant."

"That right?" The man stuck his hat back on his head. "If he does, they must not drive or they would've come through here for gas."

The girl didn't drive. Another fact in a growing list.

It was noon. Hunger mixed with nausea, and Caroline succumbed to the idea that she must find something to eat before she went to the cottage. At the town diner, she ordered a grilled cheese sandwich and sat by the window. Outside, surfers walked by carrying surfboards. Teenagers dressed in shorts and bathing suits and families with picnic baskets strolled past, all headed for the beach at the end of town.

When she finished, she left cash for the bill and got back in the car, following the directions the attendant had given her. It was when she was turning into the long dirt driveway, the two cottages waiting prettily by the sea, that it occurred to her she had no plan. Would she knock on the door and introduce herself? Or, would she wait in the car until the woman—the girl —came out and pretend to be lost? No matter how it unfolded, she wanted to see her, to know for herself what a woman who would do this to another woman looked and sounded like. Caroline would look her in the eyes and tell her that her family was ruined. She wanted her to admit what she had done and to see that pain she'd inflicted.

The cottages were twins, both white with blue shutters and flowers in window boxes. They shared a lush, green lawn. Behind the houses, she caught a glimpse of a white fence. She let the car idle for a moment. Which cottage? Right or left? Henry lived in one, the attendant had said. But which one? She looked in the mirror. Lipstick intact. She'd managed not to cry all day. Anger was her friend. She turned off the car and got out, her high-heeled shoes sinking into the soft ground. The phrase *house of sand* went through her mind.

She knocked on the door to her right. A young man, handsome, with hair the color of butter, opened the door. "Oh my God. Henry?"

"Caroline?" His face lit up in a wide smile. "What on earth are you doing here?"

She burst into tears.

"What is it? Come in. Come inside." He gave her his handkerchief then took her hand, leading her into a pleasant sitting room.

Wiping her eyes, she sat on the couch. He fetched her a glass of water, then sat next to her. "What's happened? Why are you here?"

"My husband's having an affair with your tenant." Her voice sounded cold, angry. She hardly recognized herself.

Henry's face went from concerned to shocked. "Miller Dreeser's your husband? But your last name's Bennett."

"That was my maiden name. I think you called me that and I didn't bother to correct you. It didn't seem important at the time."

Henry buried his face in his hands. "How did you find out?"

"My son saw them together in the city. My *fifteen-year-old* son saw them in a restaurant. Then, my father did a little investigating," she said. "Discovered her whereabouts. Thus, my arrival here this afternoon." She took a sip from her water glass to quench her dry mouth. Windows, open wide, let in the scent of the sea. How could Henry be the landlord? It was all too awful. She crossed her legs, setting the half-empty drink onto the side table, using the coaster he'd provided. The condensation had made a ring on the coaster.

"What have you come to do?" he asked.

She intended to give him a righteous response. *Confront the whore who's wrecked my family,* or something of that nature—not that she'd ever used the word *whore* before in her life. Until yesterday, she hadn't known it was in her consciousness deeply enough to be uttered from her mouth. Instead, she said, "I don't know." Her bottom lip trembled, and she bit the inside of her mouth to distract herself with physical pain. "I don't know why I've come except to say that I wanted to see her, wanted to hear her voice, wanted to see the girl my husband loves. I've only discovered all this. Just yesterday, in fact. I'm pregnant and not feeling well, not feeling myself, which might explain why I've driven here with no plan. I've never had anything like this happen to me before. I've lived a blessed life, sheltered, I suppose you could say. Up until now." Hot tears leaked from the corners of her eyes and she tried to catch them with her fingertips. "I'm devastated. I never knew what that word meant until now. It feels like a tsunami came and wiped everything out inside me. I've been married to Miller for all my adult life, and although it's been a hard marriage because of his...because of his ways, I was committed always, to our family, to him. I built my life around him. And now, to find out that he easily threw it away, easily lied to me, well, it's left me upended."

Henry nodded without comment. She wiped her eyes and blew her nose in the handkerchief. Outside, the waves crashed. She had not heard them before now; the buzzing between her ears had drowned them out. "I'm sorry, Henry. You must forgive me. This whole sordid thing is embarrassing enough without me adding to it with my tirade." She tried to smile, but the tears came instead. She wiped her cheeks.

"No need to apologize, Caroline. I'm very sorry for everything."

"What's she like?"

"She a young woman in a difficult situation and has made decisions that, unfortunately, have hurt you. Would it help you to know she doesn't love him?"

"What could possibly make a woman take up with another woman's husband if it isn't love?"

"She has no family, and a baby out of wedlock. The baby's

father died in the war. She was seventeen when her son was born. Her parents had kicked her out of the house. Your husband gave her a way to ensure the little boy's well-being."

Caroline's heart beat so loudly that she could, once again, no longer hear the waves. A child. A man who died in the war, leaving a pregnant sweetheart at home. An innocent little boy who needed shelter and a home, which Miller provided. The woman was a prostitute for her child. Wouldn't she do the same if she were in the same circumstances? Most mothers would. "I've spent the last few days imagining this woman, this girl, who must be utterly in love with Miller, desperate for the small amount of time she's allotted."

"That's not how it is," said Henry.

"That's how it was for me. For the last seventeen years I've loved him very much, always yearning for one more moment with him. From the time I first met him when I was twenty years old it's been that way. And yet, he loves this girl who doesn't love him."

"Why do you say he loves her?" asked Henry.

"Because he would never risk money and esteem for a woman unless he loved her. Which makes the only conclusion that he surely doesn't love me and perhaps never did. My God, when I think how I've wasted my youth on him. And I'm having another baby. Can you believe it? Just a few days ago I believed my life was perfect and now I'm in a nightmare." She blew her nose. Vulgar to do in front of a man, but she didn't care. Not today when her world had fallen apart. "I want to see her."

"Are you sure? Perhaps it would be better to confront Miller."

"Yes, I'm sure." She stood and held out her hand. "Thank you for the water."

He jumped to his feet. "Do you want me to go with you?"

She shook her head. "No, Henry, it's not your concern. But thank you. I'm sorry it's not under better circumstances that I see you once again."

Phil Rains answered the door. Dressed in dungarees and a sleeveless shirt, she wore a scarf over rag curlers and no makeup. Despite her dowdy attire, she was beautiful and young. What man wouldn't want her? A knife sliced into Caroline's ribcage as an image of Miller in bed with this girl, this child, flooded her sight. How could he have done this? She'd been married to a stranger for seventeen years. Her life was a lie. She touched her face with her fingertips. The crow's feet that etched her tender skin were like the lines on the map she had just read. She was old, used up, and mean—violent even. Her hands quivered at her sides, itching to do damage to something. Never in her life had she felt this way. *A jealous rage.* Where had she heard that phrase before?

Caroline held out her hand. "I'm Mrs. Dreeser."

Phil Rains went pale and grabbed the door with white knuckles.

"Would you like to come in?" The girl's voice shook.

"Yes, please."

Phil opened the door wider and Caroline walked inside the cottage. It was indeed the twin to Henry's, although not decorated with the care of the other. A temporary home. A cottage by the sea. Meant for week rentals, not a permanent place to stash one's mistress.

They went into the sitting room. "Please, sit," said Phil. "Would you care for something to drink?"

"No, I've had water with Henry. I knocked on the wrong cottage door." She sat, crossing her legs. Soon her stomach would be too big to cross her legs. She would be able to prop a book on it like she had with the other three. "I know Henry, as it turns out. We have a mutual friend. It's a small world."

The girl's bottom lip quivered. She took in a long, shaky breath before speaking. "Mrs. Dreeser, what can I do for you?"

Caroline looked out the window, her heart no longer pounding. On the contrary, she wondered if she had a heartbeat at all. Was she here, speaking to her husband's mistress, or was she in a nightmare? No, she could not wake up from reality. This was her life, and she must find the strength to carry onward, with dignity. How would her mother behave? After the death of Caroline's grandmother, Mother had not cried at the funeral. She sat ramrod-straight at the church, her face betraying nothing, her long neck steady, hat placed exactly right. Later, in the privacy of their home, she had wept, but not in front of strangers. *Dignity, Caroline, is underrated.* How many times had she said that to her? More than she could count.

"I imagined what I might say to you during the drive up, but now that I'm here, I can think of nothing," said Caroline.

The girl folded her hands in her lap. "I have a son. Teddy. Every decision I've made is because of him. Miller offered me a way to keep him safe and fed. I-I had no choice."

"The only choice was being kept by another woman's husband?"

Phil Rains took such a long time to answer, Caroline wondered if she might not. Would Caroline have to carry forth with the conversation, throwing insults at her with her newly cruel tongue?

Finally, the girl spoke, her voice hushed. "I don't suppose it's possible to explain to someone like you what it's like to be hungry. To wonder if I would have a place for my child to sleep other than an alley. To wonder if the next day would be the day I could no longer feed him."

"Someone like me?"

"I mean no harm, but yes, a person like you. A rich person," said Phil. "When you're poor and alone, as I am, the difference between right and wrong is no longer as important as survival."

Caroline sat with that for a moment. The girl was correct. She had never had to worry over anything. Her entire life had been one of privilege, of love. Every morning she woke to breakfast muffins and pastries piled high on a platter. Mother always sent copious leftovers home with the staff. Jams and butter and eggs cooked however they wished. At night she went to bed under soft blankets. She could afford to ponder moral dilemmas.

"What you say is true, Miss Rains. I have been fortunate. I've also spent most of my adult life giving to others, whether it's to my children and husband or the charities that I work for. Whether you believe it or not, I have seen poverty up close."

"Up close?" The girl had the audacity to sound sarcastic.

"How dare you. You have no idea how I've spent my life," said Caroline.

"And you have no idea how I've spent mine."

"I've certainly not spent mine sleeping with someone else's husband."

The girl's eyes filled with tears. "Mrs. Dreeser, I've suffered great pangs of guilt, but the need to take care of my son has outweighed them in the end. I'm not asking for sympathy, or even forgiveness, but can you understand, at least, how I have ended up in this circumstance?"

"I'm going to have another baby," said Caroline. "Can you understand my circumstance?"

Phil's eyes widened. "Another?"

"We have three children. Did you know that?"

"Miller doesn't talk about his family. But, yes, I knew from when I worked at the factory. The girls talked. Gossiped."

"He doesn't talk about us?" She tried to breathe steadily, but it was like she was walking up a steep hill.

Phil shook her head. "I believe he wants to keep us all separate, the way men do. Every part of their lives on distinct shelves."

"How do you know what men do? You're practically a child." Caroline's voice was raspy and mean. For the second time that day, she didn't recognize herself.

Phil blushed and looked at her hands. "I loved a man once. Eddie."

"Your son's father?" asked Caroline.

"Yes. He segregated parts of his life. There was me, his family, the farm, and finally, the war. I was one part of his life, whereas for me, there wasn't a part he didn't touch. He was the past, the future, the present—in every memory, every plan for my life. He made the decision to leave for the war without consulting me—simply announced it. I would never have decided something like that without him. Women are more like messy drawers, I suppose."

"Mine certainly feels messy right now. How did you know this about Eddie? How he compartmentalized?" She let go of her anger for a moment, genuinely curious. Had the young man expressed an idea that complex? Was this young woman more insightful than she when it came to men? Was this part of her allure?

"I don't know. I just did. We'd known one another all our lives," said Phil.

Like Julius and me. Ten years old, he scraped in the sand with a skinny piece of driftwood: *Julius loves Caroline*. Salt water in his hair, he'd stood next to his declaration, pointing with the stick, grinning at her. Why had she not remembered that until now?

The girl continued talking. Caroline had the feeling it was unusual, that before her sat a quiet person, contemplative, and sad. Yes, this was a sad girl. And Miller had swooped in, taking advantage of her numerous vulnerabilities and claimed her for his own.

"Our fathers had neighboring farms in Iowa. We were going to be married when he came home from the war, but he never did. He was killed somewhere in France. I remember thinking when they told me, *France, of all places*? We figured we'd never leave Iowa. But fighting in the war, it was like an itch that couldn't be scratched. After my brother was killed, Eddie couldn't rest until he was enlisted, even though he had to lie about his age. I let him have what he wanted before he left, knowing he might not come back, and never thinking a baby would come of it. I was naïve, Mrs. Dreeser, and that's the part I'm most ashamed of. Anyway, he died before I could tell him. I had to face my parents alone. I knew they would ask me to leave. I was already packed and prepared to say good-bye to my little sister, who I loved more than anyone in the world except for Eddie, and now, unquestionably, Teddy." Phil fell silent, folding and unfolding her hands in her lap. "I suppose I'm telling you this as a way to make an excuse for what's happened." She fidgeted in her chair, a splotch of red marring her perfect complexion above her neckline. "My mother, even before I told her I was having a baby, hated me. I don't know why exactly, but she does. Or, did. She's dead now. And now my sister's here with me and I'm responsible for her. I'm sorry." A sob stopped her confession.

Confessing to the person you've harmed instead of a priest? Does that allow some relief from guilt? Pity came swooping in, dismantling some of the anger for a moment. This poor girl. Her mother was to blame, sending a child out on the streets. And Miller? What punishment was good enough for him?

Caroline brushed imaginary specks from the front of her dress. Her anger should not be at this girl, but rather, at her husband. This would be the more rational reaction. Phil Rains wasn't some floozy off the street. She was a girl in trouble. Her little Audrey, if not for the grace of God, could be in this position. This was a sister, a daughter, a mother. And yet, the rage and jealousy were too large for rational thought. It had eaten her insides, taken over, so that she was merely a red ball of anger. This girl slept with her husband, while she, Caroline, raised his children without him.

"How long has this been going on?" asked Caroline. She held her breath waiting for the answer, even though she already knew the details. It was like poking a bruise. The pain almost felt good.

"Since Teddy was born. I had no place to go that would be safe for him."

"He put you up here?"

"No. In the city," said Phil. "This was recent. At the beginning of the summer."

Three years. This had been going on for three years and she'd had no idea. What kind of fool was she? How could she not have known? Why hadn't she let herself see the signs? They were there. She was a fool. A spoiled, clueless fool. Naïve and indulged, with her head in the clouds, too cowardly to seek the truth. She had allowed this to happen. She had fostered Miller's secret with her gullibility.

Caroline stood, straightening the skirt of her dress. "I don't know why I chose to come here. I suppose I wanted to see you, prove to myself that you exist. There's not one part of this that I would've believed yesterday."

Phil stood as well. Just then, the sound of a screen door opening and closing penetrated the silence between them. "Mama." A little boy appeared, wearing short pants and no shirt, sand plastered to his bare legs. Behind him was a girl Audrey's age. They both looked like Phil. They stopped short when they saw Caroline.

The little boy crossed over to her and peered up at her with big brown eyes. "Hi."

"Hello." She couldn't get the anger out of her voice, even for this innocent child. He was not to blame, and yet, she could not soften.

"Mary, please take Teddy into the bedroom and get him cleaned up."

Mary nodded and took Teddy's hand. He dutifully followed.

"My sister. And Teddy," said Phil.

"They're beautiful." Innocent children who needed a solid home. Food and shelter. The tiniest shift toward empathy made its way into her heart.

"Mrs. Dreeser, what do you plan to do?"

"I plan on divorcing him for adultery as soon as possible. My father will fire him from his companies. And I'll take possession of the houses, as my father owns them. He can live happily ever after here with you." She waved her hand to indicate the space. "With what money, I don't know."

Phil's eyes shifted back and forth like she was frightened. "The money's all yours?"

"Yes, you're correct. It's my father's fortune. Miller has no money without me. That's why he hasn't left me to be with you, I feel quite certain."

"No, he would never leave you. He made that very clear to me." Her gaze darted upward and to the right. She was lying,

"You were content to remain his mistress? For how long?"

"For as long as it took," said Phil.

"For as long as what took?"

"Until I could figure out how to escape."

Caroline stared at her. "Escape? You want to escape?"

"More than anything."

"I have to go now. I have to be back with my family." With that, Caroline barreled toward the door and out of the house, not stopping to catch her breath until she was in the car and headed down the driveway.

Several hours later, she sat with her parents in her father's study, telling them every detail of her encounter with Phil Rains.

"Caroline, why would you put yourself through that?" asked Mother.

"I had to, Mother."

"She has nothing to do with us." Mother made a motion like she was wiping her hands. "We're done with the both of them."

"She was all alone with a tiny baby. I would do anything for my children. Who knows what I would've done in her situation. We sit here in our beautiful home and make judgments, but we don't know."

"The difference between right and wrong, villain and hero, is what you're prepared to do to get what you want," said Father.

"Well, we're not in her situation. We're in our situation, with three children who are going to have to learn a terrible truth about their father," said Mother.

"Is it right to take his children from him?" asked Caroline.

"He made his choice," said Mother. "He's never been a father. You've been both mother and father. Without Edmund, they'd have no father figure. You've made excuses for him since the day you married him."

"What was I supposed to do, Mother?"

"There was nothing *to* do," said Mother. "Without adultery, you would never have been granted a divorce." She went to the bar and poured a large sherry. "This could be a gift, Caroline. You'll be rid of him. He'll be out of our lives forever."

"The children love him," said Caroline. "The younger ones anyway. Is it right for them to see him penniless and forbidden contact with him?"

"Caroline, for once in your life, resist the temptation to make excuses for him. He's ruined your life," said Mother.

"Her life isn't ruined," said Father.

"No, no. I didn't mean that," said Mother. "I'm sorry, Caroline. I'm so angry." Mother poured another sherry and handed it to Father, then sipped from her own glass. Caroline had never seen her undone.

"I know, Mother." She held out her arms to embrace her mother. "I'm angry, too. Let's get this rolling. I want it done by Christmas."

Miller

He stopped at his office in the city to call Timmy before he headed south to his in-laws. "Why hasn't he done it?" he asked.

"She didn't take her walk. My man says he waited by that bench like you said, but she never came."

"That's impossible. You could set a clock by this walk of hers."

"Maybe something came up. He'll be there tomorrow," said Timmy.

Miller called his attorney next. "Yeah. It's me. What do you know about taking out a life insurance policy?"

The hour was nearing five in the afternoon when he arrived at the Bennetts' beach home. The sun hovered between sky and sea, as if undecided which way to go. A shiver ran down the back of his spine as he lit a cigarette and walked around to the seaward facing side of the house. The rolling lawn was scattered with lawn chairs and a croquet game that looked as if it had been suddenly abandoned. He walked to the edge of the lawn where it met the sand, sea breeze tousling his hair, and took deep drags from his cigarette, hoping for relief from this anxiety, this feeling that Henry Sayer was at this moment knocking on Phil's cottage door. Ridiculous Caroline, weak and needy. He should have gone to the cottage and kept an eye on Phil, but he must make sure Caroline took her walk in the morning.

The waves were large this evening, crashing against the sand. Seagulls screamed. The sea grasses sighed for him, rustling in the wind. He must go inside and pretend everything was fine, that he was happy to be there. *How I've missed you all.* He tossed the stub of his cigarette into the lawn, making sure it was dead before turning toward the house, and then leaned over to fetch the stub. Edmund hated cigarette stubs in his lawn.

He made his way across the grass. Seb sat on the porch with a book in his hands, staring at Miller. He raised a hand in greeting; Seb nodded in response.

When he reached Seb, the angry expression on his son's face caused another shiver to make its way down Miller's spine. What Seb could have to be angry about was beyond him. A life of privilege had spoiled him, made him soft like a woman. *He should come to work at one of the factories. Learn how to be thankful for what he had. At his age I was cleaning toilets and stacking wood at the orphanage.*

"Using the most of your time, I see," said Miller.

"How was work?"

Had he imagined a sarcastic tone and an emphasis on the word *work*? "Excellent. Thank you."

Seb looked down at the book in his lap, opening it to a page where he'd folded the corner into a triangle to mark his place.

"Are you in need of a bookmark?" This kid had no respect for property.

"Mother's in her bedroom, waiting for you." Seb met his gaze, unflinching. "Everyone else went into town for supper."

"What about family dinner?"

"Mother changed her mind," said Seb.

"You holding down the fort?"

"The fort?" asked Seb.

"Military term."

Seb stared up at him, his eyes glittering in the reflection of the sun. "The military? What would you know about the military? You didn't fight."

Miller raised his hand and brought it down hard on the side of Seb's head. He was pleased to hear the boy yelp in pain. "You want military? How about we send you to military school?"

The boy lifted his chin, eyes glassy with unshed tears. "Mother would never allow it."

"I'm the one in charge here, not your mother." What had gotten into him? He was never disrespectful like this. Miller knelt and put his face close to his son's, shoving his shoulders with the palms of his hands. "You'd best remember that."

Teeth gritted, Seb looked straight into his eyes. "I know exactly what you've done. You best remember that."

Miller rose to his feet, alarm bells sounding in his mind. He strode across the porch and yanked open the screen door. He needed to see Caroline.

The house was quiet and dim. Even the servants must have retired to their quarters. He fought a sense of foreboding as he walked down the hall to Caroline's bedroom. She sat in an armchair by the window, looking out at the view. Normally, she wore her hair loose about her shoulders in large waves, but this afternoon she had pulled it back with a pink scarf. He watched her, aware that she had not sensed his presence. A breeze lifted the soft curtains and brought the scent and the sounds of the outside world from which he'd come. She wore a simple cotton dress, loose at the waist, and no shoes. Her face, without makeup, looked pink and newly scrubbed. The collar of her dress appeared wet, as if she'd splashed her face with cold water not long before he entered the room. Her mother still kept basins and pitchers in every bedroom, in homage, she said, to a gentler time, and often had the maids fill them with cold water on warm days. Miller found it ridiculous.

As he tapped on the doorframe, he noticed how petite she looked in the oversized chair, her figure no different than an adolescent girl. The way she sat, with her hands clasped on her lap reminded him of their daughter, sitting politely in church. She turned to look at him, shifting from the window, facing him.

"Are you unwell?" he asked.

"I have something to ask you. If you lie to me, I will never speak to you again. I'll take your children from you. My father will ruin you."

His heart started beating harder. What did she know? "Jesus, Caroline. What's gotten into you?" He crossed the room, sitting on the ottoman next to the chair. He pulled his handkerchief out of his pocket and wiped the palms of his hands. "You know I couldn't lie to you."

"I assumed that was true. But now I know that was a lie I told myself."

"What is it?" Did she know about Phil? How was it possible? Joseph? No, the man was loyal to him, thankful for the extra cash he gave him to keep his secrets.

"Seb was in town with a friend two days ago. He saw you at the diner."

Seb had seen him? How was it possible? He folded his handkerchief into a neat square, all the corners matching. What could he say now that she would believe?

"The diner?"

"You had company," said Caroline.

"Oh, yes. Her. She's the wife of one of the men who works in the warehouse loading trucks—a man who's been with me for years now. He hadn't shown to work for several days. I sent my secretary to see if he was ill. Unfortunately, he'd been killed in a bar fight. She's all alone with two children now, so took them all for a meal and gave her the items from his locker, and several months' pay to get her through." This was a good story. One that would evoke immediate sympathy in Caroline. "I offered to pay for his funeral."

He expected that she would tear up in relief, open her arms and say what a good man he was to offer to pay the funeral expenses. Stupid Caroline would believe anything he told her.

"How many years was he with you?" Her face was set, hard and determined.

"I don't know. About five, I guess," he said.

"What's his name?"

"Henry Sayer." Damn if that wasn't the first name that came out of his mouth.

"Sayer? I don't remember you ever mentioning his name."

"Darling, I surely wouldn't bore you with the names of our workers," he said.

"What's his wife's name? I should call on her." Even with words he would expect to come from her, she appeared strange, her expression rigid and suspicious. The flush to her cheeks was bright pink, like a child with a fever.

"I simply called her Mrs. Sayer. I'm not certain of her first name." He smiled and dropped to the floor, kneeling at her feet. "What's the matter with you?"

She was seemingly unmoved. "Why was your arm around her?"

"I was comforting her. Jesus, Caroline, have a little compassion. A fifteen-year-old-boy, looking through a window, misunderstood what was happening."

"You're a liar."

"Enough!" He stood, shoving the ottoman against the wall with a backward kick. A vase fell from the table next to the easy chair and shattered on the hardwood floor. "This is ridiculous. I have half a mind to give Seb the beating he deserves until he learns to keep his mouth shut. There was no need to get you upset with this, especially given your condition."

She looked up at him, her tone steely. "You touch my son and you will pay. My father will make sure of that."

"I decide how to discipline my son, not your father."

"If you had been around enough to actually be his father, you could have had that privilege." Her voice was a fraction under a shout. "Now, I decide."

He stared at her. In all the years of their marriage, she had never raised her voice to him. Not once.

She took in a deep breath, as if to calm herself. "You had a secret, and now you don't. It didn't take much to figure out the truth. My father made a few phone calls and figured out exactly where you had her stashed. Right next door to Henry Sayer."

He gasped.

"Yes, that's right. I know the landlord. Henry Sayer. Lovely man and quite alive. He's a friend of Julius's from the war. He came to visit me years ago and built a beautiful hutch for us, which you would know about if you ever spent any time with us." She smiled as she rose to her feet, then leaned over, picking up the pieces of the broken vase. "This was my favorite vase. I always pick my mother's roses and bring them into my bedroom. When I'm here alone at night because you're in the city—working, yes, always working—I can put my nose into the petals and take in that sweet smell and think of you. I always remind myself how much you've sacrificed to make your way and how much I admire you for it. When I think of the excuses I've made for you to the kids and to myself, despite how lonely

I've been, and how you took my youth, it makes me feel actually murderous."

"You went to the cottage?" he asked.

"I did. After my chat with Mr. Sayer, I went next door to talk to your whore."

He flinched. "What would make you do such a thing? You're acting hysterical, you know that? You are." *Start talking,* he told himself. *Come up with something she will believe.*

"Do you love her?" she asked.

"She's no one to me. You're confused." Every word in staccato. *Shame her.* He fought rising panic. *Make her think she's crazy.* "You realize how insane you sound? Driving out to the cottages?"

"Stop. I know all your tricks. All the ways you have of making me feel like an idiot, like a spoiled child. No more. She was as Seb described her. Tall and dark. Beautiful. Young. So young, Miller."

"You're mistaken," said Miller.

"I want you out. Out of here. Out of our home in the city. I'm divorcing you. My father made sure nothing is in your name. I will not allow the children to see you ever again. You're finished."

"Caroline, don't be a little idiot."

Crossing over to the mirror, she picked up her hairbrush and fixed her hair, before turning back to him. "I understand, for the first time, what kind of man you are."

The serenity in her voice scared him more than it should. She was a different person. "What kind of man I am?" He shouted now, not caring if the servants heard him. "What kind of man I am? Stupid bitch. You sit in here smelling the damn roses while I work to make this life for you. What kind of man I am?" Near her now, he pushed into her neck with his index finger.

She shoved his hands away. "Don't touch me. You've done nothing to make my life good. This is my father's, not yours. He gave you a job for me. None of this is yours."

He grabbed the sides of her arms. "Shut your fucking mouth or you'll be sorry."

She went stiff, staring into his eyes. "There's nothing you can do to me ever again."

"You think?" He started shaking her. Behind them, the door flew open. Seb lunged into the room, holding a baseball bat above his head. Before he could comprehend what was happening, Seb smacked him in the lower back with the bat. Miller let out a monosyllabic moan and turned toward his son. "Give me the bat."

Seb, like a graceful dancer, side-stepped Miller and held the bat in front of him of like a sword. "Get out, or I'll do it again. Only this time it will be your head."

"You'll be sorry, Caroline." He kicked the door on his way out, and sprinted down the hallway toward the study. When he reached Edmund's study, he slipped inside, closing the door behind him. He picked up the phone and dialed Timmy's bar. The bartender put him through to Timmy.

"I know why she wasn't on her walk," he said into the phone. "The crazy bitch drove up to Phil's cottage."

"Oh, hell."

"Yeah. She knows everything. We need this done tomorrow morning. Whatever he has to do."

"But her family knows. You'll be out in the cold," said Timmy.

"Not with the life insurance policy I took out on her. I'll be set. Not Bennett money, but enough to take care of Phil. We'll leave town. Go somewhere they can't find us."

"Consider it done."

28

CAROLINE

After Miller left, Caroline sank into the chair. "Sweetheart, will you pour me a glass of water?"

Seb set the baseball bat in the corner of the room and poured from the pitcher on the dresser into a glass. "I've never been this tired in my life." She put her face in her hands. No tears came. Perhaps, for now, there were no more. She looked out the window. It would be another spectacular sunset. She wondered if anything would give her pleasure ever again. "The smell of the seashore is my favorite smell. Have I ever told you that?"

"Yes, Mother." He handed her the glass of water, then sat next to her on the ottoman. "We all know everything you like."

She brushed his bangs from his face. "I've never done anything better than make you children. No matter what, I have that."

"Mother, I called Julius."

"Why, sweetheart?"

"Father hit me. I was afraid for us to be alone with him. He's on his way here."

"He hit you?"

Seb's eyes clouded over as he traced the pattern in the carpet with his heel. "He's gone. He'll never be able to hurt us ever again."

"I'm sorry, darling," she said.

"None of this is your fault." His eyes were fixed on the floor, but she saw a shimmer of tears in his eyelashes.

Her breath caught in her throat. What had Miller called her? A little idiot. Emphasis on the word *little*. That's the way he'd made her feel all their marriage. A photograph of her, encased in a gold frame, stood by the water pitcher. She'd had it taken last Christmas for a gift for Miller. The black and white photo had been painted to make her cheeks and lips pink, and the diffused light in the photography studio had softened the hints of age. The picture did not tell the whole truth. She was no longer young. Her youth had been given to Miller. No amount of touching up would change that fact.

Miller was correct. She'd behaved like a little child all these years. Trusting him, putting him on a pedestal. She had participated in the lie, even abetted it with her complacency. How could she be surprised that he had a secret life when she hadn't demanded he participate in this one? She'd been an ostrich, with her head in the sand outside this window. Sunny Caroline, kind Caroline, understanding Caroline. She'd been apologizing for Miller's behavior for seventeen years. How many times had she made excuses for him to her mother and Julius? To herself, and most dreadfully, her children? If she had insisted that he be the husband and father her own father was, instead of being so damned grateful he married her, she would have seen the truth. She would have demanded more for her life, for her children's life. She *was* nothing more than a little idiot.

"It is, actually. I didn't care enough about myself and you children to see the truth when it was right in front of me."

He looked up at her, brushing tears from his cheeks. "Mother, we all love you very much."

She held out her arms. "And, I love you."

A knock on the door distracted them. Julius popped his head

inside the room. Seb crossed over to the door. "Uncle Julius, please come in." He looked back at her. "Mother, I'm going to ask Margaret to make some lemonade for you. Would you like that?"

"Yes, please. Thank you."

Her oldest son kissed her on the cheek. "I'll be in the sitting room, Mother, if you need me." He nodded to Julius and left the room.

Julius pulled the ottoman close and sat next to her. "What's happened?"

She looked at him, unable to speak.

"Caroline, please, what is it? Seb called in a panic."

"It's Miller."

"What about him?" A sharpness slipped into his voice.

"Something's happened. It's as bad as I could ever imagine."

Julius's mouth, sweet when he smiled, had become a straight line. A muscle on the side in his cheek twitched. "Another woman?"

"For years now. Three years." She told him, in stops and starts, how she had driven to Phil Rains's cottage. "I knocked on her door, Julius, like I was someone else, not me. Not me, who, last week, could not have imagined this could ever happen." After she told him all the details, including the unfortunate coincidence of Henry being Phil's landlord, she ended with the confrontation with Miller. "Seb hit him with a baseball bat." She covered her mouth, suddenly seized with nervous laughter, like in church when she was a little girl.

Laugher appeared to be the last thing on Julius's mind. His face had flushed pink while she told him her story. His voice shook as he seemed to bite out words. "A mistress, with a pregnant wife at home." That was all he seemed capable of for the moment. He stared at the wall and opened his mouth as if to say something else but seemed to decide against it as he rose from the ottoman and went to the window, pulling back the cotton curtain to peer out to the sea.

"If he's lied about this, I wonder what other lies he's told?" she asked. "He could come home to me and act as if he cared about me and our children, come to my bed, and yet all the time his heart was somewhere else. Who can do this? Who can lie this well for this long?" She wanted to stand, but was afraid her legs would not hold her. She pulled her knees to her torso like when she was a little girl. "Seb asked me yesterday if Miller could have falsified the records somehow, so that he didn't have to serve in the war."

Julius let the curtain drop from his fingers as he turned to her. "Fake his medical problems? That's impossible."

"Julius, with our kind of money, anything's possible. We can buy any lie we want to. I admit I was relieved he couldn't go. I'd already had to send you away and many of our friends were over there. So many didn't come back. I thought only, *my husband's safe from harm*. I wonder what that says about me? That I was only too happy to accept the easy way, even though it was a morally inferior decision to almost every other man I knew, including my father who fought in the first war and you who put your life on the line every day for injured and dying soldiers."

"Caroline, do you remember when we were little and helped your mother with the gifts for the orphans? Do you remember how their letters made you cry?"

"Yes. I remember."

"The girl you were, pure of heart, kind. That's the person you still are. What's happened here is not your fault. It's him, not you."

She stared at the window, watching the curtain flutter in the breeze. "I've been an idiot."

"Tomorrow is another day. The kids and your parents and me —we're all here for you. We always will be."

"I'm tired."

"Climb into bed. I'll sit here until you fall asleep." Julius pulled her to her feet and escorted her over to the bed. He pulled back the covers. "Hop in."

She allowed him to tuck the covers around her shoulders, staring up at his familiar face. "What will I tell the children?"

"The same thing my father told me when my mother left. 'This has nothing to do with you and everything to do with us. None of this is your fault.'"

"But you didn't believe him, did you? If you had, Julius, we would not be having this conversation."

"I have many regrets." He smiled, but looked so sad, she began to cry all over again. "But we have to make sure the children know this is not their fault. And your father and I will be here to take his place, as we've always done. That will matter to them in the long run. They won't feel unlovable like I did."

"Julius, you're the opposite of unlovable." She pulled one arm from the covers and reached for him. He covered her hand with his. "And tomorrow's another day."

"Yes, it is and I'll be in it, no matter what."

29

PHIL

She woke feeling like sandpaper lined her eyes, having cried herself to sleep. In the kitchen, she made coffee, then stood at the window, staring at her reflection, a sense of dread in the pit of her stomach. Mrs. Dreeser was divorcing Miller, leaving him penniless. This should have given her a way out, but she knew Miller, regardless of his fortune, he would never let her go. She was not safe. Something else was bothering her, too, a detail she couldn't work out. If Miller were to leave his wife, he would lose everything, which is why he'd always been clear that he would never be able to do so. The other day, however, he said he wanted to marry Phil. There was only one way that could happen. Caroline Dreeser had to die.

Her heart thudded. Was he planning on having his wife killed?

The children came into the kitchen. She made them french toast while Mary read to Teddy at the table. He listened to her with adoring eyes never veering from her face. After breakfast, Teddy jumped down from the table.

"Me find truck," he said.

After he left, Mary cleared the table and started to wash them at the sink. "Phil, who was the lady yesterday?"

"It was a woman. A woman who needed something from me."

"What did she need?"

"Nothing for you to be worried over. Just grown-up things."

"Is Mr. Dreeser your suitor?"

"Suitor?" Phil couldn't help but smile. "Where did you hear that word?"

"Just around, I guess."

"Mr. Dreeser's a friend."

"But you don't like him. You're afraid of him," said Mary. "I can tell."

"Mama!" Teddy was yelling to her from her bedroom. Alarmed, she ran out of the kitchen and down the hallway. Teddy was under her bed with just his feet showing.

She got on all fours. "Ducky, what're you doing?"

"Truck stuck."

His truck had lodged between the bed and the wooden box Miller had brought over. She reached in and moved the box and gave Teddy his truck. What was in that box? He'd said they were some books he wanted to keep safe. Why would he have kept them here? She sat on her heel, knowing, suddenly, there was something in that box that was important. She needed to see what.

She asked Mary to keep watch of Teddy as she bounded down the back steps and across the yard. She knocked on Henry's back door. A few seconds later, he opened the door. "Phil, is everything okay?"

"Mrs. Dreeser came."

"Yes, I know."

"She's going to divorce Miller and leave him penniless."

"Slow down, Phil. I can't understand you."

"When he left the other day he said something about how he wanted us to be together all the time, that he was working on making that happen. Given what she told me yesterday, with the money situation, how would he have done that? Unless he…" She trailed off, unable to utter the awful words.

"What're you saying?"

"I don't know. This probably sounds insane, but he's left a box under my bed. He said there's books in there, but I feel like it's something else. I feel like it's important that I see what's in there. It's an instinct I have. But it has a lock. We'd have to smash it open with one of your hammers."

He put his hands on her shoulders. "Listen to me. If we do this, you have to walk away from him."

"I have to walk away from him anyway, Henry. I just don't know how."

"Let's see what's in the box."

Minutes later they were in her bedroom pulling out the wooden box. About two by two, it was made of pine, and Henry easily pried open the lid with a hammer. Inside were a series of leather-bound notebooks placed in neat rows. "Journals?"

She picked the first one and opened to the first page. Old newspaper articles from 1921 were pasted to the pages. The articles were about the Bennetts.

Several pages in, this entry:

March 28, 1921

I saw them in the park. Fat Caroline wanted peanuts, so she got them. I want peanuts and all the rest of it, too. I will marry Caroline someday. I will become like Edmund Bennett. No one can stop me.

She knelt on the floor, turning page after page, Henry next to her. It was filled with stories of the Bennetts and more proclamations about the kind of life he would have and about how he would someday be a Bennett. "Grab a more recent one," she said.

Henry handed her another.

April 11, 1943.

I hired a new seamstress today. Philippa Rains. She's a dark-eyed beauty fresh from Iowa. Innocent but intelligent.

Page after page of remarks about her appearance or habits. And finally this: *I want her. I will have her.*

A month later: *She's obviously going to have a baby. This is my way in.*

Next to her, Henry grabbed the last in the row, opening it to the first page, titled 1946: *Somebody has to die. I have to have Phil. She has to be my wife. I cannot be apart from her. She is rightfully mine. Caroline has to die.*

"Oh no. No, no, no," she said.

He took the book from her and placed it back in the box. "All right now, we have to think what to do."

She started to rock back and forth. "He's sick. We have to stop him. She's pregnant, you know. And those children. Their mother. Oh my God, Henry, what do we do? He's ruthless. He'll do anything to get what he wants. He's told me that many times. There was something crazed about him when he left this time. He will have hired someone to do it. And he left this morning with the intent to see his family in Santa Barbara. It's going to be soon. We have to warn her."

"I know where the house is," said Henry.

"How?"

"I'll tell you in the car."

30

MILLER

Timmy handed Miller a smoke and gestured for another round from the bartender. It was two a.m. and they were both drunk. Strangely, given all that had happened that day with Caroline, and the plan in motion for the morning, the two men had talked about the old days. The days in the orphanage, words spilling from them in equal measure to the number of whiskeys.

He'd been here since eight, having driven straight from Santa Barbara, chain smoking with the window down and taking the turns too fast. He wanted Phil, but he knew he needed to be someplace public the next morning, in case he needed an alibi. Being with his mistress when his wife was being pushed over a cliff was probably not the best idea he'd ever had.

Now, the conversation changed. "You sure you don't want me to call it off?" asked Timmy. "Her dying the day she was going to file for a divorce don't look too good."

Miller took a deep drag on his cigarette. "Edmund Bennett took away the one thing I'd been working for my entire life when he gave the reins to that suck-up. I'm going to take away something he cares about and see how he likes it."

"Wait a minute now. I thought this was about Phil. Is this some kind of revenge?" asked Timmy.

"You know, man, I'm sick of being screwed. I ever tell you about my whore of a mother? All my life, no one ever wanted me. Fucking Bennetts, same thing, except for Caroline. And you know what? The fact that she's stupid like a fucking puppy makes me hate her. Makes me want to kick in her face." He was slurring his words, and the masses of anger were spewing out of his gut like black bile. "I want them all to hurt like they hurt me."

About three a.m. they both stumbled upstairs. Miller passed out on the guest room bed with his clothes on. When he woke the next morning, hungover and smelling like an ashtray, he drew back the curtains and looked out to the street below. Fuck them. Fuck them all. He was going to Phil. He was going to take what was his.

31

CAROLINE

I t was nearing seven a.m. when Caroline went downstairs
to the dining room. No one appeared to be up yet except
Margaret, who brought her some toast and tea and gave
her an encouraging pat on the shoulder. "Don't fret, my Caroline. Someday he'll get what's coming to him."

"Margaret, I'm surprised at you. Such venom."

"I wish I had a little snake venom. I could've stuck it in his
whiskey." With that, Margaret walked out of the dining room.
Caroline smiled for what seemed like the first time in days.

It was a new day and she must be courageous. She would tell
the children after lunch. Later, after they had cried, her father
and Julius would be there, filling in as they always had in
Miller's absence. It was time to somehow make a new life for
herself, one where she was no longer Mrs. Dreeser, but Caroline
Bennett, the girl who cried for orphans. Everything she'd built
her life around had been ripped away and she must start anew.
Despite Miller's absences, her family had been a source of pride.
At Christmas when they were all gathered around the table, her
heart had been full. Her beautiful children, kind and smart, and
her handsome husband had been a symbol that she'd made the

right choices. Her charity work had given her further purpose, always trying to live up to the vow she'd made to God all those years ago.

The emotional anguish still made it hard to move, like nerve-endings were exposed. She had no idea when it would get easier, but surely it would eventually. One moment at a time. She went out to the porch with her cup of tea. Fog hovered over the water, but she would go on her walk early, to be back in time for her father to take her into the city to file the necessary paperwork at the courthouse. She placed her hand on her still-flat stomach. There was another baby coming. Miller's baby. She or he would most likely never know their father. Perhaps it would be better. He could not break his or her heart like he had the other children if they never knew him in the first place.

A half hour later, Caroline walked at her usual fast pace, her shoes damp with dew. It was good to breathe heavily, to feel her lungs expanding with physical exertion. She came to the bench; the walking stick she'd found for Audrey was next to it. After her conversation with Julius, she had forgotten to take it to Audrey. She picked up the stick, leaning on it for a moment, before gripping it and continuing forth. Several miles later, at the point, she stopped, standing on the side of the cliff as the fog dissipated and mixed with light until the sky seem ethereal. She shivered, leaning on her stick companion, and pulled her sweater tighter. The sound of a twig snapping caused her to turn around. A young man, dressed in a long, black overcoat, stood about twenty feet behind her. Her stomach dropped. Pinpricks of fear shot through her body. His black hat was pulled low on his forehead. She could not make out his eyes, but his mouth had a scar that started at a spot below his nose and extended over his lips, stopping at his chin. In her heightened state, everything became immediately clear. He was here to kill her. Miller had hired him. She was certain of it. Behind her, the cliff provided the perfect opportunity to kill her and make it seem like an accident.

One push and she would fall to a certain death, her body mangled on the rocks. Audrey's sweet face came to her. And the boys, fragile still. Her children needed her. She could not die.

HENRY

P hil sat in the passenger seat, clutching her purse, as Henry roared down the highway. The children, dressed in their pajamas, were snuggled together like two sardines in the back, fast asleep.

"How long until we get there?" asked Phil.

"Another fifteen minutes."

"I can't go in there with you," she said. "You have to it."

"I understand. It's no problem," said Henry.

"Can you drive any faster?"

"Not without endangering the lives of everyone in this car."

Ten minutes later, they drove down the Bennetts' driveway. Henry parked the car and sprinted to the front door. A woman dressed in a maid uniform answered the door. "Is Mrs. Dreeser home?" he asked.

The maid looked at her watch. "She left for her walk about a half hour ago. Went early this morning."

"Is her father or mother available?"

"They're still asleep," she said.

A voice from behind the woman said, "Margaret, can I help?" It belonged to a teenaged boy.

Margaret stepped aside and the young man opened the door

wider. "I'm Seb. Are you a friend of my mother's?" He snapped his fingers. "Wait, I know you. Henry Sayer, right? You were on the USS *Corry*."

"I'm amazed you remember me, but yes, I'm Henry. I have something rather urgent I need to discuss with your mother or one of your grandparents."

A man appeared behind Seb. It was Doctor Nelson.

The doctor's eyes widened, then his face lit up with a smile as he held out his hand. "Henry Sayer, what in world are you doing here?"

Henry blinked, surprised, but he couldn't waste time with pleasantries. "Doc, I think Caroline's in trouble. I'm afraid she might be in danger on her walk. Would you show me where she usually heads? I'd like to go after her."

"Why would she be in danger?" asked Julius.

Henry took the latest journal from his jacket pocket and opened it to the passage he wanted them to read. "This is Mr. Dreeser's journal. In it are some concerning passages where he speaks of hiring someone..." He stopped, unable to say the words in front of the boy. Poor Seb. No one should have to know this about their father.

"What is it?" asked Seb. "Just say it."

"Passages that make me worried for her safety. I don't know if or when he was planning it, but it's supposed to be on her morning walk." He tapped the paper.

"Seb, let's go," said Julius.

The boy was already out the door, tearing down the grass after his mother.

CAROLINE

The man ran toward her. First instinct told her to run, but she was near the ledge. It wouldn't take him long to reach her. He could toss her over at any point for a quarter mile and she would be lost to the rocks. She raised her stick, aiming the sharp point forward like a weapon, feeling the strong muscles of her back and arm engage and ran toward him as fast as she could, her strong legs propelling her light frame, holding the stick in front of her. When she was upon him, she let out a primal scream and aimed for his chest, but his hand grasped the stick. Using it for momentum, he shoved her to the ground. They rolled, together, the stick sideways between them. If she let him get her on her back, it was all over. She would not have the strength to get him off her. She did the only thing she could think of. She bit his wrist as hard as she could. He cried out and let go of the stick. She was on her feet in an instant, the man right behind her. She swung, trying to hit him, but he caught the other end.

They battled like they were playing a game of tug-a-war, both hanging on to opposite ends of the stick. A sudden image of the children playing tug-a-war with a rope popped into her mind. One time, Audrey, at a distinct disadvantage because she was so much smaller than Seb, had abruptly let go. Seb had fallen over from the sudden release of energy. She let go of the stick and the man fell backward, onto his bottom, still holding the stick. She kicked high, like a dancer, and her foot made contact. The stick flew from his hands, landing a foot away from him. Before he could get up, his girth a disadvantage now, she snatched the stick from the ground. Using every ounce of her weight, she swung it like a baseball bat for his head. This time she hit him. The smack made an awful sound. He cried out in pain and shock, staring at her with eyes like a caged animal as he touched the side of his head. "You bitch." He tried to get up but his balance was off, and he stumbled and fell onto his back. Wasting no time, she pounced on him and pinned him to the ground with her foot on his chest. Then, without thinking, pure instinct and adrenaline coursing through her body, she stabbed the stick into the side of his throat. Blood gushed from the wound. Staring up at her with a shocked expression, he opened his mouth to speak, but blood, not words, burbled from his lips.

She continued to stand over him, traumatized into paralysis at what she'd done. In seconds, his face went completely slack. His eyes changed from frantic movement to staring lifelessly up at the sky. She'd killed him. Shaking, she moved her gaze in the direction of shouting. Seb and Julius sprinted toward her.

"Mother, Mother," said Seb.

She held out her arms and pulled her son close. "It's all right, darling." She looked up at Julius. "The stick. The end you carved was sharp. I jabbed him with it and I think I've killed him. He was coming for me. Miller sent him. It had to be Miller."

Julius knelt over the man, feeling for a pulse at his neck. "Yes, he's dead." He stood.

"How did you know to come?" she asked.

"Henry and the girl came to the house as I was walking over this morning to check on you all," said Julius.

Seb extricated himself from his mother's arms. "He had Father's journal with him."

"It indicated that he'd hired someone to kill you during your walk," said Julius.

"Push me over the cliff, isn't that right?" asked Caroline.

"Yes," said Julius.

"We were too late, though," said Seb. "You took care of it yourself."

She reached for Julius. Her legs weakened under her. Sudden cramping in her stomach caused her to double over in pain. "Julius, something's wrong."

She crumpled as everything went black.

3 4

HENRY

He waited in the sitting room with Mrs. Bennett as she looked through the journals. She didn't speak or make any noise at all. Fifteen minutes passed. He went to the window, watching the waves crash to shore. The phone rang. Mrs. Bennett jumped, then went to answer it. Her hand flew to her mouth as she listened. "Oh my God. Yes, yes, I'll tell him. I'll meet you there."

She hung up the phone. "You were right, Mr. Sayer. A man tried to kill her, but she stabbed him with the sharp end of the walking stick Julius had carved for Audrey. The man's dead."

"Dead? Mrs. Dreeser killed him?" he asked.

"I know, it's a bit unbelievable, given her size, but she's quite strong. Anyway, right after it happened, Julius and Seb reached her. Julius confirmed the man's death. Caroline fainted. She's bleeding. He thinks she's losing the baby. He carried her to the nearest house, just up the beach. Everyone knows Julius; they allowed him to borrow a car and took her into the hospital in Santa Barbara. I'm going to meet them there. Mr. Sayer, thank you. Thank you for coming here, but I must go."

"Please give my best to your daughter. I'll be praying for good news."

"Thank you."

He insisted she not walk him to the door. Once outside, he strode to the car, and opened Phil's door, asking her to get out. He didn't want the children to hear what he was about to say. He quickly summarized what he knew.

"She's losing the baby?" Phil's voice was an octave higher than usual. He knew she was close to panic by the way her entire body shook.

"The doctor believes so."

"This is all my fault," she said. "I've done this."

"Miller planning to kill his wife was not your fault," he said.

"I was complicit. I accepted his offer. What did I think would happen?"

"You didn't think he would try and murder his wife. I understand your guilt, Phil, and I appreciate your willingness to accept your part in what's happened. However, almost no one, when faced with the choice between letting their child starve or not, would've made a choice other than the one you made."

They got in the car and Henry started the drive home. No one spoke as they drove north. In the backseat, Teddy had fallen asleep with his head on Mary's lap. Phil and Mary stared out their respective windows, their hands clasped together on their laps in identical poses. The fog had cleared now, and the sun was hot. He rolled down his window and everyone's hair blew about in the breeze. As they made the turn off the highway toward Stowaway, his stomach rumbled with hunger. "I'm hungry. How about we stop in town and get some fish and chips?"

Teddy, on cue, never one to miss a meal, popped his head up, like he hadn't been fast asleep a moment ago. "Me hungry, too." His hair was wet with perspiration and he had an indentation on the side of his face from Mary's skirt.

"I'm hungry," said Phil, absently. "I mean, Teddy, you say 'I'm hungry', not 'me hungry.'"

Mary caught Henry's eyes in the rearview mirror. "I'm hungry, too."

"Excellent. Let's go to Mae's," he said, with a false cheer in his voice. "I used to dream about her fish and chips when I was overseas."

Henry parked a block from the shop and waited until everyone was out of the car. The kids ran ahead, skipping and holding hands. Phil, pales as ashes, seemed unsteady on her feet. He offered his arm. The kids found a table outside under an umbrella. Gazing at their dark heads shining under the sun, he wished life was as simple as it appeared on the outside. They made a perfect picture: a young couple out with their child and what people would assume is their niece for fish and chips, maybe ice cream afterward. He held out Phil's chair and she sat. He wondered when she'd last eaten. Mae's teenaged daughter took their order, sticking her pencil in her hair exactly the way her mother usually did. "Our cook called in sick this morning," she said. "So Mama's in the kitchen."

"You give her my best," said Henry.

"Yes, sir, I will." She gave him a shy smile. "She tells anyone who'll listen how you're a war hero."

"That's kind of her," he said.

The children went to the restroom to clean their hands. Phil lifted her chin toward the sky and closed her eyes. Her face had grown thinner the last few weeks, and she seemed fragile, like her bones might break in half at the slightest touch. He yearned to reach out and run his fingers along her face. When she opened her eyes, her gaze flickered up and down the street. "Do you think I'll ever be free of him?"

"He's going to jail," said Henry.

She shook her head. "No, you're wrong. He'll get away with it somehow, especially since the hired killer's dead. There's no way to trace it back to Miller."

"What about the notebooks? It's all in there."

"He'd rather die than go to jail. The orphanage was like a jail to him and he will never go back to it. He'll never leave me alone. I have to hide somewhere. Disappear." She rushed along, talking faster than he believed possible. "I'm going to take the children and leave this afternoon, go somewhere he can't find me. I've been stashing bits of cash away little by little that he left around the house. I've got enough for train tickets. When we get home, I'll pack what I can fit into the suitcases and head some-where on the train. Maybe north to Oregon. There are places to disappear there, don't you think? Places no one's ever heard of?"

His heart might stop. "No."

"No?" she asked.

"No, you can't go. Not without me."

She stared at him for a moment. He filled with urgency. She must understand. He must get her to agree to his plan. He couldn't lose her. The children would be back from the bathroom at any moment. He must speak now or he would never have his chance. "I'll do anything you want. Leave here and disappear with you. We can find a place in Oregon to live. I have money, Phil. We can go wherever it is you'll feel safe. I'll take care of you and the children. We can get married."

"Married?" Her eyes were wide with what looked like horror.

He wiped his sweaty palms on his jeans. "I'd like to marry you, Phil, and take care of you. You'll never have to worry about anything or anyone ever again. I'll be a father to both the chil-dren. A good father—the best I can be. That's what you do to me, Phil. You make me better, braver, full of hope. When I'm with you, I forget all the pain of the past and I forget that I'd decided joy wasn't something I would ever feel again. But you—you make me joyous."

"Henry, have you lost your mind?"

"I'll protect you." He went on, afraid to let her speak. "I don't have a ring, obviously, but I could get one quite easily. We could walk up to the jewelers after lunch and get you one. We could get married today if you wanted."

"My God, no, Henry. Look at who I am. I've ruined a family, a woman's life. Why would you want me?"

"Is it only me that feels all this." He tapped his heart. "Please tell me it's not only me. Can you imagine a life with me?"

"It doesn't matter what I feel or what I could imagine. I don't deserve someone like you. I'm damaged goods. And I don't want you in danger."

He made a small movement with his head toward his missing arm. "Aren't we all damaged one way or the other?"

She started to cry. "Do you think no one else would want you? Because of your arm?"

He flushed. Is this what she believed of herself? Of him? Reaching across the table, he tilted her face upward and peered into her eyes. "Hear this. If it were between you and anyone else on this earth, I would always choose you."

She didn't speak. Two large tears rolled down her cheeks.

"Whether you feel the same way, the offer remains. I'll take you somewhere and get you set up and leave you be once I know you and the children are safe."

She wiped her cheeks. "You've been a problem, Henry, from the very first time I ever met you. I felt this immediate closeness to you and being with you makes me feel like a normal person, not Miller's whore."

"Do not use that word about yourself again. I mean it."

"Don't you know what I would give to live here with you and raise Teddy and Mary, maybe even have another child? It's all I've wanted since the first time I met you. Miller saw it. He saw how my feelings were growing for you and it wasn't safe. I can't let anything happen to you. He would have you killed if he even knew about this conversation. There's no doubt in my mind."

"After everything I faced overseas, do you think I'm afraid of Miller Dreeser?"

She smiled for the first time. "I know you're not afraid. But you should be."

"Let's eat and go home and get some clothes. We can drive

north to Oregon and hide out until we know if he's going to be arrested or not."

The children were approaching the table. Teddy's hair had been combed and his hands and face washed. Mary was a good big sister to him. If only they could all stay like this forever.

When the food arrived a few minutes later, they ate in silence. Phil nibbled on her food, but the children devoured theirs. He wasn't hungry, either, but forced himself to eat. They could have a long night of driving ahead.

When everyone had their fill, Henry took out his wallet to pay. Phil put her hand on his arm and looked into his eyes. "I'd choose you, too."

His heart soared. There was nothing he wouldn't do for this woman. Whatever it took, he would keep her safe.

35

CAROLINE

T he walls of the hospital were the color of brown eggs. She stared at them, letting the grief overcome her, and sobbed. She'd had a miscarriage. There would be no fourth child. *Miller did this to me. He killed my baby.*

She turned over when the door to her room opened. It was Mother. "How are you feeling, darling?"

"I knew it the moment I started cramping. I hoped I was wrong," said Caroline.

"You've lost a lot of blood. Julius wants you to rest for a few days at least, but we can take you home in a few hours."

"He tried to kill me, but he killed the baby instead."

"We'll make him pay. Your father has the police looking for him. He didn't go back to your house in the city or to his office. We're not sure where he is."

"He's probably gone to her."

"They're headed there as well."

"She brought the box to Mr. Sayer?" asked Caroline.

"Yes. She and Mr. Sayer broke it open and found the journals. Sweetheart, we were part of his plan from the beginning. He wanted to become a Bennett."

"He never loved me, Mother. My entire adult life's been a lie."

"But we have the children." Mother slipped in beside her and took her in her arms, letting her cry like she was still a little girl. When the tears finally ceased, they lay together talking about the past and the future. "We will come up with a plan for the rest of your life. And you have us. You're not alone."

"The only time I was alone is when I was with Miller."

"He tricked the girl into being with him. He stole the small amount of money she'd saved for when her baby came," said Mother. "It was all laid out in his journal. He's a monster."

Julius came in, bringing a cup of broth on a tray. "The nurse sent this in and said to try to eat a bit if you can." Julius set the tray on the end of the bed and perched on the other side of the bed as Caroline sat upright. "Are you feeling better?"

"Empty," she said.

"Because you were only about eight weeks along, everything will take care of itself. It's not necessary for you to have any kind of procedure." Julius's eyes were red-rimmed, as if he'd been crying.

Tears flowed from her eyes, hot on her cheeks, and soaking the collar of her gown. "It's probably for the best."

"I know it hurts. I'm sorry." He brushed a lock of her hair from her wet face. "No one seems to be able to identify the man who tried to kill you, but the local sheriff felt certain he was a hired killer of some kind."

Caroline flinched.

Julius looked uncomfortable. "The journals that Mr. Sayer brought are fairly damning. The police detective seemed certain they could bring him in for questions and book him on attempted murder."

"They have to catch him first," said Caroline. "He's resourceful, especially when pushed against the wall."

Mother and Julius exchanged glances, but they didn't argue with her. "At least try and eat a little broth," said Mother.

"I will, Mother. But will you send the little children in? I want to see them."

Mother left to fetch Audrey and Pierce, leaving her alone with Julius. She motioned for him to come over to the other side of the bed. When he sat in the spot vacated by her mother, she took his hand. "You sharpening that stick—that was the difference between life and death."

"What made you grab it?" he asked.

"Instinct, I suppose. Instinct I've been ignoring since the day I met Miller Dreeser."

"We all see what we want to see when we love someone," he said. "It makes us blind to their faults. Sometimes it makes us liars to ourselves."

"I wish we had been honest with each other all those years ago."

"I'll never forgive myself." He continued to gaze down at her with those blue eyes like the sea. "It's all I think about—what would have happened if I'd been honest to you about my feelings."

"But we wouldn't have the children."

"Yes. And they're wonderful. You've done well with them. And, Caroline, tomorrow's another day." He brushed the lone tear cascading down her cheek with the back of his index finger. "When you're ready I'll be here. This time, I won't quit until I've convinced you to try love again. With me."

"It may take a long time."

"I'll wait forever if I have to."

36

MILLER

At nine a.m. Miller was in Timmy's booth, waiting, his mind blank. He felt detached from everything other than the sights and sounds of the bar. Other than him and the bartender, plus a couple of career drunks, he was the only one in the place. He was well into his second beer with absolutely no dent into his hangover when Timmy appeared, wearing his usual suit and looking fresh as a damn daisy. Timmy had his hand in his pants pocket, jiggling his keys. His expression seemed dour. Something was wrong. Miller went cold with dread.

"What's the matter?" asked Miller.

Timmy grabbed his forehead, and started pacing in front of the booth. "Damndest thing's happened. When my guy didn't call to let me know it was done, I sent someone else down there to see what was happening. I had a bad feeling, 'cause this guy's reliable. Always calls me first chance he can get to a phone. The police were everywhere. And my guy was in a body bag. He asked around. Found out that Caroline had some kind of sharp stick. Stuck him through the neck."

The room tipped. He broke out in a cold sweat. The beers

wanted to spew out of him as he sputtered, "He's dead and she's alive?"

"Yeah, and you gotta get out of here. My informant tells me they're looking for you. Something about journals or something. You write all this down in some book?"

He didn't answer as he rose from the booth. Phil had betrayed him. She was the only one who knew about his box. All his secrets and desires, stored and packaged so that no one would know about them. "Dammit, Phil." He picked up his glass of beer and threw it as hard as he could at the wall.

Timmy took hold of his shoulders. "Way I figure, you head out of town, get lost somewhere." He thrust a stack of bills and a box of bullets into his hand. "This'll get you by for a while. When you land somewhere safe, call me, and we'll figure out your next move." He reached into his jacket and pulled out a pistol. "You take this with you. It's fully loaded."

"I can't leave her," said Miller.

"I'm telling you to go now. You have a few hours and that's it. Do not go out to the beach. Just go. Start over. New name. New everything. You understand me? Otherwise, they're locking you up and you'll never see the light of day again."

He nodded and murmured an agreement. They embraced, and Miller headed out the door with every intention of doing exactly what his friend told him not to do. There was no way in hell he was leaving Phil behind. If he had to drag her out of that house by her hair, she was coming with him wherever he was going. It was up to her if she wanted to bring that brat with her, but he was taking her or leaving her for dead.

He hid the car in a thick wood a quarter mile off the highway and walked to the cottage, carrying his weapon. When Miller arrived at Phil's cottage, he hammered the door with his fist, but no one answered. He raced around the side of the house and banged on the kitchen door. Nothing. A basket with bread and jelly was on the back step, probably left by the annoying farmer's wife. She usually came by in the morning, which meant Phil hadn't been there for hours. Where the hell was she? Phil couldn't leave without a car. He came back around the side of the house to the front. Sayer's car was gone. She was with him. Lying bitch. He knew it all along. She'd been spreading her legs for him this whole time. After what he'd sacrificed for her. The betrayal nearly knocked him to the ground.

The sound of a car drew his attention to the long driveway. Henry Sayer's car bounced in the potholes. He hid behind a bush. Just as he assumed. She was with the landlord. He waited, his heart keeping time with the second hand on his watch.

When Sayer parked the car and got out, Miller jumped out of the bush. "I'm here for Phil, Sayer. You need to get out of the way."

In the car, Teddy crawled over the seat to his mother's lap.

Sayer put his one arm out in front of him. "We don't want trouble, Dreeser. Just move along. It's over."

"I'm happy to leave once I have Phil. She's coming with me." He pushed past Sayer and headed for the car.

Phil opened her car door with Teddy clinging to her and walked over to where he stood face to face with Sayer. "Miller, everyone knows what you did. It's too late. They'll come looking for you. Just leave while you still can."

"Pack what you want to bring, Phil. You have five minutes before we go," said Miller.

"You don't own me any longer," said Phil. "I'm staying here with Henry."

"Get your goddam things, Phil," said Miller.

"Just leave peacefully," said Sayer. "Get a head start on the police. When we left the Bennetts' they already knew it was you that tried to have Caroline killed. They'll have police all over the state looking for you if you don't leave soon."

Rage coursed through him. The muscles of his arms twitched.

He would hurt her. Strangle her until her eyes begged him to stop. Henry Sayer. He hated this son of a bitch. He reached in his pocket and pulled out the pistol, aiming it at Henry's head. "Get your things, or I'll kill him."

Teddy stared at him with wide eyes before burying his face against Phil's neck.

"Phil, take the kids inside the house," said Sayer. "We'll settle this out here."

What was this? It was Mary slinking across the yard. She was almost to Sayer's cottage. Planning to call the police, no doubt. He raised his gun and fired. Mary fell to the ground.

37

PHIL

Mary fell. Phil screamed. In her arms, Teddy clung to her as they ran to Mary. She lay crumpled on the grass, her little body twisted like a rag doll. Her eyes were open, wide and scared. Blood had soaked through the top of her dress. "Can you hear me?" asked Phil.

"Yes." Barely a whisper, but she could talk. A doctor. They must get a doctor. She fell to her knees. Teddy had a death grip around her neck. In her panic, she'd forgotten everything but Mary for a moment, but now she looked over at Miller. He had the gun pointed at Henry and was ordering him to lie face down on the ground. Miller cocked the gun and pointed it at Henry's head. Suddenly, a deafening noise shattered the silence, and Miller fell to the ground, his neck squirting blood. A gunshot. From where? She looked around wildly, unsure from which direction it had originated. Mrs. Thomas rose from behind a thicket of sea grasses, rifle raised. She ran to Mary, kneeling on the ground next to her. "It's all right, dearie, you're going to be fine. It's only a little bullet that went right through your shoulder, but the doctor can sew you right up."

Mary must be in shock because she was nodding as if everything Mrs. Thomas said was an everyday conversation.

333

Henry dropped to his knees by Miller. "He's gone."

"Oh, dear, well, this is a bit of a conundrum," said Mrs. Thomas. "Henry, go inside and call the doctor. Tell them we've got a body and a girl needs some mending. Then, call Sheriff McIntyre. Tell him what's happened. Hopefully my recent delivery of free jam will keep me out of jail."

"Where did you come from?" asked Phil.

"Mr. Thomas dropped me on his way to town. I came by to visit, but then no one was here, so I went inside Henry's to wait for Mr. Thomas to come back and take me home. I saw Dreeser walk up. It took me a moment to find Henry's rifle and bullets, or I would've been out here sooner."

PART V

DECEMBER 1947

38

CAROLINE

The day before Christmas a cold front brought clear skies, swathing San Francisco in glittering ice. Caroline and Audrey sat before the fire in their new home wrapping the last of the gifts for the orphans. Outside in the yard, the shouts of Julius and the boys tossing a football back and forth penetrated the Christmas music that played through the radio. Stockings were hung and the tree was decorated, lit up with the new bubble lights that had become popular. Caroline tied a golden bow around a box containing a doll for one of the little girls. Audrey had been adamant they find the prettiest doll in all of San Francisco. Shopping with her perfectionist daughter had reminded Caroline of the years she and her own mother had scoured department stores with similar intensity.

"Mother, do you ever think of Father?" asked Audrey.

Caroline set aside the finished present, surprised at the question. "Sometimes," said Caroline. "Why do you ask?" The children never talked about him. After the initial shock over his death and crimes, the children had seemed to forget he ever existed. She knew this was only true on the outside. The scars were hidden, as were her own. There was no escaping the damage done to them because of Miller's secret. It was a fact, just as moving forward was a necessity.

"I can't remember what he looks like," said Audrey. "And that makes me feel peculiar."

There were photos of Miller in a box in the attic, in case the children ever wanted to look at them. "Peculiar how?"

"Like I should remember what my own father looked like, even though I hate him." Audrey continued. "I don't have to love him, do I? After what he did?"

"No, but it's all right to talk to me about it anytime you want to."

"Can I tell you a secret?" asked Audrey.

"You can tell me anything."

"I always wished Julius was my dad."

Caroline looked down at her left hand. The diamonds sparkled under the lights. Julius and Caroline Nelson. Her second chance. Their second chance. "We're lucky, aren't we?"

"Do you ever miss the old house?" Audrey asked.

"No. It had too many memories. Bad ones. It was good to start over, and I wanted to pick out a house with Julius."

"Mother, the boys and I were talking, and we have a Christmas wish of our own."

"You do?" She started to worry. "Something new for your lists?"

"No, nothing like that."

Julius and the boys tumbled in through the back door, rosy-cheeked and breathless and smelling like boys do after physical exertion. "Take off your boots," Caroline called out to them. "Margaret just cleaned the floors."

"There's no mud. Too cold." Julius already had his boots off and padded over to her in his stockinged feet. She loved his feet in socks. Would her delight of the simple pleasure of his presence ever grow old? She hadn't believed it possible to be giddy in love at her age. He'd given her time, as promised. Surprising to her, it hadn't taken as long as she figured it would. After grieving for almost nine months, the dormant feelings for Julius resurfaced in a mad rush. Julius was Julius and she'd loved him all her life.

"I'm ready to see about us," she told him one afternoon in May. "Would you take me out on a date?"

"I thought you'd never ask," he said.

Julius insisted he court her the old-fashioned way, taking her out for dinners and to the movies, and sending her flowers and gifts. By the summer, they were in crazy love and decided there was no reason to wait on making it official. With the children and their parents, they were married in late September on the lawn of her parents' beach house. The passion between them was intense, but their relationship was rooted in friendship and trust. Despite everything, she found loving and trusting Julius easier than anything she'd ever done. She was happier than she ever supposed possible. Not that it wasn't still hard at times. She still jerked awake from nightmares. Sometimes, in the middle of an ordinary moment, the memory of those awful days washed over her and the horror of what Miller had done to all of them hit her anew. The contents of his journals and the knowledge of what he'd set out to do was staggering to her. Still, after all these months, it seemed impossible that someone she once loved had betrayed her to such a degree.

She gazed up at Julius as he ripped off his knit hat. His hair stood up, making him look like a kid. He held out his hand to help her up from the floor. "The gifts look beautiful." He kissed her on the cheek. "As do you."

"It took a long time," said Audrey. "I'm exhausted."

Julius laughed. "Too exhausted for delivering the gifts and going to dinner at the club?"

"Well, not that exhausted." Audrey grinned.

The boys came to stand before the fireplace. "Before we get ready to leave for the orphanage, on behalf of my siblings, we have something we'd like to discuss," said Seb. "Mother, Julius, would you please sit?"

"A Christmas wish." Audrey placed the last wrapped present in the pile and sat on the large chair closest to the fire, as Caroline and Julius sat together on the couch.

"Let Seb do it." Pierce plopped next to his sister.

"I know. Stop bossing me around," said Audrey.

"We have one wish for Christmas," said Seb. "And that's for Julius to adopt us."

"Adopt you?"

"I know I'm a little old for adoption, but I want you to be my legal father," said Seb.

Audrey bounced in the chair. "Me too, me too. And Pierce, too, but he's too shy to say it out loud. I told him I'd do it."

Pierce nodded in agreement. "I do have something I want to say."

Caroline turned slightly to peer at Julius. His eyes were glassy with unshed tears as he pulled a handkerchief from his pocket.

Pierce scooted forward in the chair, bowing his head as he spoke. "You're the one we would've chosen if we could've chosen our father, and since we can now, we choose you."

Julius dabbed at his eyes. "When I was about Audrey's age, my mother left us. I never saw her again. I was sad, like you all have been about your dad. Your mother was my best friend and she comforted me and loved me, as did your grandparents. Sophie told me something I'll never forget. 'Family isn't always blood. Sometimes, when you're lucky, you get to choose who you want for your family.' I didn't feel as sad after that." He tapped his chest. "I chose you as my own a long time ago. If I could've chosen from any kids in the world, I would've chosen you."

Audrey cocked her head to the side, observing Julius. "Does this mean you're saying yes?"

"Yes. I'm saying yes." Julius laughed as he stood up from the couch. "Now get over here and give me a hug. All of you." He held out his arms and they fell into them at once. When he extricated himself, he grabbed Caroline and held her for a moment, kissing the top of her head.

Tears made her cheeks wet. Despite all the mistakes she'd made, she got to have all this: her family, imperfect, shaped from both tragedy and joy, here in the glow of the fire.

She squeezed Julius's hand. "Merry Christmas, Julius."

"Merry Christmas, Caroline."

3 9

PHIL

P hil finished her last dress around noon on Christmas Eve. She wrapped it in tissue paper and put it in a box. It was a gift from the town doctor to his wife, and Phil had promised to drop it by his office on her way home. The back of her shop was tidy, other than the usual patterns and rolls of fabric. She'd closed the front of the shop an hour ago. No one would come in to order a dress on Christmas Eve and she wanted to get home as soon as she could. There were cookies to make and a turkey to stuff. She put away her scissors and put the top on her sewing machine, catching a glimpse of herself in the mirror. Her stomach was getting bigger by the moment. An April baby, the doctor had told her, but she had a feeling she or he might come a little earlier.

Henry and the children walked in through the back door. "We're here, Mama." Teddy ran to her, hugging her legs.

"I can't wait to get home and wrap my presents for you all," said Mary. She'd been out shopping with her friend from school and carried several shopping bags. Mary glowed this afternoon, with pink cheeks and brown eyes that danced with mischief. She was growing so fast that the dress Phil had made her two months ago was almost too short. No one would ever know that a bullet had gone through her shoulder, although she had the scar to prove it. Phil watched for signs of trauma over the events of that day, but thus far the vibrant girl in front her hadn't shown any. The bullet had entered and exited in a clean line, leaving no permanent damage to her bones or muscles.

"Did you finish the last dress?" asked Henry. He kissed her cheek. "My poor wife, slaving away the day before Christmas."

"Yes, just now." She pointed to the box, reminding him that she had to drop it off on their way home.

"I worry about you working too hard," he said, placing his fingertips on her round stomach.

"I have to admit, I'm happy to take some days off. As much as I love my shop, I'm tired." She sighed, feeling happy. "But many more customers this year than last." She had more orders for her spring designs than she had time to make them. She would have to hire another seamstress. A business of her own, with employees! What a difference a year and half could make. When she accepted Henry's offer of a loan, she had made it clear that she would pay him back in full, which she did.

After the initial shock and subsequent hospitalization of Mary were over, it had taken her a few months to let go of the awful guilt weighing her down like a gunny sack of rocks on her back. She was head over heels in love with Henry, but she wouldn't allow herself to have him, not after everything she'd done. The only thing that seemed to help was to work hard. She had buried herself in the shop. Over time, with Henry and Mrs. Thomas's steady friendship, her guilt subsided. When she accepted Henry's second proposal of marriage, she made it clear that she would always make her own money, even though he had plenty. Independence was important to her, no matter if she was a married woman or not.

Before they walked out to the car, she gazed at her beautiful family. Then, she remembered Miller and shuddered. How easily she could have lost everything. It was clear from his journal entries that Miller had ordered a hit on Henry as well as his wife.

The horror of those days and the shame of her part in it would never leave her, and yet, here she was: married to Henry, with Mary and Teddy healthy and happy, plus another baby coming. Despite all her mistakes, she had all this.

"Good, because we're all anxious to start Christmas," said Henry.

Teddy jumped up and down. "Daddy bought a tree. It's on top of the car."

"We saw Mrs. Thomas here in town. She said they'd be over around five," said Henry.

"Mrs. Thomas said she had presents for me and Mary," said Teddy. "A whole bunch of them."

"Mary and me, Teddy," said Phil.

"That's what I said." Teddy wrinkled his brow.

"Grammar, Teddy. Anyway, she spoils you both rotten." How was her baby talking this well and pronouncing his r's? Time marched forth, measured by the growth of both the children. Soon there would be another baby, and Teddy would be her big boy.

"She said we're like her grandchildren and that you can't say a word about it," said Mary.

"She did, did she?" Phil laughed. "Well, that sounds like a real grandmother to me."

Phil grabbed her purse. "All right, my loves. Let Christmas begin."

She held Henry's hand as they walked to the car. The briny scent of the sea mingled with the spicy scent of the Christmas tree tied to the top of Henry's car. He held the door for her, and as she slid into the seat, the soft coo of mourning doves nesting in the rafters of her shop called out to her. She rolled down her window, hoping to catch a glimpse of them, but they were hidden, snuggled together on this cold day before Christmas.

ALSO BY TESS THOMPSON

CLIFFSIDE BAY

Traded: Brody and Kara

Deleted: Jackson and Maggie

Jaded: Zane and Honor

Marred: Kyle and Violet

Tainted: Lance and Mary

Cliffside Bay Christmas, The Season of Cats and Babies (Cliffside Bay Novella to be read after Tainted)

Missed: Rafael and Lisa

Cliffside Bay Christmas Wedding (Cliffside Bay Novella to be read after Missed)

Healed: Stone and Pepper

Chateau Wedding (Cliffside Bay Novella to be read after Healed)

Scarred: Trey and Autumn

Jilted: Nico and Sophie

Kissed (Cliffside Bay Novella to be read after Jilted)

Departed: David and Sara

Cliffside Bay Bundle, Books 1,2,3

BLUE MOUNTAIN SERIES

Blue Mountain Bundle, Books 1,2,3

Blue Midnight

Blue Moon

Blue Ink

Blue String

EMERSON PASS

<u>The School Mistress of Emerson Pass</u>

<u>The Sugar Queen of Emerson Pass</u>

RIVER VALLEY

<u>Riversong</u>

<u>Riverbend</u>

<u>Riverstar</u>

<u>Riversnow</u>

<u>Riverstorm</u>

<u>Tommy's Wish</u>

<u>River Valley Bundle, Books 1-4</u>

LEGLEY BAY

<u>Caramel and Magnolias</u>

<u>Tea and Primroses</u>

STANDALONES

<u>The Santa Trial</u>

<u>Duet for Three Hands</u>

<u>Miller's Secret</u>

ABOUT THE AUTHOR

Tess Thompson
HOMETOWNS
and HEARTSTRINGS

USA Today Bestselling author Tess Thompson writes small-town romances and historical romance. She started her writing career in fourth grade when she wrote a story about an orphan who opened a pizza restaurant. Oddly enough, her first novel, "Riversong" is about an adult orphan who opens a restaurant. Clearly, she's been obsessed with food and words for a long time now.

With a degree from the University of Southern California in theatre, she's spent her adult life studying story, word craft, and character. Since 2011, she's published 20 novels and 3 novellas. Most days she spends at her desk chasing her daily word count or rewriting a terrible first draft.

She currently lives in a suburb of Seattle, Washington with her husband, the hero of her own love story, and their Brady Bunch clan of two sons, two daughters and five cats. Yes, that's four kids and five cats.

Tess loves to hear from you. Drop her a line at tess@ tthompsonwrites.com or visit her website at https://tesswrites.com/

Join her in her Facebook fan group, Patio Chat With Tess Thompson

Come join the party in My Book Tribe, with eleven other uplift fiction writers.

9 780998 357294